"I DIDN'T DO IT.
I DIDN'T KILL MY FATHER."

Cassidy walked back to Beau, stood right in front of him. "I believe you. Over the years, I've learned to trust my instincts. I should have done that this time. I won't jump to conclusions again." And then she did something completely unexpected. She went up on her toes and pressed a soft kiss on his lips.

Heat burned through him. Lust hit him so hard his whole body tightened. He reached for her but Cassidy stepped away.

"I'm sorry," she said. "I let my attraction to you cloud my judgment. I won't do it again."

Also by Kat Martin

The Silent Rose

The Dream

The Secret

Hot Rain

Deep Blue

Desert Heat

Midnight Sun

Against the Wild

Against the Sky

Against the Tide

Into the Fury

Into the Whirlwind

Into the Firestorm

Beyond Reason

BEYOND DANGER

KAT MARTIN

ZEBRA BOOKS
KENSINGTON PUBLISHING CORP.
http://www.kensingtonbooks.com

ZEBRA BOOKS are published by

Kensington Publishing Corp.
119 West 40th Street
New York, NY 10018

All Kensington titles, imprints, and distributed lines are available at special quantity discounts for bulk purchases for sales promotion, premiums, fund-raising, educational, or institutional use.

Special book excerpts or customized printings can also be created to fit specific needs. For details, write or phone the office of the Kensington Sales Manager: Attn.: Sales Department. Kensington Publishing Corp., 119 West 40th Street, New York, NY 10018. Phone: 1-800-221-2647.

Zebra and the Z logo Reg. U.S. Pat. & TM Off.

First Printing: February 2018
ISBN-13: 978-1-4201-4317-1
ISBN-10: 1-4201-4317-4

eISBN-13: 978-1-4201-4318-8
eISBN-10: 1-4201-4318-2

10 9 8 7 6 5 4 3 2 1

Printed in the United States of America

Chapter One

Beau could hardly believe it. His father was sixty years old! The girl sitting across from him in a booth at the Pleasant Hill Café looked like a teenager. A very pregnant teenager.

"Everything's going to be okay, Missy," Beau Reese said. "You don't have to worry about anything from now on. I'll make sure it's all taken care of from here on out."

"He bought me presents," the girl said tearfully, dabbing a Kleenex against her watery blue eyes. "He told me how pretty I was, how much he liked being with me. I thought he loved me."

Fat chance of that, Beau thought. His dad had never loved anyone but himself. True, his father, still a handsome man, stayed in shape and looked twenty years younger. Didn't make the situation any better.

"How old are you, Missy?"

"Nineteen."

At least she was over the age of consent. That was something, not much.

Her hand shook as she toyed with a long strand of pale blond hair. Though her belly was enormous, the rest of her was a little too thin for someone eight-and-a-half months along, probably from so much worry.

Beau turned his attention to the woman sitting next to her daughter on the opposite side of the booth, Josie Kessler, the owner of the café.

"You should have called me, Josie. I can't believe you waited this long."

"I wanted to, Beau, but Missy was adamant. She didn't want to do anything to upset the senator. She really believed he was going to marry her."

Beau shook his head. "You know him, Josie. You've known him for years. Did you really believe that was going to happen?"

An older blond version of her daughter, Josie sighed. "I never believed it. I tried to tell her, but every time I started to talk to her, she got so upset I worried for the baby."

Full-figured now in her forties, Josie's hair had begun to turn gray. Wrinkles formed tiny lines around her mouth from the years when she was a smoker. Neither woman was beautiful, their features slightly blunt and unrefined, but there was a sweet, appealing quality about the girl.

Beau shoved a hand through his wavy black hair and took a steadying breath. "This isn't your fault, and both of us know it. It's no one's fault but my father's."

Though Josie was outspoken and a well-loved fixture in the community, Missy was quiet and shy, exactly the kind of woman his father preyed on, using flattery and attention to woo the unwary into his bed.

Unless he flat-out paid them.

Beau had known Josie and Missy's grandmother, Evelyn, the former owner of the café, since he was a kid. Missy was just a child when he'd left Pleasant Hill to attend the university in Austin. He glanced over at the girl, whose face was pale, her eyes swollen from crying. None of the women in the family had much luck with men. Or at least that's how it seemed.

He thought of the DNA test folded up and tucked into the pocket of his shirt. Josie had handed it to him when he'd first arrived. Not that he'd had much doubt her daughter was telling the truth.

"What did my father say when Missy told him about the baby?" Beau asked.

"He wanted her to have an abortion. Missy refused."

"I told him I wouldn't do that, no matter what," the girl said, sniffing into the Kleenex. "I told him I wanted to have his child."

"It's a little girl, Beau," Josie said with a wobbly smile. "We both love her already."

A peculiar tightening settled in his chest. As a kid, he had desperately wanted a brother or sister. By the time he was five, his parents barely tolerated each other. His mother had died six years ago, but now, at thirty-five, he was going to have a little sister.

Beau felt a surge of protectiveness toward the young woman carrying his father's child.

He looked over to where she sat hunched forward on the bench on the opposite side of the pink vinyl booth. At the misery in her face, he reached across the Formica-topped table and covered her hand, gave it a gentle squeeze.

"Everybody makes mistakes, Missy. You picked the wrong guy, that's all. Doesn't mean you won't have a great kid."

For the first time since he'd arrived, Missy managed a tentative smile. "Thank you for saying that."

Beau returned the smile. "I'm going to have a baby sister. I promise she won't have to worry about a thing from the day she's born into this world." Hell, he was worth more than half a billion dollars. He would see the child had everything she ever wanted.

Missy's lips trembled. She turned her head and started softly crying.

Josie scooted out of the booth. "I think she's had enough for today. This is all very hard on her and I don't want her getting overly tired." She reached for her daughter's hand. "Let's go home, honey. You'll feel better after a nap."

Missy grasped her mother's hand and awkwardly managed to climb out of the booth. Missy lived with Josie, who had taken over the apartment upstairs as well as the café when Evelyn had moved into a retirement home.

Beau got up, too. Taking the girl's slender hands, he leaned over and brushed a kiss on her cheek.

"You both have my number. If you need anything, call me. Okay?"

Missy swallowed. "Okay."

"Thank you, Beau," Josie said. "I should have called you sooner. I should have known you'd help us."

"Like I said, you don't have to worry. I'll have my assistant send you a check right away. You'll have money to take care of expenses and buy the things you need. After that, I'll have a draft sent to Missy every month."

Josie's eyes teared up. "I didn't know how I was going to manage the bills all by myself. Thank you again, Beau. So much."

He just nodded. "Keep me up-to-date on her condition."

"I will," Josie said.

Beau watched the women head for the door, the bell ringing as Josie shoved it open and they walked out of the café to the outside staircase.

Leaving money on the table for his coffee, he followed

the women out the door, his temper slowly climbing toward the point it had been when he'd first received the call.

His father should be the one handling Missy's pregnancy. He'd had months to step up and do the right thing. Beau didn't trust that he ever would.

As he crossed the sidewalk and opened the door of his dark blue Ferrari, his temper cranked up another notch. By the time the car was roaring along the road on the way to his father's house, his fury was simmering toward the boiling point.

Unconsciously his foot pressed harder on the gas, urging the car down the two-lane road at well over eighty miles an hour. With too many speeding tickets in Howler County already, he forced himself to slow down.

Making the turn into Country Club Estates, he turned again two streets later and slid to a stop in front of the house, sending a shower of dust and leaves into the air. The white, two-story home he'd been raised in oozed Southern charm, the row of columns out front mimicking an old-style plantation.

Climbing out of the Ferrari, one of his favorite cars, he pounded up the front steps and crossed the porch. The housekeeper had always had Mondays and Tuesdays off, so he used his key to let himself into the high-ceilinged entry.

On this chilly, end-of-January day, the ceiling fans, usually rotating throughout the five-thousand-square-foot residence, hadn't been turned on, leaving the interior quiet except for the ticking of the ornate grandfather clock in the living room.

"Dad! It's Beau! Where are you?" When he didn't get an answer, he strode down the hall to the study, turned the knob without bothering to knock, and walked into the elegant wood-paneled interior.

"Well, look who's here." Recently retired state senator

Stewart Beaumont Reese, dressed in his usual dark suit, white shirt, and tie, didn't get up from behind his big rosewood desk. "You should have phoned. I might not have been home."

Beau's pulse was beating too fast. He worked to keep the anger out of his voice. "I was already in town on business—*your* business, as it turns out."

The two of them looked amazingly alike, with the same blue eyes and black hair, the senator's now silvered at the temples. Both of them were tall and broad-shouldered, Stewart only an inch shorter than Beau's six-foot-three-inch frame.

They looked alike, but they had nothing else in common—and they had never been close. Far from it. Their relationship had been hostile from the day Beau was old enough to talk back to his dad.

Stewart rose from behind his desk. "You were in town on *my* business? Since when have you had anything to do with *my* business?"

Beau took a steadying breath and forced his back teeth to unclench. "Since you knocked up a nineteen-year-old girl. Jesus, Dad. It's not like you don't have women falling all over you. You had to pick a kid?"

"I don't know what you're talking about."

Beau's temper, already nearing the edge, erupted. "Goddamn it!" Walking up to the desk, he leaned over the top and got right in his father's face. "You've got a baby on the way! I've got the DNA test in my pocket to prove it! How could you ignore something like that!"

"What's going on here?"

Forcing himself to take a deep breath, Beau turned to find a woman he had never seen before standing in the open doorway. Late twenties or early thirties, a notepad in one hand, a pair of half glasses perched on the end of a very nice nose, she was a striking brunette with a stunning figure. Dressed business professional: a russet skirt suit, printed cream silk blouse, and high heels, she had a heart-shaped face framed by the cloud of dark curls that fanned out around her shoulders, big green eyes, and a porcelain complexion. She was lovely.

Beau flicked a glance at his father, who cast him a look that said *See? You've made a fool of yourself again.*

The senator sat back down in his chair. "Cassidy, this is my son, Beau. Beau, meet Cassidy Jones, my personal assistant."

Beau's eyes went back to the woman but his anger didn't cool. Surely his father wouldn't bring one of his mistresses into the house.

But there was more than a very good chance he had.

The senator smiled. "My son and I were merely having a discussion. Nothing to worry about. Was there something you needed?"

"I heard loud voices. I just . . . I wanted to be sure there wasn't a problem."

"No problem. Everything is fine."

"I'm sorry to bother you," the woman said. "Nice meeting you, Beau."

He managed a barely polite reply. The brunette walked out of the study and closed the door.

"Tell me she isn't one of your women," Beau said.

"What she is or isn't is none of your business. Now if we're through here, I have a meeting in—"

"Screw your meeting. I want to know if you're going to sit back and ignore your own child."

"It wasn't my fault, dammit! The girl practically threw herself at me. If you want me to write a check—"

"I didn't come here for a goddamn check! I just thought you might want to be involved. Apparently you're going to ignore your own flesh and blood. Wait a minute—why does that sound so familiar?"

"I hardly ignored you. I gave you the best of everything: clothes, cars, sent you to the finest schools."

"You gave me everything except the father I needed. Now you have a second chance, an opportunity to do it right."

Stewart sighed as if he were talking to someone with a learning disability. "Be reasonable, son. I'm not interested in starting another family. The girl should have gotten an abortion as I suggested. I would have been more than happy to pay the expenses."

Beau clamped hard on his temper. "I'm taking care of the girl and your kid. You don't have to worry about it. In fact, I'd prefer you didn't involve yourself. It would be better for everyone concerned."

"Then you have your wish. Now if you don't mind . . ."

Beau's hand fisted. The more he thought about it, the better the idea sounded. He didn't trust his father—a master manipulator—not to wait a few years and decide it would be good for his image to involve himself in raising the child.

"The more I think about it, since we're all in agreement, why don't I go ahead and have papers drawn up granting Missy Kessler sole custody of the child? That way you'll be kept out of it. You won't have to worry about a thing."

"Fine. Do whatever pleases you. You always have."

True, and in this case it pleased him to do what was best for his little sister.

"Expect to see me tomorrow," Beau said. "I'll have the paperwork done and be back for your signature sometime in the afternoon." Without waiting for a reply, he turned and walked out of the study.

As he strode down the hall, he caught a glimpse of Cassidy Jones walking in the opposite direction. At least his father's latest kept woman was old enough to know better than to get herself pregnant like poor Missy.

As he made his way outside, Beau slammed the front door harder than he intended. One thing he knew for sure. In the months since he had last seen his father, nothing had changed.

Chapter Two

Cassidy Jones walked out of the main house, down the path to the guest house where she was staying. The winter day was chilly, but being a Texan, she enjoyed the break from the relentless summer heat.

As she neared the front door, her mind returned to the scene in the study and her brief encounter with Beau Reese. She had wondered when she would meet him.

The senator had told her that although his son lived in Dallas, just a little over an hour's drive away, they rarely saw each other.

Cassidy knew who he was. Everyone in Texas knew Beaumont Reese, a former top-ranked pro-am race car driver. Her dad and her brothers, Brandon and Shawn, had watched him race on TV. Close to Beau's age, her brothers both had man-crushes on him.

Beau, who was no longer racing, was now co-owner of Texas American Enterprises. Along with his business partner, Lincoln Cain, he ran a billion-dollar corporation.

Cassidy had Googled him, read everything she could find on him. Thirty-five years old, never married, dated women for a few weeks at a time but didn't seem to get seriously involved.

He was a highly respected businessman who ran the marketing side of the company with a talent that helped make it the success it was today. She'd been impressed to learn he donated heavily to charity, especially organizations for children like the Make-A-Wish Foundation and St. Jude Children's Research Hospital.

Several articles mentioned he had been a troubled teen. His juvenile arrest records had been sealed, but Beau spoke openly about his past and gave his money and time to encourage teens with problems.

According to what she'd read, something had happened at the end of Beau's senior year that had turned his life around, and though he never talked about it, speculation was that the arrest for armed robbery with his best friend and later business partner had been the catalyst. While Cain served a two-year sentence, Beau attended the University of Texas at Austin and pulled in top grades—a big change from his unimpressive record in high school.

He had graduated with honors, but a few months later, tragedy had struck when his beloved grandfather, the late Morgan Hamilton, his mother's father, had died, leaving several million to his grandson.

Beau had used the money wisely. Reese had hired Cain, who turned out to have a serious knack for getting things done, and along with Beau's marketing skills, they had built one of the most successful corporations in Texas.

Cassidy knew all about Beau Reese. Still, she hadn't been prepared for the utter beauty of the man.

Several inches over six feet, with wavy jet-black hair, brilliant blue eyes, and lean-muscled, V-shaped body, Beau was a definite heartthrob. If it hadn't been for the hard set of his features and the scar running from the bottom of his ear along his jaw, he might have looked like a pretty boy.

Instead he looked like every woman's dark, midnight fantasy. Minus the contempt for her she read in those incredible blue eyes, she might have felt a twinge of attraction herself. Apparently just being associated with his father was enough to garner his disdain.

Opening the door to the guest house, Cassidy crossed the living room she had set up as an office, arriving at the laptop on the walnut desk against the wall. Like the main residence, the guest house was done in an elegant, traditional motif, with a burgundy overstuffed sofa and chairs in front of a white-manteled fireplace, and a bedroom with a four-poster bed.

The former senator still occasionally entertained VIPs, and when he did, he did it in style. The guest house gave her a place to stay while she was in Pleasant Hill.

Cassidy had only met the senator last week, only officially started working for him last Friday. But the job as his personal assistant wasn't real. It was merely a cover, a way to explain her presence at his home.

As a private investigator with a Dallas agency called Maximum Security, Cassidy had been hired to look into concerns the senator had about his personal safety.

"I don't need a bodyguard," he had said during their interview last week. "I don't think my life is in danger and I don't want that kind of negative publicity. But I think I'm being followed. Someone has been asking questions. I want to know who it is and why it's happening. I want to know what the hell is going on."

Cassidy had assured the senator that she could find out.

"I've got enemies," he had said. "Every politician has. I'll give you some names, people I'd like you to check into."

"I can do that," she said. "Digging is my specialty. It's what I do best." She wasn't the kind of PI who carried a pistol and ran around chasing criminals the way they did in the movies—not that she didn't own a gun and know how to use it. But so far she had never needed a weapon on the job.

The senator had been satisfied with her qualifications and Cassidy had accepted the task. They had come up with a plan that would put her in Pleasant Hill and give her time to figure out if his suspicions were correct and he was facing some sort of problem.

She wondered what the senator and his son had been fighting about. She'd heard them arguing clear down the hall, Beau's voice on the edge of outright fury, his father's carefully controlled but clearly unhappy.

She'd find out. She intended to do the job she was hired for, and to do that she would have to delve into every aspect of the senator's life.

She thought of the handsome older man and bit back a smile. She had a hunch he had chosen her because she was a woman, someone he believed he could control. Cassidy had taken the job because she thought he might actually be in danger.

She was good at what she did and she intended to find out what was going on. If his safety was in jeopardy, she would advise him to hire a bodyguard while she found the person or persons who posed the threat.

She would start by finding out what the trouble was between father and son. Cassidy sat down at the computer and went to work.

It was his second trip to Pleasant Hill in the last two days, the most time Beau had spent in his hometown since his mother died.

The heart attack that had killed Miriam Reese six years ago had struck completely out of the blue. His father and mother were estranged. His mother had been an absentee parent just like his dad, so making the arrangements to bury her had mostly been a duty, an obligation rather than a deeply emotional event.

It occurred to him he felt more for his unborn half sister than he felt for either of his parents.

The front door was unlocked, which wasn't uncommon in a town the size of Pleasant Hill. But as Beau turned the knob and stepped into the entry, the house seemed strangely silent, the ticking of the grandfather clock louder than usual, the air oddly dense.

He had phoned his father a little over an hour ago and reminded him he'd be driving out from Dallas with the custody papers. Though Beau had done his best to keep the disapproval out of his voice, he wasn't sure he had succeeded.

"Dad!" he called out as he walked through the entry toward the hall, the paperwork tucked under his arm. "It's Beau!" Getting no answer, he headed down the corridor toward the study, noticed the door standing slightly ajar.

Steeling himself, hoping his father hadn't figured a way to turn the situation to his advantage or changed his mind, he rapped lightly, then shoved the door open.

His father wasn't sitting at the big rosewood desk or in his favorite overstuffed chair next to the fireplace. Beau started to turn away when an odd gurgling sound sent the hairs up on the back of his neck.

"Dad!" At the opposite end of the desk, a prone figure lay on the carpet in a spreading pool of blood. "Dad!" His father's eyes were closed, his face as gray as ash. The handle of a letter opener protruded from the middle of his chest.

"Dad!" Dropping the papers, Beau raced to his father's side. Blood oozed from the wound and ran onto the hardwood floor. He had to stop the bleeding and he had to do it now! He hesitated, praying he wouldn't make things worse, then with no other option, grabbed the handle of the letter opener, jerked it out, gripped the front of his dad's white shirt and ripped it open.

"Oh, my God! What are you—"

Blood poured out of the wound as Beau clamped his hands over the gaping hole, pressing down hard, desperate to stop the flow of blood. "Call 9-1-1! Hurry, he's been stabbed! Hurry!"

The woman, Cassidy Jones, didn't pause, just pulled her cell out of the pocket of her slacks and hurriedly punched in the number. He heard her rattle off the address, give the dispatcher the name of the victim and say he had been stabbed.

Beau's hand shook as he checked for a pulse, found none. The wound was catastrophic, a stab wound straight to the heart. No way could his father survive it.

Cassidy ended the call, ran over and knelt on the floor beside him.

"Here, use this to seal the hole." She seemed amazingly in control as she handed him a credit card, then ran to the wet bar and grabbed a towel, folded it into a pad, rushed back and handed it over. Beau pressed the towel over the credit card on top of the wound, all the while knowing his father was already dead or within moments of dying.

He checked again for a pulse. Shook his head, feeling an unexpected rush of grief. "His heart isn't beating. Whoever stabbed him knew exactly where to bury the blade." And compressions would only make it worse.

Cassidy reached down to check for herself, pressing her fingers in exactly the right spot on the side of his father's neck. She had to know it was hopeless, just as he did, must have known Stewart Reese was dead.

"I'm sorry," she said.

Beau studied his father's face. Pain had turned his usually

handsome features haggard and slack, so he looked nothing like the athletic older man who kept himself so fit and trim.

Sorrow slid through him, making his chest clamp down. Or maybe it was sadness for the kind of man his father was, the kind who'd wound up the victim of a killer.

"Just hold on," Cassidy said to him. "The ambulance should be here any minute."

His mind went blank until the sound of a siren sliced into his consciousness. Cassidy hurried off to let the EMTs into the house, and a few moments later they appeared in the study.

"You need to give us some room, Mr. Reese," one of them said gently, a skinny kid who seemed to know what he was doing. Beau backed away and Cassidy followed. He felt her eyes on him, assessing him with speculation—or was it suspicion?

It didn't take long for the EMTs to have his father loaded onto a gurney and rolling down the hall, back outside to the ambulance. Beau strode along behind them, Cassidy trailing in his wake.

It occurred to him that she could be the killer. The timing felt wrong and her shocked reaction seemed genuine, but it was possible. His gaze returned to his father and the thought slid away.

As he climbed into the ambulance and sat down beside his dad, he flicked a last glance at the house. If Cassidy Jones hadn't done it, who had? Had the killer still been inside when Beau arrived? How had he escaped? What was his motive?

The ambulance roared down the road, sirens wailing, blowing through intersections, weaving in and out between cars, careening around corners. All the way to the hospital Beau held his father's hand. It was the closest he had ever felt to his dad.

His throat closed up. When he was young, there were

times he had wished his father dead, but that had been long ago. For years they had simply coexisted, neither intruding into the other's world. Now his dad lay dead or dying and Beau wanted answers.

The ambulance turned again and Pleasant Hill Memorial loomed ahead. The vehicle slammed to a stop in front of the emergency entrance and the back doors banged open.

After what seemed an eternity but was only a very short time, Stewart Beaumont Reese was pronounced dead on arrival.

Chapter Three

Beau sat at a Formica-topped table in a small, sterile room off a long, linoleum-floored hospital hallway, waiting to talk to the police. He glanced up as the door swung open and the curvy brunette, Cassidy Jones, walked in. She was dressed in business clothes as she had been the first time he had seen her, camel slacks today and a turquoise sweater, both garments smeared with his father's blood.

His slacks and V-necked sweater weren't any better, the blood dried now into ugly dark patches. Looking at them made his stomach churn.

"I'm sorry for your loss," she said, taking a seat in the chair across from him.

He nodded, hating the trite phrase that meant absolutely nothing.

"What happened?" she asked.

Beau raked a hand through his hair, which as usual needed a trim. "You were there. Someone stabbed him." He sighed into the quiet, wishing he could turn back time, if only for a few precious seconds. "He was dying when I got there. I knew it. I just didn't want to believe it."

The woman cast him a glance that lingered a little too long. "What were you doing at the house?"

His head came up. "What do you mean? I'm his son. I don't need a reason to see my own father."

"I realize that. But according to the senator, you rarely visit. You were there yesterday, back again today. Why did you come to see him?"

Beau straightened in the uncomfortable metal chair. "What business is it of yours?"

"I'm your father's personal assistant, remember?"

Beau scoffed. "How could I forget."

Her eyes narrowed. "What's that supposed to mean?" She was way beyond pretty with her plump lips and those thick dark curls, about five-five and really put together. Then again, his father's women usually were attractive.

"It means I can't believe he had the balls to bring you into the house . . . at least not right now."

She bristled. "I don't know what you think you know, but whatever it is, you're wrong. I just met your father last week. I only started working for him day before yesterday."

So the old man was still wooing her. An attractive man, a former state senator with plenty of money, his seductions never took long. Beau wondered if she really had no clue what his father intended.

"So you walked in and he had already been stabbed," she said, pressing him again.

He glanced up at her tone. "That's right. You got there just a few seconds after I did." Those perceptive green eyes continued to assess him and a light went on in his head. "Wait a minute. You don't think *I* did it? You don't think I'm the one who killed him?"

She held his gaze a little too long. "I don't know." But she clearly had her doubts. "I saw the letter opener in your hand when I walked into the study. What was I supposed to think?"

Beau came out of his chair so fast it teetered and almost toppled over. "I didn't kill my father—but you can bet your last dollar I'm going to find out who did."

The door swung open just then and a plainclothes detective walked into the room. Beau recognized Tom Briscoe, one of the guys he'd gone to high school with. In a town the size of Pleasant Hill, everyone knew everyone.

"I'm really sorry, Beau," Tom said. He was thirty-five, same as Beau, a stocky man with thick, sandy-brown hair. "I can't imagine how you must be feeling."

"Thanks, Tom." Briscoe couldn't imagine because Beau wasn't sure himself. Angry, upset, confused, determined to find out what had happened. "Detective Tom Briscoe, this is Cassidy Jones. She was my father's personal assistant."

Tom gave her the same look Beau had, making the same assumptions. There weren't many secrets in Pleasant Hill and his dad's philandering was legendary. "That so?"

"As I told Mr. Reese, I only started working for the senator two days ago—and none of my duties involved anything of a personal nature."

Tom relaxed. If Cassidy wasn't the senator's mistress, likely she wasn't a suspect. According to her, she barely knew him. What motive would she have?

"Good to know," Tom said. He turned to Beau. "The CSIs are out at the house. It's a crime scene, so you won't be able to go inside until they're done."

He just nodded. On the rare occasion he came to Pleasant Hill, he usually stayed at Blackland Ranch, Linc's property outside Iron Springs, the next town over. Beau had yet to phone his partner and his partner's wife, Carly. It would be the next call he made.

"Why don't we start from the beginning?" Tom said, pulling up a chair and settling his stocky, muscular frame in the seat. "Mind if I record this?"

Beau shook his head and sat back down.

Tom set the recorder on the table and pushed the start button. "Why did you come to Pleasant Hill to see your dad?"

It was an ugly story, one he couldn't tell without hurting someone else. "We had some business to discuss. We worked it out yesterday. I came back today with the paperwork for him to sign."

"What happened when you got there?"

"When I walked into the study, my father was lying on the floor." He swallowed as the memory arose. "He was covered in blood. There was a letter opener buried in his chest. Whoever stabbed him must have done it just a few minutes before I got there."

"You didn't go after the assailant? Try to catch him?"

"I was trying to save my father's life so no, I didn't go after him. I didn't hear anything or see anyone—I wish I had. I don't think the killer was still in the house."

"Your father was a retired senator. He must have surveillance cameras on the property."

Beau shook his head. "My dad didn't like them. He felt they were an invasion of his privacy." And some of the people he dealt with were the sort who didn't want their visits recorded.

"Too bad," Tom said.

"Yeah."

Tom turned to Cassidy Jones. "So you were working at the house when it happened?"

"I hadn't gone into his office yet that day. I have a workspace set up in the guest house. That's where I've been staying."

Beau shot her a glance. *The guest house. Damned convenient.* He wondered if she was telling the truth about her relationship with his dad.

"So the senator was expecting you?"

"Yes," Cassidy said. "There were some things he wanted to discuss. But when I walked in, I saw . . . I saw him lying on the floor, his chest covered in blood. I saw that he had been stabbed."

"Where was Beau at that time?"

Cassidy's gaze swung in his direction, and he didn't like what he saw in her face. "Beau was leaning over his father. He had the letter opener in his hand."

"I was pulling it out!" Beau shot to his feet. "I was trying to save his life!"

Cassidy's eyes locked with his. "I don't know exactly what happened before I got there, but Beau did everything he could to save his father. Unfortunately, it was already too late."

Tom eyed him a little differently now. "I'll need to take both of your statements. I'd like to do that down at the station. You can ride with me or meet me there."

"My car is back at the house," Beau said. Where he'd left it to ride in the ambulance.

"I can drive you home to get it," Cassidy said. She looked down at her blood-stained clothes. "Would it be all right if I went into the guest house to change?"

"You can go in and get some clothes, change at the station. Take one of the officers in with you. What about you, Beau?"

"I've got an overnight bag in my car."

"So you planned to stay in town?"

"Actually, no. Just force of habit. Always better to be prepared."

Cassidy stood up from her chair, hesitated, then released a breath. "Before we go, there's something I need to tell you, Detective Briscoe."

Setting her purse on the table, she opened it, took out a leather badge wallet and flipped it open. "I'm a private investigator. I work for an agency called Maximum Security in Dallas. The senator hired me last week. He wanted me to do a little digging. He was worried. He said he thought someone was following him. He said people had been asking questions. He wanted to know who it was and why. He specifically said he didn't think his life was in danger. Obviously he was wrong."

Cassidy studied Beau as Detective Briscoe took his leave. Strong biceps filled the sleeves of his blood-stained sweater. His forearms were tanned and corded with sinewy muscle. Despite the circumstances, he looked good. *Too good*, she thought as the two of them walked out of the hospital into the sunlight.

Two months ago, her relationship with Richard Shelton, a successful Dallas attorney, had come to an end. She had enjoyed Rick and he had enjoyed her, but they weren't in love, and when work began to hold more appeal than an evening at home with Rick, it was clearly time to move on.

Since then she hadn't dated. Which was probably the reason Beau Reese pushed all her hot buttons. Or maybe it was just because he *was* hot, an extremely good-looking, incredibly sexy male.

Whatever the reason, now wasn't the time or place, and a wealthy celebrity with dozens of women chasing after him wasn't worth the trouble.

Cassidy opened the door of her silver Honda hatchback and slid in behind the wheel. Beau climbed into the passenger seat, pushing it back to accommodate his long legs. They buckled their belts and she started the engine.

The late January weather was chilly, but a blue sky curved overhead. Still, it was Texas. It wouldn't be long before the weather changed.

"So you're a private detective," Beau said as she pulled out of the parking lot.

"I'm mostly an investigator. I rarely carry a weapon. I specialize in digging up information, asking questions, figuring things out. Sometimes I work with a bounty hunter friend of mine. I do the tracing, he brings in the skip, and we split the fee. One of my least favorite jobs is finding out if a spouse is cheating, but it pays the bills."

Beau didn't smile. She knew his mind was still back at the house, going over and over what had happened to his father. Her instincts said he hadn't done it. And when she replayed the scene, the timing seemed slightly off. She trusted her instincts and her judgment, but she needed to be sure.

"I wish I'd had a few more days," she said, regaining his attention as the car rolled down the road. "Maybe I could have found something that would have given us a warning, something that would have prevented his death."

Intense blue eyes went to her face. "He must have told you something, said something that could lead the police to the killer. He hired you because he was worried. What did he say?"

"He gave me a couple of names, business associates. There was also a woman. He said their relationship hadn't ended well."

Beau scoffed. "His relationships rarely ended well. My father wasn't the sort of man who stayed friends with the women he dated. He used them, then discarded them like old shoes."

Cassidy filed the information away. "I know the two of you didn't get along. I read that in more than one account. I got a firsthand look yesterday when I heard you arguing."

He scoffed. "He was a terrible father and a rotten husband. My mother wasn't any better. I think she got pregnant because she thought it was a necessary part of being married, but she didn't really like kids. She and my dad believed as long as they gave me money, they could go on with their lives as if I didn't exist."

"Was that the reason you got in trouble in high school? Nobody around to take care of you?"

He cast her a dark look. "Hey, I didn't kill him, so you don't need to be investigating me."

"Sorry." But she wasn't really sorry at all. Yesterday Beau and his father had had a vicious quarrel. Today Stewart Reese was dead. Was it possible Beau had lost his temper and stabbed the older man in a fit of rage?

"How'd you get interested in becoming a PI anyway?" he asked.

"Lot of cops and military in my family. My granddad, my brothers. My grandfather died in the line of duty when I was a kid. I was never interested in joining the force, but I liked the idea of catching bad guys, so I studied criminology in college. I apprenticed for a while with a friend of my brother's in the security business in Houston. I liked it. Investigative work seemed to be a good fit."

The entrance to Country Club Estates loomed ahead. She pulled into the area of luxury homes and drove along the golf course to the big white house with the columns out front. Several white-and-blue police vehicles were parked on the street, and yellow crime-scene tape stretched across the porch, reminding her that a man had just died here and that man was Beau's father.

Silence fell inside the car.

"Thanks for the ride," Beau said a little gruffly, his features drawn and grim as he opened the door and ducked out of the car. He and his father weren't close, but the senator was still his dad.

Cassidy watched him walk toward the Ferrari she had spotted parked out front when she'd left to follow the ambulance. With his long, lean-muscled build, wide shoulders and narrow waist, the man was definite eye candy.

She knew he was in great physical condition. She had

read he trained in mixed martial arts, and apparently he was good at it—like pretty much everything else he did.

She went around to the guest house, walked up to the uniformed patrolman standing out front and told him Tom Briscoe had said she could get something to wear. The officer escorted her inside and waited while she grabbed a pair of jeans, a yellow scooped-neck sweater, and a pair of sneakers.

"We should be done with the guest house in a couple of hours," said the patrolman, a skinny young guy with light brown hair. "You'll be able to come back then."

"Great." Because she planned to stay for at least a few more days—unless Beau Reese threw her out. She had only begun her investigation into the three names the senator had given her. She needed more information, needed to look into the senator's personal records, into his life.

By now the police would have taken his computer and the folders in his file drawers, but she had a hunch there was more. From the little she had gleaned since she'd met him, the senator was a secretive man, not the sort to leave his personal information lying around.

If her hunch was right, there would be a place he kept his important documents, his personal records, and she intended to find it.

Carrying the change of clothes, she returned to where her car was parked, surprised to see Beau Reese sitting in his Ferrari waiting for her. Apparently Beau was a gentleman, the last of a dying breed.

As she started the Honda and turned it around in the street, Beau fired up the powerful Ferrari engine, waited for her to drive in front of him down the road, then fell in behind her.

She knew where to go. When she had first arrived in Pleasant Hill, she had passed the police station, downtown on a side street off Main. Most of the buildings were false-fronted brick structures, the drugstore had dark green awnings out front, and the streets all had angled parking.

She pulled into the lot next to the station and got out of the car, waited for Beau to park and catch up with her, and they walked inside together, both of them cordial and friendly.

Cassidy planned to keep it that way—unless Beau Reese had cold-bloodedly murdered his father.

Chapter Four

The police station was busy today. Murder had a way of stirring things up. Men and women in dark blue uniforms strode in and out with purpose. Tom Briscoe was waiting when Beau walked in with Cassidy Jones. Opening the swinging half door attached to the counter, Tom motioned for them to follow him down the hall.

"You can change in the ladies' room," Tom said to Cassidy.

"Thank you." She pushed open the door and disappeared inside, came out a few minutes later in clean jeans and a yellow sweater, her bloody clothes in the bag she had brought with her. Briscoe didn't take them as evidence, since it was clear whose blood was on the clothes. Instead, he ushered the woman into an interview room, leaving Beau to cool his heels out in the hall.

Cassidy was a private investigator—he still found it hard to believe. Then again, maybe his dad was just working a con that backfired on him, hiring a woman he wanted to seduce, figuring he could get a little work out of her while he was at it.

It wouldn't have been the first time.

Beau couldn't help wondering if Cassidy had been

attracted to his dad. She was somewhere near thirty, which meant the senator was almost twice her age. With her classic features, heavy dark curls, and those big green eyes, she was a beautiful woman. His dad had always liked a woman with substantial cleavage, and it was clear Cassidy Jones had more than her share.

But she obviously had brains, too, and that was a big negative to a man who needed to believe he was the smartest guy in the room.

Beau wondered what she was in there telling Tom Briscoe. So far she had done her best not to convict him with her words. Why, he had no idea, but he hoped that didn't change. He was a well-known figure in the community, well liked by most. He gave to a number of local charities and had always been supportive of police.

He figured those things would help. He didn't think the cops would rush to judgment, which would give him some time. Exactly what he would need if he was going to find the man who had murdered his dad.

The image of his father's ashen face and blood-covered body appeared in his head. *What did you do, Dad?*

Who had his father cheated? Who had he pissed off enough to get himself killed?

It was going to take time to dig through the maze that was Stewart Reese's life. Beau thought of Cassidy and what she might be telling the police. Finding his father's killer could be even more important now. It might be necessary to prove him innocent of murder.

Beau decided not to call an attorney—at least not yet. Instead, after Cassidy Jones had finished her interview and left the station, Beau had given a clear and concise statement of events leading up to and including the discovery of his father's body. Exactly the same story he had told before.

The only thing he'd glossed over was why he had come to Pleasant Hill in the first place.

On the phone yesterday, Josie had told him that Missy didn't want anyone else knowing the name of her baby's father. She was ashamed of having been duped by a man old enough to be her grandfather.

If the girl wanted to keep the name secret, Beau sure as hell wasn't going to tell anyone. Not unless he had no other choice.

As he walked out of the interview room, relieved to be finished, he glanced up at the sound of high heels clicking on the linoleum and saw his former stepmother walking toward him down the hall. Two years after his mother died, Stewart Reese had remarried a forty-five-year-old woman from Dallas named Charlotte Mercer. They had divorced last year.

Though she was as elegantly dressed as always, Charlotte's dove-gray designer pantsuit looked slightly rumpled. Her mouth was tight, her blond hair not quite as perfectly groomed as it usually was. She looked . . . *shell-shocked* was the word that came to mind.

"Oh, Beau, I'm so glad you're here." Charlotte's eyes welled as she approached. "The police called. They wanted to let me know what had happened before I heard it on the news. They said they had some questions. I told them I would be happy to help in any way I could. I told them I would drive down right away."

Beau closed the distance, leaned in to kiss her cheek. "I'm sorry, Charlotte."

She took a shuddering breath, but didn't hug him. She wasn't the hugging type. It was strange how much she reminded him of his mother.

"You know we still cared about each other," she said, pressing a linen handkerchief beneath her nose.

He nodded, though he had no idea one way or the other. Maybe they actually had.

"It's hard to imagine him dead," Charlotte said. "Stew was a lot of things, some of which I despised, but he was a man who knew how to live."

"I'm going to find out who did it," Beau said. "You don't have to worry about that."

Her head jerked up. Hazel eyes zeroed in on his face. "What are you talking about? You have to let the police handle this. I want this over as quickly as possible. In the three years we were together, your father caused me enough grief to last a lifetime. I don't need any more scandal."

"He was murdered, Charlotte. That isn't going to change. I'm going to find the man who did it. I won't rest until I do."

Her lips thinned. "You listen to me, Beau Reese. Your father is gone. There's nothing either of us can do to bring him back. It's best for all of us if this whole thing disappears as quickly as possible."

"You'll only be marginally involved, Charlotte. Your marriage has been over for more than a year."

"I know how this works. Your father was an important man. Reporters will show up at my door. They'll be trying to dig up dirt on Stewart, and that will rub off on me."

She wasn't wrong there. Their divorce had been messy, to say the least. Infidelity was always a juicy subject for the tabloids. In this case, the tables had been turned on his dad. The senator had come home to find his wife in bed with a much younger man.

"I'll be attending the funeral, of course," Charlotte was saying. "But after that, I'm going to disappear for a while. Betsy Durant has invited me to stay with her for as long as I want." Betsy Durant was a mega-wealthy patron of the arts, a Dallas socialite who owned a house as big as a palace in the exclusive Highland Park district.

"Betsy knows how trying all of this is going to be for

me," Charlotte said. "She insists I stay with her at least for the next few weeks, perhaps longer."

Relief filtered through him. Charlotte would be busy in Dallas while Beau planned to stay in Pleasant Hill. He'd get a room at the Holiday Inn for the night and hope the crime scene was released sometime tomorrow. As soon as that happened, he would move into the house.

He needed access to his father's study, to his private personal files. He knew where they were, had walked in on his father once when he was a kid, while his dad had had his special hiding place open. Beau had gotten a good talking-to for coming in without knocking, and neither of them had ever mentioned it again.

He'd decide whether to turn the information over to the police after he had looked at it. He needed to find out who benefited from Stewart Reese's death. He needed to know the names of his father's associates—and enemies.

Which one of them had hated the senator enough to kill him? Or hire someone to do it?

He thought of the pretty lady investigator and hoped to hell she didn't cause him too much trouble.

"What about the funeral service?" Charlotte asked, regaining his attention.

It had to be done, but he wasn't ready to think about it. "I'll take care of it."

She took a step closer, rested her hand on his arm. "I could take care of it for you, Beau. Get things lined up and then get your approval. I know how difficult this must be."

It seemed like a cop-out, letting someone else make the arrangements for the last major event in his father's life. On the other hand, finding his killer was far more important than handling inconsequential details.

"I could make sure it's done in a tasteful style, something befitting a senator." Of course she would think of that.

"I could call his former assistant in the senate," she said, "get a list of all the people who need to be invited."

He nodded. "All right. When you have everything tentatively set up, let me know and we'll go over it together."

"Of course," Charlotte said.

Beau looked up to see the door open and Tom Briscoe walk into the hall. Tom spotted Charlotte and headed in her direction.

"Mrs. Reese. I'm Detective Briscoe. I'm terribly sorry for your loss."

She dabbed her handkerchief against her eyes. "Thank you, Detective. You know, even after our divorce, the senator and I remained close."

"I appreciate your coming so quickly. The sooner we can find out what happened, the sooner we can get justice for Senator Reese." Tom glanced at Beau over Charlotte's head. "You can go now, Beau. I have your cell number. But don't leave town just yet."

"I'll be staying out at my dad's," Beau said. He'd be busy. Along with finding a killer, he had a company to run.

He still hadn't called Linc. His business partner would take care of things back at the office, he knew. He was a man you could count on. Truth was, Beau hadn't called Linc because his best friend was the one person in the world who would hear the pain in his voice.

Beau headed out to his car, a million questions circling around in his head. For an instant he considered hiring the lady detective. She knew how to go about finding answers. Digging was what she did for a living. Then he thought of her pretty face, heavy dark curls, and sexy curves, and knew he couldn't afford the distraction.

Better he figure things out on his own.

* * *

Darkness hung over the flat East Texas landscape by the time Cassidy returned to the guest house that evening. Dampness seeped through her clothes and a chill wind sent gooseflesh over her skin. Clouds crept past, obscuring the stars. The front door of the main house was still blocked off with yellow crime-scene tape but when she went around to the guest house, the police officer was gone and no tape blocked the door.

A few things had been moved around inside, drawers had been opened and closed, but she had only been there a few days and she hadn't brought much with her from Dallas.

The police would have been looking for anything out of the ordinary, anything that might indicate she was connected in some way to the murder. She was a licensed PI, hired by the victim, a minor suspect with no apparent motive. But she had been at the crime scene and the police would be looking at every possibility.

She walked over and turned on the TV, found a news channel. The murder of a former Texas state senator dominated the news broadcasts. A reporter relayed the story, adding that Stewart Reese's son had found his dying father; no suspects were yet in custody. There was a number to call at the bottom of the screen if anyone had information.

In the final portion of the broadcast, Beau walked out of the police station, head down, jaw set as he strode across the parking lot. Several reporters shoved microphones into his face, but he just kept walking, sliding gracefully into his low-slung sports car, leaving the media in his dust as they ran after him down the road.

She wondered if the police had insisted he stay in Pleasant Hill or if he would be returning to Dallas. He was head of marketing for Texas American Enterprises. Beau was a very busy man.

But the police would have more questions. Cassidy certainly did. She wanted to know exactly what he and his father had been fighting about the day before, wanted to know if the argument could have continued, could have led to a violent murder.

Wishing she could get into the main house, see if she could find the files she had a strong feeling were there, she sat down at her computer, which fortunately the police hadn't taken, and went to work.

The senator had given her three names to look into. George Larson was his partner in Green Gables Realty, a chain of real estate offices that stretched east from Dallas to Texarkana and south as far as Tyler. Three months ago, the senator had insisted on selling the company, and apparently Larson wasn't happy about it.

The second name on the list, Jess Milford, was the recently terminated foreman of Alamo, Stewart Reese's construction and real estate development company, a man who had worked there for nearly twenty years. He might be carrying a grudge, the senator had said.

Last, Reese's ex-wife, Charlotte Mercer Reese. According to the senator, Charlotte had never recovered from their divorce. She was fixated on Stewart and wanted them to get back together.

Cassidy had mentioned the senator's suspicions to Beau but hadn't given him her name or the others'. He'd been overwhelmed by his father's death, but sooner or later he'd want to know. She hoped he hadn't said anything to Briscoe. She wanted to do some preliminary research first, which would be a whole lot harder once the police got involved.

Then again, maybe the cops would get lucky and find the killer right away. The police force in a town of fifteen thousand was small, but Police Chief Eric Warren had a good reputation and Briscoe seemed capable.

A little before midnight, she pushed away from the

computer. Her neck hurt and her eyes felt gritty, but she had the basics on all three people. She'd need more to figure out if any of them could be suspects.

Tomorrow she would head into town, have lunch somewhere the locals ate, and do a little shopping. In a small town, shopkeepers and restaurant owners knew pretty much everything about everyone. As long as it looked like you were going to spend money, they were happy to talk. You never knew what sort of useful information might surface.

She would see what she could find out about the murder, about the senator, and the three people on her suspect list. Well, four if she counted Beau Reese.

Thinking of him, Cassidy walked over to the window and looked out at the main house. A feeling of unease filtered through her. Beau and his father didn't get along, but that didn't mean there wasn't a chance Beau knew where his father kept his personal records. If he did, he might go after them. There could even be something in those records he wouldn't want the police to know.

No lights burned in the big house. The crime scene hadn't been officially released, but the last two patrol cars had driven off several hours ago.

Knowing she shouldn't, unable to convince herself, she turned and walked into the bedroom. After a quick change out of her yellow sweater into a long-sleeved black T-shirt, she dragged her hair into a ponytail and stuck it through the hole in a black, Maximum Security baseball cap. Her gear bag held a set of lock picks. She took the box out and stuck it into the pocket of her jeans, took out a small Maglite flashlight, and headed for the door.

It was dark out, just a sliver of moon. Dim rays threw shadowy light over the flat landscape populated with thick stands of oaks and dense leafy foliage along the creek beds. Dressed as she was, she wouldn't be easy to spot.

Making her way from the guest house across the manicured

yard, across the terrace to the back door, she used the lock picks, heard the click of the lock falling into place, turned the knob, and slipped into the laundry room.

The senator had given her the security code. She hurried to turn off the alarm. Odds were there was a wall safe hidden somewhere in the study, a problem since she wasn't a safe cracker, but the combination might be hidden in his desk. Or maybe there would be a hidey-hole inside a piece of furniture. Finding it was a long shot, but she worked with a pro, the owner of the agency, Chase Garrett, so she knew where to look.

She wasn't about to interfere in an ongoing police investigation by accidentally destroying evidence that might help solve the case. But there was a chance the senator kept his files somewhere else. The master bedroom would be her second choice.

Cassidy turned on her flashlight and followed the glowing yellow circle down the hall.

Chapter Five

Crime-scene tape fluttered in the breeze, but it was almost midnight and the police cars were gone from in front of the house. Beau parked his Ferrari in a spot half a block away, a place in the trees he used to sneak off to when he was in high school, a place his friends could park and wait for him to join them without being seen.

He'd been wild back then, always pushing the limits, trying to prove himself. He and Linc and a kid named Kyle Howler, the sheriff's son, were constantly in trouble. Then one night, Kyle had goaded them into robbing a convenience store.

Beau, who drove a suped-up red Mustang his dad had bought him, agreed to act as the wheelman. Linc and Kyle wore ski masks and carried revolvers when they went into the store around midnight. But they were kids, not killers. When old man Lafferty brought a shotgun out from under the counter, they put down their weapons and all three of them were arrested.

Linc, who had just turned eighteen, spent two years in

prison. A few months younger, still seventeen, Kyle and Beau had had their juvenile records sealed.

What happened that night had changed all of their lives.

The memories slid away as Beau climbed out of the car. No dome light went on, a trick he'd learned as a kid. Grabbing a flashlight out of the Ferrari, he stayed in the shadows as he walked toward the house.

After he'd left the police station, he had checked into the Holiday Inn, but he hadn't been able to sleep. Even after drinking a couple of beers he had picked up at the store and brought to the room, he couldn't calm his mind enough to block images of his father lying on the study floor covered in blood.

He had planned to postpone his search until he moved into the house tomorrow, but he was sure the cops wouldn't find whatever was in his father's secret place, and the information could be extremely important.

And what if the murderer also knew about the hiding place? What if he went back to the house and took whatever his father kept there before Beau had a chance to look at it?

Giving in to temptation, he'd left the motel, climbed into his car, and driven to the house that had been his childhood home.

He kept walking, crossed to the other side of the road, and made his way around back. No lights on in the guest house. He figured Cassidy had probably returned to Dallas, wondered if he'd ever see her again and felt a surprising flicker of disappointment.

He hadn't met an interesting woman in weeks, longer really, and especially not one who appealed to him physically as much as Cassidy Jones.

He was crossing the yard toward the back door when he spotted a dim light moving around behind the curtains in the master bedroom. Adrenaline shot through him. Clicking off the flashlight, he ducked out of sight behind the thick trunk of an oak tree.

Someone was in the house, and the way the light was circling, that someone was searching for something.

Moving quietly through the darkness, he reached the terrace and crossed to the back door, found it unlocked, turned the knob, and slipped into the laundry room. Beau headed down the hall toward the master bedroom, pausing just outside the door to listen for movement inside. The sound of footsteps crossing the deep cream carpet in the bedroom signaled the intruder was heading in his direction.

Beau flattened himself against the wall behind the door, muscles tense as he waited. The knob turned and the door swung open. Beau stepped out and grabbed the intruder around the waist, heard a gasp as he slammed the man against the wall.

The guy was small but he didn't go down easy. Beau blocked an elbow jab, jerked his knee up to stop a kick to the balls that would have done serious damage to his masculinity, did a quick turn, and used the side of his foot to sweep the guy's feet out from under him.

They both went down on the floor of the hall, Beau landing on top, pinning the guy in a wrestling move that took less than three seconds, with the intruder's legs splayed and his arms immobilized above his head. It was the lush, pillow-soft breasts pressing into his chest that said the intruder was a woman.

The height and feminine curves said it was Cassidy Jones.

"Cassidy, what the hell?"

"Beau." Recognizing his voice, she stopped fighting and relaxed a little, shoved hard at his chest. "Get off me. I can't breathe."

Nestled in the soft vee between her spread thighs, his body felt perfectly fine where it was. Seeing it as payback for the trouble she'd caused, he dipped his head to catch a whiff of her soft perfume, shifted a little just because she felt so good, then lifted himself away before he started getting hard.

As he came to his feet, gripped her hand and pulled her up beside him, his irritation returned. It was followed by a shot of suspicion.

"In case you've forgotten, this is a crime scene," he said. Since neither of them were supposed to be there, he tugged her down the hall into the powder room, where he could safely turn on the light. "What the hell are you doing here?"

She hesitated just long enough for him to know she was going to lie.

"The truth, or I'm calling the cops." Not that it wouldn't cause him as much trouble as her.

Resigned, Cassidy sighed. "I was looking for your father's private papers."

"The police took his laptop and all his files. You must know that. What makes you think there's something more?"

"I got the impression the senator wasn't the type to leave his personal information lying around. He liked his privacy. He didn't even have security cameras outside the house. My guess is he kept his important papers somewhere safe." She cocked a dark eyebrow. "If there's nothing to find, what, exactly, are you doing here?"

Instead of answering, Beau studied her face, trying to come to a decision. He had looked her up while he'd been sitting in that motel room. Twenty-nine years old, graduated at the top of her class from the criminology program at the University of Texas in Dallas, worked for the past five years for a firm called Maximum Security.

She'd been born and raised in Houston, came from a family of decorated cops and soldiers, just like she'd said. Reputation as an extremely competent private investigator. More importantly, no connection to the senator or any of his cronies.

"If you'd found the files," he asked, "what were you going to do with them?"

"Depends on what was in them. Stewart Reese hired me. That means my loyalty belongs to him. I wouldn't divulge anything personal I found in the files unless it was relevant to catching his killer."

"So you're planning to investigate his death on your own?"

"That's right. I was on the job when he was killed. That makes it personal. As far as I'm concerned, I'm still on the job and will be until the man who murdered him is in custody."

"What about money? How do you plan to get paid? Because if you think you can use whatever you find out in exchange for some kind of payoff—"

She stiffened. "This isn't about money—not for me—not anymore. It's about justice. I'll do what needs to be done."

He was good at reading people. It was one of the reasons his company had become so successful. She felt responsible in some way for the senator's death and she was determined to make it right.

Of course, it wouldn't be the first time he'd been wrong about a woman. He had good instincts, but hell, it wouldn't be the first time he'd been wrong about a man.

The powder room was beginning to feel confining. Or maybe it was Cassidy's soft perfume. Or that if he leaned just a little closer, he could brush against those magnificent breasts. He forced himself to concentrate.

"So let's say I know where those papers you're after might be—if they exist at all. I'll tell you what I'll do. You're a private investigator—I'll hire you to help me find my dad's killer."

"Are you serious?"

"You take the job, I'll pay you double your usual fee, but

we work together, and you don't hand anything over to the police without my say-so. And my decision is final."

Interest sparked in those big green eyes. She was watching him as closely as he'd been watching her. "I won't do anything illegal."

"You ever heard of breaking and entering? You broke into someone else's house. You're here without permission."

She glanced down, toyed with her heavy Maglite. "Point taken, but I still won't—"

"Fine. Nothing illegal." But she had better be prepared for what his father might have done. Odds were his dad was involved up to his silver-threaded eyebrows in God-only-knew what. Beau figured he'd handle the problem if or when it arose.

"Where's the stuff hidden?" Cassidy asked.

"Unfortunately, it's in the study."

She rolled those big green eyes. "I was afraid of that."

"You agreed we wouldn't do anything illegal," Cassidy hissed as they headed down the hall to the study. "Interfering with a police investigation is a criminal offense."

"So is burglary, but you didn't seem to have a problem with that."

She was only planning to *look* at the documents, not steal them, maybe take some photos with her cell, but she didn't say that. Not when she had just been hired to do exactly what she was going to do without being paid.

Plus, she'd have Beau's cooperation—at least to a point.

Following his long, lanky strides down the passage, she couldn't help remembering the leashed power of his body as he'd taken her down with an ease that was frightening. She couldn't help remembering the hard, sinewy muscles that had pinned her to the carpet in some kind of wrestling move, her legs splayed, Beau nestled intimately between them.

She had heard of women who harbored rape fantasies. Cassidy definitely wasn't one of them. Still, there was a split second when she had realized it was Beau, realized she was completely at his mercy, that she had really been turned on.

On the other hand, there were probably a dozen women who would want to have wild monkey sex with Beau Reese.

He paused at the study door, reached down and turned the knob, carefully eased the door open. Fingerprints wouldn't be a problem. Both of them had been in the study. Their prints would be all over the room.

Beau's black, high-top sneakers squeaked as he crossed the gleaming hardwood floor, stopping next to a small oak four-drawer stand against the wall. Pulling the stand a few feet away, he knelt in front of the spot where the furniture had been sitting.

Long tanned fingers slid over the surface of the wood floor, feeling for a break in the boards. Finding it, he took out his pocketknife and opened the blade, used it to pry out a square of wood so perfectly fitted it had been completely invisible.

A two-foot-by-two-foot opening about eighteen inches deep appeared in the floor. When Beau shined his flashlight inside, Cassidy could see a stack of manila files, along with what appeared to be a small box containing a pair of USB flash drives.

Her pulse quickened. She'd been right about the senator. Whatever was in that hole could very well lead them to his killer.

Beau scooped up the files and handed them over, grabbed the flash drives and stuffed them into the pocket of his jeans, then replaced the panel in the floor. He slid the furniture back into place, motioned for her to retreat, and both of them stepped out into the hall.

A few minutes later, they were standing in the living room of the guest house, the curtains closed, the files spread open on a table in front of the granite counter along a wall of appliances that served as a compact kitchen.

"There's a lot of stuff here," Cassidy said. "It's going to take some time to go over." But she was already thumbing through the files, searching for anything that involved the names the senator had given her.

Beau caught on in a heartbeat. "You're looking for something that pertains to the people he mentioned."

"That's right."

"Since we're supposed to be working together, be a good idea if you gave me those names."

She glanced up. "Sorry. I'm not used to sharing." She pulled out a manila file labeled Green Gables Realty she had spotted in the stack.

"George Larson," Beau said, correctly guessing one of the names. "Larson was my father's partner in the real estate business."

She nodded, tapped the file. "Three months ago, the senator insisted they sell. Apparently Larson wasn't happy about it."

Beau frowned. "*Insisted?* If Larson didn't want to sell, my father must have coerced him. He must have had something on him, something he was holding over his head."

"You're saying Larson was blackmailed into selling?"

"That's right." The bluest eyes she had ever seen fixed on her face and a little curl of heat slid into her belly. *Not good.*

"If you're going to work this case," Beau said, "you had better start seeing my father as the man he really was. He was ruthless and conniving, willing to do just about anything to get what he wanted. His list of enemies is going to be way more than three. Who else did he mention?"

"The other man's name is Jess Milford. He worked for Alamo, the construction and development company your father owned."

"I don't know him. Until yesterday, I hadn't seen my father in nearly a year. I talked to him on the phone when it was necessary, but I never got involved in his business dealings and he didn't get involved in mine."

"Milford was fired from an apartment construction job. He'd been with Alamo for years, foreman for the last five."

Beau scoffed. "Loyalty wasn't part of the senator's makeup. Not unless he got something in return."

Cassidy eyed him with speculation. "You really hated him, didn't you?"

A muscle tightened in Beau's cheek, pulling up the thin scar along his jaw. "Hate's too strong a word. I didn't respect him. I didn't approve of his business dealings or the way he conducted himself. Did I dislike him enough to kill him? No. He was still my father and I'll always be his son."

"You realize the murder weapon tells us a lot. A letter opener, something probably lying on top of his desk."

"It belonged to him. The end of the handle was an eagle with its wings spread. I've seen him use it dozens of times."

"That's just it. It wasn't a gun or a knife. The murder wasn't planned. It probably happened in the heat of the moment, a crime of passion, they call it. Which brings me to the third name. Your stepmother, Charlotte Mercer Reese."

Surprise flashed in his eyes. "I saw Charlotte yesterday at the police station. As I understand it, their divorce was messy but agreeable. Dad found Charlotte in bed with a younger man and insisted on ending the marriage. My father slept with any woman he wanted, but he couldn't handle it when his wife returned the favor."

"He said she never got over him, that she wanted them to get back together."

Beau frowned, shook his head. "I'm not buying it. Dad gave her nothing but trouble. From what I could tell after the divorce, she was glad to be rid of him. When I saw her yesterday, she seemed stunned but not brokenhearted, though she did say they had remained close after the divorce."

"I guess we'll see."

Beau reached over and closed the file. "It's getting really late. We can work on these again tomorrow. I presume you'll want to continue staying in the guest house."

"If you don't mind."

"Seems the best solution. I've got to make a quick trip back to Dallas, but I'll be staying in the main house until this is over."

"Oh." She hadn't considered he might do that. The idea of Beau being in such close proximity was somehow unsettling. It was possible he had murdered his father, yet he managed to spark the first real attraction to a man she had felt in months—longer, really, considering her relationship with Rick had been more of a convenience than anything with real physical heat.

He started to leave with the files tucked under his arm and the flash drives in his pocket. *Not happening.* No way was she giving him the chance to purge information that could connect him to the crime.

"You know, I'm not really sleepy," she said, stopping him at the door. "Why don't you leave that stuff here and I'll work on it a little longer?"

A slow, sexy smile curved his lips. It was the first real smile she had seen and the effect trapped the breath in her lungs.

"You don't trust me," he said.

She shrugged. "Let's just say I'm the cautious type."

"You're a smart lady. I like that. Tell you what. Since

neither of us completely trusts the other, you keep the manila files and I'll take the flash drives." Setting the files back on the table, he crossed the living room in that long-legged stride of his and paused at the door. "Let me know if you come up with anything and I'll do the same. Good night, Cassidy. I'll see you tomorrow."

When the door closed behind him, Cassidy felt as if the heat had suddenly been turned down and she could actually breathe. Aside from his dark good looks and amazingly hot body, there was something intriguing about Beau Reese.

She knew he had dated some of the world's most beautiful women, but he had also had affairs with a college professor, a female CEO, and a lady stockbroker. Clearly women with brains didn't intimidate him.

She liked his honesty, the fact he didn't try to sugarcoat his father's shady dealings or their rocky relationship. She liked that he wanted justice for his dad even though the two of them had never gotten along.

Assuming what he'd told her was the truth. Assuming he wasn't just trying to turn suspicion away from himself.

Assuming it wasn't Beau who'd committed the murder.

Chapter Six

Beau thought about driving his car from the motel to the house the next morning and calling for the Tex/Am helicopter to fly him the twenty-five-minute ride into Dallas. The Pleasant Hill Golf Course backed up to the house, providing enough open space for the chopper to land, but driving had always been a stress reliever, and the time on the road would give his head a chance to clear.

By the time he pulled up to the Texas American Enterprises building, a six-story mirrored glass structure on North Central Parkway, the tension had drained from between his shoulders and he was coming to terms with his father's death.

Stepping out of the elevator on the executive floor, he crossed the deep, beige carpet. The low tables in the reception area were of smooth, rust-grained teak, a warm contrast to the nubby oatmeal fabric on the sofas and chairs.

He waved at the feisty redheaded receptionist, Leslie Bingham, who had once held high hopes of snaring Linc but had given up after his recent marriage and now seemed to be crushing on Beau.

"Good morning, Mr. Reese. I'm so sorry to hear about

your father." She was bright and ambitious and good at her job. And aside from an occasional over-adoring smile, she was a very good employee.

"Thank you, Les." On the drive to the office he had geared himself up for the dozens of condolences he would be receiving over the next few weeks. Whatever he thought of his father, Stewart Reese was an important man and Beau was his son.

He stopped to speak to Linc's personal assistant, Millie Whitelaw, who worked in a private area at the back of the reception area. Staff worked in cubicles nearby.

"Is he in?" Beau asked.

"Yes, and he asked me to let him know when you got here. He said for me to send you right in. I'm really sorry, Beau."

"Thanks, Millie." He had phoned Linc from the motel and told him what had happened, asked him to take charge for a while, till he got things handled in Pleasant Hill. Linc was probably the only person in the world who understood the mix of emotions he was feeling.

He opened the door to his partner's private office, which was surrounded by a wall of windows like the ones in his own. The room was done in the same teak décor as the reception area, but with caramel leather sofas and chairs instead of fabric.

As the door closed, Linc stood up from his desk. A big man, six foot five, two hundred twenty pounds of solid muscle, he was good-looking, smart, and loyal to a fault.

Rounding the desk, he grabbed Beau's shoulder and drew him in for a brief man-hug. "I'm sorry, bro. I know how hard this must be. Carly sends her sympathies. And Josh called when he saw it on the news. He said to let him know if there's anything you need." Joshua Cain was Linc's younger brother, just out of the Marines and home from the war after a near-fatal injury.

Beau just nodded. He paced over to the wall of windows, stared out at the sprawling city of Dallas. Cars buzzed along the busy streets below and a stiff wind shifted through the branches of the trees.

The words seemed to just spill out. "He was murdered, Linc." He walked back to the desk. "Jesus, what the hell did my old man do to get himself killed?"

"You'll find out or the cops will. One way or another you'll make sure whoever did it pays."

"I'll find him. I won't be able to move on from this until I know what happened." An image arose of the woman who had been with him the night before in the study. "Believe it or not, I'm going to have some help. I hired a lady detective. I mentioned her when I called."

Linc nodded. "Cassidy Jones. You said she walked in just as you found your dad. They mentioned her on the news."

"She got there just as I was pulling the letter opener out of Dad's chest. The way things went down, I don't think she believes I did it, but she's smart enough to reserve judgment until she's sure."

"She'd have to be smart or you wouldn't have hired her."

Beau told Linc how he had gone out to the house last night to look for his father's secret files and found Cassidy prowling the master bedroom, searching for the same thing. He didn't mention the wrestling match in the hall that had felt way too good, so good just thinking about it stirred him up all over again.

"How'd she know about the files?"

"She told me she'd pegged the senator as secretive and private, not the kind of guy to leave his personal info lying around."

"You don't think she was involved with him in some way?"

"Nothing points in that direction. She was right about

my dad and about the files, and if she's lying about their relationship, sooner or later, I'll find out."

Linc eyed him with speculation. "What's she look like? Your father was a notorious womanizer."

Beau felt the pull of a smile. "I'll admit she's hot, but she's a little too bright for my father's taste. So far, everything about her checks out."

"Be good to have a professional working with you on the case, and you know what they say—"

"Yeah, keep your friends close and your enemies closer."

Linc nodded. "Anything I can do?"

"You're doing plenty keeping things running here. I'll let you know when the funeral is scheduled."

Linc gave a curt nod, his features grim.

Beau headed for his office, the only other private space on the top floor. He paused just outside to speak to Marty Chen, a fine-boned Chinese-American in his midtwenties who had recently become his personal assistant after his longtime female assistant retired.

The kid shot up from his desk. "I heard about your father, Beau. You have my deepest condolences."

"Thanks, Marty." He was always a little too formal, but it was kind of a nice change, and the kid was great at his job. "I'm going to need you to step up your game for a while. I'll be staying in Pleasant Hill while the police conduct their investigation. You'll be able to reach me, but I'd appreciate if you'd clear my calendar as much as you can. If it's something important, I can always chopper back to the city, but I'd rather not do it unless I have to."

"I'll take care of it."

Beau left him and went into his office. It was different from Linc's, the desk, tables, and bookcases made of gleaming black lacquer, the sofa and chairs a cream raw silk with pale blue accent pillows. It was sleek and modern and somehow soothing.

Anxious to get back to Pleasant Hill, Beau made his first call to the tech department. He pulled the flash drives out of his pocket and set them on the desk. He had tried to open them when he got back to the motel last night, but couldn't make it happen. He figured Rob Michaels, his techno whiz kid, was the guy for the job.

Michaels sauntered into the office. Red-haired and freckled, he wore wire-rimmed glasses and would have looked like a typical geek if he hadn't been pretty-boy handsome.

"Sorry about your dad, sir."

"Thanks." Beau handed over the flash drives. "I need you to understand that the information on these is highly personal. No one's to know what's in them but me."

"Goes without saying," Rob agreed. "I'll get back to you on this as quickly as I can."

"I'll be staying at my father's house in Pleasant Hill till I get things settled." He wrote his cell number down on a piece of paper and handed it over. "Call me direct when you have something. Make it a priority."

"Yes, sir." Rob walked out of the office with the flash drives in his hand.

Beau went back to work. Returning calls that couldn't be postponed, he spoke to friends who wanted to convey their sympathies, spoke to some of the employees, had a brief staff meeting, then went over his revised schedule with Marty.

As soon as he finished, he left the office, heading for his home in the Bluffview area north of Dallas, a white, flat-roofed, single-story contemporary on four heavily treed and landscaped acres bisected by a meandering stream.

Built around a free-form swimming pool, the house had twelve-foot ceilings, light hardwood floors, and black granite fireplaces and countertops. Pastel blue, green, and turquoise lent soft accents, and bright-colored modern art hung on the walls.

Parking the Ferrari in the four-car attached garage, he went inside to pack enough clothes for at least a week. Twenty minutes later, he was ready to leave, sliding into a low-slung, slate-gray Lamborghini that fit his restless mood. With its 740-horse V-12 mid-engine, the car was one screaming machine.

Unfortunately, since he was already on the radar as a possible murder suspect, he didn't dare go faster than a few miles over the speed limit.

Still, the roar of the powerful engine and the vibration of the wheel beneath his hands eased some of the tension humming through him. He found himself wondering what Cassidy would think of the incredible car, wondered if she'd be interested in going for a ride.

Which brought to mind their encounter in the hallway and another sort of ride he'd like to give her.

Not the right time, he reminded himself, not when his father's body lay on a cold slab in the morgue. Beau felt a shot of guilt for even thinking about a woman when he should be thinking about finding a killer.

By the time he reached the house, his mind was clear, his thoughts focused. He wasn't leaving Pleasant Hill until his dad was buried and his murderer brought to justice. It was a resolve forged in steel.

Cassidy did a little research, then set out to dig up as much information in the small town of Pleasant Hill as she could. Earlier that morning, the police had released the crime scene and removed the yellow tape from across the front porch. The housekeeper, Florence Delgado, had arrived, along with a cleaning crew that specialized in suicides and other traumatic events.

Cassidy had met Florence last week when she had first arrived. Flo, as the senator called her, was a round-faced sixty-year-old who had been in his employ for fifteen years. Cassidy figured Flo knew plenty about what went on in the residence but was smart enough to keep her mouth shut about it.

Cassidy approached her in the kitchen, where she stood at the sink washing dishes. She looked pale and shaken, understandably so.

"How are you doing, Florence?" Cassidy made her way toward the glass coffeepot sitting on the counter. "I know this must be very difficult for you."

Flo glanced up and her eyes filled. "I still can't believe it. I know there were people who didn't like him, but he was always good to me." She was Latina, with olive skin and chocolate-brown eyes.

"Everyone has enemies, I guess. A senator probably more than most."

Florence nodded. She reached up, took a mug down from the cupboard and handed it to Cassidy, who filled it to the brim. "Do you think the police will catch the man who did it?"

Cassidy nodded and took a sip. "They'll find him sooner or later. Beau and I are working together to help them."

"You are a private investigator. I heard you and the senator talking about it."

Cassidy wondered what else the woman might have heard. "That's right." She took another sip. "Beau is the one who found the senator. You don't think there's any chance he could have been the one who killed him?"

Flo's dark eyes widened in shock. "Mr. Beau? *Never*. He was a good boy, a good son. Oh, he got in some trouble in high school, but what boy doesn't? And look how he turned out. He has become a great success."

Cassidy watched the woman over the rim of the mug. "I know he and his father didn't get along. I heard them arguing. I guess it wasn't the first time."

Florence waved her hand as if it meant nothing. "In some ways they were alike. Both strong men and very hard-headed."

Easy to believe that. "I heard them fighting the day before the senator was killed. The police will probably ask if you have any idea what they were arguing about. Now that the senator is gone, there's no reason for you to keep silent, and it might help us catch the killer."

Florence tossed her dishrag into the sink and wiped her hands on the terry-cloth apron around her waist. "I haven't seen Mr. Beau in nearly a year. I don't know why they were fighting this time, but it always seemed to happen when they were together."

"Did they have an argument the last time you saw him? Is that the reason Beau hasn't been back?"

Flo shrugged. "Always it happens. I remember that time it had something to do with tires, a plant Mr. Cain wanted to build a few miles from Iron Springs." It was the next town over and the county seat.

"What happened?"

"Mr. Beau found out the senator intended to stop the plant from going in. They argued something awful. I could hear them clear through the walls. Mr. Beau never came back. Not until this week."

Cassidy wanted to know what father and son had been arguing about this time. So far Beau had been cooperative. She hoped that continued. A memory arose of him striding out of the guest house in that long-legged, easy gait of his, the muscles in his back moving beneath his dark blue T-shirt, his jeans hugging a round, very nice behind.

She wondered when he'd be moving into the house, wondered when she would see him again, then wished she could make herself stop wondering.

"Is there anything you can think of that might help us figure out who killed the senator?"

Flo's eyes welled with tears. She brushed at a drop that slipped onto her cheek. "Lots of people came to see him. Some came in the evenings after I went home. I would find dirty dishes in the study in the morning. I wish I could help you, but there is nothing that I know."

Cassidy finished her coffee, but the conversation was pretty much over. From the house, she drove into Pleasant Hill, curious what the locals would say about the senator and his son. On Main Street in front of Big Value Hardware, she saw a parking spot and pulled her car into the angled space.

Along a row of false-fronted brick buildings, a little dress shop named Marley's Boutique sat between Tina's Treasures—a thrift shop—and the Pink Blossom flower and gift shop, which also sold baby clothes. At the end of the block, Pleasant Hill Drugs had dark green canvas awnings over the front windows.

She started with the drugstore, wandering in, picking up a tube of lipstick that looked appealing, chatting with the teenage girl at the checkout counter, who was more inter-ested in texting than talking to customers. No help there.

The thrift shop next door yielded nothing. Pushing through the door of the boutique, ringing the bell above the door, she stepped inside and a slender woman in her thirties with a cap of light brown hair sailed toward her, a wide smile on her face.

"Hi, I'm Marley. What can I help ya'll with this fine mornin'?"

"I'm looking for something to wear out to dinner, nothing too fancy, you know? Something nice enough to wear in Pleasant Hill, but not overly expensive."

"I think we can help you with that." Marley drew her over to the dress rack. "I haven't seen you before. Are you new to the area?"

"Yes, I am." Cassidy sighed. "Unfortunately, I'm not

sure how long I'll be staying. I just started a job working for Senator Reese a few days before he was killed."

"Oh, my, such a tragedy. Do the police have any suspects? Any idea who might have done it?" She rolled heavily lashed blue eyes. "There's all kinds of rumors floatin' round. I'm sure you can imagine."

Cassidy smiled at the woman. A real Chatty Cathy. "No suspects yet, I'm afraid."

"I heard Beau was the one who found him. Why, there's talk he might even have been the one who killed him. Crime of passion and all that—you know, what with the letter opener and all. You don't suppose that could be true, do you? I mean, everyone in town likes Beau, but then the two of them did fight like cats and dogs."

Marley slapped a hand over her mouth as she realized how much she'd been talking. "Here I am, rattlin' on and on, and you just wantin' to find a dress."

"Oh, no, I'm enjoying the conversation. I don't really know anyone in town yet and I just feel so bad about what happened." She leaned closer. "You really think Beau might have done it?"

Marley glanced around. "Like I said, him and his daddy never did get along. There's lots of speculation. Winnie Barker, over to the library, said it coulda had somethin' to do with Missy Kessler, her comin' up pregnant and all, and no one knowin' who's the daddy. Missy's only just turned nineteen, you see, and such a sweet little thing. Lollie Tilford down at the flower shop said she saw Beau and Missy sittin' together in the café the day before the murder. Lollie overheard Beau sayin' something to her about money. Missy's mama was there with them—Josie? She owns the café, you see."

"I think I'm beginning to."

"Well, Beau's got all that money, and last year when he was coaching Little League out at the baseball diamond,

I saw him without his shirt—oh, that man has the most glorious muscles *ever*—not to mention the sexiest blue eyes of any man alive on this earth. If Beau paid her the slightest attention, poor Missy woulda been toast."

Cassidy tried to block the images those words created but instead her mind conjured fantasies of Beau in bed with her, his naked body pressing her down in the mattress, those incredible blue eyes gazing down at her as they made love. Furious with herself, she told herself that stories linking Beau to a pregnant young girl were nothing but gossip, not something he would actually do.

Marley seemed to get her second wind. "Why, there was a time, you know, if Beau Reese had asked, half the women in Pleasant Hill woulda dropped their panties for him." She took Cassidy's hand and started along the rack. "Now let's find you that dress."

An hour later, her mind spinning with local gossip on every subject from the mayor's drinking habits to the principal's affair with the president of the PTA, Cassidy left with a couple of casual tops and a little black cocktail dress with a short, floaty skirt that was inexpensive and didn't look half bad.

Determined to find out more about Missy Kessler and the remote possibility that Beau was the father of her unborn child, she headed for the Pleasant Hill Café.

Sitting in a pink vinyl booth sipping a Diet Coke gave her time to watch the young woman with the enormous belly waiting on customers seated at the counter. Missy Kessler wasn't beautiful, but with her long blond hair and blue eyes, she had a certain appeal. When Cassidy finished her Coke and walked up to pay the bill, she gave the girl a friendly smile. "You're Missy, right?"

Missy returned the smile shyly. "Yes, that's right."

"I'm Cassidy Jones. I was working for Senator Reese before he was killed. Beau mentioned you."

The girl's face turned paper white. She swayed like a blow-up clown on paper feet. "He . . . he did?"

Cassidy resisted the urge to reach out and steady her. "Yes, he did. You're . . . umm . . . friends . . . aren't you?"

Missy didn't miss the implication. Her chin wobbled an instant before her lips firmed. She rang up the check and gave Cassidy her change. "Excuse me. I have to get back to work."

As Cassidy took the money, guilt swept over her. The last thing she wanted was to cause the girl more pain. But she had a job to do, a killer to find, and to do that she needed information.

Leaving a double tip on the counter, she headed out the door, satisfied she had accomplished what she'd come for. She had met Missy Kessler and seen her reaction to the mention of Beau's name. Clearly they knew each other and it wasn't just a casual acquaintance. Add to that, he had been seen with her at the café, been overheard talking to her about money.

The hard truth was—there was every chance Beau Reese was the baby's father.

By the time she got into her car and drove back to the guest house, Cassidy was quietly seething. If Beau and his dad had been fighting about the girl, the argument could well have gotten out of hand. The letter opener must have been right on top of the desk. Had the senator's accusations sent his son into a violent rage? Had he picked up the letter opener and stabbed it into his father's heart?

Cassidy paced the living room of the guest house, her thoughts in turmoil. She remembered the articles about Beau, the way he'd turned his life around after a rocky start, his philanthropy, his support for troubled teens. She thought about the attraction that seemed to grow every time she was with him.

Was the image she had built completely false? Was he a cold-blooded killer? She told herself to stay calm, do her job, behave like a professional. It wasn't her place to condemn Beau Reese for taking advantage of a naïve teenage girl.

When Beau knocked on her door, she reminded herself that aside from discovering his guilt or innocence, what he did was none of her business.

She was telling herself not to overreact as she walked to the door and pulled it open, warning herself to hold on to her temper—the instant before she drew back her hand and slapped his handsome face.

Chapter Seven

Beau's arm flew up in surprise but it was too late to block the blow. His cheek stung and anger tightened every muscle in his body. As she stood in front of him, Cassidy's dark eyes flashed with fury.

Beau gritted his teeth to control his temper and took a step forward, forcing her back into the living room.

He slammed the door behind him. "Why the hell did you just hit me? And your reason better be good."

She didn't back down, didn't show a trace of fear. Instead her pretty mouth curved in a hard-edged smile. "I know why you came to Pleasant Hill."

"Is that right? Well, don't keep me guessing."

"That girl, Missy Kessler. She's pregnant."

He nodded. "Very pregnant. So what? How is that any business of yours?"

"It's motive, Beau. Missy's just a kid. You took advantage and got her pregnant. When you came over that day, you and your father started fighting about it. The fight got out of hand and in a fit of rage, you picked up the letter opener and stabbed him to death."

He closed his eyes, trying to block the terrible image of

his father on the floor, his chest soaked in blood. "That's what you think happened?"

Her expression didn't change. "Isn't it?"

"My father had already been stabbed when I walked into the study. But you're right, we did have a fight about the baby—the day *before* he died. And it wasn't about my being the father. Missy's baby is my half sister. My father is her dad."

Silence fell in the room. The blood drained from Cassidy's face. "Oh, my God."

"I got him to agree to give Josie Kessler full custody so she and her daughter could raise the child together."

"You . . . you offered to give her money," she said. "You wanted to help her."

"That's right. I told Josie I'd pay the expenses, make sure the child and her mom were taken care of properly. I came back to the house the next day to get the custody papers signed. Missy didn't want anyone to know, so I kept quiet about it. I guess it's too late for that now."

Cassidy bit her lip. Her eyes were dark with regret, but there was something more. She reached up and gently set her palm over the red mark on his cheek. "I'm so sorry, Beau. I've never done anything like that before. I don't know what happened."

He caught her wrist, holding her hand in place against his cheek, feeling the soft throb of her pulse beneath his fingers. "Maybe you were starting to like me, maybe even trust me. Then you heard about Missy and you thought I'd let you down." He let go of her wrist and she eased her hand away, but her eyes remained on his. "I didn't kill my father, Cassidy. And if you trust me, I won't let you down."

She stared at him a few seconds more, then turned and walked over to the window. Sunlight glinted on her thick dark curls and he noticed the fine ruby strands running through them. His cheek still stung where she had slapped him. She was passionate and beautiful and in that moment, he realized how much he wanted her.

She turned to face him. "It won't matter to the police. It's still motive, Beau. You and your father could still have been fighting about the baby. You could have gotten so angry you picked up the letter opener and killed him."

Beau started shaking his head. "I didn't do it. I didn't kill my father."

Cassidy walked back to him, stood right in front of him. "I believe you. Over the years, I've learned to trust my instincts. I should have done that this time. I won't jump to conclusions again." And then she did something completely unexpected. She went up on her toes and pressed a soft kiss on his lips.

Heat burned through him. Lust hit him so hard his whole body tightened. He reached for her but Cassidy stepped away.

"I'm sorry," she said. "I let my attraction to you cloud my judgment. I won't do it again."

It took all his control not to cross the distance between them and haul her into his arms. His hand fisted as he fought for control. "I want you," he said. "I have since the moment I saw you in my father's study. That day, I did the same thing you did—I misjudged the situation because of the attraction I felt for you. Now that we've cleared the air, we can—"

"No." She shook her head, shifting those dark curls around her shoulders, making him ache to grab a fistful and drag her mouth back to his for a deeper, far different kind of kiss.

"That isn't going to happen, Beau. We need to stay focused. I'm not sure you realize the trouble you're in. So far you're the primary suspect. Until we find the real killer, that isn't going to change."

"There isn't any evidence, Cassidy. There never will be because I didn't do it."

"You're on their radar. You had method and opportunity. The police will find out about Missy and that'll give you motive. We need to find the killer. We have to if you're going to clear your name."

Since she was right, he didn't argue. But now he had two objectives. One was to find the man who had murdered his dad. The other was far more personal. It had nothing to do with murder and everything to do with Cassidy Jones.

Malcolm Vaughn leaned back in the chair behind the desk in his office as the door opened and the visitor he'd been expecting walked in.

Clifford Jennings smiled, lifting the edges of a closely trimmed blond mustache that did nothing for his pale complexion. "The letter opener was a stroke of genius. According to my information, the cops have nothing—no prints, no DNA, nothing. And their only suspect is Beaumont Reese."

Mal steepled his fingers, not bothering to get up from his chair or offer to shake hands. "That's why you hire a professional. It might be expensive but you get what you pay for."

"I couldn't agree more. We may have a problem, though."

One of Mal's brown eyebrows went up. "You're talking about Reese?"

"Reese has the money, but it's the woman I'm worried about. Cassidy Jones is a private investigator and word is she's way better than good. You remember that serial killer down in Houston—the Night Watchman? The credit for his arrest went to a bounty hunter in her office named Jason

Maddox, but Jones was the tracer. She's the one who actually tracked the guy down."

Mal just shrugged. "Even a blind pig finds an acorn once in a while."

"Yeah? You remember Oliver Graves, the guy who ran that hedge-fund pyramid scheme in Dallas? One of his investors got wind of what was going on and hired Jones to prove it. She compiled enough evidence to get the feds involved. Graves is currently serving fifteen to twenty in a Texas state prison."

Malcolm straightened in his chair, not liking the news but sure he could handle any problems that might come up. "We'll keep an eye on both of them. If it looks like the woman's getting too close, we'll do something about it. An accident of some sort wouldn't be hard to arrange."

"What about Reese?"

He shrugged. "Reese is a businessman and a world-class playboy. He and his old man weren't even close. Eventually, he'll get tired of the drama and move on. And there's always a chance the DA will decide to prosecute. We can nudge things in that direction if we have to. Defending himself against a murder charge ought to keep Reese busy and out of our hair."

Jennings nodded. "All right. If anything comes up, I'll let you know." Turning, he walked out of the office.

As soon as the door closed, Mal took out the disposable phone he kept in the bottom desk drawer and punched in a number.

"There's no need for concern," he said. "Everything has been taken care of exactly as you wished."

On the other end of the phone, the connection ended and the line went dead. Just like Senator Reese.

* * *

Later that same day, Beau moved into one of the guest rooms in the main house. His boyhood bedroom had long ago been painted and redecorated. His parents had never been the sentimental type. Avoiding the study, he set up his laptop on the desk in the room, surprised to find it more difficult to be in the house than he had imagined.

He hadn't expected to feel the weight of depression settle over him, hadn't expected the dark memories of his childhood to hover in the silence inside the house. The past seemed to hang like dust in the air, making it hard to breathe.

As a boy, he had escaped the house every chance he'd gotten, had left for good as soon as he'd turned eighteen. His parents had been glad to be rid of him, one less obstacle in their drive for success, both socially and politically, as well as financially.

Beau hated to admit he had inherited a lot of that same drive. He loved his work and he loved his successes. But he also valued his friends and the people who worked for him, and he tried to give back to the community for the satisfying life he lived.

Once he had wanted a wife and family, but that time was past. He'd been deeply in love with his college sweetheart, Sarah Mills. In some ways he had never completely recovered from Sarah's death or the torturous year they had spent together while she fought a losing battle with cancer. Even now, thirteen years later, the thought of a wife and children with anyone else seemed incomprehensible.

Which didn't mean he couldn't have an enjoyable relationship with a woman. He'd had several over the years and still considered the women friends.

For an instant, Cassidy's beautiful face and sexy curves flashed in his mind. He intended to take her to bed and soon. That brief kiss and her admission of the attraction she felt for him said more than any denial. He wanted her and he was a man who got what he wanted.

His cell rang as he finished the last of his unpacking. Pulling the phone out of his pocket, he pressed it against his ear.

"It's Rob," the caller said. "Sorry, sir, but those files you wanted me to open are encrypted."

"Encrypted? You sure? Forget it, stupid question, of course you're sure." But they were talking about his father, not some high-tech genius.

"It'll take me a little time," Rob said, "but I've got some . . . umm . . . software I can use to get into them if that's what you want."

Software. Rob could do just about anything. Beau had never asked for details. "Do it," he said, and hung up the phone.

It was late by the time he went to bed. He should have been sleepy after such a stressful day, but instead his mind refused to quiet. When he finally fell asleep, he dreamed of Cassidy, of a deep, hot, wet kiss that seemed to have no end.

He woke up with a throbbing hard-on, feeling nearly as tired as he'd been the night before. He rolled out of bed, showered and dressed in jeans and a blue button-down shirt. Rolling the sleeves up to his elbows, he sat down at his computer and began running through emails.

Footsteps sounded, coming down the hall. A light rap, and Beau looked up to see Cassidy in the open bedroom doorway. "I knocked on the kitchen door but no one answered. It was open so I came on in."

He rose from his chair and walked toward her. "I told Flo to go on home, take a few days off. This can't be easy on her."

"Are you going to let her go?" She spotted the laptop, sitting open and turned on, and wandered farther into the room.

Beau forced himself not to glance at the bed. "Flo was

with my father for fifteen years, so no. I'll find something for her to do."

Cassidy smiled and he felt it like an electric shock to his system.

"I'm glad," she said, showing a soft side he found extremely attractive. Hell, there were a lot of things about the lady detective he found damned attractive.

"I found something in one of those manila files we took out of your father's study." She walked past him to the computer, and he managed to look beyond the sexy, dark blue skinny jeans and blue knit top to the manila folder tucked under her arm.

"What is it?"

She leaned over the desk to set it down. When she turned, he caught a glimpse of soft pale cleavage above a white lace bra and stifled a groan. Jesus, he never should have hired her. *Distraction* wasn't a strong enough word.

She flipped open the folder. "This is the file on the sale of Green Gables Realty."

"George Larson. He was one of the names my father gave you."

"That's right, the senator's partner in the business. There's something else in the file—a copy of a deed to a building in Iron Springs. It's from the buyer of Green Gables, granting title to your father. The thing is, the deed wasn't recorded until a month after the sale closed. I hate to say it, Beau, but I think your father took the building as payment on the side. It wasn't in the escrow, so he wouldn't have to divide the money with his partner when he sold it."

Beau wasn't surprised. He'd been suspicious of his father's shady dealings half his life.

She pulled out another document. "This is a deed showing the sale of the Iron Springs building to a man named Robert Durant. I think your father sold it to him and took the money for himself."

Beau leaned over to study the documents, trying to ignore the faint scent of gardenias that reminded him of their wrestling match in the hall.

He checked the dates and location of the property, glanced up. "He basically had no conscience, Cassidy. I warned you of that from the start."

"Maybe he needed money."

Beau opened his mouth to argue, then paused. "I guess it's possible. We always had money when I was a kid. It wasn't until I was in high school that I began to wonder where he was getting it. I started snooping through his papers, sneaking down the hall to eavesdrop on the late-night meetings going on in his study. It didn't take long to figure out a lot of what he was doing wasn't strictly on the up-and-up. It was just one more reason for me to get the hell out."

She put the document back in the file. "Maybe Larson found out he'd been cheated. Maybe they fought about it, Larson lost his temper and killed him."

Beau knew George Larson, who seemed a little too easy-going to stab a man in the heart. But money had a way of bringing out the worst in people. "We need to talk to him, find out if he has an alibi for the time of the murder."

"Why don't we give the information to Detective Briscoe? Let him talk to Larson."

Beau sighed. "Because in a couple of weeks, my father is going to have a daughter. Pleasant Hill is a small town. Eventually everyone will know the senator was her dad. I don't want her growing up with the whole town gossiping behind her back about the kind of man he was."

"It might come out anyway, Beau."

"If it happens, we'll deal with it. First let's find out where Larson was the day of the murder."

"Do you know where we can find him?"

"I know where he lives." He flicked her a glance. "You want to go for a ride?"

For an instant, something flashed in those sexy green eyes, as if she'd had the same lustful thought he'd had earlier. His blood surged, began to head south.

"I'm ready when you are," she said, sending another hot rush through him.

"Okay . . . let's go." Beau clamped down on his inappropriate thoughts and urged Cassidy out of the room. He pulled his car keys out of his pocket as they walked through the house toward the door in the kitchen leading into the garage.

Cassidy grinned and snagged the keys from his hand. "How about letting me drive? I've never driven a Ferrari."

Beau snatched the keys back. "I'm not driving the Ferrari. I'm in the Lambo. If you liked the Ferrari, you're gonna love the Lamborghini."

She hurried to keep up with him. "So you're letting me drive?" she asked hopefully.

"Not today. It's a little tricky. You'll need a lesson first."

She glanced up, that same hot spark back in her eyes. "A lesson sounds good. Always something new to learn."

As he led her out of the house, Beau couldn't help wondering if they were talking about cars or something a lot more personal and a helluva lot more interesting.

Sooner or later, he intended to find out.

Chapter Eight

Ignoring the senator's Mercedes, also parked in the garage, Cassidy slid into the burnt orange leather seats of the Lamborghini. The doors slid down from above and locked solidly into place.

The gleaming, low-slung, slate-gray vehicle looked like something from *Back to the Future*, only far more advanced. The cockpit belonged in a high-test airplane and, amazingly, there were no carpets, just industrial steel floors.

As she clicked on her seat belt, she couldn't help thinking how much her two brothers would love the gorgeous sports car that had to cost hundreds of thousands of dollars.

Beau pressed the start button and the powerful engine roared to life. It growled like a predator as it idled in the garage. Beau backed out, then pulled onto the road and drove out of the subdivision.

"We could take the long way," he said, tossing her a hopeful glance. "Get up a little speed."

She couldn't stop a grin. "Oh, yeah." She watched his big, suntanned hands on the paddles next to the steering wheel, shifting gears with perfect precision as the car shot forward down the road.

What was it about a hot guy in a hot car that was such a turn-on? She glanced down at the big black high-topped sneaker on the gas pedal. "Where's the clutch?"

Beau shifted and the engine whined into a higher gear. "Semiautomatic transmission. Clutch is electronically controlled. You can shift manually or drive it in automatic mode."

She itched to try it, wondered what it would take to convince him, then clamped down on where that thought led. One-night stands weren't her thing and she didn't have time for a fling, especially not with a heartthrob like Beau, a guy half the women in Texas drooled over.

They hit an open stretch of road just outside town and Beau let the sleek gray panther out of its cage. The acceleration pressed her back in the seat and adrenaline shot through her blood. She liked speed and she liked beauty and the Lamborghini had both. She could definitely get used to a car like this.

"Wow," was all she said.

Beau grinned, making him look even more appealing and sending her pulse up again. It was the first time he had let down his guard and shown a side of himself he mostly seemed to keep hidden.

"She's just getting warmed up," he said. "We'd need a track to really give her a run."

"*Her?* You think of your car as a woman?"

"Sure. She's got plenty of fire but she's hard to control. You gotta keep her in hand or she won't behave the way you want her to."

A flash of heat rolled through her. She closed her eyes to banish an image of them naked together. Dear God, what was wrong with her? She had certainly never had these kinds of thoughts about Rick.

She kept her gaze determinedly on the road. If she looked at Beau, he might guess what she had been thinking, and nothing would be more embarrassing. Slowing the Lamborghini, he turned and started winding his way back toward town.

"Why did you quit racing?" she asked as her blood pressure returned to normal. "According to what I read, you loved the sport more than anything else in your life."

He cast her a glance. "I did love it. Racing was my passion, still is and probably always will be. It's just . . . sometimes life throws you a curve you aren't expecting."

"Like what?"

"I got hurt pretty bad in Le Mans a few years back, spent three weeks in the hospital."

She'd seen that in an article she'd read. "That's why you quit? You got hurt?"

"Not exactly. As much as I loved the sport, I had other things I wanted to accomplish. I wanted to build Texas American into a company I could be proud of. I never intended to make racing my life. But I quit after Le Mans because the guy driving one of the four cars involved in the crash—one of my best friends—was killed in the collision. The report said I wasn't responsible, but there's no way to know for sure. I couldn't handle the thought of being the guy who got another man killed."

Emotion moved through her. She couldn't resist touching the big hand curled around the steering wheel. Her instincts were right about Beau. He was one of the good guys. No way was this man capable of killing his own father.

They parked in front of a redbrick house with white trim. Beau turned off the engine and the Lamborghini doors slid up. He rounded the vehicle as Cassidy climbed out, and they walked up the path to the front door together.

Beau rang the doorbell. A few minutes later, the door swung open and a balding man with glasses and a paunch stood in front of them.

"Hello, George," Beau said.

"I heard about your dad," George said. "I'm sorry for your loss, Beau."

"Thanks. You know how it was between us, but still, finding him that way was hard." He turned. "George, this is a friend, Cassidy Jones. May we come in?"

Clearly reluctant, Larson stepped back, silently allowing them into the house. He led them through the living room into a family room comfortably furnished with a dark green overstuffed sofa and chairs. A flat-screen TV hung above a redbrick fireplace.

"Myra's out shopping," George said. "You want something to drink?"

"No, thanks. This won't take long." He and Cassidy sat down on the sofa while Larson sat in one of the chairs. "Cassidy's a private investigator, George. The cops haven't found the guy who killed the senator, so we're trying to help them tie up loose ends. Can you tell us where you were on Thursday morning about eleven o'clock?"

George's eyebrows pulled into a frown. "I don't like your asking, but since I wasn't anywhere near your old man when he got pretty much what he's deserved for years, I'll tell you. I was in Iron Springs, in the middle of a meeting with my attorney, Phil Wheeler. You can call and verify if you want."

Beau just nodded.

Cassidy looked at Larson. "You said he got what he deserved. You must have known about the side deal he made when you sold the business—the money he got that he should have split with you?"

"I found out later." George focused on Beau. "I guess your

father has cheated me for the last time. Strangely, I'll miss the challenge of catching him at it, which I usually did."

"How did you find out about the building?" Cassidy asked.

Larson shrugged. "It's a small town. Stuff like that gets around. I figure I was lucky it wasn't worse."

"Why is that?" Beau asked.

"Your dad needed money, Beau. He always lived above his means and it finally got away from him. He told me he owed someone a chunk of money and he needed to pay it back. He pressured me to sell, and eventually I agreed. Now that it's done, I'm glad I'm out of it. Maybe I can actually enjoy my retirement."

"You know the guy's name?" Beau asked.

"Stew didn't say. He mentioned some guy in Dallas once, but it was years ago."

"What was the name?"

"Dooley Tate. It was just odd enough I remembered."

Cassidy's stomach tightened. Dooley Tate was a notorious loan shark, a bottom feeder of the worst sort, not the kind of man she would have imagined the senator to be connected with. But if he'd borrowed money from Tate and hadn't repaid him—

Cassidy mentally added Dooley Tate to her suspect list.

Beau stood up from the sofa. "We appreciate your talking to us, George. I never really thought you were involved. Now we can take you off our list."

Without replying, George rose and started walking, leading them back to the front door. "Be careful, Beau. Your father knew some very powerful people. Whoever murdered him isn't going to like your asking questions. You don't want to wind up dead, too."

Cassidy felt a chill. Anytime you tracked a killer, there was a chance it could turn deadly.

She walked in front of Beau down the path to the

Lamborghini. He helped her inside, then rounded the car and slid in behind the wheel.

Once he'd clicked his belt into place, he closed the car doors. "George said my father borrowed money from a guy named Dooley Tate. You ever heard of him?"

Cassidy nodded. "He's a loan shark. He's a real scumball, Beau. I can't imagine your father being involved with someone like that."

"George said it was a long time ago."

She sighed. "It might be worth a try. At least it would give us a place to start. If your father owed Tate money and didn't pay him back—"

"You think he'd go as far as murder?"

"I don't know. Maybe."

"How do we find out if my dad owed him money?"

"If you're up for a trip to Dallas, we ask him."

Beau checked the time on his expensive gold wristwatch, a Patek Philippe. The man definitely had expensive taste. So did his father, she recalled, thinking of the perfectly tailored suits Stewart Reese wore and the Mercedes in the garage.

"The afternoon's shot," Beau said. "I'll call for the chopper in the morning, arrange for a pickup. We can be in and out of the city in a couple of hours."

"George is right, Beau. We need to be careful."

He turned to look at her, blue eyes searching her face. "You can go back to Dallas, Cassidy. I won't think any less of you."

Ignoring him, Cassidy leaned back in the burnt-orange leather seat. "We can cross off Larson's name," she said as she clicked her belt into place. "Dooley Tate is next."

Beau's features hardened. "Tate and the other two names on my father's list."

* * *

As Beau turned the Lamborghini off Country Club Lane onto Fairway Drive and drove toward the house, he spotted an unmarked dark brown police car parked in front. Tom Briscoe unfolded his sturdy frame from the vehicle and walked toward them as Beau drove the Lambo into the garage next to his father's Mercedes, making a mental note to put the cover on the vehicle so he wouldn't have to look at it.

Briscoe waited while the doors slid up and Beau and Cassidy got out.

"Beautiful car," Tom said, eyeing the Lamborghini.

Beau's gaze went to one of his most prized possessions and he couldn't help a smile. "It has 740 horses, V-12 engine, zero-to-sixty in 2.7 seconds. Tops out at two hundred seventeen miles an hour. Not that I plan to drive it that fast around here."

"Good thinking," Tom said.

"Let's go inside." Beau led Cassidy and the detective in through the kitchen, closing the garage door behind them. He continued into the open family room, where he and his parents had spent most of what little time they had ever shared together.

"You want something to drink?" Beau asked. "A Coke or some water?" Not alcohol, not for Tom while he was on duty. Beau knew him well enough to be sure of that.

"I'm fine." Briscoe seated himself on one of the taupe and brown plaid overstuffed chairs, Cassidy sat down on the matching sofa, and Beau took a seat beside her.

Like most of the house, the room was done in a traditional style, with high molded ceilings and plush beige carpets. The Pleasant Hill *Sentinel* rested on the walnut coffee table. Brass lamps sat on matching end tables next to the couch.

"I might as well cut to the chase," Brisco said, taking a small, lined spiral notebook out of his coat pocket. He was wearing an inexpensive dark brown suit and wing-tip shoes that needed polish.

He looked down at his notes. "No DNA found at the crime scene. No one else's blood." He glanced up. "No evidence of a struggle, so we expected that."

"What about fingerprints?" Beau asked.

"Just yours and your father's on the letter opener."

"So the killer wore gloves," Beau said. "Or wiped the handle clean."

"Maybe. There was no forced entry, Beau. That means the killer had to have been someone your father knew. He must have invited the man into the study."

Beau's stomach began to churn.

"Not necessarily," Cassidy said, flicking him a glance. "I took a look at the locks on these doors. A simple set of picks would open them in about five seconds." Which Beau figured Cassidy knew firsthand, since she had let herself in the night of the murder to search for the hidden files.

Tom flashed her a look of respect. "It's possible. There's still the alarm."

"He didn't turn it on during the day."

Briscoe looked down at his notes. "The housekeeper was off that day. Good chance the killer knew that."

"The murder weapon indicates the murder wasn't planned," Cassidy said, "just something that happened on the spur of the moment. So maybe the housekeeper not being here was just coincidental."

"I'm not big on coincidence," Briscoe said.

Neither was Beau.

"What about the senator's phone?" Cassidy asked. "Did you find anything on it?"

"We're still looking for the phone. So far we haven't found it." Tom turned in Beau's direction. "When we talked at the station, you didn't tell me the reason you came to Pleasant Hill."

"I told you I came to get some papers signed. That's why I was here."

"I'd like to take a look at them, Beau."

The adoption papers. "It was personal business between my dad and me. I'd rather it stayed that way."

"I'm sure you would, but in a town the size of Pleasant Hill, word gets around pretty fast. Currently, the hot topic is you, Beau, you and Missy Kessler. And of course that includes Missy's baby. Gossip has it that baby is yours. People think maybe you and your dad were fighting about it. You lost your temper and killed him."

The knot in Beau's stomach went tighter. When he made no reply, Cassidy spoke up. "The baby isn't Beau's, Detective. Senator Reese is the father."

He should have been angry; the information was private. But all he felt was relief. He didn't want to betray Missy, but he didn't want to go to jail, either.

Briscoe settled back and drilled Beau with a glare. "That's what Missy told me. Might have been better if you'd told me, Beau. Might not look like you had a reason for wanting to keep the information secret."

"He was trying to protect her," Cassidy said.

"It's all right, Cassidy," Beau said softly. "I should have told Tom the truth from the start." He spoke to Briscoe. "Missy was afraid of what people would think if they knew she'd had an affair with a man so much older than she is. I figured she'd suffered enough. Since her pregnancy had nothing to do with the murder, I was hoping no one would need to know."

"When did you find out?" Tom asked.

"Josie called me a couple of days ago. She asked me to meet her at the café, which I did the day before the murder. She gave me a copy of the DNA test that proved the father of Missy's baby was my dad."

"How did that make you feel?"

Beau could see it coming, feel the trap closing in on him. "I was angry. I couldn't believe my father would take advantage of a girl that young. I drove out to the house to talk to him. We argued. He agreed to give Missy full custody. I went back to Dallas and had the paperwork drawn up, then came back to get it signed the next day. When I walked into the house, I found my father lying on the study floor." He clenched his jaw against the painful image that hadn't left him since that morning.

"You realize, Beau, you're the only suspect we have. The only person who had access to the house, to the weapon that killed him—the only person who had a motive to want him dead."

Beau came up off the sofa. "I didn't want him dead! We didn't get along. I didn't approve of his relationship with Missy. That doesn't mean I killed him."

Briscoe slowly rose from his chair. "Then there's the fact Ms. Jones saw you leaning over the body with the letter opener in your hand."

Cassidy stood up. "I've had time to think about that, Detective. Yes, I saw Beau with the letter opener, but his hand wasn't wrapped around the handle in a manner that would have been used to strike down a victim. He was pulling the instrument out in an effort to save his father's life."

Beau could feel his heart beating a loud, rapid cadence inside his chest. She was changing her story to protect him. Taking a terrible risk.

Briscoe stared at her, his gaze unwavering. "Are you sure you want to go down that road, Ms. Jones? Giving a false statement to the police is a criminal offense. So is aiding and abetting."

Cassidy's chin inched up. "I'm a private investigator, Detective. I'm trained to look for those sorts of clues. I saw Beau Reese removing the letter opener from his father's chest in an effort to save his life. I was upset when I gave my initial statement. I hadn't had time to process what I'd witnessed, go through the sequence of events. What I just told you is exactly what I saw, and should it come down to it, exactly what I'll tell a jury."

Clearly unhappy, Briscoe closed his notepad and tucked it back into his coat pocket. "I'd suggest you get a lawyer, Beau. Unless something new develops, you could be in serious trouble." He turned to Cassidy. "As for you, Ms. Jones, since you're so convinced Beau is innocent, I suggest you use your investigative skills to find the person who killed Senator Reese."

Briscoe turned and walked out of the house. The door slammed shut behind him.

Beau turned to Cassidy. Neither of them had moved. "You shouldn't have done that."

She just shrugged. "We needed some time. I bought us some time. You're innocent, so I don't have to worry. We just need to find the person who killed your father."

She looked so damn determined. Beautiful, smart, incredibly sexy, and fiercely determined. Wanting hit him, deep and primal, stronger than ever.

"I'd really like to kiss you," he said. Though he wanted to do far more than that.

Cassidy just shook her head. "I'm not going there with you, Beau. I'm not sleeping with you now or anytime in the future. I'll help you clear your name, but that's it."

"You said you were attracted to me. You admitted it. Why shouldn't we act on our mutual attraction?"

"I'll tell you why. Because you're Beaumont Reese, Texas heartthrob. You're famous for your love-'em-and-leave-'em affairs, and I'm not interested in becoming one of your statistics."

He grinned. "Heartthrob. I've been called a lot of things but never that."

"I'm not kidding, Beau."

He ran a finger down her cheek. "I want you, Cassidy Jones. You have no idea how much. If you did, it might scare you."

Her chin firmed the way it had when she had faced Briscoe. "I'm not scared of you, Beau."

"Good, because I'm the kind of man who goes after what he wants. I don't stop until I get it. It's only a matter of time, Ms. Jones."

A flush crawled up Cassidy's throat and spread over the cleavage above the bodice of her soft knit sweater. He could see a tiny pulse beating wildly on the side of her neck.

"We have to find Dooley Tate," she said. "And I want to know as much as possible before we talk to him."

Her reminder of the murder hit him like a pail of cold water, sweeping away his need and putting his head back on straight. "You're right. For the moment I have more to worry about than taking you to bed."

A tiny sound escaped Cassidy's throat before she turned and walked toward the sliding glass doors leading out of the family room on her way back to the guest house.

Beau just smiled and fell in behind her.

Chapter Nine

Cassidy could sense Beau's tall, broad-shouldered frame close behind her as she stepped up on the porch and opened the door to the guest house. Her heart was beating too fast. Her palms felt damp. She couldn't stop thinking about what he had said, that it was only a matter of time until she wound up in his bed.

Just hearing him say it turned her on, the conviction in his voice, the way his mouth edged into a faint, sexy smile when he spoke. Beau was right. She wanted him. It was impossible to deny. She fought the urge to just stop and turn around, grab the front of his shirt and drag his mouth down to hers for a scorching-hot kiss.

Beau was determined to get her in bed and the more she was around him, the more she wanted exactly the same. She couldn't remember feeling such a powerful attraction to a man. *Ever*. The sparks between them could set off a dynamite charge. Maybe she should just give in. So what if she slept with him? There would be emotional consequences, yes, but maybe it would be worth it.

What would sex be like with a gorgeous, incredibly hot

male like Beau? Experiencing the kind of white-hot lust she read in those amazing blue eyes could be an exciting new adventure.

Or maybe not. Maybe sex with Beau wouldn't turn out to be any more thrilling than sex with Rick or the other few men she'd had brief, unfulfilling affairs with over the years.

A slow, deep kiss might give her a clue. Maybe she should try it. Just once. If it wasn't pure melting heat—

"How will you find him?" Beau asked, jerking her back to reality and sending a second flush into her cheeks. "I wouldn't think a lowlife loan shark like Tate would be listed in the yellow pages."

"You're right. But he's fairly well-known in Dallas. It shouldn't be that tough to come up with his location. First, let's try it the easy way. I need to make a phone call."

Pulling out her cell, she hit the contact button for Jason Maddox, the bounty hunter she worked with in her office. Jase knew every underworld figure in the city. His contacts were one of the ways he located the scumball bail skips he brought to justice.

Cassidy's tracing skill was another source he used. She had helped him bring in the Night Watchman, a notorious serial killer. The reward was big-time. Cassidy had received a fat percentage for tracing the killer to the half brother in Phoenix no one had known existed.

She pressed the phone against her ear. "Jase, it's Cassidy."

"Hey, darlin'. What's up?"

"Jase, I need a favor. I'm looking for a loan shark named Dooley Tate. I figured you might know where I can find him."

"Ruthless, conscienceless, five-foot-eight piece of shit Dooley Tate? That the guy?"

A smile tugged at her lips. Jase wasn't known for his tact. "That would be him. Any idea where he is?"

"Works out of a strip club called Barbie's out on Northwest Highway. Got an office upstairs. Best time to find him is early evening, not too crowded then. But he's bad news, darlin'. You don't want to go there by yourself. I'm in Albuquerque following a trail, but maybe you can get one of the other guys in the office to go with you."

She glanced over at Beau, six-foot-three-inches of lean, solid muscle, a man trained in mixed martial arts. From what she had read, he had even done some cage fighting when he was in college. She wondered if that was how he got the scar along his jaw.

"I've got someone with me. I'll be okay."

"Think about taking that little gun of yours just in case. I know you don't like to carry, but—"

"I'll give it some thought."

"All right," Jase said. "Just be careful."

"I will." Cassidy hung up the phone.

"Who was that?" Beau asked, the lines of his face intense.

"Jason Maddox. He's a bounty hunter who works out of my office. I do tracing for him sometimes. We're friends."

The scar tightened along his jaw. She noticed it happened when he was irritated or upset. "*Friends?* You mean like friends with benefits?"

She smiled, enjoying the edge of jealousy in his voice. "I'll admit Jase is a good-looking guy, but no, not that kind of friends. I was living with someone when we met, and even after I moved out, we just never clicked in that way."

"You moved out. So you aren't involved with anyone at the moment?"

She shook her head, unable to bring herself to lie, though it might make things a lot easier. "No, not for quite some time."

The tension eased in those wide shoulders. "Good," was all he said.

"I need to work up a profile on Tate. I'm not sure what I'll find, but I'll do my best." As she sat down in front of the computer, Beau's cell phone rang.

He checked the caller ID. "It's Charlotte. She's making the funeral arrangements." He walked a few feet away. "Yeah, I can do that. No problem. I'll be there in fifteen minutes."

Beau hung up and walked back. "She's got things lined up at the funeral home. She wants to get my input and approval."

His face looked so strained, Cassidy rose from the chair. "You want me to go with you?"

He shook his head. "You have things to do. You don't need to do that."

"I can work on Tate's profile when we get back." She let the offer hang in the air. It was Beau's decision.

Those beautiful blue eyes searched her face. "You really wouldn't mind going?"

Her heart pinched at his hopeful expression. "I wouldn't mind at all. It'll give me a chance to check out Charlotte. She's on our list, remember?"

He relaxed. "Yeah, good idea. Let's go."

Cassidy grabbed her purse and they headed out the door. Ten minutes later, the Lamborghini pulled up in front of the Fremont Funeral Home. For several seconds Beau just sat there, and Cassidy's heart went out to him. Whatever the senator had done, he was still Beau's dad.

With a quiet glide upward, the car doors opened and they got out. Cassidy hadn't expected to feel a quick flash of pain, a memory of the last time she had been to a place like this, the arrangements she and her two brothers had helped her dad make for her mother. Cancer was a brutal killer, a heartbreaker for everyone.

"Are you okay?" Beau asked when she stopped at the front door.

Cassidy shook off the memories. "My mom died of cancer. It was rough. For an instant, I remembered."

He glanced off into the distance. "I lost someone that way. You never forget the pain."

Surprised she hadn't read about it during her research, she started to ask who it was, but Beau just shook his head. They stepped into an entry lit by a crystal chandelier. Soft music played in the background as a well-dressed, efficient-looking woman with silver hair pulled into a tight chignon walked toward them down the hall.

"Mr. Reese?" she asked.

"That's right. And this is Ms. Jones."

She gave them a smile that had seen better days. "I'm Mrs. Dennison. Welcome to the Fremont Funeral Home. If you will, please follow me."

Beau looked down at Cassidy and there was something in his face. "I'm glad you came with me," he said softly as the woman reached the office and came to a stop.

For reasons she couldn't explain, Cassidy reached for his hand. She laced her fingers with his, and Beau's hand tightened around them.

"The funeral is set for Saturday," Mrs. Dennison said. "If that is agreeable to you."

"What about the autopsy?" Beau asked.

"Chief Warren has assured me it will be completed well before then."

Beau swallowed and nodded. Mrs. Dennison opened the office door. "I'll give you a moment of privacy, then we'll go over the arrangements." As they walked inside, she stepped back out of the room and closed the door.

Across the room, Charlotte Mercer Reese rose gracefully from her chair. Her smile slipped a little when she noticed their linked hands. Cassidy released her hold and Beau stepped forward. He bent and brushed a light kiss on his stepmother's cheek.

"Charlotte, you're looking lovely as always." He turned. "Charlotte, this is Cassidy Jones. She's a private investigator. She's helping me look into the murder."

Blond and slender, at forty-nine Charlotte Reese was still a remarkably attractive woman. In a navy pantsuit accented by a pink and blue silk scarf, her feet in a pair of designer mid-heeled pumps, she exemplified the role of a widowed senator's wife.

One of Charlotte's blond eyebrows went up. "I thought we discussed this, Beau. We agreed it was better to let the police handle the murder investigation."

"No, Charlotte. I didn't agree to anything. I told you I intended to find the man who killed my father and that is exactly what I plan to do."

"Your father is dead, Beau. Can't you simply let him rest in peace?"

"You think he wouldn't want the man who murdered him brought to justice? If you think that, you never really knew him at all."

"We're only asking a few questions," Cassidy soothed. "Just eliminating people who knew him, anyone who might have had some sort of disagreement with him. Perhaps it wasn't murder. Perhaps things got out of hand and his death was an accident. That's all we're trying to find out."

Charlotte made no reply.

"If you could tell us where you were Tuesday morning, we could take you off the suspect list," Cassidy pressed.

Charlotte's mouth thinned. "How dare you imply I had anything to do with Stewart's murder! Beau, are you going to stand there and let this woman insult me that way?"

"Cassidy's been hired to do a job, Charlotte. Just answer the question and be done with it."

"Fine. I was in Dallas. I drove to Pleasant Hill as soon as

Police Chief Warren called to tell me what had happened. You were at the police station, Beau, when I arrived."

"Dad told Cassidy someone had been asking questions about him around town. He said he was being followed. He thought you could have had something do with it."

"Why in the world would I be following your father?"

"If not you, then someone you hired."

"That is ridiculous."

Cassidy spoke up. "He thought you might still be harboring romantic feelings toward him, Mrs. Reese. After all, you were once husband and wife."

Charlotte scoffed. "I can't imagine he believed that. Our divorce wasn't entirely pleasant. It was fortunate we were able to remain friends. And if you persist in questioning me as if I am a suspect—"

"That's all we needed to know," Beau interrupted. "I appreciate your honesty, Charlotte, and your help making the arrangements. I trust your judgment in this completely."

Some of the steam went out of her. Her hand ran over the outrageously expensive navy Chanel bag she carried. "I'm glad to help in any way I can. As I said, we were friends."

Just then the door opened and Mrs. Dennison walked back into the room. "If you're ready, why don't we start with the casket Mrs. Reese has chosen?"

Cassidy glanced at Beau, whose features once more looked tense. He nodded.

"If you will please follow me." Mrs. Dennison walked out the door and Beau's stepmother fell in behind her.

Cassidy started walking next to Beau. She was surprised to feel his hand searching for hers, then his long, tanned fingers taking hold.

They walked out into the marble-floored hall, their footsteps echoing, then entered a silent, windowless room that carried the faint scent of white lilies. The casket Charlotte had chosen was polished rosewood with ornate gold handles.

It was regal and tasteful and extremely expensive. Beau looked at his stepmother and nodded.

They returned to the office and went over the remainder of the arrangements.

Beau never let go of Cassidy's hand.

Chapter Ten

Beau spent a restless night in the empty house he had been raised in, which at this point in his life seemed completely unfamiliar.

During the long hours before dawn, his mind had run through possible murder scenarios, names of people his father had known, people he'd had business dealings with. One thought followed another, among them the haunting question: If his father needed money as badly as George Larson said, why hadn't he come to his son?

The fact they had clashed so many times over the years wouldn't have prevented Beau from giving his dad whatever money he needed. He'd been a lousy father, but they were family and Beau owed him a great deal. Without the first-class education Stewart Reese had paid for, Beau might not have gone on to become the success he was today.

He was grateful for the drive and intelligence he had inherited from his father. And there were the opportunities the senator's standing in the community had provided when Texas American had been newly founded and struggling.

Not that Beau dismissed Linc's amazing contributions to the company's success.

But deep down, Beau knew the senator would have gone to any length to keep his troubles secret from his son and the rest of the world.

Or maybe his death had nothing to do with money. The crime seemed unplanned. A crime of passion, the police believed. Maybe the murder had been committed by one of his father's many women. If it wasn't Charlotte, who else could have done it?

The thought drove Beau's thoughts in a direction he didn't want to go. What if Josie or Missy had killed him? Missy's condition seemed to rule her out, but Josie? Missy's mother couldn't have been happy about the way the senator had treated her daughter. Could she have gone to the house to confront him? Could Josie have lost her temper and killed him?

Anything was possible, and those possibilities had kept him awake late into the night.

That and the constant lust he felt for Cassidy Jones. He had dreamed of her lush body beneath him, of filling her and taking her deep. He'd awoken in a cold sweat, hard and aching, cursing the reputation he had with women that he didn't really deserve.

He didn't put time limits on relationships as the tabloids implied. They just seemed to fizzle, then slowly fade away. Maybe it would be different with Cassidy. He was determined to find out.

Unfortunately, at the moment he was the prime suspect in a murder. Finding the killer and proving his innocence had to be his first priority.

He was thinking about it when he got the call from Briscoe the next morning.

"Beau, it's Tom. The autopsy results came in last night. Nothing we didn't expect. Death a result of a fatal stab wound to the heart. The body's been released to the funeral home."

Beau's chest felt tight. "The service is Saturday. Charlotte handled the arrangements. I spoke to her about an hour ago. She's decided to keep the funeral relatively small, just friends and family. There'll be a few state senators and congressmen. The governor sent his condolences but he won't be there. I'm sure he's keeping his distance until the case has been solved."

"I'm sorry, Beau."

"Thanks, Tom." Beau hung up the phone. It went unsaid that Briscoe would continue to do his job, even if the murder trail ended with Beau. Beau respected him for it.

His next call went to Marty, who arranged for the Tex/Am chopper to pick him and Cassidy up in an open area off the golf course late that afternoon. Her bounty hunter friend, Jason Maddox, had said their best chance of speaking to Dooley Tate would be in the evening. If they went in a little early, he could get some work done at the office.

Now they were both strapped in, the chopper rising into the air. The whir of the helicopter blades took his mind off the murder and returned his attention to the moment.

Cassidy sat in the seat beside him. When he looked in her direction, he saw that she was grinning, completely caught up in the flight. He found himself smiling, too. That she could make that happen under the dire circumstances he was facing was enough to renew his determination to have her.

"I guess you like flying," he said over the com system, adjusting his headphones to hear her reply.

"I hate flying," she said. She looked down at the colorful patchwork of land and subdivisions disappearing beneath them. "Somehow this is different."

"Kind of like the Lambo, right? It isn't just driving."

Her grin returned. "Exactly."

The helicopter neared the city, circling then landing on the roof of the Texas American building. He would take care of business; then they could head out to Barbie's. Beau led Cassidy into the rooftop elevator and pushed the down button, heading for his private office on the executive floor one story below.

As the elevator door opened and Cassidy walked ahead of him into his spacious office, his gaze dropped to the sequined pockets on the skinny jeans stretching over her perfect ass, disappearing into mid-heel black knee-high boots. A pink silk blouse tucked into the top of the jeans softened the look enough to be presentable at the office. The short, black leather jacket she carried would give her the sass she needed to fit in at Barbie's.

Beau took a last look, felt his groin tighten, and forced himself to look away.

"Nice," she said, admiring the view through the wall of glass windows looking down on the streets of north Dallas. She turned to survey the black lacquer desk and bookshelves, the cream silk fabric on the sofa and chairs.

"Your domain suits you. It's kind of . . . I don't know . . . calming."

"I think so."

"I imagine that would be helpful in a business that requires so much from you."

Not many people got that, how much it took out of you to stay focused, stay productive, keep all the balls in the air. It was satisfying, challenging, but also a constant headache.

He'd wanted her to meet Linc, but his friend was in New Mexico, checking on a highway project they had under construction. He introduced her to Marty Chen, who brought her a cup of tea while she waited for Beau and his assistant to catch up on some unavoidable business.

As soon as Marty left, Beau called Rob Michaels. "I need those encrypted files, Rob. Any progress?"

"Yes, sir. It would be good if we could talk in person."

"Come on up."

Dressed in his usual chinos and sneakers, his red hair moussed up in the middle, Michaels walked in a few minutes later.

"Rob's the company whiz kid," Beau said to Cassidy. "Rob, meet Cassidy Jones. She's a private investigator helping me look into my father's death."

Rob nodded. "Ms. Jones."

"So you were able to get into the files?" Beau asked.

"Yes, sir." He handed the flash drives to Beau. "I made them more easily accessible. You can open them now."

Beau sat down at his desk, shoved one of the drives into his computer and opened the index. He caught the soft scent of gardenias as Cassidy walked behind him to study the screen over his shoulder.

"What am I looking at?" Beau asked.

Rob glanced at Cassidy. "May I speak freely, sir?"

Did he trust Cassidy with this kind of information? He didn't know for certain, but he needed her help—which meant he didn't have a choice. And if he didn't tell her, he wasn't sure she wouldn't find a way to get the information on her own. "Go ahead."

"They're offshore accounts, sir. Cayman Islands. You can follow the transactions, money going into the accounts, then coming out."

Beau looked at the column of numbers, dates of deposits, dates of withdrawals. Numbers that added up to millions of dollars. He'd look them over later when he had more time. "What's on the other drive?"

Color washed into Rob's cheeks, making his freckles stand out. "It's a list of names, sir, alphabetical. I only read enough to realize it contained very personal information, things the people on the list wouldn't want known."

Beau looked at Cassidy. *Blackmail* was the word that hung between them. His father's means of getting what he wanted, both politically and personally. The second flash drive seemed to burn into his hand.

"I'll need to study the drives more closely," he said. "I don't need to remind you how confidential this information is."

"No, sir, not at all."

"Thanks, Rob, you did a great job."

"Thank you, sir. Let me know if you need anything else." Rob walked out of the office and quietly closed the door.

Beau pulled the first drive out of the computer and shoved in the second. Cassidy moved a little closer, the curve of her hip just inches from his shoulder. He forced himself to concentrate.

"I have a feeling if we look under the name George Larson," she said, "we'll find the reason he agreed to sell his half of Green Gables Realty."

Beau scrolled down the list and sure as hell, there was Larson's name. He opened the file and saw a photo of George with his arm around a curvy blonde in her twenties. Myra Larson would not be pleased.

Beau looked at Cassidy. "You realize the names on this list are all people who might have a reason to kill him."

"We'll need to look at them before we can make that determination."

Frustration rolled through him and he shoved up from the chair. "For chrissake, Cassidy, how many people wanted my father dead?"

"Your father was a successful politician. I'm sure some of the information he collected was only a means of understanding his political opponents, people he needed to win over to his way of thinking. I imagine amassing that kind of information isn't uncommon."

A sigh whispered out. "God, I hope you're right. Otherwise we may never figure out what happened."

Cassidy's shoulders straightened. "Oh, we'll figure it out." Her determined expression had a smile tugging at the corners of his mouth. Leaning down, he pressed a soft kiss on her lips.

He meant for it to be quick and fun, but instead of ending the kiss as he'd planned, he sank in, tasting the softness, feeling the heat rush over him like a fiery wave.

Cassidy made a little sound in her throat. Her soft lips parted and his tongue swept in. Her arms went around his neck, her fingers slid into the black hair curling at the nape of his neck, and the next thing he knew he had her up against the wall and he was kissing her the way he had kissed her in his dreams, deep and hot and erotic.

He wanted to rip off her pretty pink silk blouse, wanted to free those lush breasts and bury his face between them. He wanted to taste the fullness, suckle her nipples, find out if they were dusky rose or pale mauve, see if they were as bold as a quarter or as petite as a dime.

He was hard. Aching and pulsing until he couldn't think. He had to have her, now, this instant or he was going to explode.

The intercom buzzed. His foggy brain heard Marty's voice but he couldn't tear himself away. His personal quarters lay behind a paneled wall, a place he went to change when there wasn't time to go home, or to nap between meetings. There was a bed in there, a small living room with a sofa and chair.

It seemed a million miles away. Cassidy's head fell back as he kissed the side of her neck. Then he took her mouth again. Something buzzed at the edge of his mind but he ignored it. If he hadn't felt slender, determined hands pressing against his chest, he might have pulled her down on the floor and taken her right there.

She shoved again and Beau broke free, breathing too hard, his arousal throbbing, his mind a foggy blur.

"It's . . . it's your assistant," Cassidy said, trembling as she began refastening the buttons on her blouse he didn't know he'd undone.

He just looked at her.

"You need to answer, Beau. Marty's going to think something's going on."

His head began to clear. A slow smile stretched over his lips. "Yeah, we wouldn't want Marty to think something's going on."

She almost smiled, instead gave him a little nudge toward his desk. He sat down, grateful for the chance to compose himself, spoke to Marty while Cassidy wandered over to the windows.

He answered a question about an important meeting with the CEO of the Wayne Corporation, which he had been working on for weeks and now had to reschedule, then leaned back in his chair.

Blotting the memory of the wildest, hottest kiss he could ever recall, clenching his jaw so he wouldn't get hard again, Beau walked over to where Cassidy stood in front of the windows.

"I didn't plan for that to happen," he said. "I hope you know that."

She turned. "It was my fault as much as yours. I should have stopped you."

He wasn't completely sure she could have. He almost couldn't stop himself. "Maybe we'd both be better off if we just let things take their natural course."

Cassidy looked up at him. "We can't, Beau. We don't have time. If we don't find out who killed your father, you could be arrested. Think what that will do to your reputation, how it will affect your business."

His stomach pulled into a hard, tight knot. Dammit, she

was right. He had to get his head on straight and he had to do it now. Besides hurting himself and the business that meant so much to him, he had Linc to consider. Cain had just gotten married. He and Carly wanted to start a family. Linc didn't need the kind of trouble Beau's arrest would bring down on all of them.

"You're right. I wasn't thinking." He managed to smile. "It seems to happen a lot when I'm around you."

She glanced out the windows. "Maybe I should come back to Dallas, work out of my office in the city."

Beau shook his head. "I want you to stay in Pleasant Hill. I need your help. We'll do better working as a team." He reached out and touched her cheek. "I won't rush this. Whatever's happening between us, we'll wait to figure it out. First we'll find the man who killed my father."

Cassidy held his gaze for several long moments; then she nodded. "All right."

Beau caught her hand and tugged her toward the elevator. "We'll go over the files when we get back to the house. In the meantime, we came to talk to Dooley Tate. You ready for that?"

She looked up at him. "I'm ready."

Beau pressed the elevator button and waited for her to walk inside. He pushed the button for the parking garage. It was time to find a killer.

Chapter Eleven

Cassidy stepped out of the elevator into the underground garage. Her pulse was back to normal, the flush gone from her cheeks, but her lips still tingled, along with other feminine parts of her body.

One thing she knew, Beau Reese was the best kisser on planet Earth.

She sighed, not daring to let herself go where that thought led. Not right now. Not when they were in hot pursuit of a killer.

She stood next to Beau as a valet brought up a sleek black BMW coup. "How many cars do you have?" she asked.

"Counting this one, four. Besides the Ferrari and the Lambo, I've got a Jeep Rubicon I drive when I want to spend time outdoors. This is the car I use for business."

He helped her into the passenger seat, then went around and slid in behind the wheel. "Sometimes my job calls for long hours. There's a small private apartment connected to my office. If it gets late, I can sleep in there, shower and change and go back to work."

"I saw photos of your home in *Architectural Digest*. It looks beautiful. Doesn't sound like you get to use it much."

He smiled. "Not enough, that's for sure. I had it custom built. I thought I'd spend more time there, but if I stay too long, I don't know . . . sometimes it gets kind of lonely. My schedule's pretty full, so it doesn't happen that often."

Cassidy made no reply. With his amazing looks and a net worth in the hundreds of millions, *lonely* wasn't a word that should pertain to Beau Reese. And yet somehow she believed him. There was something about Beau, something mysterious that kept him slightly aloof. Cassidy was determined to find out what it was.

He turned on the headlights as the car rolled along the highway. It got dark early this time of year. The temperature was in the sixties, the skies clear. It was a little after six when they followed a guy on a Harley into the parking lot next to a sign that read BARBIE'S.

The lot was already half full with customers stopping on a Friday night on their way home from work. Sex was always a draw, no matter what time of day it was. Add to that, another sign boasted the cover charge was only a buck until 7 P.M. Afterward, it went up to five dollars.

"You ready for this?" Beau asked, surveying a group of bikers who pulled in behind them.

Cassidy raked her hands through her hair, fluffing the heavy dark curls into a big-hair, slightly trashy look. On the drive over, she had added more makeup. She adjusted the snug, waist-length black leather jacket she'd put on after they'd left the office. "I'm ready."

Cassidy glanced at Beau. He was wearing jeans and a navy-blue Henley, a casual look that showed off his hard-muscled chest. She wouldn't have imagined him in a pair of black cowboy boots, never guessed how good he would look in them.

They'd both fit in just fine, she figured. "Come on, cowboy, let's go."

Beau didn't smile. He was busy watching the bikers, who were parking and dismounting their bikes. Cassidy got out of the car, and she and Beau walked toward the front door. The biker who had arrived in front of them, big and burly with inky, slicked back hair, leaned against the railing around the front porch.

"Hey, sweet cheeks, why don't you ditch the pretty boy and let a real man show you a good time?" He grabbed his crotch and made a lewd gesture.

Cassidy sneered. "I only see one real man here and you aren't it."

Beau turned, exposing the scar along his jaw, which should have been a warning. Instead, the guy took a threatening step toward her. Beau lifted his boot a fraction, the biker tripped and went down hard, landing with a foulmouthed curse. Cassidy felt Beau's hand at her waist as they walked inside the club.

"You shouldn't have done that," she said.

His mouth edged up. "Probably not."

Just inside the door, a big, dark-skinned bouncer stood with his arms crossed over his massive chest, surveying the interior for any sign of trouble. Beau walked up to the counter, where a buxom blonde accepted two crisp dollar bills for the cover charge.

Music blared inside. A long counter lined with men in jeans and work boots or wearing black leather sat next to women with too much makeup, short skirts or tight jeans. The stage spread across the opposite end of the room and there were smaller stages on each side, though only the main stage had entertainment this early in the evening.

The décor was flashy and modern, bright lights in neon orange, blue, and red. There was an empty dance floor in front of the stage where a woman in a leopard-skin thong and sequined pasties danced to Katy Perry's "Roar."

The waitresses, exemplifying the club's name, were all dressed like dolls, in barely there, white ruffled skirts and bibs held up by red suspenders.

The women's nipples were covered but not much more, and when one of them bent over to set drinks on a small round table nearby, nothing but a tiny thong covered the twin globes under her skirt.

Beau urged Cassidy up to the bar. A twenty appeared in his hand, which he shoved across the counter at the approach of the bartender, a tall, skinny guy with a thin goatee.

"We're looking for Dooley Tate. He in tonight?"

The bartender took the twenty. "He's here. Who wants to see him?"

"Beau Reese."

"I'll let him know." The guy disappeared, then returned a few minutes later. "Dooley's upstairs. You can go on up."

Beau pushed another twenty across the bar. "Thanks."

Cassidy walked in front of him toward the staircase she had spotted when they walked in. The bouncer gave them the eye but made no move to stop them.

When they reached the top of the stairs, Beau opened the door and Dooley Tate, short and stocky with thinning light brown hair, rose from the opposite side of his desk.

"Beaumont Reese," Tate said. "Used to watch you on TV. Never thought to see your pretty face in a place like this."

Beau closed the door. "You never really know what the wind's going to blow your way, do you? I gather you were a friend of my father's."

"On occasion." As Dooley sat back down, he gestured to a pair of battered oak captain's chairs in front of his wooden desk. "Have a seat."

They sat down across from him.

"So who's the lady?" Dooley asked.

"My name's Cassidy Jones. I'm a private investigator."

"I've heard of you. You helped that bounty hunter, Maddox, track down a serial killer . . . What'd they call him?"

"The Night Watchman."

"Yeah, that was it. So what do you two want?"

"I want to know if you loaned my father money," Beau said. "If you did, I want to know if he paid it back."

Dooley chuckled. "Been some time since your old man was hurting bad enough to come crawling to me for favors. Even if he was, the last few years, the kind of money he needed was too big for me to handle."

Cassidy caught the tension that crept into Beau's shoulders. "If he wasn't getting money from you, who made him the loans?" he asked.

"I don't know for sure. Years ago, a guy named Sanford Cummings could play in the big leagues, but he had an untimely run-in with an eighteen-wheeler a couple of years back. There's a guy name of Malcolm Vaughn. Looks down his nose at a small-potatoes operator like me. Thinks his shit don't stink because he's got connections, people who can handle the big money loans he brings in. Your old man might have gone to him."

"You think he did?"

Dooley shrugged. "Could be. You'd have to ask him."

Beau sent Cassidy a glance and they rose from their chairs. "Thank you. I appreciate your help."

"Your dad was a good customer. Always paid his debts—one way or another."

"What do you mean?" Beau asked.

"Sometimes a favor is just as good as cash." Dooley rounded his desk, walked over and opened the door. "A word of advice, Beau. Vaughn's not a guy you want to piss off. Do yourself a favor. Let sleeping dogs lie, if you know what I mean."

Beau stood back as Cassidy walked out of the room.

He walked out behind her and closed the door. She could almost hear the wheels spinning in his head.

"We need to talk to Vaughn," he said.

"We have to find him first. Once we do, we'll have to be very careful. Like Tate said, if he's got those kinds of connections, he could be a very dangerous man."

The bouncer was absent when they reached the bottom of the stairs. They made their way out to the parking lot and headed for the car. Unfortunately, the bikers who had pulled in behind them formed a human wall across the rear of Beau's BMW; one of them Cassidy recognized as the guy Beau had tripped on the porch.

"Here we go," Beau said softly, and she couldn't mistake the gleam in his eyes. Cassidy opened her mouth to tell him to chill, try to talk the situation down, but it was too late.

"I'd appreciate it if you gentlemen stepped away from my vehicle," Beau said pleasantly, but there wasn't a hint of friendliness in eyes that now looked cold as ice.

The biggest of the three, barrel-chested with a long, pointed beard, just grinned. "Yeah, well, I'd appreciate it if you'd hand over the keys. Me and my buddies want to go for a little test drive. You'll get your car back when we're finished."

The smile Beau gave them looked utterly feral. "I don't think so. The only ride you're going to get is on the end of my boot." Cassidy gasped as Beau's foot shot up, catching the biker full force in the groin. He dropped like a stone, hugging his privates and moaning, which galvanized his friends.

With the click of a switchblade, a knife glinted in the overhead lights of the parking lot. "You shouldn't have done that," the guy from the porch said. "Now your pretty face is gonna get carved up even more than it already is."

Beau's features hardened. He whirled, his foot shot out,

and the knife went flying. The guy from the porch rushed forward and threw a punch. Beau ducked and elbow-jabbed him beneath the chin, then threw a hard punch that landed in his midsection, doubling him over.

The third guy rushed forward. Beau's knee jerked up, landing in the man's solar plexus, then a hard right sent him flying backward.

Beau clicked the locks on the car and started the engine remotely. "Get in!" he shouted, which Cassidy would gladly have done if the fourth man hadn't quietly slipped behind her, locked an arm around her neck, and dragged her back against his chest.

"Let me go!"

"I'll let you go, sweetheart, after we've all had a little fun." He cupped her jaw. "Such a pretty mouth. I can think of all sorts of things to do with a mouth like that."

"Last chance," Cassidy warned.

The guy just laughed. Cassidy didn't hesitate a second time, just pulled the little .380 nestled in her jacket pocket, aimed the gun at the big foot she could see on the ground between her legs, and fired.

The man howled and started dancing, and Cassidy broke free. Running for the car, she jumped into the passenger seat just as Beau slid into the driver's side. He jammed the car into gear and the vehicle shot backward. She heard the roar of a motorcycle firing up, then another.

"Hang on!" Beau cranked the wheel, and the next instant they were tearing out of the parking lot, tires spinning, careening around a corner and shooting off into the darkened streets. A single headlight appeared behind them, followed by two more.

"They're coming after us!" Cassidy's heart thumped wildly. Gripping the seat belt, she dragged it across her chest and clicked it into place.

Beau downshifted, the car slowed to round a corner, then he hit the gas and the BMW shot forward with the speed of a gazelle. The BMW roared full-throttle down the road. Beau turned into an alley, turned again as they shot out the other end. He rounded two more corners, hit the gas, and just kept going.

"I don't see them," Cassidy said, still peering through the rear window. Beau didn't slow. In minutes he was heading up an on-ramp, pulling onto the freeway, merging into the traffic. Keeping his speed even with the rest of the cars on the road, he wove in and out, staying on the freeway for a couple of miles, then taking an off-ramp. He wound his way through the streets, following a circuitous route back to the office, where the helicopter was waiting.

"I think we lost them," Cassidy said, relaxing back into her seat, finally able to breathe.

"Kid's play," Beau said, slanting her a sideways grin. "I could have lost those guys when I was fifteen." His grin widened. "I can't believe you shot that guy."

Cassidy huffed out a breath. "I aimed for his foot. He's lucky I didn't aim for his family jewels."

Beau laughed. "I thought you didn't carry a gun."

"Jase suggested it. I'm licensed. Since I wasn't sure what we might run into, I thought it wasn't a bad idea."

Beau chuckled and just kept driving, finally pulling into the underground garage.

"We should probably report the incident to the police," Cassidy said.

"Or not. Guys like that don't want trouble with the cops any more than we do."

Cassidy didn't argue. Beau was right. And even though she was the one who had fired the weapon, it could still mean trouble for Beau.

"One thing's for sure," he said as they rode the elevator

up to the top floor and walked out onto the roof. "No one can say you're boring."

She turned, propped her hands on her hips. "You're the one who started the fight. If you hadn't tripped that guy, it wouldn't have happened."

"Yeah? It was your sweet little ass in those tight jeans that sent the poor guy over the edge."

Cassidy couldn't stop a smile.

Twenty minutes later, the helicopter landed on the golf course, returning them to Pleasant Hill. Beau walked her toward the guest house.

"We need to look at those flash drives," she said, "see if we can find out where the money went. Maybe it'll tell us if there's a connection to Vaughn."

His light mood shifted, darkened. "I'd rather take you to bed, but I guess that isn't going to happen."

"Not tonight."

He glanced away. "No. Not tonight. Tomorrow's my father's funeral. I need to deal with that." He stopped at the front door and his eyes fixed on her face. "Saying 'not tonight' isn't exactly a *no*. I'll settle for that for now."

Her stomach lifted. "Beau . . ." But his determined look said he wasn't giving up on his seduction. Cassidy wished she weren't glad.

"It's been a long day," he said. "We need to get some sleep."

She nodded. Now that they were home and safe, exhaustion settled over her. Before she could turn away, he bent and brushed a kiss on her cheek. "Good night, Cassidy Jones." Turning, he headed back to the house.

Cassidy watched him walk away, wanting to call him back, act on the feelings for him that continued to grow. A jumble of emotions ran through her. She wasn't ready to deal with them. Not yet.

She closed the front door and headed for the compact

kitchen, suddenly hungry. Searching the fridge, she found a frozen orange-chicken Lean Cuisine, popped it into the microwave, and ate it in front of the TV.

As soon as she finished, she sat down at her computer. The name she typed in was Malcolm Vaughn.

Mal leaned back in the chair behind the desk in his study. Outside the windows, it was dark, just a sliver of moon winding between the clouds. Seated across from him, Clifford Jennings dug a finger into his short, kinky blond hair to scratch an itch.

"What's going on?" Mal asked.

Cliff crossed a leg over his knee. "I got a phone call a little earlier from one of our sources, guy who works for Dooley Tate."

Tate being a competitor of sorts, Mal kept tabs on him and a couple of others in the business. The cost of information was usually worth the price and there was always someone who had something to sell.

"Apparently Reese and that female detective were out at Barbie's snooping around," Cliff said. "Reese wanted to know if Tate had loaned his father money. I guess he thought Dooley might have offed the old man for not repaying the loan."

Mal scoffed. "The senator's needs were way out of Dooley Tate's league."

"What if they keep digging, Mal? Sooner or later they'll come up with your name. They'll be coming here to talk to you."

"Let them come. I helped the senator get a loan and he repaid it. Where's the problem?"

"I don't like it," Jennings said.

Malcolm steepled his fingers and leaned back in his chair. "Neither do I. I don't want them getting too close.

Maybe we can give Reese a little more trouble, something else to worry about."

Cliff's blond mustache curled up at the corners of his mouth. "Good idea. Maybe we can kill two birds with one stone, so to speak. I know exactly what to do."

Chapter Twelve

The day was overcast and grim, matching the dismal mood of the mourners standing around the magnificent rosewood coffin on top of the open grave. The air was damp in the churchyard, the wind biting through the layers of Cassidy's clothes, the black wool skirt and plum cable-knit turtleneck beneath her peacoat.

Beau wore a black Italian designer suit with hand-stitched lapels he'd had his assistant bring out to the house. A diamond tie tack kept his black-and-blue striped tie in place against the breeze. Without an overcoat, he had to be freezing, but he didn't move, just stood with his back straight and his shoulders squared, staring at the casket draped with white roses.

The first part of the service, held in the chapel, had been packed wall to wall, filled with both locals and members of the Texas political community, people the senator had worked with at the capitol in Austin. There would have been more if Stewart Reese hadn't been a murder victim, the motive for his death not yet clear, the culprit not yet apprehended.

As they had left the chapel for the graveyard portion of

the service, a handsome, powerfully built, broad-shouldered man at least six-five and his attractive blond wife walked up to Beau. Cassidy had seen photos of Beau's partner, Lincoln Cain, on the Internet. The woman had to be his new wife, Carly.

"I wish there was something I could do," Cain said, gripping Beau's hand, leaning in for a brief man hug.

"I'm so sorry, Beau." Carly rose to kiss his cheek.

A third man walked up, with dark brown hair, about the same height as Beau but younger and a little more muscular through the chest and shoulders.

"If there's anything you need," the man said, shaking Beau's hand, "I'm not that far away. All you have to do is ask."

"Thanks, Josh." Beau turned. "I'd like you all to meet Cassidy Jones. She's the lady I told you about."

Cassidy smiled at the group of friends, who seemed to be sizing her up. "Nice to meet you."

"We're glad Beau has you helping him," Carly said.

Beau turned to the younger man. "Cassidy, this is Josh Cain, Linc's younger brother."

"Pleasure, ma'am," Josh said, shaking her hand. She had a hunch he was a soldier. Or had been. She had a brother in the army. There was something different about servicemen. The way they stood, the way they moved, the way they spoke. Something.

She could see reminders of Linc in the hard line of his jaw, the slight cleft in his chin. Unlike his older brother, whose eyes were brown, Josh Cain's eyes were a dark shade of blue.

The small group spoke in low tones as they crossed the grass toward the green canvas tent erected in front of the coffin. Cassidy stood next to Beau, and though they weren't touching, she hoped he could feel her presence, silently lending him support.

Charlotte Reese stood on his other side, looking regal in a black skirt suit, blond hair swept up beneath a pillbox hat, a fine veil of black netting over her face.

At the edge of the crowd, Josie Kessler stood next to her daughter. Beau had spoken to her and Missy when they had arrived at the chapel, had invited them to sit with him, but they had declined.

Cassidy had taken a moment to speak to the girl, to apologize for her misunderstanding at the café and explain that she was a private investigator working on the case.

"I'm a friend of Beau's," she finished. "I'd like to be your friend, too."

Missy managed a shy smile. "I'd like that."

As the minister continued his sermon, every once in a while she noticed Beau's worried gaze going over the heads of the mourners to the pregnant girl and Josie. Missy was more enormous than ever. She looked ready to pop, her face puffy and still a little too pale.

Whatever happened, Cassidy was certain Beau would take care of her and her baby.

The minister's voice pierced her thoughts as the brief, graveside portion of the funeral came to a close.

"And so we deliver into God's hands, this man, Stewart Beaumont Reese, who dedicated his life to the service of the people he represented. Shall we pray?"

Cassidy bowed her head, let the minister's words wash over her. He had only begun to pray when a sharp cry sliced through the quiet. Cassidy's head jerked up in time to see Beau's tall figure leap into action, long legs moving him through the crowd, which parted like sheaves of wheat in a storm as he strode toward Missy.

Cassidy hurried behind him, racing to keep up, spotting the girl's prone figure writhing on the ground.

"Call 9-1-1!" someone shouted. Cassidy dug out her cell, but at least three people were already on their phones. Beau was kneeling, scooping the girl up in his arms, striding across the churchyard toward the black stretch limo that had carried him and Cassidy to the service that morning.

The driver opened the door and Beau ducked his head and disappeared into the back seat, Missy still in his arms. Josie jumped in and so did Cassidy.

"Drive!" Beau commanded. "She's having a baby. You need to get to the hospital as fast as you can!"

The driver—Andy was his name—didn't hesitate. As soon as the door slammed shut, he hit the gas. When the limo had arrived that morning, Andy had recognized Beau as the celebrated race-car driver.

Now, as the limo careened down the road, bounced out of the churchyard, and speeded toward the hospital, Andy seemed determined not to let his racing hero down.

Beau cradled Missy in his lap. "You're gonna be all right, sweetheart. The doctors are going to take care of you."

Cassidy made sure of that by calling ahead and letting them know they were bringing in a woman in labor and that they would be there any minute.

Missy whimpered. "Oh, God, it hurts."

Her mother gripped her hand. "Do your breathing, honey. Remember how they taught you in class? Take deep, focused breaths, then pant through the contraction. In and out through your nose." Josie started breathing, panting, then breathing. Missy closed her eyes and joined her mother.

By the time they got to the hospital, all of them were panting and breathing, including Beau. Cassidy could read the fear in his eyes, the worry lining his forehead.

"It's going to be okay," he kept saying to Missy. "Everything's going to be all right."

Cassidy felt a pinch in her chest at the concern in his voice. Clearly he was going to be a great older brother to Missy's baby girl.

The doctors were waiting when the limo pulled up in front of the emergency entrance. The car doors flew open. Beau helped Missy out, then helped the nurses lift her up on the gurney. Her water had broken and his slacks were damp and wrinkled but he didn't seem to care. Reaching down, he wrapped his fingers around Missy's hand and walked beside the gurney till the nurses shooed him away and the gurney disappeared down the hall.

"Are you the father?" a tall, black-haired nurse asked.

Beau just shook his head. "I'm the baby's brother."

It took a moment for the nurse to figure that one out, then she smiled. "Women have babies every day. Missy's going to be fine. Her mother's going into the delivery room with her."

"Good," Beau said, nodding. "That's good."

"The baby's coming a little early," the nurse said. "I understand Missy was attending a funeral. If she was upset, it might have brought on the contractions."

Beau looked up, color washing out of his face. "So the baby is premature? Is she going to be okay?"

"The doctor is in with them now. It's only a week or so early. I'll let you know how things are going. There's a waiting room just down the hall." The nurse smiled. "I have to warn you, this may take a while. First babies tend to take longer."

"How long is longer?" he asked.

"I think the average is something like eight hours. As I said, I'll keep you posted." The nurse left them standing in the hallway.

Cassidy squeezed Beau's hand, which felt icy cold. "Why don't I have Andy drive me back to the house so I can get you some fresh clothes?"

He looked down, seemed to finally notice how completely disheveled he was. "All right. I keep a go-bag packed. It's got jeans and T-shirts, toiletries, everything I need. It's in the closet in the guest room."

"I'll find it. I won't be long."

He looked down at her. "I keep having to say thank you."

She smiled. "It's all right. I'll find a way for you to repay me."

For the first time that day, Beau looked at her and his eyes gleamed. His mouth edged into a sexy smile. "I think I know exactly the way."

Seven hours and forty minutes later, Beau had the sibling he'd always wanted. A baby sister, Evelyn, named after Missy's grandmother. Evie, they planned to call her. Six pounds thirteen ounces, ten miniature fingers, ten miniature toes, perfect in every way.

After a long, exhausting day, the first time Beau saw the infant, nestled against her mother's breast, a feeling moved over him unlike anything he had ever known. So tiny, so sweet, so completely dependent on the people who cared for her. A fierce surge of protectiveness rushed through him. He would protect this child with everything he had.

His thoughts must have shown on his face, for when he looked over at Cassidy, she smiled at him softly and wiped a tear from her cheek.

Though the birth had gone well, the doctors decided to keep Missy and Evie overnight for observation. He and Cassidy said their good-byes, left the hospital, and drove back to the house in Cassidy's Honda, which she'd driven to the hospital when she'd brought him clean clothes.

He was tired clear to the bone. His emotions had run the gamut from deep sadness to wild elation. Now he felt utterly drained.

Go-bag in hand, he walked Cassidy to the door of the guest house before heading for his own bed in his father's big, empty residence across the lawn. She paused on the porch, turned and looked up at him.

"Rough day," she said.

"Yeah."

"Are you okay?" Concern shone in her face, and when she looked up at him with worry in those big green eyes, suddenly he wasn't okay. He wasn't okay at all.

"No." He glanced away, shook his head. "I don't know . . . I just . . . I feel like everything is so screwed up." His gaze returned to her pretty face and desire hit him like a fist. The go-bag slipped from his fingers. He slid a hand into her thick dark curls and drew her toward him. "I need you, Cassidy. So much."

She leaned into him. "Beau . . ." Going up on her toes, she kissed him. "I need you, too."

Everything tore loose inside him. Hunger, pain, joy, need, all mixed together. Beau caught her face between his hands and kissed her, a deep, yearning, taking kiss he felt in every cell in his body. Cassidy kissed him back, opening, giving him access, holding nothing in. He ravished her mouth, plundered her greedily, endlessly.

He barely remembered walking her backward into the living room, kicking the door closed, pulling her turtleneck over her head, unfastening her black lace bra, letting it fall to the floor.

He paused to look at her breasts, full and beautiful, tipped slightly upward. He cupped them, ran his hands over her dark rose nipples. She moaned as he bent his head and took the fullness into his mouth, suckled greedily, bit the end. Cassidy shoved off the lightweight jacket she had brought to him at the hospital, grabbed the hem of his T-shirt, and pulled it off over his head.

Her fingers traveled over his chest, dipped into the ridges and valleys, over the ladder of muscles down his stomach, moved restlessly back up to his shoulders. He took a moment to look at her, the flush in her cheeks, the tousled dark hair. Pale, lovely breasts rose and fell with every ragged breath. A small waist flared to womanly hips.

"God, I want you." He kissed her again, couldn't seem to get enough. Cassidy leaned into him, her arms going around his neck, her fingers sliding into his hair. Her tongue tangled with his as he backed her up against the living room wall and shoved up her black wool skirt, smoothed a hand over her hip, down to the thin strip of lace between her legs.

She was wet. So hot and wet. He wanted to be inside her more than he wanted to see another sunrise.

He let go of her long enough to retrieve the condom in his wallet, kissed her as he freed himself and rolled it on.

"I need you, baby. Now. Here. I don't want to wait." His fingers caught hold of the lace between her legs; he gave a sharp tug and the delicate fabric tore free.

Cassidy moaned as he lifted her, wrapped her legs around his waist. He heard her shoes hit the carpet, then he was filling her, sliding deep inside.

For a moment he paused, letting her tight, wet heat envelope him. Her fingers dug into his shoulders as he started to move, began to take what he wanted, what he so desperately needed.

Propping her back against the wall, he took her deep, rode her hard, the little whimpers in her throat driving him on, making him hotter, more needy.

"Cassie, baby," he said. "Sweet God, I want you. I don't know how long I can last."

She made a soft sound in her throat and rode him, didn't back away from the hunger burning through him. Her head fell back as he surged deeper, and her body tightened around him, sucked him even deeper. Her climax hit hard, gloving him so sweetly it drove him over the edge. Pleasure rolled through him, deep and saturating, washing away the pain, the darkness.

For seconds he just held her, his face buried in her silky dark curls, inhaling the faint scent of gardenias.

Neither of them moved for the longest time. When he finally set her back on her feet, Cassidy leaned against him and Beau smoothed back her hair. "You okay?"

She just nodded. He moved away long enough to deal with the condom, returned to find her standing exactly where he'd left her.

"I hope I didn't hurt you." With her skirt around her waist and her perfect breasts tilting wickedly up at him, she looked beautiful and completely wanton, and he started getting hard again.

"You didn't hurt me. That . . . that was amazing."

He couldn't stop a smile. "I thought so. I'm really glad you did, too."

She looked down at herself and warm color rose in her cheeks. "I'd better get dressed."

Beau shook his head. "No way, baby." Hauling her back in his arms, he very thoroughly kissed her. "Wait right here." Crossing to the door, he walked out on the porch and retrieved his go-bag.

He held up the bag and walked back into the living room. "Now I'm bedding you good and proper—like I should have done in the first place."

When she just stared at him as if he had lost his mind, he bent, scooped her over one shoulder, walked into the bedroom and settled her on the bed. Unzipping the go-bag, he grabbed a handful of condoms and tossed them on the nightstand.

Cassidy didn't move.

"Probably be a good idea if we finished getting undressed," he said.

"Yes . . . of course. I'm . . . uh . . . not very good at this."

His head came up as she eased to the side of the bed. "You don't think so?"

"I don't know. Tonight was the best sex I've ever had, so maybe I'm getting better."

Beau laughed. "If you get any better, honey, you're liable to kill me."

She smiled at that, seemed to relax. "I could umm . . . really use a shower."

He closed his eyes to block the image. "Good idea. It's been a helluva day." Beau waited till he heard the shower go on, heard Cassidy open and close the glass door, then followed her into the bathroom.

If that was the best sex Cassidy Jones had ever had, Beau figured she was in for some really nice surprises.

Chapter Thirteen

Beau stirred at a sound in the darkness and awoke from the depths of the most restful sleep he'd had since his father had been murdered. The familiar ring of his cell phone dragged him fully awake and he reached toward the nightstand to quiet it before Cassidy awoke.

The digital clock on the nightstand read 1:00 A.M. He checked the caller ID but didn't recognize the number. Slipping out of bed, he padded naked into the living room. "Reese."

"You want to know who killed your father?"

His hand tightened around the phone. "Who is this? How did you get this number?"

"Drive to 516 Brookdale Road. Go in through the back door. You've got twenty minutes. No police and you'd better be alone."

"Tell me who this is."

The line went dead. Beau glanced toward the bedroom. After a third round of incredible sex, Cassidy was deeply asleep. Which was probably good since he had been warned to come alone.

Quietly returning to the bedroom, he grabbed his jeans

and a long-sleeved T-shirt out of his go-bag, grabbed his sneakers and went back into the living room to put them on.

Cassidy's car keys sat on the table in the entry. Driving the Lambo didn't seem like a good idea, so he picked up her keys and slipped outside, quietly closing the door behind him. He headed for the Honda, slid inside and started the engine, then punched the address he had been given into the nav system in the dash, a necessity, he imagined, for a detective.

The map showed the house was on the south side of town. Driving the speed limit, careful to stop at all the lights, he still made his destination in eighteen minutes.

No lights on in the single-story redbrick house. Clouds covered the moon, making it a pitch-dark night. He headed around to the back of the house and walked up on the patio. No movement inside, no lamps went on.

Reaching for the doorknob, he turned it, found the door unlocked, opened it and slipped inside. He owned a gun, kept it in his home for protection, had learned how to handle a weapon in his bad-boy days. If Cassidy's little pistol had been handy, he would have brought it, wished he had it now.

He tried to see through the darkness, caught the gleam of a stainless dishwasher next to the sink in the kitchen. He'd taken a couple of steps before he noticed something sticky on the floor.

"Anybody home?" he called out.

No answer. There was an odd smell in the air, coppery and dense. His pulse hammered. A trickle of sweat rolled between his shoulder blades. A bad feeling crept over him, warning him to beware. "Anybody here?"

No answer, nothing but the lingering smell and the darkness. He had two choices. Turn on the lights or turn around and leave as quietly as he had come. Leave without the answers he had been promised.

"I'm leaving!" he called out.

Still no answer. He turned, started to retrace his steps when the back door flew open and the kitchen light went on. Two uniformed patrolmen, guns drawn and aimed at his chest, stood in the doorway. "Don't move!" one of the officers called out. "Put your hands in the air!"

Cautiously they stepped into the kitchen. Beau's gaze shot from the policemen to the thick pool of blood spreading over the kitchen floor. His stomach heaved when he spotted the man's lifeless body. His eyes were open, a neat hole in the side of his head.

"It's not what you think," Beau said. "I got a phone call. I was told to come to this address."

"Move away from the body and get down on your knees," ordered the cop. "Keep your hands in the air."

"I didn't kill him. I don't even know who he is." Keeping his hands raised, he got down on his knees at the edge of the pool of blood, which was beginning to congeal. The second officer, younger, fresh faced and pink cheeked, rushed toward him, grabbed one of his wrists and twisted it behind his back. Beau could have stopped him with a single movement. Instead he felt the click of metal around first one wrist then the other.

"You're Reese, aren't you?" the first cop said. "Beau Reese?"

"That's right." The younger cop was on the radio calling it in, giving the location of what appeared to be a break-in that had ended in murder.

"Look, I walked in just a few minutes before you got here." Beau's pulse raced, throbbed in his head. "Someone called my cell and told me to come to this address. They said they had information about the man who killed my father, Senator Reese."

The cop walked toward him. "So I guess it's just another coincidence, same as before." He jerked Beau to his feet and shoved him toward the door. "You just happen to be around when somebody ends up dead."

Beau closed his eyes. He hated to think what Cassidy was going to say when she found out he was involved in a second murder. He hated for her to think he'd been stupid. Which clearly he had been.

He looked up at the older cop. "I'm not saying any more till I talk to my lawyer." From the way the guy looked at him, it was the first smart thing he'd said since he'd left the guest house.

Beau had been sitting in a holding cell for two hours when Tom Briscoe arrived. Tom let him make a phone call. He called Linc, told him what had happened, and asked him to hire an attorney.

"I'll call Nate Temple," Linc said. "He's the best criminal defense lawyer around. He'll have you out of there as fast as humanly possible."

"It was a setup, Linc. I can't believe I got sucked in. Stupid. Stupid. Stupid."

"You had no idea this was coming. You wanted information. You went after it. What about the lady detective? Why didn't you call her, take her with you?"

"She was asleep. I didn't want to wake her." There must have been something in his voice.

"Asleep? Where, in your bed?"

He didn't deny it. Linc was his best friend. "Not exactly. Look, this wasn't her fault. I made a bad decision; now I need to fix it."

"Take it easy, all right? I'll call Temple. Just stay cool until he gets there." The line went dead.

Linc was there for him, the way he had been since high

school. Beau, the spoiled rich kid ignored by his parents, and Linc, who lived with his mother and drunken, abusive father in a seedy apartment down near the railroad tracks.

Linc had been the official town bad boy, tough as nails and loyal to a fault. He was a Texas multimillionaire now, but he hadn't really changed.

At sixteen, Beau had been tall but still gangly. He was being bullied by a couple of varsity football jocks till Lincoln Cain, the biggest, strongest kid in class, had befriended him. He'd taught Beau how to defend himself, which led to boxing lessons his father had gladly paid for—anything to keep him busy and out of the house—martial arts lessons after that.

Beau had grown into his tall, lanky body, which was now hard-muscled and well-defined; if it came to it, he had no trouble defending himself.

Which might be useful if murders kept happening wherever he went.

He looked up as a police officer walked toward him. The cop returned him to the same bare-walled interrogation room he had been in before. Tom Briscoe was waiting, looking sleepy-eyed, ticked-off, and disappointed all at once.

"What the hell happened, Beau?"

Beau shook his head. "I should probably wait for my attorney."

"It would look better if you cooperated—assuming you're innocent."

"I'm innocent. For chrissake, I didn't kill him. I don't even know his name. Who was he, by the way?"

"Guy named Jess Milford. Ring any bells?"

A muscle ticked in his cheek, which Briscoe must have noticed.

"I can see that it does. Milford worked for Alamo, one of your father's companies. He lost his job a little over two months ago. Did you know that?"

He knew it. Milford was one of the names his father had hired Cassidy to check out. "I'm not answering any more questions, Tom. Not until my attorney arrives. In the meantime, I'll tell you what I told those two cops." Beau recapped the events of the night, starting with the phone call he had received and ending with the police showing up exactly in time to catch him at the murder scene.

"Someone had to have called 9-1-1. The cops arrived right on time. It was a setup, Tom. I've been digging around, asking questions about my father's murder, and somebody doesn't like it. That call is bound to show up in the dispatcher's log. Maybe they can track the number, see who made it. The call alone ought to be enough to convince you it was a setup."

"Look, Beau, it's not that simple. The call came in as an anonymous tip, a possible burglary at 516 Brookdale Road. When the police arrived, they found you and a dead guy. That makes two dead guys, Beau, both connected to you."

Beau glanced at his watch. He needed to call Cassidy. He had no idea what she'd think when she discovered him gone, along with her car. He wondered if Linc had been able to line up an attorney. If Temple took the case, how long would it take him to get to Pleasant Hill? How much time would Beau have to spend in jail before Temple could bail him out?

He looked at Briscoe and tried to focus. "What about my father's murder? Any new suspects? Anything new on the case?"

"Not so far."

"Did you ever find my father's cell phone?"

"No. We tried to ping it. Last call went through a tower in the area. We figure the battery's gone dead."

"Or the killer disabled it. Look, Tom, we both know the senator had enemies. Have you checked that angle, tried to figure out who else had motive?"

"If you're thinking of Josie Kessler, she and Missy were both working at the café at the time of the murder."

"I wasn't thinking of Josie . . . well, I admit she crossed my mind, because she definitely had motive. I didn't think it could have been Missy, because of her condition. I'm glad it wasn't either one of them."

"So am I. Anything else you want to add before you go back to the holding cell?"

"Only that I didn't kill Jess Milford or my father. I'm counting on you, Tom, to figure out who did."

Briscoe made no reply. Which didn't make Beau feel any better.

Cassidy got to drive the Lamborghini. Beau had called. He was in jail, being held on suspicion of murder. The police could hold him for forty-eight hours before they officially had to file charges. Cain had found him an attorney.

Cassidy's emotions had been in turmoil from the moment she had awoken and found herself alone. Beau was gone. She'd been sure he'd left to escape the awkward *morning-after* conversation, the way a lot of men did.

Self-loathing rushed in. She'd been a fool. She'd allowed Beau to use her when she had known what a heartbreaker he was. After a long, hot shower and time to think, she'd finally admitted it wasn't all his fault. She had wanted him every bit as much as he'd wanted her.

Whatever happened, she finally decided, the night had been an incredible experience, one she would never forget. She told herself it didn't matter that one night was enough for Beau.

Then she'd gone in search of her car keys and discovered them missing. Glancing out the window, she realized her car was gone and a whole new set of worries swept in.

It wasn't until later in the morning that Beau had finally

been allowed to make a second phone call, this one to her. When he'd explained what had happened, she'd felt the most unsettling combination of fear and relief. Fear for Beau and relief it wasn't over between them.

Beau told her where to find the keys to the Lambo and she promised to be there as quickly as she could.

"You don't have to hurry," he said darkly. "It doesn't look like I'm getting out of here anytime soon."

She'd done her best to lighten his mood. "I don't have to hurry? What, are you kidding me? It's a Lamborghini, Beau. It doesn't know how to go slow."

He chuckled, though she thought it sounded forced.

When she got to the Pleasant Hill police station, Beau's attorney had already been there awhile. He was making arrangements for Beau to be released.

"You must be Cassidy," he said as he walked toward her, not a wrinkle in his navy pinstripe suit. "I've spoken to Beau. He said you'd be coming. You're the private investigator working on his father's case."

"Cassidy Jones." She extended a hand, which he shook.

"I'm Nathan Temple. I prefer Nate. Linc called, asked me to handle Beau's case." Nate Temple was older than Beau by at least five years, an attractive man with traces of silver threading through his light brown hair.

"I understand Beau called you and explained what happened," Temple said.

"That's right. He said he got a phone call around one P.M. The caller promised information about his father's death. He was given a location and twenty minutes to get there. It had to be a setup. He didn't even see the body until the police came through the door."

Temple was nodding. Cassidy figured he was looking for possible discrepancies in Beau's story. He led her a few feet away where they couldn't be overheard.

"The victim is a guy named Jess Milford," he said. "Do you recognize the name?"

Beau had mentioned it when he'd called. She nodded. "Milford was one of the people the senator hired me to check into. He thought he was being followed. He said someone had been asking questions. Milford was the foreman of Alamo, the senator's construction and development company. He was fired a few months back. Senator Reese thought he might be holding some kind of grudge."

"And now Milford's dead."

"Yes, and Beau was set up to take the blame."

"You seem sure of that. You don't have any doubt of Beau's innocence?"

She stiffened. "No. Do you?"

Temple relaxed. "I've known Lincoln Cain and Beau Reese for years. I don't believe Beau killed anyone. We just need to prove it. Or in more legal terms, make sure the police *can't* prove it."

"We need to do better than that. Beau's reputation will be ruined unless he's completely exonerated. To do that, we need to find the killer."

"It would certainly be the best solution."

"What evidence do they have against him?"

Temple tossed her a look. "Besides being found at the murder scene? The second one in a week?"

"Besides that."

"The police found the weapon, a Smith and Wesson forty-caliber semiauto. It was on the floor under the kitchen table. The good news is, the gun was wiped clean, no prints, nothing. So far Beau's only connection to Milford is that the victim worked for the company owned by Senator Reese and his ex-wife."

Surprise lifted one of her eyebrows. "Charlotte was the senator's partner in Alamo?"

"That's right. Beau says he isn't sure what happened after the divorce, whether one of them bought out the other or they still owned it together."

She wondered why Beau hadn't mentioned Charlotte's involvement, but then they hadn't had time to work the Milford angle yet.

She glanced toward the door leading to the holding cells, willing Beau to appear. "Will you be posting bail? How long before you can get him out of jail?"

"Chief Warren isn't ready to charge him. Too many loose ends. In a high-profile case like this, the DA wants to be sure he's got all his ducks in a row. Doesn't mean it won't happen, but until it does, they're letting him out. Beau has agreed not to leave town."

The attorney glanced toward the door and smiled. "Here he is now."

Cassidy turned to see Beau walking toward them. Instead of his usual straight posture, his shoulders slumped and a curl of black hair fell over his forehead. She wanted to go to him, put her arms around his neck and tell him everything was going to be okay.

Instead, she stood quietly next to his attorney. Her heart constricted when he reached for her, pulled her into his arms and buried his face in her hair.

"I was an idiot," he said. "I'm sorry. I didn't kill Milford. I hope you know that."

Her hold tightened. "I know you didn't kill him. You were clearly set up." A shudder of relief ran through his body. Cassidy leaned back and finger-combed the dark curl away from his forehead.

Beau looked at Temple. "We finished here?"

"For now."

Beau took her hand. "Let's get out of here." The three of

them walked out of the police station and headed for the parking lot.

"Why don't we go back to the house where we can talk," Nate suggested. "We need to develop a strategy. Unfortunately, I don't have much time. I've got to get back to Dallas."

"You aren't staying?" Beau asked.

"They haven't pressed charges. There's nothing I can do for you here. I'll come back if you need me."

Beau nodded. Cassidy spotted her silver hatchback parked in the lot. She had worried the police would hold it as evidence.

"They've already searched the Honda," Nate said. "They didn't find anything so they released it." He pulled her keys from the pocket of his suit coat and held them out to her. "I gather these belong to you."

She glanced at Beau, whose eyes looked bleaker than she had ever seen them, no longer a beautiful blue but more a faded gray. "Why don't you drive the Honda, Nate? I'll drive Beau back to the house in the Lambo. You can follow us—if you can keep up."

Beau's head jerked in her direction. He stared at her and something shifted in his features. A slow smile spread over his lips. "The lady's driving the Lambo. You've got the address. We'll see you back there."

Nate smiled and just shook his head.

A soft buzzing sounded on his desk. Mal leaned over and picked up his cell phone, pressed it against his ear. "I'm listening."

"Two birds with one stone—just like I said. Milford won't be flapping his mouth and Reese has more trouble than he can handle."

"I doubt they have enough to convict him, but at least

he'll be out of the way for a while. What about the woman? You think she'll back off or try to dig deeper?"

"She won't quit," Cliff Jennings said. "She'll press even harder. But with Milford gone, she'll just run into a bunch of dead ends."

"And if she doesn't?"

"We handle it."

"We can't afford another murder. Sooner or later someone will find a way to connect the dots."

"So we make it an accident, just like you said."

"Maybe it won't come to that," Mal suggested.

"Yeah, maybe."

"Make sure there are no unexpected complications." Mal hung up the phone.

Chapter Fourteen

Beau sat down across from Nate at the table in the kitchen of the main house. Since no one had eaten all day, Cassidy fixed ham and cheese sandwiches from food she found in the fridge and made a pitcher of iced sweet tea.

Beau picked at his meal. He should have been hungry, but his appetite had vanished. As they sat around the table, Nate explained what might or might not happen over the next few days and warned them not to speak to anyone outside their immediate circle, especially not the media.

"They're going to be after you like bloodhounds on the scent of fresh meat, Beau. Just stick to *no comment*."

He sighed. "I plan to avoid them as much as I possibly can."

"It won't be easy," Nate said. "You might want to hire some security."

Beau just nodded.

After Nate had answered his questions, the Tex/Am chopper landed on the golf course to pick the attorney up and whisk him back to Dallas.

"What'd you think of him?" Beau asked as he padded back into the kitchen and returned to his seat at the table.

Cassidy took a sip of iced tea. "I like him. He doesn't waste time or words, just tells it like it is."

"Linc knows him better than I do. He says he's one of the best criminal lawyers in Texas." He shook his head. "I can't believe this is happening. I keep thinking I'm going to wake up."

Cassidy reached across the table and set her hand over his. It was warm and soft and he remembered how smooth her skin had felt when he'd touched her last night. It made him want to touch her again. Arousal slipped through him. He wanted more of her, way more, but he couldn't think of that now.

Cassidy squeezed his hand. "We're going to find the killer, Beau. We're going to prove you're innocent."

"How? Where do we even start?" He scrubbed a hand over the beard stubble on his jaw. "We only had three leads to begin with. George Larson has an alibi and Jess Milford is dead. We don't even know if the same person killed both of them or if it was two different people. Hell, my father was stabbed. Jess Milford was shot in the head."

"We have a third lead, Beau. Charlotte Mercer Reese— your stepmother. She was your father's partner in Alamo. I'm surprised you didn't tell me."

"It didn't seem important, not until today. I didn't even think of it until Nate and I were discussing Milford's connection to my father. I can't see Charlotte as a killer. Besides, she was in Dallas when my father was stabbed."

"We don't know that for sure. We haven't had time to check it out. We also need to look at your cell phone, see if we can figure out who called you last night."

"The police took it. They're holding it as evidence." He ran a finger through the condensation on his half-empty iced tea glass. "I wonder how the caller got my number. It's supposed to be unlisted."

"Charlotte would have had it. I know you don't like the idea, but we really need to talk to her."

Beau sat forward in his chair. "There's another possibility, and the closer I look at it, the more plausible it seems."

"What's that?"

"My father had my number, and his cell phone is missing. I'm betting the killer took it. If he did, maybe the murder wasn't the spur-of-the-moment crime of passion it appeared to be."

Cassidy fell silent as she pondered the notion. "Milford's death would certainly support that theory. He and the senator were definitely connected. Let me do some digging, see what I can find out about Alamo."

"Good idea. There's too damned much we don't know. Two men are dead and we have no idea who killed them or why." Frustration rolled through him. "This whole thing just seems to be spiraling out of control."

"I know this is difficult, Beau, but you've got good people around you. I'm good at what I do. Temple is good at what he does. Add to that you're smart and determined. Together we can put the pieces together. We can do this, okay?"

Some of his frustration eased. "You're right. I'm sorry. I'm out of my element here. I need to have some patience and I've never been a patient man." He tossed her a look and felt the faint tug of a smile. "Except in bed. I'm guessing you figured that out last night."

Cassidy blushed. It was the first time he'd mentioned what had happened between them. If things had turned out the way he'd planned, they would have had plenty of time to talk about it this morning—hell, time to do a lot more than talk.

Cassidy glanced away. Sex was the one thing she seemed shy about. He kind of liked that.

"Apparently you have endless patience in certain matters."

She rose from her chair. "I need to get to work. As soon as I have something, I'll let you know."

Beau stood up, too. After a night in jail, he could really use a shower and fresh clothes. "While you're at it, I'll take another look at the information on those flash drives."

He watched her walk out the back door, heading for her computer in the guest house. He wished he could go with her, take up where they had left off last night. It wasn't going to happen, at least not right now.

Exhaustion rolled over him. He'd slept less than an hour last night. It didn't matter. The clock was ticking. There were things he needed to do.

The media arrived. Cassidy was surprised it had taken them this long. Vans filled with reporters from the local news channels as well as Dallas, Austin, and Houston lined up in front of the house, waiting for a glimpse of Beau Reese, former champion race-car driver, multimillionaire, murder suspect in two homicides, and the hottest news story in Texas.

He was pacing back and forth in the living room of the guest house, where he had managed to escape. The curtains were drawn. Cassidy tried to ignore him and finish her work on the computer.

"I feel like a caged cat," he growled, as if he really were one. "Don't they have something better to do than stand outside and gawk at someone's home?"

"They're just doing their job, Beau. You should be used to it by now."

He snarled something she was glad she couldn't hear. Walking over to the window, he peered through the crack in the curtains. "We can't stay here. Not with those jackals swarming all over the property. My place in Dallas is a lot more secure. There's a first-class alarm system and security cameras. I could arrange for guards to keep the media away, but I'm not supposed to leave town."

"Call Temple. See if he can get them to let you go back to your own home. You work in Dallas and the city's only an hour and a half away. It's not an unreasonable request."

"Good idea. If they agree, we can talk to Charlotte."

"And Malcolm Vaughn. I found him. We can follow that lead, too."

Since Beau's phone was still at the police station, Cassidy had entered Nate's number in her cell. She handed Beau the phone, watched as he punched the contact button and waited for Temple to answer.

Cassidy kept typing, working to dig up information on Alamo as Beau explained the situation to his attorney. He listened to Nate's reply and hung up the phone.

"He's going to call me back."

Cassidy got up from the computer and walked over to where he stood by the window. She could feel the tension humming through him, sense his frustration. She wished she could touch him, soothe his worries in some way.

When he turned to look at her, the darkness in those cobalt eyes changed to glittering heat. The answering rush of warmth she felt warned her to keep her distance.

"Did you . . . umm . . . turn up anything new in those flash drives?"

"I only got through the one containing personal information. You were right. Most of it was stuff about people my father worked with in Congress, names of their wives and children, their interests and hobbies, sports their kids were involved it. Stuff that made for good conversation."

"And the rest?"

"He kept that flash drive hidden for a reason. Some of it was similar to the information on George Larson—personal, intimate, and extremely incriminating. If he used it to get what he wanted, it was blackmail. As soon as this is over, I'll destroy it."

Beau hadn't exaggerated his father's lack of ethics. As they dug deeper, Cassidy wondered how much worse it was going to get.

"If he was blackmailing someone," she said, "they would definitely have a motive for wanting him dead."

"There were notes typed under the names. I didn't see anything posted recently. George Larson was the last file he opened and the last entry he made, and that was a couple of months back."

Her cell rang. Beau checked the caller ID, then pressed the phone to his ear. He started talking and some of the tension eased from between his shoulders. "Okay, that's good. We'll chopper in so they can't follow us."

He hung up the phone. "Chief Warren agreed to let us go back to Dallas."

"That's great, Beau."

Since his pilot's number was in his cell, he called Marty Chen and told him to have the chopper return to Pleasant Hill.

"I need my car," Cassidy said. "I've got some things I need to do back in Dallas. I can meet you there."

"We've got work to do. I need you to come with me. I'll send people down to pick up both our cars and bring them back to the city."

She was ambivalent. She needed to go into her office, do some follow-up with some of her clients. She needed to stop by her apartment and pick up fresh clothes. But she didn't want to clash with those reporters any more than he did. And there was the problem of Beau, himself. If she stayed with him, she'd end up back in his bed. As she'd said, he was smart and he was determined, and she was wildly attracted to him. She was a woman and in no way immune to that magnetic Beau Reese charm.

Figuring she could make up her mind once her car arrived in the city, she went to pack her things. Beau had managed to escape the main house with his computer and the flash drives. Cassidy packed up her laptop, along with the manila files they had found, which she still hadn't had time to go through completely.

When she went back and looked out the window, she was surprised to catch a glimpse of two police cars rolling down the block toward the house. A few minutes later, she heard a knock on the guest house door.

Beau had seen the cars, too, and worry tightened his shoulders. He strode over to answer the knock and found four uniformed patrolmen on the porch.

"Afternoon, Officers. What can I do for you?" The reporters had followed the police, trespassing across the backyard and swarming into position around the guest house front door. A dozen cameras waited to catch a glimpse of Beau.

"Chief Warren sent us," one of the patrolmen said. "We're here to help with crowd control."

Beau relaxed. "Thanks, I appreciate it."

It was getting noisy outside. It seemed even the cloudy weather and threat of rain couldn't deter the news hounds.

"Hey, Beau! How about a story for old times' sake?" An attractive blond reporter smiled and waved. Cassidy wondered how well he knew her.

A chorus of others started shouting. "Beau, tell us what happened! Did you kill your father? What about Jess Milford? Give us the scoop, Beau!"

The dull roar of an aircraft engine and a depression of air signaled the arrival of the chopper, circling, then descending, the noise covering the boisterous shouts of the crowd.

Beau turned to Cassidy. "You ready?"

"More than." One of the officers grabbed the handle of

her carry-on. Cassidy slung the strap of her computer over her shoulder and grabbed her purse.

Beau grabbed his computer and the manila files. "Let's go."

One of the patrolmen stepped outside, into the throng of pushing, shoving reporters. Beau followed, keeping her close beside him while the other three officers blazed a trail through the unruly mob toward the edge of the golf course, where the helicopter had landed and sat with its blades slowly spinning.

They were still yelling Beau's name as he and Cassidy climbed inside, strapped themselves into their seats, and the chopper lifted away. Cassidy's stomach swooped up as the ground dropped away beneath them and the helicopter rose into the air.

"You okay?" Beau asked through the headphones. He seemed more himself now that they had formulated a plan, far more in command of the situation. Beau was a man who liked being in control, another thing she had learned about him last night, a thought that made her face heat up again.

"I'm fine," she said, though of course she really wasn't. She was just as worried as he was, maybe more so. Men were dying. No one knew why. Until the killer or killers were caught, Beau could be in danger.

It didn't take long before the chopper landed on the roof of the Tex/Am building. Beau hurried her into the elevator and they went straight down to the parking garage.

"My house is only seven miles away," he said as the valet brought up his black BMW. "We'll be there in less than twenty minutes."

We. Clearly, he wasn't giving her a choice. She could argue, make him take her to her apartment, but she was still working the case and it would be easier with his input.

He drove through the Bluffview district, an area of big, beautiful, very expensive homes. No one was around when he turned into the long, curving driveway toward the sprawling, white, flat-roofed contemporary house up ahead.

"Looks like we're safe for the moment," Beau said.

Safe? Cassidy thought of last night, caught the hot gleam in those fierce blue eyes, and knew she wasn't safe at all.

Chapter Fifteen

"Your home is lovely," Cassidy said, ambling through the modern interior. Twelve-foot ceilings, lots of white with accents of cool tones: blue, green, turquoise. Beautiful modern paintings to brighten the walls. The windows at the back of the house looked out on the aqua waters of a free-form swimming pool.

"If it was warmer, we could go for a swim," Beau said as he walked up behind her, bent and nuzzled her neck. Little slivers of heat shot through her.

"It's nice and private," he said. "We wouldn't even need swimsuits." Another nibble, followed by the warm press of his lips against the sensitive spot below her ear. "Or we could get in the whirlpool down at the end. Nice and hot in there."

Hot. She was already on the verge of bursting into flames. She closed her eyes, imagining what it would be like to make love with Beau in the warm water of the hot pool.

She turned, rested her palms on his chest as she looked up at him. "We need to be working the case. Besides, it's starting to rain."

She hoped her refusal didn't sound as half-hearted as she was afraid it did. They didn't have time for sex. Every moment was crucial. "By the way, I found something. It might be important."

Beau bent his head for a soft, lingering kiss, then drew away. "I hope you're giving me points for self-control here, because working is the last thing I want to be doing right now."

"You haven't had much sleep. Maybe we could take a nap later."

His eyes gleamed. "Now there's an idea I like." He grabbed the files he had set on the table, grabbed the handle of her carry-on and rolled it down the hall. "Let's get you settled, then we can talk about what you found."

She should tell him she couldn't stay. She didn't need to get involved even more deeply with Beau. Instead, she followed him, ignoring a pang of disappointment when he walked past the master suite and tugged her carry-on into the bedroom next door.

"You've got your own bathroom. Do you need to unpack first, or should we set up your computer?"

She glanced around the room, which continued the modern theme of the house. The platform bed was low, the bedspread chocolate brown with bright orange and red throw pillows. "I don't see a desk. Maybe the kitchen table or someplace else would work."

"There's a partners' desk in my study. It's handy if you have someone working with you on a project. Linc used to come over at least once a week. He's home most nights now that he's married."

Beau led her back down the hall, opened a ten-foot door that matched the others in the house, and walked her into the study.

"So how come you never got married?" she asked.

Beau turned. His smile had faded, his features closed up. Any hint of heat in his eyes was gone.

"I was engaged once. It was a long time ago."

Clearly it was a sensitive subject. His hard look warned her not to press for more, but she was a detective. Discovering secrets was part of her DNA.

"What happened?"

His mouth tightened. "She died," he said flatly. Definitely end of topic.

Grabbing the computer out of her hand, he walked to the opposite side of his freestanding desk. Built of the same blond wood as the hardwood floors, the desk was lovely, all smooth lines and perfect angles. On top sat a masterwork of modern computer technology that had to cost thousands of dollars.

She walked over to study the equipment. Two Mac Pro six-core computers with matching 33-inch monitors perched next to a pair of Sennheiser HD 800 wireless headphones. Cassidy silently swooned at the 78-inch curved Samsung television with Bose SoundTouch audio. It was good to be king.

Her gaze moved away from the expensive technology to the modern fireplace, the sleek brown sofa and chair in front of it, then to the built-in blond credenza and bookshelves behind the desk. She moved toward them like a zombie, compelled to know what Beau read.

Winning: The Racing Life of Paul Newman rubbed bindings with a book of racing photos by Louis Klemantaski. On another shelf, sat a row of how-to books on marketing and sales. He was, after all, the head of marketing for a billion-dollar corporation. She recognized Zig Ziglar's *Selling 101*. Next to it was *Social Media Marketing for Business*.

There were a number of contemporary art books: Picasso, Miro, Jackson Pollack. Current artists like Cattelan, Cindy Sherman, and Jeff Wall were included.

She turned to him with a smile, found him no longer scowling. "You can tell a lot about a person by what they read."

His mouth edged up. "That so? What do you like to read?"

She shrugged. "I'm into fiction. I like to escape the problems of the world. I read everything from literary fiction to mysteries, thrillers, and romance."

He started smiling. "Romance, huh?" The gleam was back in his eyes.

"Yeah . . ." She looked at him and hoped he didn't hear the little hitch in her voice. The men in romance novels were sexy as hell, but Beau Reese had them beat by a mile.

He tipped her face up and very softly kissed her. "We'd better get our work done, so we can take that nap."

Heat washed through her. She had never met a man who affected her the way he did.

"One last question," she said, and he stiffened, definitely not wanting to talk more about the past. "How did you get that very sexy scar on the side of your face?"

Beau relaxed. "Fistfight in high school. Guy was wearing his senior class ring."

"Who won?"

"I did." He rubbed the side of his face. "Not sure it was worth it."

"I think you owe him. Otherwise you might have been too pretty."

Beau smiled and just shook his head. As Cassidy went to work setting up her computer, then plugging her cell phone in to charge, Beau brought over another desk chair. She sat down and adjusted the seat, opened her laptop, and brought up the file she'd been working on.

"Here's what I've got so far," she said. "As you know, Alamo was jointly owned by Stewart and Charlotte Reese. That didn't change even after the divorce. But the company is no longer in business. Alamo closed its doors after a fire destroyed a three-hundred-unit apartment project they were building in Iron Springs."

Beau frowned. "The company went broke? There must have had been insurance money."

"There was. The building was still under construction when the fire occurred. The insurance company paid the claim, but Alamo decided to cancel the project. They said the rental market had changed. Demand was low. The project was no longer viable, so they took the money and closed the doors."

"When did it happen?"

She looked down at the monitor. "November twenty-first of last year."

"So about two months ago."

"That's right. The thing is, Beau, the blaze was deemed arson by vandals. There was writing on the unfinished walls, piles of workplace debris were set on fire. But the police never caught the vandals."

Beau kept watching her. "There's something else. What is it?"

There was definitely something else. She wasn't sure she liked the way he was beginning to read her. "From what I can tell, the senator was right about the market. If they had completed the project, they never would have been able to fill that number of rental units. Alamo would have lost millions of dollars. Instead, Stewart and Charlotte took the insurance money, paid off any debts against the property, sold the land to a guy who wanted it for part of a subdivision project, and came out with a very nice profit."

His gaze remained on her face. "So you're saying my dad was behind the fire."

She shrugged, though that was exactly what she thought. "Maybe he just got lucky."

"My dad had a way of getting lucky that always seemed to cost other people money." He walked over to the window that looked onto a stretch of manicured lawn. A narrow creek carved its way through the land.

Beau paced back. "What about Milford?"

"For the last five years, Jess Milford was foreman of the company."

"So Milford would have been working on the apartment project. I'm wondering if my dad got rid of him so he'd be out of the way when the fire was set. It would certainly be easier without the foreman around. You know the date he was fired?"

"No, but I can probably find out."

"How?"

"Unemployment benefits. Maybe your friend Rob could go into the records, see if Jess Milford signed up for unemployment. That would give us roughly the date he was let go. Or I guess we could just ask Charlotte."

His mouth edged up. "Better idea. Way better than hacking into government records."

Cassidy just smiled. "If Alamo fired Milford before the arson, he probably wasn't involved. So why would they kill him? And if they did, why did they wait so long?"

"Milford had to be pissed when he was let go," Beau said, frowning. "He was a longtime employee. He would have heard about the fire after it happened—it would have been in all the papers and on TV."

"Let's say Milford had his suspicions, but he didn't have any proof. Then something happened. Maybe he kept digging, turned up some kind of evidence. He found out who'd set the fire, went to them and . . . I don't know . . . tried to get them to pay him to keep quiet?"

Beau started nodding. "Maybe my father's murder was the catalyst. Milford believed it was connected, went to the men responsible, and pressed them for money. But instead of paying him, they murdered him and set me up to take the fall."

"They wanted you out of the way. They don't want you asking any more questions." Cassidy sighed. "Of course, at the moment, it's all just conjecture."

"Yeah, but it makes a helluva lot of sense."

She had a hunch they were on the right track, but they needed more. "Let's go see Charlotte. We want answers and Charlotte might have them."

Beau pulled her up from the chair and into his arms. He kissed her so thoroughly her toes curled inside her sneakers.

"The day's shot," he said. "Tomorrow we go see Charlotte, find out how much she knows." He caught her hand, brought it to his lips, then started tugging her down the hall. "In the meantime, I really need to get some sleep."

When they reached the master bedroom, he scooped her into his arms. "You promised me we'd take a nap and I can't think of a better idea."

Cassidy slid an arm around his neck as he carried her over to his big king-size bed. He settled her in the middle, then eased down on top of her and his mouth settled hotly over hers.

She barely remembered Beau stripping off her clothes, then removing his own. She focused on his amazing body, loved running her hands over the hard muscles in his chest, across his flat abdomen, loved the way they bunched when she touched them.

She knew he was exhausted. He had barely slept last night, but he refused to rush. Beau Reese clearly liked sex and he made certain his lover enjoyed it, too.

He settled himself on top of her, propped himself on his elbows as he kissed her. His heavy weight pressed her gloriously into the mattress as he nibbled the side of her neck, kissed his way down her body, taking his time, making her moan with need.

By the time he was inside her, she was begging, pleading

for the sweet, simmering pleasure he had given her the night before. Beau surged deep and she clung to him, arched her back to take him deeper, dug her fingers into the muscles across his shoulders.

"That's it, baby, just hang on."

A soft moan escaped. His rhythm increased, faster, deeper, harder, carrying her upward, closer and closer to the peak. No matter how much he took, she wanted more, wanted all he could give her, gave back all she had.

Then she was flying, trembling and crying his name.

Beau came hard, following her to release, every muscle rigid. For long seconds they drifted down, floating, returning slowly to their surroundings. Beau kissed her softly one last time, then left her a moment before he padded back to bed.

Lying on his side, he curled her spoon-fashion against him. He was asleep the minute his head hit the pillow, but Cassidy lay awake.

She had never understood the world's fascination with sex. Now she knew. Now she realized the kind of power amazing sex could have over a person. Now she understood, and it scared her.

The way she felt about Beau was completely new to her and utterly frightening. Part of her wanted to slip out of bed, put her clothes on, leave and never look back. Another, stronger part wanted to stay right where she was and never leave.

Even if she found the will, she couldn't go. Not with the trouble Beau was facing. He was embroiled in murder, bone deep. His father was dead, and one of his father's employees. Beau had been at both crime scenes. His troubles weren't going away anytime soon.

Not unless they found the killer, and Beau needed her to help him do that.

Cassidy began to ease away, to let him rest while she went back to work on the computer, but his arm tightened around her and he shifted her back against him, needing her even in his sleep.

She took a deep breath. Maybe a short nap would be okay. She was nearly as exhausted as he was. Surely a little more time in bed with him would be all right.

But Cassidy was beginning to wonder if a little more time with Beau would ever be enough.

Chapter Sixteen

A jagged bolt of lightning followed by the crack of thunder split the air, jarring Beau from a deep, troubled sleep. He glanced at the clock on the nightstand. Nine A.M. His hand shot toward the other side of the mattress but the sheets were cold, no sign of Cassidy. He dragged himself out of bed, surprised to discover he could still be tired after so many hours of sleep.

He yawned. Well, at least he'd slept off and on. After their nap, which had stretched into late evening and included another round of incredible sex, they had gone into the kitchen to find something to eat. While he'd rummaged through the pantry and found what he needed to make spaghetti, Cassidy had come up with the ingredients for a seriously delicious Greek salad.

There was always food in the house. His housekeeper, Marge O'Halloran, came by a couple of times a week. She and a helper took care of the cleaning and, like Flo, Marge made sure to keep his shelves well stocked, even resupplied the wine cellar if he left her a list of what he wanted.

After their late supper, they'd gone back to bed, made love again, and he'd fallen asleep. One bad dream had followed another, most of them hazy now, no longer disturbing. He'd finally gotten some rest, but unlike Linc, who was an early riser, Beau preferred late hours and rarely got into the office before nine in the morning.

There was another crack of lightning as he pulled on a pair of sweatpants and padded barefoot down the hall. One of his nightmares had been that Missy had lost her baby, which had jarred him awake in a cold sweat. He needed to call the hospital, make sure Missy and Evie were okay, make sure there was nothing they needed.

He continued along the hall in search of Cassidy, but she wasn't in her bedroom. She wasn't in the study. He found her in the kitchen, reading the *Morning News* on her iPad and drinking a cup of coffee. He owned a Keurig, but he liked the taste of freshly ground beans. The familiar rich aroma led him to the pot on the black granite counter.

"Looks like we're getting a storm," Beau said, pouring himself a mug, his gaze going from the dark clouds outside the window to the sexy brunette who had been in his bed last night.

She had showered but still wore the white terry robe she'd found hanging in the guest bathroom. Damp mahogany curls fanned around her shoulders, a stray lock clinging to the side of her neck. She looked beautiful and desirable, and a shot of lust hit him so hard, the muscles across his stomach clenched.

It was crazy. He'd made love to her for hours, yet he wanted her again. A faint streak of color rose in her cheeks and he knew she had read his thoughts.

"You . . . umm . . . need to call Charlotte," she said. "See if you can convince her to talk to us."

He took a sip of coffee, strong, the way he liked. "It's after nine. I'll give her a call. First I want to phone the hospital, see how Missy and Evie are doing."

"I called earlier. The nurse said they were doing great. The doctor's releasing them today."

"That's good." But he wanted to check for himself. Padding across the kitchen, he picked up the wireless phone on the counter and dialed information. The hospital put him through to Missy's room, and he smiled at the sound of her voice.

"It's Beau," he said. "How are my girls doing?"

Missy giggled. She was still such a kid. If his dad were alive, Beau would love to kick his ass.

"Evie's fine. She's so sweet, Beau. I have the sweetest little girl."

Emotion filled his chest and his heart felt funny. "Yes, you do," he said gruffly. "I'll come see you both as soon as I can."

She sniffed. He could hear the tears in her voice. "I'm not sorry, Beau. I'll never be sorry."

Beau cleared his throat. "I'm not sorry, either. I'll see you both soon."

He glanced over at Cassidy, caught her soft smile, and a rush of something hit him that he didn't want to feel. He turned his attention to the next call he needed to make, found Charlotte's cell number in the address book on the counter, and punched the numbers into the phone.

It rang three times before she answered.

"Charlotte, it's Beau. I need to talk to you. I'm hoping I can come over this morning. It won't take long."

"All right. I'm available at noon. We could have lunch, or you could just come over to Betsy's house."

"I'll come to the house. Is eleven too early? Cassidy's with me."

"Oh. Well, all right. Eleven is fine. I'll see you then."

He hung up the phone. When he turned, Cassidy was staring at his naked chest. He stayed in shape. Worked out with a martial arts trainer, still boxed a little, ate healthy food. Beau knew women. This one was different, but still easy enough to read.

He smiled. "Honey, I hope you're thinking what I think you're thinking. We can always put off our meeting for another hour or two."

She jerked her gaze away, but the color returned to her cheeks. "We can't do that. We have an appointment." She got up from the kitchen table and headed for the door. "I'd better get dressed. With all the rain, traffic might be bad. It could take us a while to get there."

He chuckled as she left the kitchen. Not only did he lust after this woman, he liked her. It was a rare combination.

It rained hard during the next hour, water slashing against the windows, pounding on the roof. By the time they were ready to leave, the wind had died down and there was a break in the weather, though the sky remained a dull, pewter gray.

It didn't take long to reach the exclusive Highland Park neighborhood, which wasn't that far away. It was exactly eleven A.M. when Beau drove the Beamer through the ornate, gilded gates of Chateau Durant.

With its mansard roof and manicured French gardens, the mansion looked as if it belonged in Versailles, not Texas.

"Plenty of room for guests," Cassidy said sarcastically as he pulled the car around the circular drive. Beau figured twenty thousand square feet.

He parked in front of the steps leading up to a pair of massive carved front doors. "Betsy Durant is the queen of Texas society," Beau said. "Her house is definitely fit for a queen."

"I see her picture in the *Morning News* about once a week. Her husband's death didn't seem to slow her down."

"Betsy had all the money. Albert was her second husband. He was just along for the ride."

A butler formally dressed in black welcomed them into a marble-floored entry lit by a crystal chandelier.

"Mrs. Reese is expecting you. If you will please follow me." Nose in the air, he led them into an elegant salon done in ivory and gold. Charlotte waited across the room, blond hair upswept, not a wrinkle in her floor-length, navy pleated wool skirt and matching sweater.

She rose from a gold velvet Louis XIV chair next to an antique rosewood table. "I'm afraid you just missed Betsy. She had a meeting with the garden society."

"That's a shame," Beau said, barely able to hide the relief in his voice. "You remember Cassidy?"

"Of course. Hello, my dear."

"Mrs. Reese."

The door opened again and the butler wheeled a tea cart across the inlaid parquet floor, onto the thick Persian carpet in the seating area.

"Would you like a cup of tea?" Charlotte was in her element. French nobility could live in Chateau Durant. The only problem was the house belonged to someone else.

"That would be lovely," Cassidy said. She wore beige slacks, a cream silk blouse, a tweed jacket, and low-heeled boots. She was good at reading people, had guessed what would impress his stepmother. Cassidy looked as if she belonged in the house.

Charlotte poured and served, passing the delicate gold-rimmed porcelain cups around. Beau took a seat beside Cassidy on the gold velvet settee and worked not to fumble as he balanced the cup and saucer on his lap.

"We just have a couple of questions, Charlotte," he said.

She sat back down in her Louis XIV chair, took a sip of tea and set the cup in its saucer. "Apparently you're still investigating Stewart's death."

"That's right," Beau said.

"I saw you in the news. It seems your digging for clues

has managed to embroil you in yet another murder. I wish you had listened to me, Beau. Now all you have done is make matters worse."

"Maybe. But it isn't going to stop me from finding Dad's killer. I came here to talk about Jess Milford. He was the foreman of Alamo."

"That's right. I can't believe someone killed him. But then I still can't believe your father is dead."

"Why did the senator fire him?"

Charlotte looked uncomfortable. "I don't know. He was already working for Alamo when I married Stewart. Your father convinced me to invest my savings in the company and we became partners, but Stew made the decisions. I remember him saying something about Jess slacking off, no longer doing a good job."

"When did Dad let him go?"

"I'm not sure exactly. Sometime in late November. I remember he gave the man a month's severance, but Jess was still angry about it."

"So Dad fired Milford just before the apartment fire that took down the business."

She shrugged, but her eyes slid away. "I suppose that's right."

Cassidy set her cup and saucer down on the gilded table in front of the settee. "Which brings us to why we're here. The fire was arson. There's a good chance the building was destroyed so that you and the senator could claim the insurance money."

"That's ridiculous."

Beau leaned over and set down his tea. "Charlotte, you and I both know Dad was responsible for that fire. The rental market tanked and the project was going to fail. My father wanted out. He hired someone to make that happen. There's no use lying about it."

Charlotte's lips trembled and her hand shook, rattling the cup in her saucer. He could see she was about to cave.

"Come on, Charlotte. Tell me the truth. If you don't, I'll just keep digging until I find out."

She took a shaky breath, slowly released it. "I didn't know Stewart was involved until later. I thought it was vandalism, just like the police said. I suppose I should have suspected. I knew he had borrowed a large sum of money from someone. But we were divorced. I didn't put the pieces together until after we'd sold the company and he'd paid me my share."

Her mouth thinned. "Well, slightly less than my share. You know how he could always manipulate things in his favor."

Cassidy spoke to Charlotte. "Senator Reese hired me because he thought someone was following him, asking questions about him. He believed you might have had something to do with it. If you were no longer interested in a relationship, why did you hire those men?"

Charlotte's spine went stiff. "For heaven's sake! What makes you think—"

"This is all going to get worse before it gets better," Beau said. "I'll do my best to keep you out of it if you'll just tell us the truth."

Charlotte sat there for several long moments. She took a deep breath. "All right, fine. I hired a man to follow Stewart because I wanted to make him nervous. I wanted him to know I meant business."

"In what way?" Cassidy asked.

"I needed money. I told him I knew he was involved in that fire. I told him if he would just give me a little more of the profit he made from the sale of the property, I'd keep quiet about it. Stewart only laughed. He said if his reputation was ruined, mine would be, too. He knew how I felt about that. He wasn't the least bit afraid I would pursue it."

Cassidy leaned forward. "You said the senator borrowed a large sum of money. Do you know who made him the loan?"

"No. I'm sorry. He was always borrowing money from someone, always robbing Peter to pay Paul. He was never good with money."

"Thank you, Charlotte." Beau rose from the settee. "As I said, I'll keep you out of this if I can."

Cassidy rose and Charlotte led them out of the salon, but it was the butler who showed them to the door.

"Well, we got answers," Beau said as the door closed firmly behind them. "But not enough."

Cassidy tugged on his arm, leading him down the wide front steps. "We need to talk to Malcolm Vaughn." She smiled. "And I know where to find him."

Cassidy buckled her seat belt as Beau drove the BMW around the circular drive, then out through the ornate gates of Chateau Durant.

"So tell me about Malcolm Vaughn," Beau said.

Cassidy leaned back in the passenger seat. It started raining again, spotting the windshield, and Beau turned on the wipers. She loved the way his hands looked, wrapped around the steering wheel, the confident, almost arrogant way he handled the car.

"Vaughn owns a company called Equity Advance," she said, settling back in her seat. The swish of the blades seemed somehow soothing. "They make nothing but commercial loans so they don't fall under the same regulations as residential mortgage brokers."

"Vaughn's the sole owner?"

"That's right. The company specializes in big-money loans to people who have credit problems or the project is something out of the norm. He charges eighteen-and-a-half percent interest, in some cases possibly more. The loans are usually secured by some sort of real estate, but from what I could find out, the notes aren't always recorded. If the borrower falls behind in his payments, the company doesn't hesitate to foreclose."

"Sounds like Dooley Tate was right. He's not a guy you want to piss off."

"Of course we don't know for sure the senator borrowed money from Vaughn since there was no construction loan recorded on the property. Even if Vaughn made the loan, he might not be willing to tell us."

But Beau kept driving, heading for the address she had given him, an office in a high-rise building on Main Street in the downtown financial district.

They parked in a garage beneath the towering glass structure. Cassidy noticed there were security cameras everywhere and several uniformed guards. The elevator took them up to the twenty-second floor.

The office of Equity Advance was impressive, with dark wood furniture and deep cinnamon carpets. A busty blond receptionist seated behind the front desk rose to greet them.

"May I help you?" The woman eyed Beau up and down, taking in the fit of his dark blue jeans and navy tweed blazer, noticing the leather patches on the sleeves. The wind had ruffled his wavy black hair, giving him a rakish appearance that only made him better looking.

"We're here to see Malcolm Vaughn," he said. "My name is Beau Reese. This is Cassidy Jones."

Beau got a smile that didn't extend to her. "I'll see if Mr. Vaughn is available. Please have a seat. Is there anything I can get you, Mr. Reese?"

"No, thanks, we're fine." They sat down on a dark gray leather sofa in front of a glass-topped coffee table. Beau picked up a *National Geographic* and began to thumb through the pages.

The blonde returned a few minutes later. "Mr. Vaughn is

between appointments. He can speak with you for a few minutes."

She gave Beau another exuberant smile. "I'm sorry I didn't recognize you, Mr. Reese. Everyone in Dallas knows who you are. We've all watched you on TV." Cassidy thought she might start drooling any minute.

"It's been a while since I've been on the track," Beau said, his return smile not encouraging.

"All right, then." The blonde barely hid her disappointment. "If you will please follow me."

She led them into a plush office done in the same dark wood tones. A tall, slender man in his late forties, attractive, with light brown hair and dark eyes, rose as they walked into the room. He came around to greet them.

"I'm Malcolm Vaughn. We've never met, Beau, but I knew your father. I'm sorry for your loss."

"Thank you," Beau said, accepting the hand Vaughn offered.

"Ms. Jones." He shook Cassidy's hand, as well. "Please sit down. I'm afraid I don't have much time. What can I do for you?"

They sat in stylish gray leather chairs in front of the desk and Vaughn returned to his ergonomic chair on the opposite side.

"I'm trying to clear up any of my father's unresolved business. I understand he may have had dealings with you."

Vaughn steepled his fingers. He seemed to be sizing them up. "If you're asking if Equity Advance loaned him money, the answer is yes. On more than one occasion. The senator always paid it back."

"So your company financed him on the apartment project in Iron Springs?"

"I didn't say that. But as it happens, yes, some of the money he borrowed went into that project. It didn't work out the way he planned, but I understand he survived the unfortunate fire without much of a loss."

"And you got repaid?"

"That's right."

"Just to be clear," Cassidy pressed, "the senator no longer owes you any money."

He shot her a look, clearly not liking her interference. "No."

"Is there anyone else you can think of the senator might have borrowed money from?" she asked. "Another company or individual, someone who might not have gotten repaid?"

Vaughn leaned back in his chair. "I understand the senator's murder remains unsolved. I assume your questions have something to do with his death?"

"That's right," Beau answered. "I intend to find out who killed him. To do that, I need to know what was happening in his life at the time he was killed."

Vaughn rose from behind his desk, a graceful man, almost effeminate. "The senator and I were business associates, nothing more. I wouldn't know anything about his finances, aside from those that pertain to Equity Advance, nor would I have any idea who might be responsible for his death."

His gaze remained on Beau. "After what I've read in the newspapers, I should think you would be wise to let the police handle the investigation."

A muscle tightened in Beau's cheek. He rose and Cassidy stood up, as well. "Thanks for your time," Beau said. "I appreciate your seeing us on such short notice."

Vaughn made no reply, but Cassidy could feel his dark gaze following them as they walked out of the room.

Chapter Seventeen

"I probably should have been a little more diplomatic," Beau said as he opened the passenger door and waited for Cassidy to settle herself in the seat.

She looked up at him. "You're kidding? Really?"

He slammed the door and rounded the car to the driver's side, slid in behind the wheel and fired the engine. "So I baited him a little. Maybe it'll stir something up. I don't know what it was, but I didn't like him. I felt like he was telling us part of the truth but not all, like he was leaving something out."

"Malcolm Vaughn brokers big-money deals. The men who bankroll his loans are the kind who can make people disappear. You should have stuck with your story, Beau, that you were clearing up your father's accounts. You shouldn't have said you were investigating his murder."

She was right, but he didn't like hearing it. He wasn't used to someone else calling the shots, even if he respected that person's opinion.

"Maybe not, but we were getting nowhere and I warned you before—I'm not a patient man."

She flicked him a sideways glance. "Except in bed."

He looked at her, saw the amusement in her eyes. A curl of heat settled low in his groin and a smile tugged at his lips. "Yeah, except in bed."

Just thinking about it had his blood rushing south. He glanced at Cassidy, spotted an unruly curl at the base of her neck, and wanted to nudge it aside with his tongue. He wondered what she'd say if he pulled into the Adolphus, took a suite, and hauled her back to bed.

Inwardly he sighed. Not going to happen. He was a suspect in two murders.

"It's too late to worry about it now," he said. "And you never know, maybe Vaughn will panic and do something stupid. Maybe we'll actually get a break in the case."

Her brow arched, warning him not to get his hopes up. "Let's go back to your house. We need to take a look at the bank records on that other flash drive. We've got a little more information now. Maybe we can make more sense of what we see."

But when he neared the driveway, he spotted the media, out in full force. He said the F-word under his breath, then glanced at Cassidy. "Sorry."

"They would have shown up sooner or later. I'm surprised they waited this long."

"The bad weather probably helped for a while." He muttered another swear word. "I need your phone." He turned the corner before anyone spotted the car, and pulled over beneath the spreading branches of a magnolia tree.

Cassidy handed him her cell and Beau called Marty Chen. "I need you to get some security over to my house ASAP. There's media all over the place. I'll need men round the clock, at least for a while."

"They're already there. Should be a couple of black SUVs parked out front. Oh, and I brought back the Lamborghini. Rob drove Ms. Jones's car back."

"Great. Anything else?"

"A detective named Briscoe called the office earlier this morning. He said they'd gotten what they needed off your cell phone. I picked it up at the police station on my way out of town. You'll find it in your car."

"Thanks, Marty. Can you call whoever's in charge at the house and tell them we're coming in?"

"His name's Will Egan, works for Citywide Security. I'll give him a call."

Marty hung up and Beau turned to Cassidy. "Security's in place. They'll clear the way for us. Marty also brought back our cars."

"That's great. I have some errands I really need to run." A smile curved her lips. "Marty seems superefficient. I hope you pay him well."

"I pay him a small fortune and he's worth every dime." He pulled the car away from the curb. "He even retrieved my cell phone."

"On second thought, no matter what you're paying him, I think he deserves a raise."

Beau chuckled and drove the car down the street toward the house. Two black SUVs sat on the road opposite the driveway while four uniformed men urged the crowd of reporters out of the way as the Beamer approached. Beau ignored the shouted questions, nudged aside a few persistent reporters with the bumper of the car, and turned up the drive while the guards fell in behind the vehicle, blocking the way.

A few seconds later, he drove past Cassidy's silver Honda hatchback, sitting out front.

"Marty is a prince," she said. "I've got things I really need to do."

Beau pulled into the garage, parking between the Lambo and the Ferrari. The garage door slid closed as they got out and walked into the house.

"We need to look at those files," Cassidy said, heading

for the study down the hall. Beau enjoyed the view from behind, the sexy way her stretch jeans curved over her tight little ass. He tried not to think how much he wanted to peel her out of them and haul her back to bed.

He sighed, forcing his thoughts back to finding a killer.

Mal looked up as the door opened and Clifford Jennings walked into the office.

"You wanted to see me?" Cliff sat down in a chair on the opposite side of his executive desk and crossed a leg over his knee. Jennings was his right-hand man, his go-to guy when he wanted something done. He was smart and he was ruthless, a man Mal could count on.

"Reese and that female PI came to see me," Mal said. "Wanted to know if the senator had borrowed money and if he'd paid it back."

"What'd you tell them?"

"I told them the debt had been repaid, but I don't think Reese was satisfied. I may have underestimated him. Beau Reese was a winner on the track. It takes balls to drive a race car two hundred miles an hour. Still, I have a hunch once the girl is out of the way, he'll back off."

"So you want me to have her taken care of?" Cliff smoothed his fingers over his mustache as if he relished the notion.

Mal leaned back in his chair. "As I said before, only if it can be made to look like an accident. Make sure that's understood."

"I'll handle it." Clifford rose from his chair. "We finished here?"

"For now."

Jennings turned away and ambled out of the office.

Mal thought of the disposable phone in the bottom drawer of his desk. He should probably make the call, bring his client up to speed and inform him of his decision. On the other hand, if things were handled properly, the problem would be solved and his client would never need to know.

Mal leaned forward and buzzed his receptionist. Pamela didn't have much in the brains department, but she had other talents. He didn't like problems, and after his conversation with Reese and the woman, he needed some stress relief.

The door opened and she sashayed in, sporting big hair and pouty lips, ass swinging in her short tight skirt, cleavage on display. He was surprised she wasn't chewing gum, the way she usually did.

"You need something, Mr. Vaughn?"

He didn't have much use for women, paid this one too much for the ridiculously easy job she did, but she had skills more valuable than answering phones and taking messages.

He reached down and unzipped his trousers. "I think you can guess what I need."

She tossed her long blond hair over her shoulder. "Oh, yes, Mr. Vaughn. I think I know exactly what you need." Pamela rounded the desk and dropped to her knees.

Now that they were safely back in the house, Beau retrieved the flash drives he had brought with him when they'd left Pleasant Hill. He checked the labels he'd put on the back and found the one he wanted. When he turned, he saw Cassidy examining the photos on his desk.

She held up a picture of him in his orange-and-black fire suit displaying a first-place trophy, Cain's arm over Beau's shoulder. "You and Linc. Where was this taken?"

"*Los Angeles Times* Grand Prix."

She picked up a photo of him and his college roommate, an African American student with a wide, goofy grin. "Ronnie

Jackson," he said. "He was my best friend at UT-Austin. Great basketball player."

"He looks like he would be. He's even taller than you."

His nerves began to build as she moved to the next photo, last Christmas with Linc and his brother Josh. Next to it was a photo of him and Sarah back in his senior year of college.

His chest clamped down when she picked it up, studied the slender girl with the long, silver-blond hair and the face of an angel. "She's beautiful."

His jaw went tight. "Yes." Cassidy's head came up at the harsh note in his voice.

"Is she the woman you were engaged to?"

Memories rolled over him, the joy of finding her, the love and laughter they had shared, the cancer diagnosis and long months of suffering, the despair of losing her. He felt a sharp instant of pain before he managed to nod.

"What was her name?"

"Her name was Sarah. Look, Cassidy. I prefer to keep my private life private. Besides, it's all in the past." He held up the flash drive. "This is the drive with the bank account information. Let's see what we can find out."

Cassidy didn't press for more, just set the photo back down and walked over to her side of the partners' desk. She was letting him off the hook, at least for now.

He handed her the flash drive. "So far this whole mess seems to revolve around money. Let's see if the insurance payment shows up in my father's bank accounts. If it does, let's see where it goes."

"Follow the money. Always a good place to start."

He relaxed, grateful she was accepting the change of subject. Sarah's death wasn't something he discussed. Not with anyone.

"We can use my laptop. I've got the senator's current

banking information in there. We can cross-reference, see how the accounts interconnect."

He felt a smile edging aside the dark mood that had claimed him. "I'm not even asking how you got into my father's banking records."

Cassidy smiled. "Good idea."

Beau rolled his chair around to her side of the desk while Cassidy sat down and plugged in the flash drive. She opened it, brought up the files, and went into the senator's offshore Cayman account records.

"Let's go back a ways," she suggested. "See if we can see the bigger picture." She began to scroll down slowly, reading each line as it passed. "Look at this. Seven months ago, a big chunk of money was deposited directly into the offshore account. Three million dollars. Those accounts are extremely sophisticated. No way to know for sure where it came from."

"I've got a pretty good idea," Beau said.

"Equity Advance."

"AKA Malcolm Vaughn. He admitted he'd loaned my father money for the construction project."

Cassidy opened a tab on her C drive and brought up the records from the United Bank of Dallas. "Here's the transfer. From the looks of those foreign currency charges, it was money from the Cayman account."

She studied the pages. "Over the next few weeks and months, the money gets dispersed to Alamo."

"He's using the funds to build the apartments," Beau said.

"That's right. He's also using the money to pay his living expenses. His car payments, mortgage payments, credit card bills. Since your father lived the good life, he was rapidly depleting the account."

Beau pointed to a line on the screen. "There's another sizable deposit."

"That's about the time he sold Green Gables Realty. He got half the money, George Larson got the other half. There's another deposit here, got to be the sale of the building he took in that side deal. The senator transfers all of it into the Cayman account, then uses it to make payments to the original lender."

"Equity Advance," Beau said.

"Presumably. He pays down the loan, but he still owes them a chunk." Cassidy scrolled through the Dallas account. "In December, the senator makes a deposit that doesn't go to the Caymans. It goes directly into his stateside account."

"The fire was in November," Beau said. "Got to be his share of the insurance settlement."

"Okay, so after his claim gets paid, he takes the money, sells the land the apartments were being built on, closes Alamo, pays off Charlotte, and deposits his share into the Dallas account."

Cassidy pointed to another line. "Here's where he transfers the money from the Dallas bank into his Cayman account."

"He moved the money so he could pay off Equity Advance. They would have called the loan. When the fire destroyed the project, he no longer had any collateral."

Cassidy studied the screen. "Here's the payment, but it wasn't enough to repay the total amount of the original loan."

Beau leaned back in his chair. "Malcolm Vaughn said my father repaid the money, but according to this, he didn't have enough to repay it all." Beau's gaze swung to Cassidy. "So Vaughn was lying. And if he didn't get paid back, he had a reason to murder my dad."

"Maybe."

"What, you don't buy it?"

"Once Stewart Reese was dead, there was no way Vaughn could get the rest of the money."

"Maybe he was making a point. You don't pay me, you're dead."

"Maybe."

Beau tipped his head back in frustration. "I still think he was involved."

"If he was, we need to prove it."

He sighed. "So I guess we keep digging."

"We do, but not today. Now that my car is here, I need to go into my office. I want to change into something more casual, then I've got some business I need to take care of."

"So do I. Linc has more than enough on his plate without trying to handle my job, too. Why don't I pick you up later and take you out to supper? I know a place I think you'll like."

She tipped her head toward the front of the house. "What about your paparazzi?"

"I'll take care of them."

"All right, but I'd rather meet you there. That way I'll have my car."

Beau reluctantly agreed. He was getting used to having Cassidy around. He thought of her sweet curves and big green eyes and how much he enjoyed her company.

It bothered him to think that once this was over, they would go their separate ways. But he wasn't good at long-term relationships. He'd been down that road and it was just too painful. Sooner or later, the inevitable was bound to happen. The thought depressed him.

He brightened a little, thinking about dinner and the place he intended to take her. And afterward he'd convince her to come home with him instead of going back to her apartment—after all, they still had a murder to solve.

He left the house first, driving the Ferrari, purposely drawing the media away so Cassidy could escape. He lost them a couple of miles down the road and continued on to the office.

It was late afternoon by the time he arrived at the Tex/Am building. He had plenty of catching up to do. He went over his schedule with Marty, agreed to a dinner with the CEO of the LEN Corp. and his wife. The sales team had pitched LEN's manufacturing division on Tex/Am Transport's taking over their freight contract. All Beau had to do was schmooze the big boss a little, give him a nudge in the right direction.

He'd need a date for the evening. With any luck he could convince Cassidy to go with him.

Two hours after he got to the office, a light knock sounded and Linc walked into the room. "Thought I'd drop by, see how you're holding up."

Sitting behind his black lacquer desk, Beau leaned back in his chair. "I'm hanging in, I guess you could say. You were right about Temple. He's a good man. I just hope I won't need him again."

"Maybe the police will come up with something."

"Yeah. Cassidy and I talked to Charlotte this morning." He looked up at his friend, a man he would trust with his life. "You remember that big fire last fall in Pleasant Hill?"

"I remember. Apartment project Alamo was building."

"That's right, though I didn't know about it at the time. Jess Milford was foreman. My dad let him go just a few days before the fire. We think the fire may be connected to the murders."

"We?" Linc, who rarely missed a thing, picked up on the reference. "You and Cassidy?"

"That's right. She's a PI, remember? That's why I hired her."

"Beautiful girl. Apparently she's smart, too. We both know she's more than just your employee. I think you really like this girl."

"Cassidy's a lot of things and yeah, I like her. Won't change the outcome."

"Why not? Because you're determined to grieve for the rest of your life?"

Beau came out of his chair, braced his hands on top of the desk. "In case you don't know, grief doesn't have a time limit."

His friend looked at him with a trace of pity. "Not if you don't want it to." Linc started for the door, turned back. "You don't need to worry about the business. I can handle whatever comes up. You just need to focus on clearing your name."

Beau sat back down in his chair. "You're right." A long sigh escaped. "Sorry about . . . you know. I've got a lot on my mind right now."

"I know you do. Just remember, I'm here if you need me."

As he always had been, since back when they were in school.

The phone on his desk rang. No matter what Linc said, there were things he needed to do. As for Cassidy, he intended to enjoy the time they had together. He wouldn't let the past interfere. Tomorrow he would deal again with the murder.

Tomorrow—if he wasn't on his way back to jail.

Chapter Eighteen

Cassidy pulled the Honda into a parallel parking space in front of Maximum Security and turned off the engine. All the way to the office, she'd been thinking about the woman in the photo on Beau's desk. *Sarah*. She tried to tell herself the burning in the center of her chest wasn't jealousy. Sarah was dead. Had died years ago. Surely she couldn't be jealous of a dead woman.

But the bitter truth was, she didn't want to share Beau with another woman, even if that woman was no longer living. Clearly, Beau had been in love with the beautiful, statuesque blonde. By his reaction, some part of him still was.

From the beginning, Cassidy had known Beau wasn't a long-term kind of guy. Which had been fine with her. If her past relationships were any indication, she wasn't a long-term kind of gal.

And yet, her feelings for Beau continued to grow, changing little by little into something far from superficial. She was involved with him on a deeply emotional level and the more she was around him, the worse it was going to get.

She wondered what Beau felt for her. Certainly not the

pain-filled, heartbreaking, deeply abiding love he'd felt for Sarah.

Rubbing a fist against her chest as if it could make the burning go away, she climbed out of the car and headed into the office, which was simply furnished, with sturdy oak desks and pictures of Texas cattle ranches on the walls. A hooked rug on the floor in front of the brown leather sofa in the reception area gave it a homey feel the guys all liked.

The usual crew was there: PIs Jase Maddox, Dante Romero, Ford Weatherby, and Lissa Blayne. There were some part-time contractors who worked for the agency, but they weren't in at the moment. The owner, Chase Garrett, sat in his office on the far end of the room, while a plump older woman, the widow of a cop who had died in the line of duty, manned the receptionist desk.

Connie Thurston did way more than run the office. Chase was the backbone, but Connie was the heart.

"Where you been hidin', girl?" Connie called out in a voice tinged with her African American heritage and her Detroit upbringing. "That ex-boyfriend of yours, Richard What's-his-name, stopped by three times in the last two days. Said to tell you he's had time to think. Wants to talk things over."

She barely paused. "If he comes in again, tell him I'm not interested." They'd been finished as a couple weeks before they'd actually parted, and that had been several months back.

"Hey, Cass, honey," Jase called out. "Wait up!" He was a big man, hard-bodied and handsome. Rising from his desk, he caught her in two long strides, reaching her just as she set her laptop down on her desk.

"What's up?" she asked.

"Just wondering how it went with that scumball, Dooley Tate. He didn't give you any trouble, did he?"

Jase looked down at her with a pair of steely blue eyes

that rivaled Beau's, but she didn't feel the slightest twinge of attraction. She had never dated any of the guys in the office. Not only were they dedicated bachelors, but it was her personal rule.

Since they liked and respected her, they hadn't pushed for more than friendship. Instead, they'd taken on the role of protectors, which was a little irritating at times since she was fairly good at protecting herself.

"No trouble with Tate. Beau tangled with a bunch of bikers. He handled himself like a pro."

"Beau Reese, right? Hotshot race-car driver?"

"Not anymore."

"So what happened?"

"Beau took care of three of them. One of them came after me and I shot him in the foot. Aside from that it was fairly uneventful."

Jase grinned. "The poor sonofabitch should have known better than to tangle with Hopalong Cassidy Jones."

She rolled her eyes. "Very funny."

"Let me know if you need anything else." He winked and ambled back to his desk.

Cassidy went to work making follow-up calls to recent clients, just to make sure everything was okay. She had a couple of messages from people who wanted to hire her, one that required going undercover as a CPA to find out if an employee was embezzling money, another from a distraught housewife who wanted her husband followed.

Cassidy referred Lissa for the CPA job and Dante for the housewife. "Romeo" Romero had a way of cheering up lonely, abandoned women.

Beau called once, but he was still working, which gave her time to go home and change before they went out. Her apartment was only a few blocks away, walking distance unless she needed her car or the weather was bad, and close to the neighborhood gym she hit three or four times a week.

It was dark outside by the time she was finished and ready to leave. By then, everyone was gone except Jase. Her phone rang again and she checked the caller ID, smiled as she pressed it against her ear. "Hey . . ."

"Hey, baby, you ready for something to eat?"

The endearment rolled over her and her stomach floated up. Sometimes when they made love he called her Cassie. She liked it way too much.

Dammit to hell, why did it have to be him? Why not someone else? Someone not in love with a ghost?

She had always wanted the kind of relationship her parents had, both of them madly in love till the day her mom had died. She could still remember hearing them upstairs at night, laughing softly in the darkness. Remember the summer holidays, the two of them lying on the beach side by side, her mom feeding him potato chips, him grinning. He would call sometimes just to tell her he loved her.

Her throat tightened. Maybe someday . . .

Cassidy bit back a sigh. "I'm definitely hungry," she said. "Even a greasy burger sounds good right now."

Beau chuckled. "You won't believe the food in this place I'm taking you."

"I can't wait to try it. I'm heading out right now, on my way home to change." Slinging the strap of her laptop over her shoulder, Cassidy tucked the phone beneath her chin, grabbed her purse, and headed out the door.

"How about you wear something like that little black dress I saw in the guest-house closet. That and nothing else would be good."

Oh, wow. The little black dress was still hanging in Beau's closet, but going out with no underwear was such an erotic thought her belly clenched. "You are a very wicked man."

He laughed as she arrived at her car door. She was digging for her keys when she heard the roar of an engine, followed by the squeal of tires. Glancing up, she saw a

...t-up brown sedan roaring toward her, the car weaving, the driver obviously drunk.

"Oh, my God!" There was no escape, no time to run and nowhere to go. The phone slipped from her nerveless fingers and clattered to the pavement. Fear slammed through her as she dropped to the asphalt and rolled beneath the car, banging her head in the process, feeling the sharp sting of broken glass slicing into her arm.

The sound of grinding metal and a rush of air hit her as the car plowed into the side of the Honda, careened off and kept going, speeding on down the road. For several moments, Cassidy lay under her car, breathing in the smell of motor oil and rubber, trying to stop trembling.

"Cassidy! Cassidy!" Heavy footfalls pounded toward her; a pair of long legs and big feet in cowboy boots appeared in her line of vision. "Cassidy!"

She turned her head to look at Jase, who crouched down next to the car. "I'm . . . I'm okay." Trying to avoid bits of hot metal and more broken glass, she eased herself out from under the vehicle.

Jase stared down the road but the car was long gone. "Crazy fuck." He led her over to the sidewalk and eased her onto the curb. Glancing down at herself, she saw that her sweater was torn and covered with grime, the knees of her leggings ripped open and the skin scraped bloody underneath.

Jase saw the gash in her forearm and swore again. Pulling a handkerchief out of the back pocket of his jeans, he wrapped it around the cut on her arm. "Press down on this. You might need stitches. I'll drive you to the emergency room and you can get it checked out."

Her head was spinning, her pulse still hammering. Suddenly she remembered she'd been on the phone with Beau and realized he had probably heard the accident as it happened. He'd be frantic.

"Can you find my cell? If it still works, I need to make a call."

A siren sounded in the distance. The cops were on the way. Beau had probably called them. Jase retrieved her purse and laptop and set them down on the curb beside her. He handed over her phone, which was battered but still working, and she punched in Beau's number. There was panic in his voice when he picked up.

"Cassidy! What the hell happened? Are you okay?"

"I'm . . . I'm okay. Some drunk nearly ran me over. I'm pretty banged up, but I'm . . . I'm okay."

His voice steadied. He was back in control. "The cops are on the way. So am I. I'll be there in just a few minutes." She could hear the roar of the powerful Ferrari engine, knew he was driving like a maniac to get there.

She nodded, though Beau couldn't see. "Okay."

"I'm coming, baby. Just hang on." The line went dead. Her head hurt. Her arm throbbed and her knees burned. Jase's handkerchief was covered with blood. When her hand started shaking, he took the phone and tucked it into her purse.

"Come on. Let's go get the docs to take a look at you."

She shook her head, blotted the blood on her arm with his handkerchief. "It's not that bad. I'll be okay. Besides, I want to wait for Beau."

Jase's piercing blue eyes sharpened. "You're cut and bruised and you might have a concussion. Reese can pick you up at the hospital."

"Beau's coming from his office. It's only ten minutes away. Less, the way he drives."

Jase swore softly. A police car rolled up just then and Jase walked over to talk to them, but the beat-up brown sedan had long since disappeared and catching the driver wouldn't be easy. Still, she wanted to make a report. They needed to stop this maniac before he seriously hurt someone.

She heard the squeal of tires and her head jerked up. The Ferrari slid to a halt in the middle of the street, the door flew open, and a tall, black-haired man ran toward her. A car horn honked, but Beau didn't stop.

"Cassidy!" He pulled her up from the sidewalk into his arms and hung on tight, buried his face in her hair. "You scared me. Jesus, you scared me."

She wasn't the crying type, but for once she wished she could just let go. She clung to him, only for a moment, then forced herself under control. A shudder ran through Beau's hard body as he eased away.

He looked down at the bloody handkerchief, her torn leggings and skinned knees. "Christ, I'm calling an ambulance."

"Wait! It isn't as bad as it looks. I'll be okay."

He tipped her chin up, saw a smudge of blood on the side of her head. "You might have a concussion. I'm taking you to the emergency room."

Jase walked up just then. He was nearly as tall as Beau. "I told the cops you'd give them a statement at the hospital." He turned a hard look on Beau. "'Bout time you got here. I tried to take her to emergency but she wanted to wait for you."

"I'm here now. Who are you?"

"Jason Maddox." Neither man moved or looked away.

"He's the guy who helped us find Dooley. Now do you two think you could postpone your pissing contest until later?"

Beau just turned, swept her up in his arms, and started striding toward the Ferrari. Jase brought her laptop and purse, settled them in the low-slung sports car.

"Thanks."

Jase just nodded.

Once Beau had her belted into the seat, he roared off

toward Baylor Medical, which wasn't all that far. Along the way, Cassidy filled him in on what had happened.

"I swear, that car came out of nowhere—I only had a split second to react. The way it weaved toward me, I could tell the driver was drunk."

"The bastard could have killed you. I'd like to get my hands around his neck."

Cassidy made no reply. Wasn't much she could say to top that.

A few minutes later, she was sitting on a table behind a curtain in the emergency room while an older doctor with thick gray hair looked her over. Aside from a slight headache, she didn't have any sign of a concussion, no confusion, no memory loss, no dizziness, nausea, or vomiting.

"Will you have someone with you tonight?" the doctor asked.

"I'll be with her," Beau said, leaving no room for doubt. The doctor seemed satisfied. A nurse finished up, putting ointment on her scrapes and scratches, bandaging the cut on her arm.

The police arrived just as the woman finished. "She's all yours," the nurse said to them as she left.

"Your friend Maddox told us what he saw. But he didn't actually see the collision. Can you tell us what happened?"

Cassidy took her time, trying to remember those few moments before she had hit the ground, but she hadn't gotten a license plate number. An old, battered, brown sedan wasn't much of a description.

"It might have been a Ford," she added, which didn't seem to impress them.

"We'll do our best, Ms. Jones," said an officer who had red hair and a crooked nose that looked like it might have been broken. "But Dallas is a big city."

"Could have been an illegal," the other officer said.

"They hit somebody then keep driving because they don't want to get deported. It's a huge problem out in LA."

"You never know, maybe we'll get lucky," the red-haired cop said. "Car might show up on a street cam somewhere."

But Cassidy knew the chances were slim.

Beau led her back to the Ferrari and they drove off toward his house.

"So I guess the little black dress with no panties isn't going to happen," he said, trying to lighten the moment.

Cassidy managed to smile. "Not tonight. I'm kind of out of the mood."

Beau cast her a glance. "*Not tonight* isn't exactly a no, so I'll settle for that for now."

Cassidy laughed, her tension easing. He'd said that about taking her to bed, and look how that had ended.

As they neared the house, Beau used the hands-free to phone Will Egan, head of security, telling him they were on their way home.

Egan's voice came over the speaker. "They're all gone, Mr. Reese. Reporters headed out for a bigger story. I guess you haven't seen the news."

Beau glanced at Cassidy. "What's going on?"

"Terror attack in Houston. Some nutcase strapped on a bomb, went into a restaurant and blew himself up. Luckily, as a bomb maker he wasn't much good. Managed to kill himself and injure half a dozen people who were there for supper, but nobody else got killed."

"I guess that's something."

"You want my team to stay here in case the media comes back?"

"Go on home. I can always call if there's a problem."

"All right, that sounds good. Have a nice evening."

"You, too." Beau ended the call.

"Saved by a terror attack," Cassidy said. "There's something wrong with that."

"I guess." Beau fell silent. No more teasing conversation as they neared the house. She had a feeling he was more upset about the accident than he had let on. Now his adrenaline rush was wearing off and a black mood had settled over him.

He'd feel better tomorrow, Cassidy told herself. Both of them would. But as she studied the dark look in his eyes and the grim set of his features, she wasn't completely sure.

Franco Giannetti drove the beat-up old Ford into the junkyard and parked it among a row of wrecked cars headed for scrap metal. He turned off the engine, leaned back in the seat, and slammed his hand down hard on the steering wheel. Dammit, he'd botched the job. He couldn't believe it.

Fuck, it should have been easy. He'd found the Jones woman at Reese's house—not hard to do when it was all over the news. Late in the afternoon, he'd followed her to her Uptown office on Blackburn Street: Maximum Security, an office full of PIs.

He'd staked the place out, planning to follow her when she left, hadn't really figured the opportunity to finish her would come so soon. But he had been ready. This wasn't his first rodeo. Hit-and-run was one of his specialties, which was the reason Cliff Jennings had called him.

Franco pulled a disposable phone out of his pocket. He needed to make the call, bring Jennings up to speed.

He punched in the number, then paused before hitting the send button. What if he didn't make the call? He'd gotten away clean. The car would soon disappear, never again to be seen. He and Pete Rodriguez, the owner of the scrap yard, had an understanding. As soon as the vehicle was disposed of, Franco would give Pete his usual fat fee and another old car would be readied for when it was needed.

Pete didn't ask questions and Franco didn't give answers. But he had managed to turn deadly car accidents into a very lucrative business.

Unfortunately, not this time.

He looked down at the phone, trying to prepare himself for Jennings's wrath. What if he waited? Jennings hadn't given him a time limit, just a job that needed to be done fairly soon. It had to look like an accident—that was the only condition.

On the other hand, if Jennings somehow found out . . . Franco ignored the shiver that ran down his spine, and hit the send button, listened to it ringing.

He was good at what he did. No way the woman had any idea she was a target. He'd come up with a new plan, figure the best way to handle things.

Next time he'd get the job done.

Chapter Nineteen

Beau helped Cassidy into a long white-cotton nightgown. She was battered and bruised, cut and scraped, but she was okay. He should have insisted she sleep in the guest room, where she could get a good night's rest, but he wanted to be able to check on her, make sure no problems came up. And after what had happened, he couldn't seem to let her out of his sight.

The doctor had given her a couple of pain pills. Beau fixed her a glass of warm milk. After she drank it, she climbed into his bed, he tucked her in, and she drifted into a quiet sleep. For a while he just stood there watching her, grateful the accident hadn't been worse.

Finally he undressed, eased onto the mattress beside her, and eventually fell asleep.

He wasn't sure what time he started to dream. The nightmare, hazy at first, turned sharply vivid, an endless stream of images, all incredibly real. Sarah, standing beside a pond in the moonlight in a sheer white nightgown, brilliant rays shimmering on her long, silver-blond hair. She was so beautiful and he was so happy to see her.

The dream suddenly shifted and Sarah was in the city,

standing in the middle of the street. A car was speeding toward her. He heard the squeal of brakes, the sound of shattering glass and the whine of twisting metal.

Images flashed, colors and sounds in his head, and Sarah was lying in the hospital. She was dying and it was no longer a dream—it was a memory. A terrible, aching memory of pain and suffering and death.

Then the dream changed again, and it wasn't Sarah in the hospital bed, it was Cassidy. And she wasn't sickly, she was vibrantly beautiful, with her big green eyes and soft dark curls. But she was dying, just like Sarah. Fresh pain sliced through him, an agony so deep he could feel it in every cell in his body. Pain and loss that lived eternally inside him and never went away.

Panic pumped adrenaline through his blood. Silently he screamed out to her, but it wasn't Sarah's name on his lips. It was Cassidy's.

His eyes shot open. Beau scrubbed a shaky hand over his face. He was covered in perspiration, the dream still clear in his head. The accident had triggered the nightmare, the phone call to Cassidy, the fear in her voice, the utter horror he'd felt when he'd heard the screech of tires, the sound of breaking glass and grinding metal. He'd imagined the worst, imagined her body crushed beneath the weight of an oncoming car.

Somehow he'd managed to hold himself together enough to call the police as he'd driven like a madman toward her office. He'd found her alive, injured but okay.

For the first time, he realized how much he cared for her. How much she meant to him. He was in deeper with Cassidy than he'd been with any woman since Sarah.

In way too deep, and he couldn't let it continue. If something happened to Cassidy, he couldn't handle it. He never wanted to go through that kind of pain again.

It was still dark outside when Beau eased out of bed and

padded naked into the kitchen. He poured himself a glass of water and drained the glass, felt a little better. He could handle this. He just needed to keep her at a distance, make sure he didn't get in any deeper.

True, they were good together. He appreciated her sharp mind and enjoyed her company, and they were fantastic together in bed. But eventually the sexual attraction would fade. She was a smart woman. She'd be prepared for that, be able to handle it when the time came for things to end.

His chest clamped down at the thought of her leaving. He took a deep drink of water and forced himself to relax. It wasn't over between them yet. He needed Cassidy's help to prove his innocence. He'd just have to be a little more careful, keep his feelings in check.

He thought of the beautiful woman asleep in his bed and found himself moving in that direction. It would all work out, he told himself.

He and Cassidy could enjoy each other for as long as it lasted. All he had to do was make sure he didn't fall in love.

Her mind felt fuzzy and something was ringing in her head. Cassidy roused herself, managed to wake up enough to realize the pain pills had worn off and Beau's cell phone was ringing.

She glanced around. Beau's bedroom was as sleekly contemporary as the rest of the house, with a sitting area in front of a modern fireplace off to one side. The furniture was dark wood, not light like most of the house. The ultra-modern bathroom was amazing.

Beau fumbled with the phone, managed to grab it off the nightstand as he swung his long legs to the side of the bed. "Reese."

With his back to her, she admired the long muscles

moving beneath his smooth skin, his broad shoulders and tight round behind. A tug of desire pulled low in her belly.

She focused on Beau's conversation, couldn't tell who was on the other end of the line, but Beau was frowning.

"Cassidy's with me. Eleven o'clock will work. We'll see you there." He hung up the phone, set it back down on the nightstand.

"Who was it?" she asked.

"Tom Briscoe. Chief Warren wants to see me. I told Tom we'd drive out. We're meeting them at eleven."

Cassidy sat up in bed, pulling the sheet up to cover herself. Beau's gaze went to her breasts and her face went warm. She tried not to think of sex for the second time that morning.

"How are you feeling?" he asked.

"Headache's gone. I'm a little sore but I'm okay. Did Briscoe say what he wanted?"

"No. I guess we'll find out when we get there." He reached out and grabbed his jeans, pulled them on. "There's a couple more pain pills in that bottle the doctor gave you. You want me to get them?"

She shook her head. "They make me sleepy and I really don't need them. I'm feeling much better today."

She dropped the sheet, grabbed her robe off the chair, and slipped it on, felt Beau's gaze following her every move. Need swelled again. She had never met a man who could make her want him with a single glance.

"I need a shower," she said, dragging her gaze away from all the glorious muscles in his chest. "I wish I'd had time to go by my house and get some fresh clothes. And I need to have my car towed to the garage."

"I'll have Marty take care of your car. And there's a washer and dryer in the mudroom if you need to wash your clothes. Or we can send the stuff out to the dry cleaners.

Mrs. O'Halloran will be in this morning. She can take care of it."

"Are you sure about my car?"

"You're working. Your car needs fixing. It won't be a problem."

"I can take care of my clothes later. It's just . . . it would have been nice to have something different to wear."

He drew her against him and kissed her, sliding his hands inside the robe to cup her breasts. Her nipples went instantly hard.

"I like you best in nothing at all," he said, kissing her again. Heat rolled through her. She draped her arms around his neck, then winced as he bumped the cut on her arm.

Beau instantly stopped. "Dammit, I'm sorry. I don't want to hurt you."

Cassidy checked the bandage, saw the cut wasn't bleeding. "I'm okay." She wished he'd go back to kissing her, but it looked like that wasn't going to happen. "I really do need that shower." She tossed him a sexy glance and took hold of his hand. "We could save water if you joined me."

Beau's beautiful eyes gleamed for an instant; then he shook his head. "Give yourself a chance to heal. Besides, we don't have that much time."

Cassidy ignored a trickle of disappointment. He was probably right. Of course, taking a shower with Beau would certainly keep her mind off her aches and pains.

Half an hour later, dressed in brown tights under a tunic-length beige turtleneck sweater and her knee-high brown boots, she was ready for their drive to Pleasant Hill.

On the way out to the garage, Beau stopped in the kitchen and introduced her to Mrs. O'Halloran, his gray-haired housekeeper, who seemed only a little surprised that Beau had a woman in the house. It wasn't the first time,

Cassidy figured, but from the respectful way the woman treated her, it didn't happen that often.

Beau chose the Lambo for the hour-and-a-half trip to Pleasant Hill. Cassidy settled in the seat as the doors slid down and locked into place and Beau backed out of the garage. God, she loved this car. Just riding in it made her smile.

But as the distance rolled past, Beau grew quieter and quieter. He was obviously worried about what might happen when they got there, and so was she.

"You don't think they brought me back here to arrest me, do you?"

It could happen. He was the only suspect in two homicides. "It's possible, I guess. But you have a very powerful attorney. I think they would have informed him if that was the case." But there was always a chance they would wait to call Temple until after Beau was in custody.

"You think I should have phoned, asked him to meet us there?"

"Probably. If the police start asking questions, you can always refuse to answer until he arrives."

They drove on in silence. Cassidy turned her attention to the passing landscape along Interstate 30. The ground was mostly level, small farms and open country crossed by intermittent streams heavily lined with oaks and other deciduous trees, wild berries, and shrubs.

The day was clear, with big white clouds in a brilliant blue sky, but the temperature was in the fifties and the forecast called for late-afternoon rain.

"What about this guy in your office?" Beau finally asked, cutting into the silence. "Maddox. He seemed to have more than a passing interest in you."

"It's not that. Jase can be a little overly protective. So are the rest of the guys in my office."

"The rest of the guys?"

"It's a detective agency, Beau. Only one other female investigator works there."

"So you've never dated Maddox?"

"No. I told you that."

"Why not? He's a good-looking guy."

"Jase is too wild for me. He's a good friend, just not my type."

She wished she had the nerve to ask him about Sarah, but he had enough on his mind without being dragged into the past. They continued down the highway and entered Pleasant Hill. The Lamborghini rolled down Main Street and Beau pulled into the parking lot next to the single-story brick building that housed the police department.

Beau held the door as she walked inside. The minute they reached the counter, Tom Briscoe strode toward them.

"Chief's waiting," he said simply. "His office is this way."

They followed Briscoe to a door off the main room, several uniformed officers passing them along the way. Cassidy recognized the skinny young cop who'd stood guard outside the guest house the night of the murder. He gave her a nod of acknowledgment as he passed.

Briscoe knocked, then opened the door. As they walked into the office, Police Chief Eric Warren rose from behind his desk.

"Thanks for coming in, Beau," the chief said.

"Nice to see you, Chief, though I would have preferred different circumstances."

Cassidy should have guessed the two would know each other. Beau had been raised in Pleasant Hill, which made him a local celebrity.

"And you're Ms. Jones?"

"Cassidy will do."

"Nice to meet you." He was a nice-looking guy in his forties, brown hair and a solid jaw, just a few wrinkles at the corners of his hazel eyes. He looked capable, Cassidy thought, and if so, maybe he had something good to report.

"Have a seat." Chief Warren gestured toward the metal chairs in front of his desk, then sat down behind it.

"I hope you called me out here because you have good news," Beau said. "Like maybe you found the murderer or at least another suspect."

"Not yet. I can tell you what we *have* found. We confirmed you received a call on your cell twenty minutes before you were found at the scene of Jess Milford's murder. We were, however, not able to trace where the call originated. Looks like it must have been a disposable."

"So you know it was a setup."

"One phone call doesn't prove anything. However, the CSIs believe the direction of the blood spatter found in Milford's kitchen indicates some of it would have shown up on the shooter's clothes. The only place you had blood was on your shoes. Also, there was no gunshot residue on your hands."

Beau released a slow breath. "That's because I didn't shoot him. Did they find any prints in the house?"

"Nothing out of the ordinary. Yours were on the doorknob but nowhere else."

He nodded. "I didn't touch anything else. I walked in just seconds before the cops showed up. I hadn't even turned on the light. What about Milford's phone or his computer? Find anything there?"

"Nothing useful. Detective Briscoe canvassed the area but nobody saw or heard anything that night."

"Not even the gunshot?"

"No. Lots of trees around the house. Might have helped muffle the sound."

"So where does that leave me?"

"I've known you awhile, Beau. I know you and your dad

didn't get along. I could buy the theory you argued, lost your temper, and killed him."

"I didn't kill him."

"Let me finish. But I don't buy the idea that you took a gun that had the serial numbers filed off to Jess Milford's house and for no apparent reason, shot him in the head. And you managed to do it without getting any gunpowder on your hands, or his blood anywhere but on your shoes. I think something else is going on here. Unfortunately, at the moment we have no idea what it is."

Beau settled back in his chair. Cassidy read the relief in his face, though he was still the main suspect in the death of his father.

"Is there anything you can think of, Beau, that could give us a clue as to why your dad and Milford were murdered?"

"I've been thinking about it, believe me. Cassidy's an investigator. She's been helping me try to find out. So far, the only connection we've come up with is Alamo. My dad owned it and Milford was a former employee."

"We've been working that angle. You know about the fire that destroyed the apartments Alamo was building?"

Cassidy caught Beau's glance. He didn't want his father's reputation ruined. He was worried about Missy and the baby. He was afraid it would affect little Evie as she was growing up in Pleasant Hill.

But two men were dead. He needed to give the police something they could use.

"The fire was arson," Beau said. "No secret about that. The investigation concluded it was vandalism. We think Milford might have stumbled onto something, somehow found out who was responsible. Maybe my father did, too, and that's why they were killed."

"You think they were killed to keep them from talking?"

Beau shrugged. "At this point, it's the only thing that makes any sense."

He wasn't mentioning the money the senator owed, or his belief that Malcolm Vaughn might have murdered his father for not repaying the loan.

Chief Warren rose in dismissal. "I wish I could tell you this is over, Beau. There's not enough to hold you for Milford's death, but you're still the primary suspect in the senator's murder. At this point, there's no way to know if the two are even connected. Maybe someone tried to pin Milford's death on you because you were already a suspect in the first murder. Until the senator's killer has been found, we're still looking hard at you."

Beau's features darkened. He nodded.

"Stay close," Chief Warren said as Beau held the door and Cassidy preceded him out of the office.

"Well, that was good news and bad," he said glumly as they crossed the lot toward the Lamborghini, which had drawn a small group of teenage admirers.

"Good news is they don't think you killed Milford. Bad news is they still think you might have killed your dad."

His face looked grim. As they reached the car, a teenage boy with shoulder-length black hair wearing baggy jeans and a striped T-shirt stepped up to Beau. "Dude, your car is totally awesome."

Beau relaxed for the first time that day. A smile lifted the corners of his mouth. "Yeah, it is." He clicked the remote and the doors slid up. "Have a look inside."

"Wow, cool!" a gangly blond boy said as the whole gang rushed forward, all of them clustering around the car. Peering inside, they checked out the futuristic wheel, control panel, and industrial steel floors.

The black-haired teen looked at Beau. "You're Beau Reese, right? My dad and me used to watch you drive when I was a kid."

Cassidy smiled and so did Beau because the teen was still very much a kid. "I'm him."

"How fast does one of these babies go?" the blond boy asked.

"This one tops out at about two twenty."

His pale eyebrows shot up. "Two hundred twenty miles an hour?"

"That's right."

"You ever drive it that fast?" the black-haired kid asked.

"Just on the track. That's the only place it's safe to drive a car at those speeds."

They were looking at Beau like he was a race-car god. Cassidy supposed to a racing fan he was.

"We gotta go, guys." Beau slid in behind the wheel. Cassidy climbed in and Beau closed the doors. He waved to the boys as he pulled out of the parking lot.

"You're good with kids," Cassidy said.

"I like kids. I was an only child. I always wanted a brother or sister. I used to want a big family of my own."

"You can still have that."

Beau just shook his head.

Cassidy's heart went out to him. He was never going to get over Sarah. She wished it didn't bother her as much as it did.

"What about you?" he asked. "You want kids someday?"

She glanced away. Of course she wanted kids, though she wasn't sure it would ever happen. "Depends on the guy. I'm not interested in being a single mom. I'd want my baby to have a father."

Beau fell silent. She knew he was thinking of his own dad and the relationship they'd never had.

"Before we head back," Beau said, "I want to check on Missy and Evie. They're home from the hospital. I want to make sure they have everything they need."

"Good idea. But if we're going to see them, let's make a stop at the Pink Blossom, pick up a little gift. It's just down the street."

"I should have thought of that myself. And I could really use something to eat."

"Me, too." Cassidy leaned back in her seat. Whatever happened between them, she was glad Beau had his baby sister and Missy. Maybe, in time, he would understand it wasn't too late to have a family of his own.

She wanted that for him, she realized. She wanted him to be happy. Even if that happiness came at her own expense.

Warning bells went off in her head. Every day she was falling harder for Beau. She needed to end things now, before she got hurt.

Unfortunately, she wasn't willing to leave until he was no longer a murder suspect.

She sighed as the car rolled down the block. The sooner that happened, the better off both of them would be.

Chapter Twenty

Carrying a stuffed pink giraffe and a pair of tiny pink crocheted booties he couldn't resist buying, Beau followed Cassidy up the stairs to the apartment above the Pleasant Hill Café. A Minnie Mouse baby bouncer Cassidy had picked out waited in the car, in a box that would barely fit inside.

After a quick stop at Burger King, he'd called Josie, so she and Missy were expecting them. Josie pulled open the door at his knock, but instead of a smile, a worried frown darkened her face.

"Come on in. Missy's in the bedroom nursing Evie. She'll be finished in just a minute."

Nursing. He swallowed. Babies were completely foreign to him. He handed the booties to Josie, along with the giraffe, as he and Cassidy walked into the living room. He spotted a bassinet in the corner with a mobile made of tiny seahorses dangling above it. A soft pink blanket was draped over one end of the couch and there were stuffed animals scattered around, probably other gifts from friends.

"There's a baby bouncer in the car," Beau said.

"If you don't already have one," Cassidy added.

Josie smiled tiredly. "I loved the one I had for Missy when she was a baby, but we don't have one for Evie. Room's a little crowded, but we can make it work."

"Let me just go get it." Beau went back down to the car and brought the box upstairs. "It plays music and vibrates," he said, hoping that was a good thing as he set the box down.

"It's a wonderful gift. Thank you both very much." She looked tired and frazzled, her blond hair dull and lifeless. It occurred to him that she was working full-time at the café, running the place one employee short without Missy, and trying to help her daughter care for her newborn.

"I'm forgetting my manners," Josie said. "Would either of you like some coffee or a glass of iced tea?"

"Coffee sounds good," Beau said.

"It's chilly out." Cassidy smiled. "Coffee sounds great. Let me help you with it."

While the women were in the kitchen, Beau took the bouncer out of the box. It didn't need tools for the assembly so he started putting it together. While he worked, he thought of Missy and mentally formulated a plan.

Hearing laughter and the rattle of glassware, he set the assembled bouncer aside as the women walked back into the living room.

"Oh, you put it together!" Cassidy grinned excitedly and handed him a steaming mug, then sat down on the sofa beside him.

"Minnie Mouse," Josie said, looking at the design on the seat cushion. "That is so cute."

Beau took a drink of coffee, felt the warmth spread through him. "How're they doing? Is the baby okay?"

"The baby's doing fine." Josie sat down in an over-stuffed green chair that matched the sofa. "Such a sweet little thing. But Missy's tired. She has to get up at all hours of the night to nurse. She doesn't mind it, though. She loves her little girl."

"You look tired, too, Josie," Beau said. "I know it can't be easy, taking care of Missy and Evie and trying to run the café. I was thinking . . . How would you feel about getting some extra help in here? I could find someone. Or maybe you know someone who'd be good with the baby."

Josie just shook her head. "We don't have enough room for someone else, Beau. It's nice of you to offer, though."

He sipped his coffee. "I've got an even better idea. How about moving into a bigger place? Sooner or later Missy is going to need a house of her own. It might as well be now."

"We can't afford that, Beau," Missy said as she came through the bedroom door.

He looked at the little pink bundle in the slender girl's arms and something shifted and softened inside him. "I know you can't, but I can. Do you think you and your mom could carve out enough time to look at a few houses? You could pick out something big enough for you and your mom and someone to help with the baby. We could close the sale as soon as possible. What do you think?"

Missy looked dumbfounded. "You can't be serious. You want to buy me a house?"

"Why not? I can afford it, and you and my little sister need a place to live."

Missy sat down in the other chair, the baby cradled gently in her arms. "It's too much, Beau. I wouldn't feel right about it."

Beau glanced at Cassidy for support, but she was clearly staying out of it. He turned to the older woman. "What do you think, Josie? We could find something that isn't too far from the café."

Josie's gaze went to her daughter, relief clear in her face. He'd known she was worried. He hadn't been sure what about. "If Beau wants to do this for you and his sister, I don't see why you should refuse."

Missy's eyes filled with tears. For the first time, he

understood what his father had seen in the girl. There was something unpretentious about Missy, something wholesome and good.

"Do you mean it?" she asked.

"Of course I mean it. Josie, you must know a Realtor who'd do a good job for you. Can you line someone up?"

"Diane Ellison is good. I can give her a call."

"I'll call her, too," Beau said. "Explain how this is going to work. All right?"

Missy rose and walked to where he sat on the sofa. Leaning down, she settled the sleeping baby gently in his arms. He looked down at the innocent face and felt as if a tiny hand had reached out and touched his heart. His gaze went to Cassidy. She was watching him with misty eyes.

He looked back down at the baby, sat there for several minutes just staring, studying the miniature fingers and tiny bow-shaped mouth. By now he should have had a child of his own, more than one, if he'd had his way. He glanced back at Cassidy. If things were different . . . if he were a different man . . .

He handed the baby back to Missy and rose from the sofa. "You got the check I sent?" he asked a little gruffly.

"We got it," Josie said. "Thank you."

Beau leaned over and kissed Missy's cheek. "Take care of our girl, okay?"

She just nodded. "Thanks for the presents, Beau, especially the bouncer. I really wanted one, but I didn't want to spend the money."

"That's from Cassidy," Beau said, glancing her way. Didn't matter that he had paid for it; she was the one who had picked it out.

They walked outside together, headed back down the stairs to the Lamborghini.

"You're a good man, Beau Reese," Cassidy said as she slid into the vehicle.

Beau thought that if he were a better, smarter man, he would latch on to Cassidy Jones and never let go. It wasn't going to happen. For now, he needed her to help him prove his innocence. He needed her and he wanted her, but he would never risk the closeness he had shared with Sarah.

"We have to go back and figure out what to do next," Cassidy said, putting the conversation back on track as he pulled onto the highway and headed for Dallas. "We need to go over what we know, and figure things out."

Figure things out. Beau wished it were that easy.

"No paparazzi," Cassidy said as the Lamborghini turned into Beau's driveway. "How does it feel to be yesterday's news?"

"It isn't the first time. I was dead to the press the minute I stopped racing, which was fine with me."

Beau drove into the garage and turned off the engine, the Lamborghini's doors slid up and they climbed out of the car.

Pausing in the kitchen to grab a couple of Diet Cokes, they headed down the hall to the study. Instead of sitting at the partners' desk, Cassidy retrieved a yellow legal pad from her briefcase and grabbed a pen; then she and Beau sat down at a table in the corner.

She set the pad down in front of her. "Not exactly twenty-first century, but it'll give us a chance to organize our thoughts." They needed to go through the information they had come up with, look at it from different angles.

She picked up the pen. "Okay, let's start with what we know—and keep in mind this is only a working theory. The more we find out, the more it's likely to change."

Beau took a long drink of his Coke. Cassidy watched the muscles in his throat move up and down and tried not to think how sexy he looked. God, she had it bad.

"All right," Beau said. "We have two murder victims, but we can't be sure the murders are connected. Briscoe could be right—someone could have set me up because I was already a suspect in my father's death. Milford's killer thought he could blame it on me and get away clean."

"It's a possibility. But in both cases, the killer was extremely efficient, leaving no fingerprints or DNA. In Milford's case, the bullet to the head was neat and efficient. Whoever did it, had to know the police wouldn't have enough to prosecute you for Milford. More likely, the killer or killers wanted you out of the way so you wouldn't keep digging, trying to find out who murdered the senator." Cassidy jotted down a few notes.

"So we'll assume the murders are connected," Beau said.

"For now. It makes the most sense. Your father and stepmother owned Alamo. Milford was a longtime employee. We know there was an arson fire that destroyed Alamo's unfinished apartment project and that Milford was fired two days before it happened, probably to get him out of the way."

"Charlotte was convinced my father was responsible for the fire. The real estate market changed, the project would have tanked, and my father would have lost a lot of money."

"Instead, he made a profit," Cassidy said.

"Money he used to pay off Vaughn's Equity Advance construction loan."

"Some of it, but not all."

"Which gave Vaughn a motive for murder," Beau finished.

Cassidy jotted down a few more notes, but she was still unconvinced. "Let's back up a little. What about Milford? Vaughn wouldn't have had a motive for killing Jess Milford."

Beau rubbed the back of his neck as he pondered the thought. "Maybe he would have. Vaughn would have wanted his money back, right?"

"Absolutely. No way was he setting a bad precedent by letting your father skate."

"So maybe *Vaughn* arranged the arson. My dad would collect the insurance money and Vaughn would get paid. Maybe Jess Milford found out Vaughn was involved, tried to blackmail him, and Vaughn killed him. Or more likely, had someone else kill him."

"What about your dad? You still think Vaughn is the man behind his murder?"

"My father used the money he borrowed to live the high life he was accustomed to. He didn't pay it all back, so Vaughn took care of him, just like Milford."

Cassidy tried to convince herself, but doubt must have shown in her face.

"You still don't believe it." Beau released a sigh of frustration.

Cassidy took a sip of her Coke and set it back down on the table. "Something's off. I can feel it. I'm just not sure what it is."

"Maybe, but I know one thing. Two men are dead. If Vaughn was behind the arson, there's a good chance both of the murder victims had some kind of run-in with him."

"You realize, if Vaughn's behind the murders and you keep pursuing this, you're taking a very big risk."

"I'm going to find the man who killed my father. If it's Vaughn—"

"I'm not suggesting we quit, just warning you of the danger."

Beau scowled. "Okay, I get it. We need to be careful. You still in?"

"Of course. I do this for a living, Beau."

"All right, then we're going to need to step up our game."

A faint shiver ran through her as she thought of the man she had met at Equity Advance. There was something disturbing about Malcolm Vaughn, something in his eyes. It was the look of a predator, one who relentlessly pursued its prey.

She glanced over at Beau. "I keep thinking about what Dooley Tate said."

One of his black eyebrows went up. "Tate said favors are as valuable as money. It's crossed my mind, too."

"Your father was a senator. He traded in favors. That's how political deals are made. Surely he could have come up with something Vaughn wanted in exchange for the rest of the money he owed. If he did, Vaughn would have had no reason to kill him."

Beau took a swallow of his Coke. "So how do we find out?"

Cassidy tapped her pen on the yellow pad. "I need to call Jase. He always has an ear to the ground. Maybe he's heard a rumor, something Vaughn might be involved in that will help us figure things out."

The thin scar along Beau's jaw tightened. "I don't like it. I don't want you in debt to Maddox."

"You don't have to worry. It's quid pro quo. Sometimes I help him. Sometimes he helps me. Sometimes we work together."

"I still don't like it."

Cassidy eyed him with speculation. Was that jealousy she heard in his voice? Surely not. "You just don't like Jase. You're afraid he'll poach on your territory."

Beau's gaze ran over her, as blue as the tip of a flame and just as hot. Desire clenched the muscles across her belly.

"Do I need to worry?" he asked.

"About Jase? No."

He frowned. "What the hell does that mean?"

Cassidy just smiled. "It means you still owe me that dinner and tonight would be a good time."

Beau relaxed. "Dinner it is. It's getting late. We'll put this aside for now and go get something to eat."

"First I want to shower and change." And Cassidy knew exactly what to wear.

Chapter Twenty-One

Beau changed into a pair of tan slacks, a light blue button-down shirt, and a navy-blue sport coat. While Cassidy was getting dressed, he called the restaurant he had in mind and made a reservation.

Half an hour later, he was beginning to get antsy, pacing in front of the living room windows, tempted to pour himself a drink. On the other side of the glass, underwater lights illuminated the clear blue water of the swimming pool, which he usually found soothing.

Tonight he had too much on his mind.

He turned at the click of high heels on the hardwood floor, spotted Cassidy walking down the hall in the short black cocktail dress with the floaty little skirt he had seen hanging in the guest-house closet. Thick dark curls bobbed against her shoulders, making him want to grab a fistful and drag her mouth to his for a deep, burning kiss.

The bandage on her skinned knee had him frowning, but the cleavage displayed by the neckline and those fuck-me heels had his blood running hot. Grateful he was wearing a jacket that helped hide the bulge beneath his zipper, he smiled and started toward her.

"You look gorgeous." He bent and pressed a soft kiss on her lips and they parted in invitation. Beau deepened the kiss, taking his time, enjoying the rush of heat. Just as he was settling in, Cassidy pulled away.

"I'm starving," she said. "Looks like you're ready to go."

He was ready, all right. But not for supper. He sighed as she took his arm and they started for the car parked in the garage. Her soft breasts brushed his chest and he realized she wasn't wearing a bra.

Beau slammed to a halt. "You're wearing your little black dress. What are you wearing underneath?"

She grinned wickedly. "I bet you can guess."

"*Jesus*. Seriously?"

She took his arm again and urged him toward the door. "As serious as a heart attack, honey."

"Which is what you're going to give me if I have to sit through dinner imagining you across the table without anything under your skirt."

She laughed. "It was your idea."

For which he could kick himself right now. He smiled. Later, however, it would certainly make things interesting.

They reached the door to the garage. When he opened it, a low light came on, dimly illuminating the interior.

"You have the cleanest garage I've ever seen," she said. "Not a spec of dirt on the floor, not a trace of oil or gasoline. How many times a week does somebody clean it?"

"My handyman washes the cars and keeps the garage clean. Vehicles like these deserve to be treated with care."

She laughed. "That's right, you think they're human. I forgot. So where are we going for dinner?"

He pressed a button and the doors on the Lambo began to slide up. "A place called Antoine's. It's a little ways out of town, but the food's worth the drive."

He helped her settle into the car, her dress riding up just

inches from a glimpse of heaven. Inwardly he groaned. At this rate, it was going to be the longest evening of his life.

Beau backed the sports car out of the garage, drove down the driveway and turned onto the street, heading for the little French restaurant owned by a friend.

Antoine De la Croix ran one of the best restaurants in the Dallas area. Antoine's was intimate, with only fifteen tables, white linen tablecloths and fresh flowers on each one.

"It's lovely," Cassidy said as he guided her through the door. Pale amber lighting lent a soft glow to the dining room, and French music played softly in the background.

"Beaumont, *mon ami*!" Antoine, a big, burly, bearded Frenchman, was a racing fan. Beau couldn't remember exactly how they had met, but it had something to do with the classic Bugatti that was Antoine's pride and joy.

He clapped Beau hard on the shoulder. "It is good to see you, my friend. It has been far too long."

"Yes, it has," Beau agreed. He didn't come here often. It was a place he brought only his closest friends. It occurred to him he had only brought one other woman, a lady stockbroker he had dated, a woman he still admired and respected.

"Antoine, I'd like you to meet my friend Cassidy Jones."

Antoine, in his usual overblown manner, took her hand and kissed the back. "Such a beautiful woman. It is a pleasure to meet you, Ms. Jones. My friend's taste in women is as excellent as his taste in automobiles. Come. I have saved for you the best table in the house."

He led them to a quiet corner. Beau seated Cassidy, then took a seat across from her.

The big Frenchman beamed. "Perhaps you should let Antoine make the selections tonight so that you will not be disturbed. I promise, my friends, you will not be disappointed."

Beau looked at Cassidy, who smiled. "That sounds wonderful."

"You heard the lady," Beau said. "Looks like tonight it's up to you."

Antoine shot him a devilish grin, then turned to one of the waiters and snapped his fingers. "Champagne! The best in the house for my friend and his lady!"

Antoine strode off and Beau smiled at Cassidy. "He can be a little overdramatic, but he's a good guy, and his chef is one of the best in Dallas."

"I'm looking forward to his selections." She tossed him a glance from beneath her thick lashes. "I just hope they won't be too filling."

Beau silently groaned. There was no mistaking her meaning or the challenge in those big green eyes. "You *are* trying to kill me."

"Not at the moment." She grinned. "I can't promise what might happen later."

He felt like tossing down his napkin and dragging her out of there right now. Instead, he forced himself to smile. "If you don't behave, this is going to be the shortest dinner in history."

Cassidy laughed. "I'll behave . . . for now."

God, he liked this woman. She gave as good as she got and never backed down.

For the next two hours, they drank champagne and ate some of the most incredible French food he'd ever tasted—though both of them were careful not to eat too much.

They skipped dessert, which Antoine pouted about, but Beau had been aroused for most of the evening and enough was enough.

He drove Cassidy back to the house, wishing he could just pull over somewhere and satisfy the hunger they both were feeling; would have if the weather had been warmer.

As it was, he drove into the garage and closed the door, rounded the car to help Cassidy out. Her skirt slid up just to torture him. He set a hand at her waist and urged her toward the house just as her phone began to ring.

She cast him a glance. Both of them knew it might be important. Cassidy dug her cell out of her little black purse and pressed it against her ear, started nodding and talking.

"Okay, yes . . . that would be great, Jase."

Jase. The big, overprotective cowboy who worked in her office. Irritation rolled through him.

"I'll be in tomorrow," Cassidy said. "We can talk about it then." She laughed at something Jase said, and Beau's irritation grew. "Okay, fine, I'll buy lunch. See you tomorrow."

Lunch? No way.

Cassidy ended the call, stuck the phone back in her purse, and looked up at him. "I left a message on Jase's phone before we left. He's going to make a few calls, see what he can find out about Vaughn that might be useful."

"And then the two of you are going to lunch," Beau said darkly.

"I told him if he found something, I'd buy him lunch. It's no big deal."

"Is that so?" He barely recognized the emotion sliding through him as jealousy, but it made him angry and hot all at once. Cassidy squeaked as he dragged her into his arms and slanted his mouth over hers. She could go to lunch with Maddox, but she'd be thinking about a different man while she was there. Beau intended to make sure of it.

He deepened the kiss, wanting more of her, all he could get. He thought she might pull away, but her arms went around his neck and she pressed herself more fully against him. He could feel her soft breasts against his chest, moved his thigh between her legs, lifted a little and heard her moan. His tongue slid into her mouth, tangled with hers, and heat rolled through him. He was rock hard and aching, wanting her and determined to make sure she wasn't thinking of anyone but him.

The kiss went on and on, both of them making little erotic noises and gasping for breath. His hands found their way inside the bodice of her dress to cup her breasts, massage and caress them. Her nipples were as hard as he was, and he knew she was ready, wanting this as much as he did.

He nipped the side of her neck as he turned her around, a hand drifting between her legs. "Brace your palms on the hood of the car," he said softly.

"What?"

"Do it," he commanded.

Cassidy made a sexy little sound in her throat, bent over and flattened her hands on the still-warm Lamborghini. When he flipped up her little black skirt, the vision of hot, half-naked female against an equally hot car made one of the sexiest pictures he'd ever seen.

Moving behind her, he lifted her silky dark hair and pressed his mouth against the nape of her neck, gently kissed a bruise he found there. Sliding the straps of her dress off her shoulders, he kissed each little scrape and scratch he found on her back.

Cassidy whimpered.

Beau ran his hands over the firm little globes of her bottom and nudged her legs apart. He could feel her trembling.

"You want this?" he asked.

"Yes, Beau . . . please . . ."

She whimpered as he entered her, seated himself and began to move. Cassidy arched her back to take him deeper and he nearly lost it, took a deep breath and fought for control. Gripping her hips, he drove into her, determined to make it good for both of them, make it a ride she wouldn't forget.

She cried out as she started to come but Beau didn't stop, not until she came again. Clenching his jaw, he finally allowed his own release, a hot tide that swept through every muscle and bone in his body.

When they finally drifted back to earth, he eased her dress back into place, turned her into his arms, and just held her. She felt so good, fit him so perfectly. Such a beautiful woman—*his* beautiful woman.

Beau shook himself. What the hell was he thinking? Cassidy wasn't his woman. No way was he letting himself go where that thought led. He pressed a last soft kiss on her forehead. "You okay?"

She smiled at him softly. "Way better than okay."

"Yeah, me too." He kissed her one last time. "It's getting late. We've got work to do tomorrow."

Cassidy just nodded.

For a while he'd been able to set his troubles aside and enjoy the evening. He'd thought of nothing but Cassidy and how much he wanted her. Now his worries were back full force.

Was Malcolm Vaughn behind his father's murder? And if he was, how the hell did they prove it?

Chapter Twenty-Two

Cassidy started the day with a faint headache. A little too much champagne. But what a romantic night it had been. Romantic and *hot*. Her face heated at the memory of what had happened in Beau's garage. She loved sex with him. No man had ever made her feel the way he did. She had a feeling no man ever would.

It was dangerous to let herself be drawn in any deeper, but she couldn't seem to help herself.

It was late morning when she showered and dressed in the bedroom next to his. For the first time, it occurred to her today was February third—the anniversary of her mother's death. With everything that had been happening, somehow the date had slipped her mind.

Despair settled over her. She hated this day. No matter how bright it started out, she couldn't avoid the sadness that grew hour by hour as her mind filled with memories of the warm, loving woman who had raised her.

For the last six years, on this day, she had gone to the cemetery to put flowers on her mother's grave. Being there gave her time to remember the way things were when they were a family, the joys they had shared. It gave her time to appreciate all the things her mother had done for her, a way to feel closer to her mom.

She headed for the study. Beau was sitting at his desk when she walked in. His eyes swung to hers and heated. He was thinking about last night and for an instant, she thought of it, too.

But darker memories swept in and her smile slowly faded. Beau must have noticed because the heat dimmed in his eyes and concern replaced it.

"You okay?"

She smoothed a hand over the stretch jeans she had put on with a V-necked sweater. "Not a good day for me, I'm afraid. Six years ago today, my mother died."

Beau rose from behind his desk and walked toward her. "I'm sorry, baby. I know how that feels." He wrapped her in his arms, lending his warmth and strength.

"Sarah was sick for most of my senior year in college," he said, surprising her. "She died in June, right after graduation. It's been thirteen years, but I still remember how I felt the day she died."

Cassidy slid her arms around his waist and rested her head on his shoulder. Beau had never brought up Sarah before. She told herself it was a good sign. "Sarah had cancer, right? Just like my mother."

She could feel the movement as he nodded. "She fought it. We both believed she could beat it, but in the end she lost the battle."

"I'm sorry."

"It gets easier as the years pass. Sometimes I forget for weeks at a time. Then it all comes back and it's like it happened yesterday."

She hung on to him a little longer, wishing she could make him forget, knowing he never would. Just like she would never forget the six months she had nursed her mother before she'd passed away.

Cassidy let him go. "I always drive out to the cemetery, put some flowers on Mom's grave. Since my car's in the shop, I was hoping you might let me borrow the BMW."

"You want me to go with you?"

She shook her head. "Thanks for the offer, but I'd rather go by myself."

"I understand that. I'll tell you what. Why don't you take the Lamborghini? That might cheer you up a little."

Her eyes widened. "Really? The cemetery is a ways out of the city. Are you sure it would be okay?"

"You've driven it before. The trip'll do you good."

She threw her arms around his neck. "I'm driving the Lambo! I'm cheered up just thinking about it."

He chuckled, eased back, and softly kissed her. "The keys are on the hook in the garage. Go visit your mom. Do whatever else you need to do. I've got some catching up to do at the office. I'll meet you here later."

"When I get back, we can finish going through those manila folders we found in your dad's study. There's a couple we haven't looked at."

"Sounds like a plan."

Cassidy hurried back to the bedroom and grabbed her jacket, then left the house in Beau's Lamborghini. It was hard to stay depressed when you were driving a car that felt like you were flying.

She wondered what her dad would say if he saw it, and made a mental note to call him and her brother Brandon later. Maybe she could Skype Shawn in Afghanistan when she got back to Beau's house.

She'd only gotten as far as Lemmon Avenue, heading for Uptown, when her phone rang. Careful to keep her eyes on the road, she pulled her cell out of her purse, saw it was Jase, and found a spot to pull over.

"Have you found something?" she asked.

"Maybe. I'm at the office. What time are you coming in?"

"I'm on my way now. I'll be there in just a few minutes." She ended the call. She hadn't reminded Beau she was stopping at the office before she left town. He didn't like the idea of her meeting with Jase, even though she'd told him there was nothing going on between them. As soon as she was finished, she could drive out to the cemetery.

Jase was sitting at his desk when she walked in. He and Connie were the only ones there, but with the odd hours they all worked, someone else could show up anytime.

Cassidy waved at Connie, who was on the phone, then crossed the room and sat down in the chair next to Jase's desk. "Tell me you got something."

"I got something. Not sure it'll help." He leaned back in his chair, shoved his boots out in front of him. "I can tell you Vaughn is connected to some very powerful people, but you probably knew that already."

"It's not surprising, with the big-money loans he makes. He's getting the money to make those loans somewhere. What else?"

"His right-hand man is a guy named Clifford Jennings. He's not on the company payroll. He works directly for Vaughn."

"That's news."

"Jennings doesn't know squat about the loan business. He handles collections, makes sure the money gets paid back. Usually a threat from Jennings is enough to get it done. If there's a problem, word on the street is Jennings will do whatever it takes to make his boss happy."

"Does that include murder?"

"He's not a killer. He just handles things. He knows who to call to get it done."

"Senator Reese owned a construction and development company. They were building a big set of apartments in Iron Springs when an arson fire burned the project down. Reese collected the insurance money, which went to pay

Vaughn. Do you think Jennings could have arranged the fire?"

"I think he can make just about anything happen."

"So Vaughn controls Jennings. Any idea who pulls Vaughn's strings?"

"He uses three or four different people to fund those big loans. I don't know their names, but they'd be able to exert plenty of pressure."

"There's an old saying: 'He who holds the gold, rules.'" Jase chuckled.

"There's a chance Jess Milford found out who arranged the apartment fire," she said. "Good chance Vaughn was behind it. Milford might have tried to blackmail him, and Vaughn had him killed."

"If you could get something on Jennings, maybe he'd roll on Vaughn."

She nodded, thinking the same thing. "It looks like the senator had only paid back part of the money he owed Equity Advance when he was murdered, but I can't see Vaughn killing him over the debt. Reese recently retired from politics. He still carried plenty of juice with people in Texas, even kept files with information he used to get what he wanted. He had to have something Vaughn could have used."

"I know the cops are looking at your friend Beau for the murder," Jase said. "But from what you've told me, I think both men were killed by the same guy. No prints, no DNA, both hits quick and deadly. Gotta be a pro, and if it was, could be Vaughn was involved."

"Sounds about right," Cassidy said.

"So maybe there's two different things going on here. Maybe Milford was killed to keep him quiet, but the senator was killed for a completely different reason."

"Like what?"

Jase grinned. "I got no idea, sweet thing. It's your job to

find out." His grin slid away. "Be careful, Cassidy. Guys
like these play for keeps."

Franco Giannetti eased out of his parking space on Blackburn Street, following the flashy metallic-gray sports car. It
sure as hell wasn't hard, not with the careful way the
woman was driving. He couldn't believe her boyfriend had
let her borrow his fancy Lamborghini. Damn thing had to
be worth a fortune.

He'd been watching Reese's house since he'd come up
with his new plan. Today he'd followed the woman from
the house to her office, where he'd made a run at her before.
He'd watched her park and go inside, found a spot and settled
in to wait.

An hour slipped past. He fidgeted, shifted in the torn
vinyl seat, trying to get comfortable. It was chilly in the
truck, but when a payoff was involved, Franco could be a
patient man.

He turned on the engine, ran the heater to take off the
chill, amazed it worked in the old beater truck. All he
needed was to catch a break and the job would be done.

He was beginning to get bored when she finally came
outside and climbed into the pricey sports car. He followed
the vehicle at a safe distance, but no way was she going to
spot him, not in the old white Chevy pickup he'd driven out
of the junkyard. The way he did business, all the car needed
was an engine that would run.

He pulled over when she slowed and parked in front of
a flower shop down the street. She ran inside and came back
out a few minutes later carrying a pretty yellow bouquet. He
followed her again, saw her turn into the parking lot of a
four-story brick apartment building and waited while she
went inside.

He still hadn't completely formulated a plan. He was keeping his options open, a technique he preferred. Today might not work, but if he got the chance, he was taking the woman out.

Franco felt a rush of excitement as he leaned back in his seat. This job was right up his alley, a way to make a sizable score all at once. But the challenge, the adrenaline rush of getting away with it . . . well, sometimes it was just downright fun.

Though Jase had pressed her for the lunch she owed him, Cassidy had put him off, promising she'd make it up to him next week. After leaving the office, she'd stopped at the flower shop, then swung by her place to retrieve some fresh clothes.

She fumbled with the key to her loft apartment, finally got the door open, and walked inside. She'd been gone so long the place smelled musty. She cracked some windows, although it was chilly outdoors, went into the bedroom and packed a rolling duffel, adding a few less conservative, sexier outfits than she'd taken to Pleasant Hill.

Her stomach was growling so she heated a can of chicken noodle soup, popped the top on a Diet Coke, and sat down at the counter in her small galley kitchen.

The apartment had a nice open feeling enhanced by the high ceilings and living-dining combination. Eventually, she'd get around to buying some accent pieces to brighten the plain beige sofa and chairs she had purchased when she'd first moved in.

She finished her lunch and was ready to head for the cemetery, but before she left, she wanted to call her dad. He was retired from the police force, but still worked part-time in the security business. They chatted awhile, which always lifted their spirits on this dismal day.

She phoned Brandon, a cop in New Orleans, but he didn't pick up, so she left a message. She hoped she could reach Shawn in Afghanistan. She'd try to Skype him when she got back to Beau's.

It was late afternoon by the time she was in the car, driving toward the small country cemetery outside Kaufman, about forty minutes south of Dallas. The sky had darkened as heavy clouds rolled in, but it hadn't started raining yet.

The little cemetery occupied a piece of land outside the city limits of the town where her mother had been born, and other members of her family were buried there, too. There was a place for her dad already paid for next to her mom, but she didn't want to think about that.

It was peaceful as she wandered among the tombstones. Only two other people were in the cemetery and they were standing around a headstone some distance away. She set the flowers on her mother's grave, stood there awhile, and found herself talking about Beau.

"He's a terrific guy, Mom. You would really like him. The thing is, he's in love with someone else, a woman who died a long time ago. Since I deserve a man who's in love with me, not a dead woman, I don't think it's going to work out."

Just saying the words made her heart pinch. She was already more than half in love with Beau. But talking to her mom seemed to help, so she sat there awhile longer. She hadn't realized how late it was getting until she noticed the sun dipping below the horizon and it began to rain.

Hurrying to the car, she climbed in and started the powerful Lamborghini engine, settled back and strapped herself into the seat. The sound of the engine made her smile, along with the sweet gesture Beau had made in letting her borrow one of his most prized possessions. Knowing how valuable the car was and how much he loved it, she still couldn't believe she'd had the nerve to accept his generous gift.

It was raining hard by the time the Lambo rolled through the tall wrought-iron gates enclosing the graveyard. There was another car parked just outside, an old Chevy pickup with WASH ME traced through the dirt on the door. Maybe the rain would give it a long-overdue cleaning.

She wondered who the driver had been visiting, wondered if he had lost a member of his family, too, and felt a twinge of pity.

The pickup lights went on as she drove the Lamborghini along the narrow road down the hill. The truck pulled in behind her. The pavement was slick and the road was curvy, so she was taking it slow.

Too slow, apparently. The old Chevy speeded up behind her, coming up fast in her rearview mirror. She pressed down on the gas, but the road was too twisty to go very fast and no way was she risking a crash in Beau's expensive car.

She made the first of a series of turns, but the pickup stayed right on her tail.

Idiot. Any trace of pity fled. There was nowhere to pull over, no way to get off the road, and with him so close, no way she could stop. What the hell did he want her to do? She speeded up a little more, but so did he.

She was beginning to get mad. She drove a little faster, then braked for the curve ahead. There were lots of trees, so she needed to be careful, but the pickup didn't slow, just kept coming, roaring up behind her. She couldn't believe it when he rammed her bumper hard enough to jolt the car, denting the back for sure.

Oh, God, Beau was going to kill her.

She never should have borrowed it. What in the world had she been thinking? She glanced in the mirror, saw the pickup rushing toward her again. Was he drunk? On drugs? A chill went through her. Or was it something else?

She thought how close she had come to being killed in front of her office. This wasn't the same vehicle, but if the hit-and-run hadn't been an accident, this could be another attempt.

Cassidy fought the wheel. Adrenaline poured through her—not the fun kind, the scared kind—and her hands started sweating. If Beau had been driving, the sports car could have handled the speed and the curves, but she wasn't a race-car driver, and the pavement was wet and slick. She had to go faster, told herself she could do it.

She had two brothers. Brandon had taught her to drive in his souped-up '66 Chevelle. He and Shawn had goaded her until she'd learned to handle the car to their satisfaction.

As the truck raced up behind her again, she hit the gas and the Lamborghini shot forward as if it had wings. For a moment, she left the pickup behind and satisfaction rolled through her. But there was a sharp curve up ahead that dropped off into a field on one side, and no way could she keep up her speed.

She slowed and the pickup roared up on her tail. He rammed her just as she went into the turn. The rear end fishtailed, she hit the gas to correct the slide, which worked until the car hit a pothole and skidded sideways.

The pickup rammed into the passenger door, sending the Lamborghini careening off the road. The car shot into the air, spun, hit the ground, flipped and rolled, and there was nothing she could do. She clung to the wheel, kept her head down as the sports car landed on its roof and the airbags went off, but the car just kept rolling.

On the third roll, something hit her in the head and she blacked out for a moment, came to as the Lambo righted itself and jarred to a halt. She was dizzy, her mind fuzzy, but the pickup seemed to be gone. She couldn't see any headlights in the mirror anywhere behind her, but she'd wrecked Beau's beautiful car.

Cassidy felt the warm trickle of blood running down her forehead and tears filling her eyes. Then the world went black and she felt nothing at all.

Chapter Twenty-Three

Beau paced the floor outside the intensive care unit of the Presbyterian Hospital in Kaufman. He thought of the crash and felt sick to his stomach.

He'd driven home from the office, thought Cassidy might get there ahead of him, but when he arrived, the Lambo wasn't parked in the garage.

He'd tried her cell, but it had gone straight to voicemail. He purposely hadn't called her earlier, determined to give her some space. He understood what she was going through, figured she'd feel better by the time she got home.

He had just begun to worry when the police called. They said there'd been an accident, that the victim was a woman named Cassidy Maryann Jones. She was in intensive care at the Presbyterian Hospital in Kaufman. That was all they knew.

He'd been frantic. He'd called the hospital but he wasn't immediate family so they wouldn't tell him much. He'd driven the Ferrari the forty miles to Kaufman like a madman, phoned Linc on the way—he had no idea why—and told him what had happened.

His friend's deep baritone had calmed him a little. "Take

it easy," Linc had said. "You'll find out what happened when you get there. Carly and I are staying in Dallas this week so we aren't that far away. We'll meet you there."

"You don't have to do that. I'm okay."

"We'll see you there." The line went dead.

Beau's hands tightened around the steering wheel. He should have known his friends wouldn't let him handle this alone.

The evening traffic and the heavy rain forced him to slow down. He'd considered taking the helicopter, but making the arrangements, then meeting the chopper, would have taken as much time as driving, and he preferred just getting on the road.

The minutes dragged past. By the time he arrived, his stomach was tied in knots. He pushed through the doors of the two-story brick building, strode up to the reception counter, and asked for a patient named Cassidy Jones who had been in a car accident.

Behind the counter, a gray-haired receptionist with reading glasses perched on her nose checked the name on her computer. "The patient is in intensive care. Take the elevator up to the second floor. Check in at the nursing station. Someone there will tell you where to go."

He turned and started walking, skipped the elevator, and took the stairs two at a time to the second floor. When he arrived, he went straight to the nursing station, spoke to a nurse in green scrubs with short auburn hair.

"I'm here to see a patient named Cassidy Jones. They said she was on this floor."

"She's here. The doctor is in with her now. What's your relationship to the patient?"

"I'm . . ." *A friend* didn't sound right. Cassidy was way more than that. They might not let him see her if he was only a friend, and he sure as hell wasn't going to pretend to be her brother. "I'm her fiancé," he said. "Can you tell me her condition?"

"She's listed as stable. That's all I know. As I said, the doctor is in with her now. He'll talk to you as soon as he comes out. There's a waiting room down the hall."

Beau thanked her and headed in that direction. There was no one else in the room when he pushed through the door, but he couldn't make himself sit down. He swallowed, replaying the day in his head, wishing he hadn't let her borrow the car. He'd been sure she could handle it. She'd driven the Lamborghini before and hadn't had any problems.

What if she'd died? What if he'd gotten her killed?

His eyes burned. He pressed his thumbs into the sockets and rubbed them. He remembered the crash at Le Mans, remembered lying in the hospital bed, waiting to find out if his friend had survived the crash. Remembered the terrible moment he'd found out Joe Markham had died.

His breath hitched. He sank down on a blue vinyl sofa, elbows on his knees, his head dropping into his hands. He didn't pray often, but he said a prayer for Cassidy, hoped it would somehow help.

His head jerked up when the door swung open and Cain and Carly walked into the waiting room. At six-foot five, two hundred twenty pounds of solid muscle, Linc seemed to take up all the space in the room. Carly was blond and pretty, strong and competent, the perfect match for his best friend.

She walked over to Beau, sat down next to him, put an arm around his shoulders, didn't say a word.

"How is she?" Linc asked.

"Stable. That's all I know." He blew out a breath. "It's my fault. I shouldn't have let her drive the car. It was raining. Sometimes a powerful car like that can get away from you. I just . . . today was the day her mother died. I wanted to cheer her up."

Linc sat down in a chair and leaned toward him. "It's too early to blame yourself, Beau. You don't know what actually happened."

His throat felt tight. He didn't care what had happened. He just wanted Cassidy to be okay.

The door opened again and a pair of uniformed police officers walked into the waiting room, one older, with a fringe of light brown hair, the other young and dark, probably Latino.

"Beaumont Hamilton Reese?" the older cop asked.

Beau came up from the sofa. "I'm Beau Reese."

"You're the registered owner of the Lamborghini involved in the accident?"

"That . . . that's right. Cassidy borrowed it for the day. Do you know if she's okay?"

"The doctor's still in with her."

"Can you tell me what happened?" Beau asked.

The officer pulled a notepad out of his pocket and checked his notes. "Apparently a farmer was working outside his barn when the car went off the road. He called 9-1-1, then went to see what he could do. She was unconscious, but he could tell she was breathing. The car was upright so he decided to wait for the ambulance."

Beau tried not to think of Cassidy, strapped in and unconscious, surrounded by darkness in the middle of a muddy field.

The officer studied his notes, looked back at Beau. "The first officers on the scene thought it was a single car accident. Driver missed a tricky turn on a slick road in the rain. But now that they've had a chance to examine the site more closely, it doesn't look like that's what happened."

Beau frowned. "What do you mean?"

"It looks like the Lamborghini was hit from behind. The driver of the other car wasn't paying attention or maybe he was drunk. We don't know. The Lamborghini spun out, slid sideways, and was T-boned by the car behind. Looks like the vehicle slammed directly into the passenger side door. The Lamborghini flipped and rolled a couple of times. The accident happened on a curve, so the car landed in the field beyond. The ground had softened with the rain, which helped."

"The farmer didn't see the accident," the Latino cop added; Rodriguez was printed on his name tag. "He just saw the vehicle go into the field. He was there when the police and ambulance arrived."

Beau thought of Cassidy inside the spinning car, the vehicle completely out of control. He knew what a crash that bad felt like, knew the fear.

A wave of nausea hit him. "Do you mind if I sit down?"

"Sure, no problem."

He sank down on the vinyl sofa, leaned back and raked his hands through his hair. A thought struck. "What happened to the driver of the other vehicle?"

"The car, a white Chevy pickup, was found abandoned a few miles down the road. Turned out to be stolen, reported a couple years ago. No sign of the driver."

A chill went down his spine. "The driver fled the scene?"

"That's right. Car was stolen. Like I said, he may have been drunk. We don't know. We've got no description so we can't put out a BOLO."

The knot returned to Beau's stomach. The police believed it was an accident, but Beau now knew it wasn't. Cassidy had been a target. It was the second attempt on her life in the last few days. Someone was trying to kill her.

He thought of her hooked up to some machine in intensive care, and prayed whoever had done it hadn't succeeded.

Cassidy opened her eyes. A bag of fluid hung next to the bed, dripping liquid through a needle into her arm. A heart monitor beeped a steady rhythm. That, at least, ought to be good news. But her head was banging as if her brain was trying to escape her skull, and her eyelids weighed a thousand pounds. She reached up, touched the bandage on her forehead with a shaky hand.

She was in the hospital. She was injured but still breathing. The final moments of the crash came flooding back. The pickup slamming into the side of the car; the Lamborghini flying through the air, spinning, rolling, landing in a muddy field. She didn't remember anything after that.

Her mind went to Beau and she tried to imagine what she would say to him. The door was pushed open even as the thought formed, and there he was, so handsome and dear her heart squeezed. His face was lined with worry, his black hair mussed, his gorgeous blue eyes intense.

"Cassidy . . ." He walked toward her, took hold of her hand, and brought it to his lips. "You're going to be okay, honey. You've got a concussion, some bruised ribs, cuts and scratches, but they've moved you out of intensive care into a private room. The doctor says you're going to be all right."

Her eyes burned. Tears welled that she couldn't stop. "I ruined your beautiful car. I wrecked the Lamborghini. I'm so sorry, Beau."

His jaw went iron hard, stretching the narrow scar down the side of his face. "You think I care about the car? I don't give a fuck about the goddamn car! I can buy ten more Lamborghinis if I want them. All I care about is you, baby. I was so worried." He swallowed, glanced away. "I'm just so glad you're going to be okay." He bent and softly kissed her lips. "You just get well, okay? Don't you worry for a second about the frigging car."

She tried to smile, but her lips barely curved. "He was trying to kill me, Beau."

He nodded, looked grim. "Yeah, I figured that out."

The pounding in her head worsened. Her eyes felt gritty, the lids heavy. "The first time . . . the hit-and-run? I thought it was an accident. But it . . . wasn't. We need to tell the . . . police."

"I'll talk to Briscoe, bring him up to speed. We'll figure this out."

She moistened her lips, which felt dry as cotton. Her mind was just as fuzzy. "I'm not . . . not sure telling them is going to change anything."

He squeezed her hand. "We can talk about it later." His worried gaze remained on hers. "The police found your phone. Do you want me to call your dad and your brothers?"

"No . . . please don't. If I'm going to be okay . . . there's no need for them to . . . worry."

"You sure?"

She moved her head in a nod. The pounding increased and she bit back a groan.

He bent and kissed her cheek. "You need to get some sleep. I'll be right here if you need me."

She relaxed. Beau was there. She didn't have to worry. She let her eyelids drift closed. Tomorrow she would feel better, be able to think more clearly. Find a way to keep from getting killed.

As she started to edge into sleep, a final thought occurred. If someone wanted her dead, maybe they wanted Beau dead, too. She had to warn him, tell him before it was too late. But even as the idea took root, it drifted away, her mind sliding into the sweet, pain-free darkness that she had been in before.

Beau looked up to see Linc and Carly standing in the doorway of Cassidy's hospital room. He walked over to join them.

"You spending the night?" Linc asked, though it wasn't really a question.

"I want to be here if she wakes up. The doctor says her memory might be fuzzy for a day or two."

"She got lucky," Linc said. "A concussion, a few bruised ribs, some lacerations. Could have been a whole lot worse."

"I'm glad she was in the Lamborghini. It's built around a carbon fiber monocoque. You know, like a Formula One race car. The driver's in a cage so the weaker parts of the car break first. It allows the energy from the crash to disperse."

"So the rest of the car fails before the cage breaks up."

"Yeah," Beau said, his gaze going to the pale form lying in the bed. "The doctor says they want to make sure the concussion isn't worse than it appears. No swelling on the brain, nothing like that. She might need to stay another day or two, but if she seems okay in the morning, there's a chance they'll release her."

Linc nodded. He clamped a big hand on Beau's shoulder. "Listen, we need to talk. Carly's going to stay here while we grab a cup of coffee."

Beau flicked a last glance at Cassidy, then forced himself to move toward the door. They walked out into the hall and made their way down the corridor to the cafeteria, passing doctors in white coats and nurses in scrubs, hearing the rattle of carts going in and out of hospital rooms. The acrid smell of ammonia burned his nostrils.

As they walked into the cafeteria, weary visitors and family members, some trying to keep their kids under control, wandered among the staff, heading for the food lines or just there for coffee and a break from their worries.

Beau and Linc each grabbed a coffee and made their way over to a table.

"Looks like you've got a problem," Linc said, taking a seat across from him.

"Yeah." His friend was no dummy. Two accidents, both

nearly fatal, weren't accidents at all. Beau took a sip of his coffee, set the paper cup down on the table. "If this wasn't an accident, the hit-and-run wasn't either."

"Someone tried to kill her. You got any idea who it is?"

"We've been digging around, turning up a lot of dirt on a lot of people. One of them's a guy named Malcolm Vaughn. Ever heard of him?"

"I've met him. Owns a company called Equity Advance. Makes high-risk, big-money loans."

"That's him," Beau said.

"I don't know much about him, other than he donates heavily to charity. Gives him a chance to rub elbows with the Dallas elite, drum up business. He was at the Dallas Art Gala last year."

"You and I were both there, but I didn't know who he was back then."

Linc took a sip of his coffee. "So what's your plan?"

Beau leaned back in his chair, blew out a tired breath. "Take Cassidy off the case. Get her out of town, somewhere she'll be safe."

"You could take her out to the ranch. Carly and I are picking out stuff for the new house, so we're staying in the apartment. We'll be in the city for the next two weeks, which leaves the ranch house empty. And Josh is close by if you need him."

Beau remembered the way he'd felt when he'd found out Cassidy had been in a car accident. Terrified she might die. Sick with dread, his stomach knotted, his emotions in turmoil. He was in too deep. The last thing he needed was to spend more time with Cassidy. He needed to distance himself. Protect himself.

But he couldn't let Cassidy down. If she was killed because of him . . .

He closed his eyes for a moment to clear the unwanted thoughts. "Whoever went after her tried to make it look like an accident. I don't think they'll come straight at her. Maybe I could talk to Vaughn, see if I can convince him to back off, leave Cassidy alone."

His phone rang just then. He dug it out, saw the blocked caller ID, pressed the phone against his ear. "Reese."

"What the hell's going on? I just got a call from the office. Chase said he heard about the wreck on the news. Tell me Cassidy's okay."

"Maddox. Good of you to call." There was a faint edge in his voice. He wondered how Maddox had gotten this number, but it didn't seem to be much of a secret anymore. "Cassidy's banged up, got a concussion, but she's going to be all right."

"She was with me at the office just a few hours earlier, met me there looking for intel on Malcolm Vaughn."

"Did she find any?"

"Vaughn's smooth. He's a businessman on the surface, but ruthless underneath. He's a bad dude to have for an enemy. That's what I told her. What happened wasn't an accident—you get that, right?"

"I get it. Trying to figure out what to do about it."

"Get her out of town, take her somewhere safe—or I will."

Beau straightened. "I'll take care of Cassidy."

"You better. I just got into Phoenix, but I'll come back if you need my help."

"Good to know," Beau said darkly, not happy to find out Cassidy had gone to see Maddox without telling him about it. He tamped down a fresh surge of jealousy that was completely unlike him. "You find out anything that could help us?"

"I told her about Vaughn's man, Clifford Jennings. He takes care of things for Vaughn. If Vaughn wanted Cassidy dead, Jennings is the guy who'd make the arrangements. That's all I know. If I hear anything more I'll call you."

"Appreciate it."

"She's a good lady, Beau. Keep her safe."

The words hit him hard. "I will," he said gruffly, and no matter the emotional toll he'd have to pay, he meant it. He wasn't letting anyone hurt Cassidy again.

He hung up the phone and turned back to Linc. "That was Jason Maddox. He's a PI and bail enforcement. Works with Cassidy at Maximum Security. He's afraid they'll come after her again."

"You realize it might not just be Cassidy they're after."

"I've considered it." He was no dummy, either. "I think they figure if my PI is out of the way, I'll give up the search."

"Will you?"

"My father is dead. Nothing is going to bring him back. I won't risk getting Cassidy killed, too."

"Now you're being smart. The trouble is, it might be too late."

He nodded. "Yeah, I've considered that, too."

"I realize you've been off the streets for a while—we both left that life behind years ago. But knowing how to handle yourself isn't something you forget. You still got that old Browning forty-five you used to shoot out at the dump when we were kids?"

Beau smiled faintly at the memory of their high school days. The smile faded as his mind shifted to the attempted robbery, the two years Linc had spent in prison, while Beau's dad had been able to wipe his underage record clean.

"I traded the Browning a few years back for a Glock seventeen. Haven't been on the shooting range for a while."

"Good weapon. As I recall, you used to be a crack shot."

Beau didn't deny it. When he took on a challenge, he didn't stop till he'd mastered it. Same with martial arts. Same with racing cars. "You think I should start carrying?"

"You've got a concealed permit, right? Wouldn't hurt to be prepared. Figure out what's going on. Arm yourself and take care of your woman."

A muscle jerked in Beau's cheek. "She isn't my woman."

"Isn't she? I saw you in that hospital room. I've known you too long, bro. Don't kid yourself."

Beau made no reply. He'd brought Cassidy into this mess. Until it was finished, she was his responsibility. There was no changing that. But when it was over, it was over. There was no changing that, either.

He pushed up from his chair. "I need to get back."

Linc stood up, too. "Think about what I said, and if you need anything, just ask."

Whatever happened, Beau knew Linc would be there for him. If the situation were reversed, he'd be there for Linc. It had been that way since high school, and that hadn't changed.

As they walked back down the hall, worry dogged him. He needed to get Cassidy somewhere safe.

Beau had a bad feeling it wasn't going to be that easy.

Clifford Jennings stood on the opposite side of the desk from his boss. Mal Vaughn wasn't happy at the moment.

He looked down at the society page of the Thursday *Dallas Morning News* spread open in front of him. Vaughn picked it up and started reading.

"'A Lamborghini owned by former Texas race-car driver Beaumont Reese, valued in the hundreds of thousands of dollars, was involved in an unsolved two-car collision on Wednesday evening outside Kaufman.'"

Vaughn flicked Cliff a dark look over the top of the paper, started reading again. "'The female driver of the borrowed vehicle, identified as Cassidy Maryann Jones, was taken to a nearby hospital for treatment and released the following day. Police are searching for the driver of a white Chevy pickup found a few miles away. According to authorities, the man, who fled the scene, is wanted for questioning in the accident. Both Reese and Ms. Jones, a Dallas private investigator, refused to comment on the incident.'"

Vaughn flicked the paper, carefully closed it, folded it, and set it down on top of his desk. "You said you could handle this. It doesn't look handled to me."

"The guy I hired is reliable. I don't know what went wrong. Whatever happened, he'll take care of it."

"You think Reese and Jones will believe the attempt was an accident?"

Not after the first time, which his boss didn't know about. Cliff knew better than to lie. "No. Franco botched his first effort, too. I'll talk to him, see if he can come up with something that'll work."

Vaughn's mouth thinned. "Don't bother. He's out. I don't have time for second-raters. Call The Spear. He's a professional. He'll get it done."

"The Spear doesn't take multiple jobs this close together in the same area—it's too high risk. He's already made an exception. He won't do it again."

"Make it worth his while. Offer him double his normal fee, more if you have to. Pay him enough, and he'll take care of it. Or should I say *them*. This has gotten out of hand. I can't risk Reese and Jones finding something that could lead back to the client."

Cliff didn't argue. *Client* meant investor. He had no idea who Vaughn's investors were and he didn't want to know.

Turning, he walked out of the office. He'd make the call, phone the number of the throwaway used by the professional hit man who called himself The Spear. Cliff had never set eyes on the man, had only heard his voice, distorted by a digital synthesizer. There was no guarantee the man would pick up, but Cliff fervently prayed he would.

If he took the job, the hit would get done, but not without plenty of preparation. It was the way the man worked, the reason he was so successful. The reason he charged a small fortune.

Cliff wondered about Vaughn's motives. Jess Milford had gotten what he deserved, coming to Cliff about the arson, threatening to tell the police what he'd found out if he didn't get paid. But the senator had been one of Vaughn's customers, a borrower who always repaid his debts, in one form or another.

Cliff wondered what Stewart Reese had done to get himself killed.

Chapter Twenty-Four

For the last three days, since her release from the hospital, Cassidy had been lying in bed in Beau's guest room. She was slowly going crazy. She glanced toward the door. Her black-haired, blue-eyed prison guard was gone, at least for the moment. He'd be back, she knew, making sure she stayed in bed and got her rest.

Not today. It was nearly noon and she had too darn much to do. Easing off the mattress, ignoring the soreness in her ribs and the swirling in her head, she made her way to the bathroom and turned on the shower. She hissed at a sharp stab of pain as she stripped off her long cotton nightgown and stepped beneath the warm, rejuvenating spray.

She took her time, washed her hair twice just to have an excuse to stay in longer. Soaping herself one last time, beginning to feel like her old self again, she gasped as the shower door flew open, letting in a draft of cold air and shooting out a jet of water. She bit back a grin as Beau mopped the wetness off his face.

"What are you doing?" he asked. "You aren't supposed to be up for another day."

"Too bad. I'm up and I'm staying up. Now if you don't mind . . ."

For the first time, he seemed to realize she was standing in front of him naked, warm water trailing over the tips of her breasts, cascading into her navel, sliding through the dark curls at the apex of her legs.

Beau's gaze ran the length of her body and a familiar hot gleam came into his eyes. He cleared his throat. "Sorry." Hurriedly, he closed the shower door.

"I'll be out in a second," she said.

"Are you sure you're okay? You aren't dizzy or anything?"

"I'm okay, better by the minute." She considered inviting him to join her but as achy as she still was, that might be pushing her luck.

"Call me if you need me. I'll be just outside the bathroom door."

He was worried about her. He'd been endlessly patient and unbelievably gentle. She wouldn't have guessed he could be so sweet. Cassidy finally gave in and turned off the water, climbed out of the shower and toweled herself dry. She combed the tangles out of her hair, then had mercy on her prison guard/nurse, wrapped the towel around herself, went over and pulled open the door.

"I'm okay, all right? No dizziness, nothing." She gave him a big, wide smile. "See? I'm fine."

Beau glanced away. "As soon as you're dressed, we need to talk. I'll be in my study."

She didn't argue. They had plenty to discuss—like how to keep from getting killed.

Beau had told her he'd brought Will Egan and his team back to the house, had Will beef up security to the max. There were men around the property 24/7, but that couldn't go on forever.

Cassidy partially dried her hair, leaving it damp enough to dry in soft curls around her shoulders. She took a pair of stretch jeans off a hanger in the closet, then sucked in a breath at a fresh jolt of pain as she pulled them on. She found a yellow cashmere scoop-neck sweater, gritted her teeth, and eased it on over her head.

Breathing a sigh of relief, she glanced down at her feet. The sneakers could wait. There was only so much torture a person could endure at one time.

Padding barefoot down the hall, she found Beau seated at his desk in the study. His head came up as she walked in, and his gaze ran over her once more, came to rest on her feet.

"I can't believe your bare feet are turning me on." He glanced up. "You drive me crazy. You know that?"

A little thrill went through her. She thought of his beautiful body, the ladder of muscle across his flat belly, his wide shoulders and hard-muscled chest. Yesterday he'd worked out with his martial arts trainer, then boxed with a sparring partner in his home gym behind the garage.

She wondered if there was a way to make love without hurting her ribs, imagined how good it would feel, and desire rose so hot and sweet her mouth watered.

"We need to talk," Beau said again, breaking the moment. "You're out of bed, so I'll assume you're feeling up to a change of location. I'm taking you out of town, a place you'll be safe."

She should have seen this coming. She was shaking her head even before he finished the sentence. "We need to stay in Dallas, Beau. We're starting to put things together, figure things out. That's why they came after me. There's a good chance they'll come after you, too."

"I know that. Cain's offered us the use of his ranch. We can bring in security. Deke Logan's a friend of his, former special ops. He's one of the best security guys around and he's got a great team. Plus Josh is there. Former Marine sniper. We wouldn't have to worry."

"Listen to me, Beau. I realize you're trying to protect me, but we can't hide forever. As soon as we come back to Dallas, I'll be a target again. A guy like Vaughn has plenty of patience. He'll just wait us out. We need to stay here and deal with this."

"Are we sure it's Vaughn?"

"Everything we've come up with so far points to him."

"All right, so I'll hire another detective to handle the case. Cain worked with a guy named Ross Townsend when Carly was having trouble. Townsend's good."

"So am I. And I'm not about to trust my life to someone else. We need to stay on this, keep working the case ourselves."

Beau leaned back in his chair, released a slow breath. "I had a feeling that's what you were going to say. I've thought about it, tried to look at this from different angles. Are you sure you don't want to take some time, try to get a handle on this thing before we go at it again full speed?"

She moved around to his side of the desk, stood close enough to get a whiff of his sexy cologne. "I'm dead sure. I don't want to be looking over my shoulder for the next five years. I want these guys dealt with. Which reminds me—did you talk to Detective Briscoe?"

Beau looked up at her. "I called him. He said he'd get in touch with the Kaufman police and the Dallas PD. But unless there's proof the hit-and-run and the crash are related—"

"Which there isn't. The only way the police are getting involved is if we find the proof they need. You asked me once if I wanted out. Now I'm asking you. We both know the risks. If you want out—"

"No way!" Temper sparked in his eyes. "I brought you into this. I'm not letting you deal with it alone." Beau reached across his desk, picked up the semiautomatic pistol she hadn't noticed lying there. "This belongs to me. Glock seventeen, nine mil. I'm a damn good shot and I'm permitted to carry. You want to stay in Dallas, we'll stay. But from now on, we'll be prepared."

Beau stood in front of the whiteboard Cassidy had created. He wasn't a professional investigator, but he'd read enough true crime novels and watched enough cop shows to be able to contribute to her efforts.

"All right, we've got the victims—Milford and Senator Reese." She stood at the board, one hand on her hip, the other clenching a yellow pencil, her gaze fixed on the pair of photos spaced apart at the top. "In one way or another, we think Vaughn is connected to both men."

On the Internet she'd found a photo of Malcolm Vaughn at a charity benefit, printed it, and tacked it up between Milford and his father.

"Under Vaughn we have Clifford Jennings," Beau said. "Vaughn's right-hand man." Cassidy had found a police mug shot from ten years back. Jennings had been twenty-four years old at the time. The photo showed a man of average height and weight, with tight blond curls pushed up by a headband. He'd been arrested for forging checks and promoting prostitution, meaning he'd been a pimp. Jennings had served two years in the Federal Detention Center in Houston. No arrests since his release.

Beau held up a line drawing he'd sketched because they didn't have a photo. "This represents the guy who tried to kill you." He pinned the drawing up on the board. "Assuming it was the same man both times."

"It was him," she said. "Two old cars, both of them barely running. He's getting them somewhere. A used-car lot or a junkyard someplace."

"Lot of used-car lots in Dallas," Beau said. "Not as many junkyards, but still . . ."

"It's a place to look. Maybe someone will remember the pickup."

"It was stolen, so even if they do, likely they won't admit it."

Frustration turned her mouth down at the corners. Beau wanted to see those pretty lips curve into a soft, warm smile.

"For the moment, why don't we concentrate on Vaughn?" he said. "He's the guy running the show."

Cassidy perked up. "All right. If we're starting with Vaughn, we need to know more about him. We've found the basics—divorced, never remarried, no kids. He lives in a million-plus condo in Turtle Creek. Started Equity Advance five years ago. But we need more than that."

"A lot more," Beau said.

"We need to know who he talks to, who he associates with. If we could put a bug on his car, we'd know where he goes. Maybe we could even get an audio device inside—"

"You're kidding, right? That's highly illegal."

She tossed him a look. "So's murder."

"Good point."

"So how do we get access to his vehicle?" She tapped the yellow pencil against her cheek. "The parking garage at his office has cameras all over, and way too many security people to get in and out without being seen. I know that development in Turtle Creek. It's gated, patrolled. Be like getting in and out of Fort Knox. We need some other way."

Beau ran the notion around in his head. "Linc mentioned Vaughn's a philanthropist. You found his photo at a charity event. Linc says Vaughn uses his high-society contacts to promote his loan business. Might be able to use the charity angle somehow."

Cassidy concentrated, worrying her bottom lip. Since her release from the hospital, she'd been spending her nights in the bedroom next to his. He hadn't touched her. She was recovering, healing. Even thinking about having sex was a betrayal.

She moved, shifting her thick mane of curls, and he went hard. *Damn.* He'd vowed to keep his distance, get his emotions back in check, but staying away from her was killing him.

"It's February," she said. "There's a couple of big events going on this month. The Heart Association Benefit and the Children's Home Valentine's Masquerade Ball. I saw them mentioned in the paper. Both are happening tonight. If he's planning to attend one of them, we might be able to get to his vehicle while it's parked in the lot."

"How do we find out if he's on either guest list?"

She smiled. "I'll find out."

"What, you're going to hack into their online system?"

"Of course not. I'm going to call and ask."

Cassidy found the website for tickets to the black-tie Heart Association Benefit and called the number. A volunteer answered the phone. "How may I help you?"

"My name is Maryann Jones. I was supposed to buy tickets to the benefit tonight for a friend, but I think he might have already purchased them. Can you check for me?"

"Of course. How do you spell your friend's name?"

"V-A-U-G-H-N."

The line went silent as the woman checked. "I don't see the name anywhere on the list. Shall I get you the tickets?"

"I think I'd better wait, make sure I got the information right. Thanks so much for your help." Cassidy ended the call and went to the page for the Children's Home Valentine's Masquerade Ball.

She used the same routine, but this time the woman refused to give her the information. "This isn't an open event," the woman said. "There's a very exclusive guest list."

"The person I'm calling for is a friend of Beau Reese. I'm sure Mr. Reese is on your list." She had no idea if Beau was on the guest list. He was a celebrity with plenty of money. She was just hoping his name would be enough to get the information.

"Beau Reese? The famous race-car driver?"

"That's him."

"Well, of course Mr. Reese would be welcome to attend. I'm happy to check, see if his friend has tickets. What's the name?"

"Malcolm Vaughn."

"Hang on a minute." She went off-line, then came back on a few minutes later. "Yes, it looks like Mr. Vaughn has already purchased two tickets for the event."

Cassidy shot a fist into the air. "Then I'll need two tickets for Mr. Reese."

"I'm afraid we only have VIP tickets still available." Figuring Beau could afford the extravagant price the woman rattled off, and the money was going to a good cause, she reserved two tickets. But she had to call back with a credit card within the hour to hold the reservation.

"Mr. Reese would prefer his attendance be kept anonymous," she finished.

"Of course," the woman said.

Cassidy ended the call. The good news was it was a masquerade ball. They'd be wearing costumes and masks, which would cover up the bruises on her face and allow them to move around freely. It couldn't be more perfect. Vaughn would never even know they were there.

The bad news was, since it was a Valentine's ball, not a Halloween party, the theme was romantic couples. Beau would not be thrilled. Cassidy took a deep breath, determined to convince him.

Chapter Twenty-Five

Beau was in the kitchen making sandwiches for lunch when he looked up to see Cassidy walk excitedly into the room.

"We got lucky. Vaughn's going to the Children's Home Masquerade Ball tonight. Unfortunately, the only tickets available are VIP, which cost a fortune, but I think it would be worth it. Plus it's a donation—tax deductible."

He set the mayonnaise jar down on the kitchen counter. "Tax deductible, huh? So how much of a deduction am I going to get?"

She bit her lip, which made him want to kiss her. "Seven thousand dollars."

He shrugged. "Not too bad, considering it's for charity."

"Apiece."

He laughed. "I bet no one's ever called you a cheap date."

Cassidy practically danced. Fortunately for his libido, her pretty feet were now in a pair of sneakers. "So are you okay with this?"

"Where do you plan to get the surveillance equipment?"

"My office. I've got some stuff there, plus the guys always have a stash of interesting paraphernalia. Chase pretends not to know about it. I should be able to find something. We can stop on the way to the costume shop."

The costume shop. Beau inwardly groaned. Dressing up in some garb that made him look like an idiot was the last thing he wanted. But bringing down Vaughn countered any hesitation he had.

"Fine, get the tickets, but I'm not wearing a pair of those ridiculous tights. I'm not dressing up as a court jester or Henry the Eighth, or any guy who went out in public with his privates on full display. We need to get that straight right now."

Cassidy laughed. "Okay, no tights." She glanced down at the fly of his jeans. "Though you do have a very nice package."

Beau's gaze followed hers and he actually felt himself blush.

"No tights," Cassidy said, still grinning. "I need to pay for the tickets; then we have to get going. Finding the right costume might take a little time."

Beau pulled out his wallet, slid out his American Express card and held it out to her. He caught her wrist when she reached for it. "Are you sure you're up to this? It's only been a few days since you were lying in a hospital bed."

"True enough. But since I don't care for a repeat performance, I don't have much choice. Besides, I'm not going alone, and we won't have to stay very long. As soon as we get the bugs on his car, we're out of there."

"How do we find out what he's driving?"

"Already got it. Found it in the DMV records before I made the calls."

"Hacking again?"

"I didn't have to hack. Digging up information is what I do. It's all out there. You just need to know where to look."

"So what's Vaughn driving?"

"White 2016 Mercedes S550 coupe."

"Nice car."

"Not cheap, that's for sure." She looked away. "Not nearly as much as a Lamborghini."

"Hey, take it easy. I called the insurance company. You

can help me pick out a new one after this is over." The minute the words were out of his mouth, Beau regretted them. When this was over, it would be time to end things between them. It was the way it had to be.

To take his mind off the inevitable, he grabbed the lunch plates off the counter, each with a roast beef sandwich, a handful of potato chips, and a dill pickle. He set them down on the kitchen table along with glasses of sweet iced tea.

Cassidy sat across from him and they both dug into their meals. When they finished, she picked up the plates. "So . . . what about Sir Lancelot?" she asked with a mischievous gleam in her eyes.

Beau fought a smile and just shook his head. This was one argument Cassidy Jones wasn't going to win.

They were climbing into the BMW for their trip into the city when Beau's cell phone started to ring. He flipped it open but didn't recognize the number, held the phone to his ear. "Reese."

"Hello, Beau." A woman's voice floated over the line. "This is Emily Watson, Senator Watson's wife. You probably don't remember me, but—"

"Actually, I do. My father introduced us a few years back at a chamber of commerce ribbon-cutting ceremony he and I both happened to be attending."

"That's right. I got your number from Charlotte. I hope you don't mind."

"Of course not. What can I do for you, Mrs. Watson?"

"This is a difficult time for me, I'm afraid. Were you aware my husband died almost a month ago?"

"I'm sorry, I didn't know. You have my sympathies."

"Thank you. I'd like to talk to you, Beau . . . if you could find the time. Charlotte told me you were investigating your father's death. I don't know for certain, but there's a chance I have information that might be important."

His brain went on alert. Emily Watson's husband had been a sitting Texas state senator, a colleague of his dad's. Maybe she knew something that could lead them to the answers they needed.

"I'd be more than happy to meet with you, Mrs. Watson." *The sooner the better.* "Would tomorrow work?"

"It's just Emily, and tomorrow would work very well. I take the children to church in the morning, but we'll be home by eleven."

"Eleven o'clock then. What's your address?"

She rattled off a house number on Binkley Avenue in University Park. "You know how to get there?"

"I'll find you," Beau said. "I'll see you tomorrow." The call ended and he turned to Cassidy.

"We might have just caught a break. We've got a meeting with Emily Watson, Senator Watson's wife, tomorrow at eleven A.M. She says she might have something on my father's murder."

"Wow. That could be good."

"Emily says her husband died about a month ago. It would have been in the papers, but I don't remember reading about it."

Cassidy frowned. "I think I remember seeing something on the news."

"His wife didn't say how he died. Maybe he'd been sick."

"Maybe. Then again, seems like the body count keeps rising."

Beau felt a chill at the back of his neck. "I guess we'll find out tomorrow."

One thing he'd learned—a helluva lot could happen between today and tomorrow.

* * *

They had a jillion things to do to get ready for the masquerade ball. While Beau stayed in the car to keep watch for anything that might be suspicious, Cassidy went into her office to get the surveillance equipment they needed.

Although it was Saturday, the office was humming. Connie, who took Sundays and Mondays off, came out from behind her oak desk and pulled Cassidy into a hug.

"Oh, you poor child. We've all been worried sick."

"I'm okay." Cassidy hugged her back. "Just remember the ribs."

"Oh, damn, I forgot. How you doin', girl?"

She shrugged. "I'm stiff and sore, but I'll be fine in a couple more days." Jase was still in Arizona. Ford was out, but Rome and Lissa were there. Her fellow investigators had called her at the hospital, called every day since to see how she was doing.

They knew she was staying with Beau. She had a hunch they were dying to meet him, but chances were good he was only passing through her life on his way somewhere else, so the introductions could wait.

She ignored a little pang in her heart as she walked over to Rome, who stood next to Lissa. Romeo Romero was a six-foot-tall, black-haired, dark-eyed, überhandsome Latino. Lissa was a tall, slender blonde. For months, the pair seemed to be fighting a mutual attraction neither would admit. Cassidy wondered how much longer the denial would last.

"Hey, lady," Rome said, bending to brush a kiss on her cheek. "Glad to see you're back on your feet."

Lissa very gently hugged her. "I'm so glad you're okay. We were all really worried."

"It could have been worse, that's for sure."

"They haven't found the other driver?" Lissa asked.

"Not yet." They didn't know the full story and she didn't have time to go into it now. "Listen, guys. I need some help. Rome, I know how good you are at this kind of thing. I need to get into a locked vehicle without setting off any alarms. Think you could help me with that?"

He flashed her a bad-boy grin. "Oh, yeah. I have exactly what you need—but you can't tell anyone where you got it."

Which meant it was something illegal. Rome had been a gang member before he went straight. Luckily he'd gotten out before he'd been arrested.

He dug into his bottom drawer, came out with a flat black box about five inches square. He explained how the device worked and Cassidy started grinning.

"Definite jail time if you get caught using this little beauty," she said.

"You can say that again. In the wrong hands, it's bad news for honest citizens like us."

"I'm not using it on an honest citizen, and I won't get caught. Thanks, Rome." She left him with Lissa, hoping the sparks between them wouldn't set the room on fire, tried not to think about Beau and how much it was going to hurt when he was gone.

Once she reached her locker in the storage room, she dropped what she needed into the canvas bag she kept inside, along with the device Rome had lent her, and left the office, making her way out to where Beau waited in the BMW.

"No trouble?" she asked as she slid into the passenger seat.

"Haven't seen a thing. You get what you needed?"

Cassidy unzipped the bag on the floor between her feet. "You aren't going to believe this." She pulled the small black box out first. "This little devil gets us into a car without the alarm going off. It steals the code to the key pad and unlocks the door."

"How's it work?"

She handed him the box. "An RF transmitter finds the remote entry code and sends it to the locking system. You just touch the vehicle with the device to make it work. The transmitter uses very low power so it doesn't trigger any nearby cars."

Beau whistled. "So you can get into a car and steal what's inside without anyone knowing you were there. The dome light is going to be a problem."

She grinned. "It shuts down the system so the light won't go on."

Beau handed back the box. "Does it let the thief start the damn engine, too?"

"Unfortunately, yes."

"Damn. You're talking to a guy who owns a couple of six-figure sports cars so that's not good news. What other illegal devices are in that bag?"

She smiled as she pulled out a small circular disk. "Having this little toy isn't actually illegal. It depends on how you use it."

"Like we'll be using it tonight?"

She shrugged.

"What is it and how does it work?"

"It's a battery operated, motion sensitive, magnetic GPS. We stick it under the car bumper. Lasts about twelve hours of driving time before the battery goes dead."

"So we can follow the vehicle on the computer."

"That's right. Kind of like Google Maps. We can get the addresses of wherever he goes."

"I'm likin' that."

"Me, too." Pulling a tiny black plastic square out of the bag, she held it up. "And last but not least, we have one of my favorites. A wireless, voice-activated audio transmitter.

You program it by sending a text to the SIM card in the unit, then you call it from your cell phone and you can listen to what's happening within thirty feet of the device. No rings, no beeps, no clicks to alarm the target. And there's no distance limitation because you're listening on your phone. You can call from anywhere."

Beau took the device from her fingers and studied it. "If we hide this inside his car, we can listen to his conversations, phone calls, or with passengers."

"That's right. It sends a signal to my cell whenever audio is being transmitted."

"I've got to admit, I'm impressed. There's a chance I'll wind up back in jail, but it's still an impressive bag of tricks."

Cassidy stuck the last device back into the bag and checked her watch. "We need to get over to the costume shop. The afternoon's almost gone."

The Beamer fired up as Cassidy clicked her seat belt into place. "So how about Robin Hood? I could go as Maid Marian."

Beau flicked her a glare in answer. Cassidy chuckled as he made a final check of their surroundings and pulled out of the parking lot. Her humor slowly faded. They were going to the party to try to catch a killer.

The trip to Floyd's Antiques and Costumes no longer seemed like fun.

Chapter Twenty-Six

The charity ball at the exclusive Westhaven Country Club was in full swing by the time Beau drove up in front of the entrance. A young, white-jacketed parking valet jerked open the Beamer door while another young man swarmed around the hood of the car to the passenger side to help Cassidy out.

The weather was rotten. A fine, damp mist hung in the air, and clouds obscured the moon. The dampness made the roads slick and seeped into Beau's costume, but the moonless night would provide cover as he moved through darkness.

He'd been careful to ensure they weren't followed. Will Egan and his security team hadn't spotted any unfamiliar vehicles in the area, so he wasn't expecting trouble. But Cassidy hadn't either, the night she'd driven out to the cemetery.

Beau checked his surroundings as he stepped out of the BMW, which blended in well with the Cadillacs, Jaguars, and Mercedes being valet-parked in the lot half a block from the main entrance. He'd done a quick drive-through and spotted what appeared to be Vaughn's white S550 coupe before he'd pulled up in front of the club. He'd check the registration when he got inside the car to be certain it was Vaughn's.

He rounded the car to where Cassidy waited, nervous energy sliding through him as he offered her his arm and they started up the front-porch steps toward the two-story redbrick building. Six huge white Corinthian columns spread across the front, and yellow light gleamed from every window.

Heading for the arched white double doors at the entrance, they joined the reception line behind a couple dressed as Romeo and Juliet. *Romantic couples* was the theme, which Cassidy had neglected to mention until they got to the costume shop.

Another couple wore Peter Pan and Wendy outfits. Beau bit back a grin at the poor SOB, who looked ridiculous and downright embarrassed in his ugly green tights—no question his wife had insisted he wear them.

Beau was dressed as a pirate, in a full-sleeved white shirt and black breeches tucked into knee-high jack boots. The breeches fit like a second skin, which Cassidy seemed to be enjoying a little too much. The good news was a jerkin— similar to an unbuttoned long leather vest—covered the Glock in the clip holster on the belt around his waist. A black satin head scarf covered most of his hair, and both of them had their masks in place.

Dressed as a tavern wench, in a short, black gathered skirt, an embroidered, off-the-shoulder blouse, and a red corset that cinched in her waist and shoved up her full breasts, Cassidy looked delicious. Exactly the distraction they might need.

After a heated argument about who was going to plant the bugs in and on Malcolm Vaughn's car—definitely him— Cassidy had grudgingly agreed. Mainly because he'd told her he wasn't going to the damn ball any other way.

She might be a private investigator, but she was still not completely healed. He'd noticed her quick intake of breath more than once when something jostled her ribs. He had a hunch she was still fighting an occasional bout of dizziness.

Once inside, he handed the computer-generated tickets to the matron behind the table, dressed in a medieval costume, her heavy breasts spilling over the barely there blue velvet bodice.

The woman smiled. "Welcome to the Children's Home Valentine's Ball." She glanced down at his tickets. "Oh, I see you're one of our VIPs. You'll find a table right in front of the podium reserved for our most special patrons."

Drawing any sort of attention was the last thing he wanted, but with luck, they'd be finished and on their way by the time dinner was served.

"Thank you." Beau urged Cassidy toward the doors leading into the reception room in front of the main ballroom.

"Well, we're in," she said as they walked into the big open chamber.

Beau glanced down at her, his gaze landing on the soft mounds shoved up like a feast for a king—or in this case, pirate king. He felt a surge of heat and jerked his eyes away before the breeches he had jammed himself into betrayed his lusty thoughts.

"Let's order a drink and mingle," he said. The reception room was decorated for Valentine's Day, with bouquets of pink roses on linen-draped, stand-up tables, pink and red crepe paper swirled among red hearts and cupids. Valentine's Day was still a way off, but the guests didn't seem to care.

They walked up to one of the bars and ordered drinks, champagne for Cassidy, Cutty and water for him. Another tavern wench and pirate couple stood a few feet away, the man with a patch over one eye and a head full of dreadlocks that would give Jack Sparrow a run for his money.

Among the reasons they had chosen their outfits was the hope other couples would be dressed the same way, providing even more anonymity. A third pirate and wench duo stood on the far side of the room.

"So far we're right on track," he said.

Cassidy glanced down at her wristwatch. "We've got twenty minutes before they call us in to dinner."

"Let's keep moving. Five more minutes and I'm heading for the men's room." More precisely, to a door down the hall that led outside the building.

As head of marketing for Texas American, he had been to Westhaven a number of times. Plenty of business done on the golf course. He didn't play often enough to be very good, but he had a natural knack for sports. He could play to a twelve handicap and at least not embarrass himself.

They moved toward one of the high tables and set down their drinks, smiling and flirting with each other as if they wanted to be left alone, which they did. Even with the head scarf and mask, there was a chance he'd be recognized.

The group was large and boisterous. Two hundred costumed couples in Roman togas, medieval garb, uniforms, hoop skirts, and pretty much any costume you could think of. It was impossible to tell if one of the costumed men was Malcolm Vaughn.

As the minutes ticked past, his nerves kicked up another notch. On the surface Cassidy seemed relaxed, but Beau figured she was nearly as edgy as he was.

Another minute passed. Leaning down, he whispered in her ear. "I'm heading out."

She looked up at him, whispered, "I'll phone if there's trouble."

His cell, in a case on his belt, was set to vibrate. He nodded, turned, and walked quietly away.

When he'd driven in, he'd left the surveillance devices in a paper bag under a row of hedges at the edge of the parking lot. He walked down the hall toward the restrooms and spotted the back door, which led to a cement walkway out to the golf course. Once outside, he ducked off the path toward the hedgerow at the edge of the lot, bent and retrieved the small paper bag.

Staying in the shadows as much as possible, he kept walking. The Mercedes was parked up ahead, two more rows and off to the right. The clouds were growing thicker and darker, the wind coming up, blowing trash and leaves across the lot. As he neared the vehicle, he took a pair of latex gloves out of the bag and pulled them on.

The Mercedes loomed ahead. Beau prayed the car actually belonged to Malcolm Vaughn.

Cassidy took a sip of champagne and continued her conversation with an older woman in a silver wig and an eighteenth-century gold brocade gown spread over wide panniers. Her husband wore a curly wig and gold satin knee breeches.

"Costume parties are so much fun," Cassidy said, needing to mingle so she wouldn't stand out.

"Oh, yes. And this one's for such a good cause. Roger was dead set against wearing a wig, but I think it makes him look handsome."

Roger's lips curled into a sneer. He merely grunted.

"Now, dear, don't be a spoilsport." The woman, Opal, looked to Cassidy for help.

She managed to glance at the dainty gold wristwatch that had belonged to her mother. Time was ticking away. Beau had ten minutes to install the devices, get back to the front door, and have his car brought up. She would meet him there and they could leave before the guests were seated for dinner.

She forced herself to concentrate. "I think the wig makes

you look very distinguished, Roger. After all, men like
Washington and Jefferson wore them, all the great men who
formed our country. What could be more distinguished
than that?"

Roger looked mollified. He stood a little straighter.
"Maybe you're right. I hadn't thought of it quite that way."

"Oh, look, dear! The Denbys are here. Let's go say
hello." Opal straightened her gown and the panniers holding it out on the sides, and took his arm. "It was nice talking
to you, Maryann," she said as they wandered away.

Since standing there by herself wasn't a good idea,
Cassidy glanced around in search of someone else to talk to
until it was time to meet Beau. She took a step, bumped into
a man dressed in a long white toga next to a woman simi-
larly garbed. Matching laurel wreaths crowned their heads.
Like a number of partygoers, they had removed their masks.

Cassidy's stomach dropped out when she recognized
Malcolm Vaughn.

Beau pressed the black box against the door to the Mercedes, heard the click of the locks, and pulled open the door.
As he slid into the driver's seat, he withdrew a small pen-
light, opened the glove box, found the registration and held
it under the light.

A sigh of relief whispered out. The car belonged to
Vaughn.

Beau put the registration back where it belonged and
closed the glove box, panned the light around under the
dash and found a spot to place the audio listening device.
He made sure it was firmly attached, glad he was wearing
the latex gloves.

After one last check, to be sure the device would remain
in place, he eased out of the car, quietly closed the door, and

shoved the black box into his waistband, out of sight beneath the leather jerkin.

The tendons in his neck felt tight, his nerves on edge. He checked, didn't see anyone coming. Time to attach the GPS. Moving toward the rear of the Mercedes, he set the paper bag on the ground, took out the GPS transmitter, bent and stuck the device under the rear bumper, then checked to make sure it was securely in place. He stripped off the gloves and stuck them in the bag, took a last look at his handiwork and started to rise.

"What do you think you're doing?"

Adrenaline spiked through him as he spotted a big pair of shoes. Nudging the paper bag under the car, he rose to his feet. The parking lot security guard was tall and brawny. Suspicion darkened his features.

Beau flashed him a smile. "My girlfriend and I got into a fight. I needed some air, so I came out here. I wanted to cool off—you know what I mean?" He tipped his head toward the redbrick building with the white columns out front. "Unfortunately I can't just leave her here so I've got to get back." He started past the guard, but the man didn't budge.

"Let me see some ID."

His breathing went shallow. He could take the man down if he had to. With the mask still over his face, no way could the guard identify him. But it wouldn't be easy and it could pose all kinds of problems he and Cassidy did not need.

"I don't have my driver's license on me," he said. He glanced down. "Not much room in these breeches. My girlfriend has my wallet in her purse." He managed to come up with a good-buddy grin. "That's why I have to get back. She's got my money too. Hopefully she's over her tiff by now."

The guard looked him over head to foot. The guy was three inches taller than Beau and probably seventy pounds heavier. Taking him down would be a definite challenge, but he wasn't about to let the man call the police.

"What'd you do to piss her off?" the guard asked.

Beau shrugged. "She caught me looking at a little blonde with big tits. My girlfriend's the jealous type, you know? She's kind of insecure, doesn't think her boobs are big enough." *That was a laugh.* Cassidy had the perkiest, prettiest breasts he'd ever seen.

The guard didn't relax. He tipped his head toward the Mercedes. "That your car?"

Beau's body shifted into alert mode. "Nah. Too rich for my blood. I was just checking it out. Maybe one of these days I can afford something like that."

The guard didn't buy it—this was a very exclusive affair.

"My girlfriend's got all the money," Beau added. "Makes it easier to overlook her bad temper. Plus she's good in bed."

The guard laughed out loud. "Go on back," he said, still chuckling. "Have a nice evening."

"Thanks." Beau waved over his shoulder as he walked away.

"Ms. Jones. It's nice to see you again." Malcolm Vaughn stood regally in front of the table, the perfect image of the emperor he was pretending to be.

"Mr. Vaughn. I'm . . . umm . . . a little surprised you recognized me." *What about Beau? Had Vaughn recognized him, too?* Beneath her skirt, the little .380 felt comforting in the holster strapped to her thigh.

"Mal will do," he said. "This is Ashley Stanfield. Her father is one of my clients. Ashley kindly agreed to accompany me tonight."

"Nice to meet you, Ashley."

"You as well."

Vaughn glanced over Cassidy's head, searching the

room. "This is a couples event. I can't imagine you're here by yourself. Should I assume you're here with Beau?"

She had to brazen it out, pray Beau would wait and not come looking for her before she could manage to make her escape. "That's right. He's quite a philanthropist. Beau especially loves giving to charities that help children." Which according to the information she had dug up on him, was actually true.

"So where is he? It's rude to leave a lovely young woman alone for so long."

"He was . . . umm . . . feeling a little unwell. He went to the men's room. I'm sure he'll be back in a few more minutes."

"Would you like another glass of champagne? That one looks a little flat." His expression said he knew she hadn't been drinking it. She didn't want him speculating on why they had come.

She took a sip. "No, it's fine." She turned to Mal's date, who was about her same age, a good deal younger than Vaughn. "I like your costumes," she said. "A Roman emperor and his lady. I bet Mal selected the outfits."

She figured he saw himself that way, as a ruler of men, emperor of his world. Ashley flashed him a worshipful glance, clearly hoping to become more than just friends.

Cassidy had to admit, with his classically handsome features and light brown hair, Mal Vaughn was an attractive man. Attractive, but a trifle too metrosexual for Cassidy's taste, which ran more to alpha males like Beau.

Of course, she hadn't known that until she'd met him.

She glanced at her watch, saw she was overdue to leave.

She pointedly turned to look at the hallway leading to the restrooms. "I'm beginning to worry. I think I had better go check, make sure Beau's okay."

"Allow me," Vaughn said. "You can hardly go into the men's room. I'll make sure he's all right. What costume is he wearing?"

Oh, God. She moistened her lips, which had gone bone-dry. "He's a pirate. He's got a . . . umm . . . patch over one eye." Praying the slightly misleading description might help in some way, Cassidy stood frozen as Vaughn turned and headed for the hallway.

Desperate now, Cassidy pretended to notice a couple near the door. "I think I just saw Beau talking to some friends," she said. "I hope you'll thank Mal for his help. It was nice meeting you, Ashley."

"You, too, Cassidy."

She took off at a sprint, then forced herself to slow down, make her way less frantically to the exit. When she reached the foyer, she took a deep breath but didn't stop, crossing the front porch, descending the wide brick steps to the valet stand.

When she spotted the BMW idling at the curb, her legs nearly buckled with relief. Hurrying over, she waited for the valet to open the passenger door, then slid into the seat, ignoring a painful jolt to her ribs.

She was shaking as she clicked her seat belt into place and the valet slammed the car door. Beau put the Beamer in gear, checked the rearview mirror, and drove away from the entrance to the country club.

Chapter Twenty-Seven

"You're late." Beau sliced Cassidy a glance. "What happened in there? I was getting worried. I was about to come looking for you."

"Malcolm Vaughn happened. Thank heavens you didn't come back inside. Oh, God, Beau, I was scared to death when he walked up and recognized me. I had a helluva time figuring out how to get away. If you had come back, he would have expected us to stay. It could have been extremely uncomfortable, to say the least. How about you? Did you run into any trouble?"

"Only about two hundred seventy pounds of trouble. Security guard. He would have been a real sonofabitch to put down."

Her head swiveled toward him. "Put down?"

He just shrugged. "Luckily he was sympathetic to a guy with woman trouble."

Cassidy laughed, relieving the tension both of them were feeling. "So we got it done?"

Beau smiled. "Yeah, baby, we did."

"Vaughn was there with a woman named Ashley Stanfield. He said she was the daughter of one of his clients."

"Stanfield. Name sounds familiar."

"I'll check it out as soon as we get home. We don't need to worry about the audio tonight, or at least I wouldn't think so. Not when he's got a date with him."

"As soon as we get home, I'm taking you to bed. Watching you walk around all evening in that skimpy outfit is more than any red-blooded male can stand."

Her gaze flicked across the console to the bulge beneath his tight black pants. "Good idea. No pirate ever filled out a pair of breeches better than you."

He smiled wickedly. "Hot pool or shower? We need to warm up."

"Hot pool," she said softly, and he could hear the little hitch in her voice.

"Good thinking. Easier on your ribs."

Cassidy made a sexy little sound in her throat that really turned him on. Unfortunately, as he drove back toward the house, only a few seconds had passed before a pair of headlights showed up in his rearview mirror.

His pulse kicked up. "Looks like we've got company."

Cassidy whirled in her seat to look out the back window. "How could they have found us?"

"Same way we found Vaughn, I guess. Or maybe he called them." He pressed down on the gas pedal, urging the BMW a little faster. Eventually, the road would widen and straighten out and he could pick up speed, but there were sharp curves in this area.

Beau silently cursed. The BMW was a great automobile, but for high-speed driving on this kind of terrain, it wasn't the Lambo or the Ferrari.

He checked the rearview mirror. The headlights were still behind him, rapidly closing the distance. He reached down to the compartment beneath his seat, took out the Glock and rested it on the seat beside him.

He could outrun the oncoming car, eventually lose it in traffic, and get them back home. It wouldn't be much of a problem. But he was tired of feeling like prey instead of predator. He kept the car moving at the same speed. With no room to pass in this section, the other vehicle stayed close behind. The straightaway loomed ahead, widened into a four-lane road.

He flicked a glance at Cassidy. In the glow of the dashboard lights, her face looked pale, but her expression was set in determined lines. Her hand trembled as she raised her skirt. He spotted the pistol he hadn't known she was wearing. Her hand steadied as she pulled it out and set it on the seat beside her. She wanted this over and done with as much as he.

Beau maintained his speed as he reached the straightaway. The car behind him accelerated, came right up on his bumper, a big black SUV. Clenching his jaw, he pulled into the right lane and buzzed down his window.

As the SUV approached, he wrapped his hand around the pistol. The SUV pulled up right beside him, giving him a close look at the driver's face. Broad forehead, wide nose, high cheekbones, thick black hair combed straight back. His hand tightened around the pistol grip, his finger on the trigger. For a moment through the window, he and the driver's eyes met.

Then the man hit the gas and the SUV shot forward. At the last second, Beau saw the couple in the backseat entwined like a pair of snakes. The breath he hadn't realized he was holding rushed out. Cassidy relaxed back in her seat.

"It was a limo," she said. "Someone else leaving the party early."

"Yeah."

"I feel like an idiot."

Beau cut her a look. "Don't." He set his weapon back in the compartment beneath the seat. "It could have gone the other way. At least we were prepared."

Cassidy sighed. "You're right."

Now that the apparent danger was over, his gaze slid down to the holster strapped around her pale, pretty thigh. Why the gun looked so sexy he couldn't say, but he felt a rush of heat that sent the blood straight into his groin.

Adrenaline still pumped through his veins. He planned to put it to good use when he got home. He glanced over at the sexy woman next to him. She was eyeing him like a juicy piece of meat. Seemed like the two of them were on the same page.

Beau pressed harder on the gas.

As the BMW pulled into the garage, Cassidy's body still hummed with a combination of fear, battle-readiness, and relief. Sitting in the passenger seat, she'd been certain the driver in the black SUV planned to kill them. For a moment, memories of the crash came rushing in, bringing the bile up the back of her throat. The Lamborghini sliding, flying through the air, flipping, bouncing, landing in the field with a bone-jarring jolt.

The certainty that she was going to die.

Tonight, instead of a confrontation with a killer, the SUV was a limo, holding nothing but a young couple in the throes of making love. The nausea slowly faded. In its place, something hot and needy whispered through her. She sensed Beau's gaze and suddenly felt flushed and overly warm, her breasts achy and sensitive.

Beau turned off the engine and they climbed out of the car. When they reached the kitchen, he caught her shoulders and turned her to face him. "I know you were thinking about the crash. Are you okay?"

She opened her mouth to say yes, that she was fine, but a funny little sound came out and she just shook her head.

Beau drew her into his arms and for several seconds just held her. He bent and softly kissed her. "It's all right, baby. It shook me up, too."

A breath shuddered out. "For a moment, it was like a flashback. Everything came rushing back."

"Yeah, I've been there." He eased her away a little. "It's getting late. You've had enough excitement for one night. Maybe you should just, you know, get some sleep." He kissed her forehead. "Probably be good if you . . . umm . . . slept in the other room."

She swallowed. She didn't want to sleep in the other room. She wanted to sleep with Beau. She needed him to erase those fearful moments, make her feel safe.

"Probably be a good idea," she said. "But I don't want to."

His eyes gleamed, turned a hotter, more intense shade of blue. "You sure?"

Cassidy nodded. *Oh, yeah, I'm sure.*

"The pool is private. None of the guards can see over the fence."

She leaned up and kissed him, felt the warm pressure of his lips. For an instant, Beau deepened the kiss. Then he took her hand and led her outside. The night was dark and cold, the wind whipping the branches of the trees behind the patio walls.

The hot pool sat at the far end of the swimming pool, steam curling up in hazy tendrils. Beau retrieved some towels from the cabana and set them on the cement decking next to the steps leading into the heated water. She caught the glitter of a foil packet and her belly clenched with need.

Beau stripped out of his pirate costume, then helped her undress, being careful of her ribs. He descended the steps, took her hand, and led her into the chest-deep water.

"You don't need to do anything," he said, kissing the

side of her neck. "I'll take care of everything. You just relax and let me do the work."

It sounded so good. He always seemed to take care of her. She let herself float in the water, her hair fanning out around her face, the warmth soothing her battered body, her tightly strung nerves. Beau spent long moments just kissing her, nibbling the corners of her mouth, the side of her neck. He trailed hot kisses over her breasts, her belly, between her legs.

Heated water surrounded her, buoyed her, allowed her to do nothing but feel. Beau took full advantage, sampling and tasting, building the hunger inside her. By the time he stretched out on his back on the stairs and drew her on top of him, she was on fire for him.

A little sound came from her throat as he began to kiss her again, lifted and settled her astride him. Her heart beat faster. Need sank low in her belly. She wanted him so badly.

Shifting a little, she slowly took him inside her, biting her lip to hold back a moan. She loved the feeling of full-ness, the intimacy of having him as close as two people could get.

"Easy . . ." he said. "I don't want to hurt you."

She ran a finger over his lips. "You won't hurt me." But even as she said the words she knew they weren't true. Once this was over, Beau would be gone. She loved him. When he left, the pain would cut deep.

She leaned forward, rested her hands on his shoulders. Moved a little, heard him groan.

"God, I want you," he said.

She wanted him, too. She always seemed to want him. But along with the sex, she wanted him in her life. She wanted him to feel for her the things that he had felt for Sarah.

Beau slid a hand around the back of her neck, pulled her mouth down to his for a deep, burning kiss. Gripping her hips, he held her in place to accept his thrusts, driving deep, stirring the hunger. Her skin felt hot and tight. Sensation blazed through her. The adrenaline rush returned, pumping pleasure through her blood instead of fear.

She pressed a hot, wet kiss on his mouth, her damp curls cocooning them, surrounding them in heat and darkness. His hands found her breasts as she rode him. He was mindful of her ribs, moving slowly and with care, which only excited them more.

She took him deeper, felt a shudder move through his long, hard body as he fought for control. Riding the edge of climax, Cassidy kissed him. "Let go, honey," she whispered.

Beau groaned and his muscles went tense. Gripping her hips, he drove into her, doing his best not to hurt her, building the heat, driving them both insane. Her release came swift and hard, a rush of pleasure so sweet tears stung her eyes.

I'm falling so in love with you, she thought as she began to spiral down, but she didn't say it. Beau wouldn't want to hear it. His love remained locked in the past. It was sad. It was unfair. But it was true.

Cassidy consoled herself that for now he was hers. She would enjoy their time together. When it was over, she vowed, she wouldn't look back. She would just let him go.

She pressed a last soft kiss on his lips. In the meantime, she would sleep well tonight and regain a little more of her strength.

Tomorrow they had work to do.

Beau sat at the desk in his study, going over work emails and generally playing catch-up. Running Tex/Am's sales division wasn't an easy job. No matter what was happening in his personal life, there were things he needed to do.

He typed half a dozen replies, then sent a message to

Marty, asking him to postpone a dinner engagement with one of the company's biggest customers, find a way to smooth the man's ruffled feathers. The email whooshed into cyberspace, and Beau leaned back in his chair.

Last night, after they'd come in from the hot pool and gone to bed, Cassidy had curled up beside him and fallen deeply asleep. He hadn't awoken her this morning. She needed her rest, needed to heal. He still couldn't handle thinking about the crash that had nearly killed her. He had embroiled her in this. If something happened to her, the fault would be his.

He shoved the unwanted thought away, along with the chest-deep ache that came with the idea of losing her. He didn't want to think about that, either.

He looked up as she wandered into the study yawning, looking sleepy eyed and well tumbled. He thought about making love to her last night, how good it always was between them. She walked over and gave him a peppermint-toothpaste kiss and he felt the kick.

"Good morning," she said.

Beau pulled her down on his lap and gave her a far more thorough greeting. "Good morning."

Cassidy gave a kitteny little mew of pleasure, then pushed him away. "You should have awoken me. We have work to do."

She was right, so he didn't argue, pushed thoughts of hauling her back to bed out of his mind.

Cassidy sat down on her side of the partners' desk and turned on her laptop. She yawned. "Let's start with Ashley Stanfield, Vaughn's date at the party last night, see how she fits in."

While Cassidy busied herself, Beau went in and got her a cup of coffee, which she moaned over and sipped gratefully.

"Thanks. I feel better already." She typed a few more lines, took another sip of coffee, and started reading info on the computer screen. "Ashley Stanfield's twenty-nine years old, graduated from Wellesley, does some modeling, wants to be a Broadway actress. She's all over Instagram. Has a big following on Facebook. Her father is Theodore Stanfield. He's a Texas billionaire."

Beau took a drink of coffee and studied the screen over her shoulder. "Now I remember why the name sounded familiar. I've met Stanfield a couple of times. Made his money in the beauty business."

"Theodore Stanfield owns a line of hair and skin products, and a chain of spas with salons in all the major cities."

"If he's a client of Vaughn's, he must be an investor. Far as I know, the guy wouldn't need to borrow money."

Cassidy clicked to a few different locations. "I'm not seeing any connections between Stanfield and your father or Milford."

"Can't fault a guy for hoping. Maybe we'll turn up something later."

Cassidy started typing. "Let's take a look at Senator Scott Watson." She clicked her mouse a couple of times and an article about his death popped up in the *Dallas Morning News*.

"Check this out," she said. "Scott Watson died from anaphylactic shock. According to this, Watson had a severe allergy to peanuts. Somehow one got into his lunch. He was alone when it happened. He fell unconscious, died a few hours later."

"A peanut got into his lunch," Beau repeated with mild disbelief. He sighed. "I guess those things happen. Assuming it was anything but an accident seems like overkill."

Cassidy flicked him a glance at the word. "You're right. There's no reason to suspect it was anything more sinister than a fatal mistake."

But the phrase she had used popped into his head. *Seems like the body count is rising.*

"I need to take a shower before we meet with Mrs. Watson, but first let's check my phone, see if the audio device in Vaughn's car is working." She retrieved her cell, but the indicator light wasn't on. It was Sunday morning. After a late night out, Vaughn was probably still sleeping. Or maybe he got lucky and Ashley Stanfield was keeping him entertained.

"Let's see where he went after he left the party." Cassidy brought up the GPS software and a map popped up on the screen. The GPS was working. Beau watched the pulsing signal, a stationary dot at Vaughn's address in Turtle Creek.

Cassidy went backwards to the original time stamp, the date the vehicle began to move, setting the device in motion at 12:15 P.M. last night. The dot moved along the road from the Westhaven Country Club, made a stop on Lawther Drive in Lakewood, then drove straight to the current location in Turtle Creek.

"Lakewood," Beau said. "Pricey neighborhood."

"I'm guessing the stop he made was Stanfield's house."

Beau grinned. "Looks like our boy Vaughn didn't get laid."

Cassidy chuckled. Rising, she leaned up and kissed him, then headed for the shower. Resisting the urge to join her, Beau went back to work on his emails. He needed to go into the office next week. He had sales meetings, client meetings, planning and strategy sessions.

It wasn't going to happen. Not as long as Cassidy was in danger. A memory arose of her lying in the hospital, fluids dripping into her arm, her head swathed in bandages.

Not gonna happen again. He'd be better prepared. Both of them would be.

Half an hour later, a noise in the doorway caught his attention and he glanced up. Looking far better than she had the day before, makeup covering the bumps and bruises, she walked in wearing a navy-blue sweater with a long navy plaid skirt and boots, very professional for their meeting with the senator's wife, as she always was when she was working.

"Looks like you're ready," he said, joining her at the door.

"Ready and hopeful."

They made a quick stop in the kitchen for another cup of coffee and some of the orange Pillsbury refrigerator rolls Mrs. O'Halloran kept for him that he'd stuck in the oven. Then they headed out.

Beau opened the door leading into the garage. "Time to find out what Emily Watson has to say."

Chapter Twenty-Eight

On the way down the drive, Beau stopped to speak to Will Egan. A man in his forties, Will had prematurely gray hair and an easy disposition.

"Any problems last night?" Beau asked.

"Not a thing."

"We've got a meeting, then we'll be back." He was driving the Ferrari. Maybe it was the incident last night, or maybe he just needed to clear his head. Driving a car with that kind of power always seemed to help.

With very little Sunday traffic, he easily located the address in University Park that Emily Watson had given him, and pulled up in front of the family's traditional, brick façade, two-story home. Making their way up the stone walkway to the plank front door, Beau rang the bell, and a few seconds later, Emily Watson pulled it open.

A slender woman, midforties, medium brown hair with the first fine threads of gray, she smiled at Beau, then spotted Cassidy and her look turned wary.

"I didn't realize you were bringing someone with you."

"Emily, this is Cassidy Jones. She's a private investigator

working with me on my father's murder. Anything we discuss with you will remain strictly confidential."

The woman returned her gaze to Cassidy, took in her conservative clothes and the concern in her face and apparently approved.

"Thank you for coming." Emily stepped back, inviting them inside. Hardwood floors gleamed throughout the house as they walked into the entry. The residence was immaculately clean, everything in its place, though Beau could hear children's voices coming from the second floor.

Emily started walking, expecting them to follow. "The kids are upstairs. I thought we could talk in the living room. I just brewed a fresh pot of coffee."

"I'd love a cup of coffee," Cassidy said, which Beau had learned was a technique she used to put people at ease when there were going to be questions.

They followed Emily into a modern stainless kitchen with white cabinets and granite counters. Emily poured them each a mug, added cream to hers, but Beau and Cassidy took theirs black.

From the kitchen, they made their way into a high-ceilinged living room with dark wood beams. Beau sat next to Cassidy on a sea-foam green sofa while Emily sat down in a matching chair. An ivory and green floral carpet warmed the wood floor beneath the walnut coffee table.

"I was very sorry to hear about your father," Emily said, taking a sip from her mug. "Such a tragedy. How is your investigation coming?"

"Slowly," Beau said. "We have some ideas about what might have happened, but nothing concrete. We're hoping you can help."

Emily set her mug down on a coaster next to the brass lamp beside her chair. "Perhaps I can. As I told you on the phone, Scott passed away a little over a month ago. He died of anaphylactic shock. It was terrible for all of us."

"I saw the article in the newspaper," Cassidy said. "Losing someone is even more painful when it's completely unexpected."

"Yes, it is. Which is the reason I began to question how it happened. Scott was always extremely careful. I had taken the girls to my mother's for a visit that day, so Scott was home by himself. We don't keep peanuts in the house. None of us would ever bring them home. Apparently, he made himself a sandwich and somehow the peanut got inside. I can't imagine how."

"Odd things happen sometimes," Cassidy said.

"Yes, but even so, Scott always kept an EpiPen in the top drawer of his desk. He was sitting there when they found him. He often sat at his desk to eat lunch. All he had to do was open the drawer and take out the pen. He had used one before so he knew how to do it. But no pen was found in the room."

Beau sat forward, his half-finished mug of coffee in his hand. "Did you mention that to the police?"

"Not that day. All I could think of was Scott, how I was going to tell the girls. What I was going to do without him. Later, I thought one of the EMTs must have taken it. I asked the police about it, but no one seemed to know where it was. When the autopsy came back, it showed he never used an EpiPen. And that makes no sense."

Beau looked at Cassidy, whose thoughts must have been running the same. "Is there a chance someone killed your husband, Emily?"

"I don't know." She pulled a tissue from beneath the sleeve of her sweater and dabbed it against her eyes. "I haven't pursued it. I have to think of my children. But when Charlotte mentioned you were looking into your father's murder, I thought there might be some connection."

"Why would you think that?" Cassidy asked.

Emily straightened in her chair. "Two weeks before Scott died, Senator Reese came to see him. They spoke privately. I had no idea what about. But later, when I asked Scott what the senator wanted, he said Stewart had asked him for a favor."

Favor. The word put Beau on alert. "Go on."

"Scott was chairman of the Joint Oversight Committee on Government Facilities. The members were planning to hand out contracts worth six hundred million dollars for deferred maintenance and new construction in the capitol complex."

"And the favor?"

"I'm not exactly sure. I think it might have had something to do with granting a contract to a particular company, someone your father wanted."

"Did Scott agree?"

"He didn't want to. He grumbled about it, said he didn't have any choice. Apparently he owed Senator Reese for a vote he had cast on a bill Scott wanted passed. I didn't press for more. As the wife of a politician, I've learned when to push and when to let something go. Now I wish I had pushed harder."

Beau set his mug down on the coffee table. "There's no reason to believe the favor Scott did for my father had any bearing on what happened to him or my dad. But there's always a chance it could be important. Whether it is or isn't, I appreciate your telling me."

"As an investigator," Cassidy said, "I've learned that any little scrap of information can turn out to be helpful. You never know what it might be."

They stood up from the sofa and Emily stood up, too. She led them to the front door. "Thank you for coming. I feel better just telling someone about my suspicions."

"We'll do our best to follow up," Cassidy said.

"If it turns out to be something, I'll let you know," Beau said.

Emily set her hand on his arm. "Whatever you find out, I don't want to know. Can you understand that?"

A thread of unease filtered through him. He thought of the hit-and-run driver, the man who had run Cassidy off the road. "I understand," he said.

"Thank you again," Cassidy said. Turning away, they headed down the stone walkway to the car.

"Your father wanted a favor," Cassidy mused as the Ferrari rolled toward home.

"That was definitely the way he did business."

"We know your dad visited Watson two weeks before he died, so about six weeks ago. If I remember right, that was about the time he paid back most of the money he borrowed from Vaughn."

"Most but not all," Beau said.

"Maybe he paid the rest with a favor—something Vaughn wanted."

"Yeah, like getting a big fat construction contract for one of his clients."

Cassidy started nodding. "Let's work with that. Let's assume your father got Watson to convince the members of the committee to give the contract to the company your dad wanted. Two weeks later, Watson is killed so there wouldn't be any connection."

"You're making a pretty big leap."

"Yes, I am. And here's where that leap takes us. Watson was a loose end. Your father was a loose end, too. Both of them knew about the deal. Vaughn wasn't taking any chances. He had both men killed."

His hands tightened around the steering wheel. "We

need to find out if Scott Watson recommended a particular company and if so, how much the contract was worth."

"Emily said the state was spending six hundred million for deferred maintenance and new construction. That's big bucks."

Beau's gaze sharpened on hers. "Yeah, plenty of motive for murder."

The sky was clearing, clouds drifting away, exposing patches of blue. But the streets were still wet as the Ferrari drove back toward the house.

"The contract might be public record," Cassidy said, thinking out loud. "Some kind of public filing or something."

"If it isn't, I might be able to find out. My father was a politician for eighteen years, a senator for the last twelve. I can make some calls, talk to some people I know, try to get the information we need. Tomorrow's Monday. Even the politicians will be back at work."

Cassidy sat back in her seat, enjoying the roar of the powerful engine as the Ferrari moved effortlessly along the road. They had almost reached Beau's house when his cell phone started ringing. He checked the number, answered it on the hands-free.

"Hey, Missy." He smiled.

"Hi, Beau. I hate to . . . umm . . . bother you, but you said to call if we found something."

He flicked a glance at Cassidy and his smile widened. "So did you?"

"We did. Me and Mom found the perfect little house. It's got three bedrooms and there's two bathrooms plus a little powder room off the entry. There's a park right across the street and it's just a couple blocks from the café, so Mom can walk to work. Me, too, once the baby is older. Do you have time to, you know, come and see it?"

Beau looked at Cassidy and she read his expression,

easily read his thoughts. They didn't have time. They were trying to catch a murderer. And there was the not-so-small matter of trying to keep from getting killed.

"We can be there in an hour and twenty," he said. "That work for you?"

"Oh, that would be so great. The real estate lady said anytime today would be good for her. And the house is empty, so if you like it, we could move in right away."

"You're the one who has to live there, sweetie. Let's just make sure it's in good shape, okay?"

"Okay. You should see Evie, Beau. She's the best little girl. She's already sleeping most of the night."

"That's good. We'll make this work, I promise." There was a smile on Beau's face when he hung up the phone. "She says the baby is doing great."

"I love babies. I can't wait to see Evie again."

Beau's gaze swung away from the road back to Cassidy. For an instant something warmed in his eyes; then it was gone.

The hour-and-twenty-minute drive to Pleasant Hill passed quickly. The entire time, Beau kept watch to make sure they weren't followed.

They met Josie, Missy, and the baby at the house. The Realtor, Diane Ellison, was a busty redhead with a friendly smile. As Missy had said, the single-story home on Shady Lane was just a couple of blocks from the restaurant, nothing fancy, but from the outside, at least, it appeared to be in good condition. And as Missy had said, a shady little park with benches beneath the trees sat just across and down the block from the house.

Cassidy held little Evie while the Realtor gave Beau, Missy, and Josie a tour of the interior, which, being empty, made an inspection fairly easy. The house was only ten years old, with an open kitchen, a breakfast bar and eating area that looked into a family room with an antique brick fireplace. There was a fenced yard out back and a two-car attached garage.

Cassidy gently held the sleeping baby in her arms as she glanced around the house, which had new carpet, drapes, and paint, and included a refrigerator in the kitchen, plus a washer and dryer. The house looked good, and if repairs came up, the cost wouldn't be a problem for Beau.

The tour ended and the small group walked back into the living room. "So what do you think?" Missy asked Beau. When he wasn't looking, she grinned at Cassidy, turned so she could see Missy's fingers crossed behind her back. Cassidy grinned back. It was obvious how much mother and daughter loved the house.

"If you like it," Beau said. "Then I like it, too."

Missy's eyes teared. All of them smiled in relief. Cassidy gave Missy a secret thumbs-up, growing more and more fond of the teenage girl who'd had to grow up too soon.

Beau focused his attention on the Realtor. "Make it happen, Diane, and soon. All cash. No contingencies. Just like we discussed."

Missy squealed and threw her arms around Beau's neck. "Thank you, thank you, thank you!" Half the women in town had a crush on Beau, but Missy seemed to see him more as an older brother, a healthy relationship Cassidy was sure pleased him greatly.

Missy took the baby, cuddled her, and tucked the soft pink blanket around her. "You want to hold her, Beau?" Before he could answer, the girl settled little Evie in his arms. Beau looked down at the infant and the expression on his face hurt Cassidy's heart. He should have had children in his life. He deserved it. He turned and smiled at her; then his expression slowly changed. His features went from soft to hard, and whatever he'd been thinking was gone.

He handed the baby back to Missy. "As soon as the sale closes, you can move in. Josie, you need to call the moving company, arrange for them to pack your things. Tell them to send me the bill."

Josie just nodded, a little shell-shocked at their good fortune. "I'll call them right away."

Beau checked his watch. "We have to get going." He set a hand at Cassidy's waist, urging her toward the door. "Keep me posted."

The drive home to Dallas was a mostly silent journey, though Cassidy wasn't sure why. Beau seemed to be somewhere far away, and wherever it was, it wasn't warm and fuzzy.

Unease slipped through her. Whatever Beau was thinking, she was sure it wasn't good.

Chapter Twenty-Nine

All the way back to Dallas, Beau kept replaying the scene in his head, him holding the baby, Cassidy looking at him with a soft smile on her face, him smiling back.

Like a lunatic, he thought now, a guy caught up in something he didn't completely understand and would never experience.

That kind of thinking was over, long in the past. It had died with Sarah, and he wouldn't allow it to return.

Memories arose, long summer days on campus, he and Sarah making plans, talking about having a family, how many children they wanted.

It was only a few weeks later that the cancer diagnosis had come in. Terminal. Nothing they could do but accept the inevitable. They didn't want to believe it, flatly refused to give up hope. But as Sarah slowly wasted away, there was no use denying the outcome. Sarah's anguish and suffering had been intense. In a different, less obvious way, so was Beau's.

He thought of Cassidy, his deepening feelings for her, the way her smile somehow warmed him inside. The way she steadied him, helped him deal with the problems he was facing.

The last thing he needed was to fall in love. He'd made a life for himself. One that didn't include a wife and kids. He was comfortable. Safe. He thought of the agony of losing Sarah. He'd be a fool to let down his guard and take that kind of risk again. Since he wasn't a fool, he needed to back away.

He'd talk to Linc, find a way to ensure Cassidy was protected until this was over, set up security twenty-four hours a day.

He was deep in thought, running over his options, discarding possibilities, when he pulled up to a stop light on Lovers Lane and noticed a car in his rearview mirror. It was a fairly new white Toyota four-door sedan, a family car, though the driver appeared to be the only person in the vehicle at the moment.

The Ferrari was idling, satellite radio playing soft rock tunes. A few other cars were on the busy street, a Ford F-150 facing him on the opposite side of the intersection next to a Subaru Outback, a Chevy with a dent in its right fender behind the Toyota, nothing that looked threatening.

He checked the mirror, saw the turn signal on the Toyota go on as the driver pulled into the right-hand lane on Cassidy's side of the car and came to a stop beside them. Beau glanced over at the driver, a guy in a ball cap, noticed the window was rolled down. The driver's arm came up.

"Gun!" Beau shouted. Both of them ducked as two quick shots smashed through the glass in the Ferrari's passenger window, tearing into the headrest, missing Cassidy's head by inches, the other shot shattering the window on the driver's side of the car, exactly where he had been sitting.

Cassidy popped up and fired through the broken window as the Toyota charged into the intersection, squealed around the corner, and roared off down the block.

Beau jammed his foot on the gas, punching into the intersection, slinging Cassidy hard against her seat belt just as the light changed and the F-150 lurched toward him. Beau steered hard to the right to miss a collision and stay behind the fleeing car.

"Keep low!" He pressed harder on the gas pedal, and the Ferrari leaped ahead like a panther after a gazelle, engine growling, gaining on the white Toyota at breakneck speed. He'd almost caught up when the car braked and cut in front of two slower-moving vehicles, blocking Beau's approach. He jammed on the brakes and managed to duck in behind them, followed for a few seconds before the Toyota screamed through a yellow light, turned left as the light changed to red, and shot off down the block.

Cursing, Beau downshifted and hit the gas, running the light, shooting into the intersection to the sound of blaring horns and the squeal of burning rubber, barely missing a Cadillac coming the opposite way. He cranked the wheel, made the turn, and raced after the Toyota, which cut in and out with more skill than Beau expected.

A red light loomed ahead. Cassidy kept her gun angled toward the driver in the Toyota, but there were too many people around to get a clear shot. The Toyota ran the light, but a moving van rolling into the intersection forced Beau to slam on the brakes and squeal to a stop.

"Come on . . . come on."

The van finally cleared the lane and Beau punched the gas. But as he roared down the street, there was no sign of the Toyota.

"I don't see him! Which way did he go?"

"Left!" Cassidy shouted. "He went left!"

Beau jerked the wheel and jammed on the gas, running another red light, but he didn't see the Toyota. The streets were crowded, people pouring back into the city after the weekend. He ducked in and out of traffic, but the Toyota never reappeared.

"I don't see him," he said, muscles tight across his shoulders.

"I don't either."

Beau swore foully. He turned left and cruised around the block, tried another block, but there was no sign of the car or the man in the ball cap.

"He's gone," Cassidy said glumly, slumping back against the seat.

Beau slammed a hand down on the steering wheel. "I can't believe I let him get away."

"He caught us off guard. We overreacted last time. I guess we didn't want to do it again."

"It shouldn't have happened. He was driving a fucking Toyota!" He glanced at Cassidy, saw the corners of her mouth twitch in amusement, and released a slow breath. "So I guess we're both okay."

"I'll be better when we get home."

"Yeah, me, too. We need to call Briscoe, tell him what happened. Did you get a plate number?"

"BC4 X589. I doubt it's legit."

"The guy was using a silencer," Beau said, still trying to comprehend what had just occurred.

"I noticed. Means he's a professional. I don't think he was just after me this time. I think he planned to take both of us out."

Beau's insides tightened. The guy was a professional. Which meant there was no way in hell he could back away from Cassidy now, no matter the personal cost. It was a pipe dream, anyway. He never could have gone through with it. He wouldn't have been willing to risk putting her safety into the hands of someone else, not as long as she was in such grave danger.

Beau ignored a vague feeling of relief that she would be staying with him, and turned the car toward home.

As soon as he got to the house, Beau spoke to Will Egan, bringing him up to speed on the shooting and authorizing him to hire more men. Next he phoned Tom Briscoe. Using the landline in the kitchen, he put the phone on speaker so Cassidy could join the conversation.

"It's Beau Reese, Tom. I was hoping you'd be in. Looks like we've got more trouble."

"What's going on, Beau?"

After a brief summary of the shooting, which included how close the assassin had come to killing both of them, Briscoe started asking questions.

"So we're looking for a late-model, white, four-door Toyota," he said, recapping what they knew. "You get a plate number?"

"BC4 X589," Cassidy replied.

"You sure the guy was using a silencer?"

"Dead sure," Beau said and he and Cassidy shared a glance at the pun.

"Description of the assailant?"

"Average height. Never got a look at his face. Wore a dark blue ball cap tugged down over his forehead. Dark brown hair, I think."

"Cassidy, you got anything to add?"

"Two shots fired close together. One for each of us, I'd say. Near misses. Miracle Beau caught on in time for us to duck, throw off his aim."

Which, Beau thought, he probably wouldn't have done if it hadn't been for their false alarm run-in with the black SUV.

"You think the hit was on both of you, not just Cassidy?"

Briscoe asked. "Keep in mind, whoever it was has already made two failed attempts."

"I'm guessing this was a different guy," Cassidy said. "The shooter was a pro. I think if he'd been the one to run me off the road, he would have come back and finished me."

Beau's stomach knotted. He didn't want to think there might actually be two people trying to kill them instead of just one.

"If you're right," Briscoe said, "odds are he'll make another attempt."

"I know," Cassidy said.

Beau clenched his jaw. "He can try. He won't succeed."

"We'll need statements from both of you. And DPD will want a look at the car. I'll call them, have them send someone out. And I'll ask them to keep your neighborhood on their radar."

"Thanks, Tom. I'd appreciate it if you kept this out of the media. They'll be climbing all over me again."

"I'll do my best. Listen, Beau, there's something else. I hate to be the bearer of more bad news, and it's not official. I'm probably not supposed to say, but rumor has it they're thinking about convening a grand jury. The DA is up for reelection. Your dad was a senator; you're his wealthy, celebrity son. The DA doesn't want any hint of impropriety or favoritism."

"Surely with Milford's murder and all the stuff that's been going on, they can see this is bigger than just an argument between me and my father that escalated into me killing him."

"So far we haven't got any kind of connection between your father's murder and anything else. If you have evidence, we need to see it. Do you?"

Did they? *Hell no.* They had nothing but a bunch of

theories that so far led nowhere. The hit-and-run and the crash could have been nothing more than coincidence.

"What about the guy who just tried to take us out?" he asked. "That ought to prove something."

"No proof it's related. At least not yet. We'll keep working the case here in Pleasant Hill, and the Dallas PD will be working the shooting. Until we come up with something that ties all this together, that's all we can do."

Tom was right. They had no real proof the shooting was in any way connected to anything else. "We'll keep after it, Tom, find the evidence you need." *Somehow*.

"I should tell you to back off, leave the investigation to the police, but I'm not going to. You need to find something, Beau, and you better find it soon or the DA will move forward with his plan."

Beau felt sick. It seemed things were getting blacker and blacker. Cassidy's hand settled gently on his shoulder. Beau looked at her and took a steadying breath.

"I appreciate your telling me, Tom."

"I'll run that plate number, see what turns up, but I wouldn't get too excited. Not if the guy is the pro you think he is."

"Yeah."

"Watch your back. Both of you." Briscoe hung up the phone.

Beau walked over to the kitchen table, sank down in one of the chairs. Cassidy sat down in the chair next to his.

"I know this is overwhelming," she said, "but we're getting close, Beau. That's why they're coming after us so hard. Once we figure out what's going on, it'll be clear you weren't the one who killed your father."

Beau raked both hands through his hair. "At the moment, I'm not as worried about the people who killed my father as the people who are trying to kill *us*."

"We're building a case, digging up evidence. We're

going to figure this out. Once we do, there'll be no point in killing us."

"I hope you're right."

Cassidy rose from the chair. "I'm going to take a look at the GPS on Vaughn's car. I'll check my phone, see if the audio's picking anything up." He watched her walk away, following the movement of her sexy ass in the skinny jeans she was wearing, wished he could just take her to bed and forget everything else.

He sighed as he leaned back in his chair. First thing tomorrow morning, he'd make some calls, try to get the names of the contractor Scott Watson had personally recommended.

If the cops were done with the Ferrari, he'd call Marty, have the car picked up and the shattered windows and the bullet-torn headrest repaired. Maybe the cops would be able to dig a slug out somewhere, get a lead on the weapon, but if the guy was the professional he seemed, it wouldn't matter much.

He shoved up from his chair. He was mentally exhausted, weary to the bone. He headed down the hall to Cassidy, knowing she had to be feeling the same. And there was still a police report to be made before they were done for the day. Until this was over, they needed each other. He hated to admit it, but in some ways he needed her even more than she needed him.

Beau paused for a moment in the doorway. Cassidy was sitting at her laptop, tapping away, her soft dark curls falling around her face. She was one of the most feminine women he had ever met. At the same time, there was a toughness about her, an ability to handle whatever life threw at her.

Some men might be intimated by that toughness, but Beau admired it. With everything that had been happening, he was grateful she was no delicate flower.

* * *

It was blustery outside the next day, temperatures in the high fifties, overcast with no chance of rain. Egan had patrols set up and men stationed all over the property.

Cassidy holed up in Beau's study and by midmorning had the names of all the companies awarded contracts by the oversight committee. The work, which had started January first, was already well underway.

Unfortunately, the list included everything from plaster and lathing, to electrical contractors. There were plumbing companies, painting contractors, flooring companies, lighting suppliers—six hundred million could buy a helluva lot of construction work.

She glanced up as Beau walked into the study, looking yummy in a pair of creased blue jeans and a light blue long-sleeved T-shirt. For a moment, her mind went back to the delicious wake-up sex they'd had earlier that day.

"'Morning." He leaned down and brushed a quick kiss on her lips.

"Good morning." She smiled at the recollection that she'd thought he needed a haircut when she'd met him. His glossy black hair was even longer now, curling softly at the nape of his neck. She wanted to run her fingers through it, pull his mouth down to hers for a far less platonic kiss.

"I may have found something," he said.

She brightened. "Good thing, because I've found way too much. There must be dozens of contractors working on those repairs."

"Maybe so, but only one of them was recommended by Senator Scott Watson."

Her eyebrows went up. "You got it? Beau, that's great! Which company is it?"

"Hardrock Trenching. They're based in Houston."

She looked back at her list, saw the name. "It's listed in public records. I printed the list so you could see." She circled the name. "That's good work, Beau."

"Maybe. The thing is, they're not a very big company. In order to participate in projects over a million dollars, they had to qualify under the Texas Facilities Commission Small Contractor Participation Assistance Program. Which apparently they did."

"So how big a contract did they get?"

He picked up the printed paper, looked down at the name she had circled. "That's the weird part. The job was only worth two hundred thousand dollars. The company won't actually net anywhere near that."

Cassidy frowned. "I don't get it. If Vaughn wanted a favor, why would he pick something with so little value?"

Beau's head tilted back and he stared up at the ceiling. Then his gaze, dark with frustration, zeroed in on her. "Don't you get it? We screwed up. There's no way this is the favor Vaughn wanted. Hell, maybe Senator Watson's death really was an accident. We've got to go back, start completely over."

Rounding the partners' desk, he sat down heavily in his chair, a mixture of disappointment, regret, and worry all etched into his face.

"You think we're on the wrong track," she said, not willing to give up yet.

He sighed. "We must be. Killing two people—possibly three—over a low six-figure trenching contract doesn't make any sense."

Cassidy's shoulders slumped. He was right, dammit. If there was a favor involved, it had to be something worth way more money than that.

"Okay. We'll leave it for now. We still have an audio bug in Vaughn's car and a GPS tracker on his bumper. We'll stay on top of them, monitor them twenty-four hours a day if that's what it takes. We aren't giving up until we find out if Malcolm Vaughn is the man behind the murders."

Beau propped his elbows on the desk and leaned forward, his expression a little less tense. "You're right. If Vaughn's our man, we'll catch him."

Cassidy turned back to her computer, clicked up the screen showing the GPS locator. The address for the current location appeared on the screen.

"This is Vaughn's office," she said as Beau got up and padded around the desk behind her. "His Mercedes is parked in the parking lot. We'll check it every half hour until he leaves. Then we follow his route, see where he goes."

She pulled out her cell phone, but the audio signal wasn't alerting. "We'll keep a closer eye on this, too. If he calls anyone, we'll know it. We'll phone the device and listen in on the conversation. One way or another, if Vaughn is guilty, sooner or later, we'll catch him. If he's guilty, Malcolm Vaughn is going down."

Chapter Thirty

Three days passed and nothing. The house was overrun with security people. Along with the extra team Will Egan had brought in, Beau had hired a bodyguard named Frank Marino, a redheaded former police sergeant who had worked for Linc. When Marino wasn't prowling the grounds, he was staying in the studio apartment at the other end of the house.

The only good news was the purchase of Missy's house in Pleasant Hill had closed, and Missy, Josie, and the baby had already moved in. Josie was looking for someone to help with the baby part-time but hadn't found the right person yet.

There was lots going on in the world outside the house, but inside, Cassidy was becoming claustrophobic.

"I can't take this anymore," she said glumly, sitting with Beau at the breakfast table Thursday morning. "I'm going to go bat-hat crazy if I have to stay in this house one more day."

He chuckled. "I'm happy to take you back to bed, honey, keep your mind off your troubles for a while."

A little sliver of heat washed into her belly. She'd love nothing more than to spend the day in bed with Beau, but with a killer hunting them, they had work to do. She was hoping there was a safe way to get out of the house.

She managed a grudging half smile. "You did more than your share this morning, and I have to admit it worked—for a while. But it's not fresh air. Why don't I take your guy Marino with me down to the office? I called earlier. Jase is back in town and Rome might be there. Maybe one of them has heard something that'll help us."

"You don't think they would have called? And who's this guy Rome? The former gangbanger who gave you the car door opener, right?"

"Yes, and Rome might need it." She seized the excuse like the last breath of oxygen in a roomful of poison air. "I really should take it back to him. What do you say?"

The corner of Beau's mouth edged up. "I say we hang on to it a little longer, just in case. But if you want to get out, we've got good people around us. We'll take Marino along and I'll go with you."

"You don't have to do that."

He didn't say a word, just cocked a black eyebrow, reminding her that someone was trying to kill them.

"Okay, fine. We'll both go. The Ferrari's back, all patched up and ready to hit the road."

"Be smarter to take the BMW. Blends into traffic better. The Jeep would be best—too bad it's red."

He was right, dammit. Not the Ferrari, and a red Jeep was out of the question. She bit back a smile. Beau and his flashy cars.

"Fine, we can take the Beamer. Maybe we could, you know, go to lunch or something. We can't hide in the house forever."

He scowled. "I was hoping Vaughn would make some kind of move by now. So far he hasn't gone anywhere interesting and his conversations have been way beyond boring."

They had stayed on top of the audio and GPS, but so far,

Vaughn had spent very little time on his cell while he was driving, just calls to his office—including some steamy phone sex with his secretary. Nothing they could use, and he hadn't had anyone else in the car to talk to.

They had followed his route on the computer screen, but mostly he just went to the office, then home. The man was definitely a workaholic.

They headed down to the agency, with Frank Marino following the Beamer in a black SUV. He parked behind them in a space in front of the building and stayed with the vehicles, keeping an eye out for trouble.

Connie was working at the front desk when they walked in. She glanced up, spotted Beau, and both black eyebrows shot up.

"My, my, girlfriend, now I see why you haven't been coming to work."

Cassidy just smiled. "Connie, this is Beau Reese. Beau, Connie Thurston. She runs the place and somehow manages to keep all of us in line."

"Pleasure to meet you, Connie. And I congratulate you. I know from personal experience, keeping this lady in line is a monumental job."

Connie laughed. "Oh, he's got your number, girl. I can tell you that."

There was no one else on the floor. Cassidy looked over as Chase Garret walked out of his office. He was tall and very good-looking, in his midthirties, with dark blond hair and a lean, hard body. Like Jase, he was most comfortable in jeans and cowboy boots, though he kept his boots polished to a mirror shine.

He walked straight up to Beau. "Chase Garrett." He extended a hand.

"Beau Reese." The men shook.

Chase tipped his head toward the door he had just walked

out of. "Why don't you two come into my office, where we can talk?"

Beau glanced at Cassidy, but she had no idea what her boss wanted. They followed him into the room, a smaller version of the main office, with a big oak desk, chairs, and bookshelves. Pictures of Chase's family ranch out in the Hill Country hung on the walls.

Chase closed the door. "Have a seat." Both of them sat down in comfortable brown leather chairs in front of his desk. Chase sat down on the opposite side. "I hear you two have been having some problems."

The muscles in Beau's shoulders tightened beneath his shirt. "You heard that?" He didn't like people knowing his business. He flicked Cassidy a glance, but she just shook her head. "What exactly did you happen to hear?"

Cassidy didn't tell him Chase had a way of knowing everything that went on in Dallas.

"For starters, I heard there's a contract out on the two of you. Someone with big money wants you dead. I was just getting ready to call Cassidy when you walked through the door."

Her pulse shot up. She'd known someone was hunting them, but a professional hit sounded even more frightening. "Any idea who took out the contract?" she asked.

"No, but I've got feelers out. The minute I hear I'll let you know. In the meantime, you need to get somewhere safe until this blows over."

"It isn't going to blow over," Beau said. "Not until we figure out what the hell is going on. Holing up somewhere isn't going to solve the problem."

Chase's dark gaze rolled over him, surveying the protective gleam in Beau's eyes, taking in more than Cassidy wanted him to know. "Okay, I get that. Maybe there's something I can do to help. Tell me what you've got so far."

Cassidy glanced at Beau and read his reluctance. He

didn't know Chase Garrett from the man in the moon. He didn't know if he could trust him. No way did he want to spill the information they'd been collecting.

Cassidy set a hand on his arm. "I've worked with Chase for years, Beau. He's one of the best investigators in the business. I'd trust him with my life. On a couple of occasions where guns came into play, I actually have."

Beau released a pent-up breath. "All right. That's good enough for me." For the next half hour, they filled Chase in, bringing him up to speed on the murders, including the possibility that Senator Watson's death had not been an accident. They also relayed their suspicions that Mal Vaughn was involved up to his money-lending neck.

Neither of them told Chase they were tracking the man. The PIs in the office were independent contractors. Not knowing some of the gray areas they worked in gave Chase credible deniability. She didn't want him losing his license—or worse—over something she'd done.

"If you're right," Chase said, "whatever's going on—it's big. Cassidy's had two previous attempts on her life. Now a pro has come out of the woodwork hunting both of you. If Mal Vaughn is involved, he's not the big fish. Someone with way more to lose is calling the shots."

"Any idea who?" Beau asked, leaning forward in his chair.

"I don't know, but maybe I can find out." Chase rose from behind his desk, his attention fixed on Beau. "The people who work for me, they're family. You can believe I'll stay on this. I know Jase is digging around. Rome and Lissa know about the contract. They've got their ears open for anything that might be useful. I've warned them to keep it low-key. With luck, something will turn up."

For the first time, Beau seemed to relax. He stood up and extended a hand, which Chase shook. "Thanks."

"Stay safe. Both of you. I'll be in touch."

As they walked out of the building, Frank Marino waited beside the front door. He was a lean man, fit and watchful. Cassidy didn't miss the swell of a pistol in the shoulder holster beneath his jacket. The man took his job seriously and she was damned glad he did. She and Beau were also armed.

"No sign of trouble?" Beau asked.

Marino's gaze went to the upper stories of the buildings lining both sides of the street, scanning for a shooter who might have a sniper's nest in a location above. "None so far."

Beau followed his gaze, then looked down at Cassidy and gently touched her cheek. "I don't think going to lunch is a good idea."

She sighed. "Not when we know for sure there's a hit out on us."

"Let's go back to the house, take another look at Vaughn's movements. We'll send Frank out for something to eat. He always seems to be hungry."

She nodded, checked her phone. No audio alert. "Vaughn isn't talking."

Beau's features hardened, tightening the scar along his jaw. His eyes were a fierce shade of blue. "Maybe not, but nobody's perfect. Sooner or later, Vaughn's going to screw up. When he does, we'll be ready."

Vaughn's mistake came at nine P.M. that night. It started when the GPS signal pulsing from beneath the bumper of his car began to travel from his office along the streets of the map on the computer screen.

Standing behind Cassidy, Beau watched the moving red dot as Vaughn's Mercedes headed for home the way he usually did this time of night. But halfway there, Cassidy's iPhone alerted to sounds inside the car.

She flashed Beau a look, picked up her cell and dialed

the audio bug, which made a silent connection to the device hidden under the dash. She set the phone on speaker.

Beau heard a ringing inside the car, not Vaughn's usual cell phone ringtone, but something different. "It's another phone," he said as Vaughn answered.

"I'm listening," Mal said to the caller. Silence while the person on the other end of the phone was speaking. "I told you I'd take care of it," Vaughn said. More conversation, then, "All right, if you think it's necessary. But it'll take me half an hour to get there."

The line went dead. The pulsing image on the computer screen slowed, then turned around and began to move in the opposite direction.

"He's meeting the guy on the phone," Beau said, his pulse beginning to thrum.

"It could be anyone," Cassidy reminded him, looking at him over her shoulder from her chair in front of the screen. "We shouldn't get our hopes too high."

"Vaughn took that call on a different cell phone. If he's up to no good, probably a disposable. I can't wait to see where he's headed."

It took thirty minutes for the Mercedes to arrive at its destination, and Beau's nerves were on edge the whole time. The car slowed, then stopped, the device still pulsing, but no longer moving.

"He's out in Westlake," Beau said, studying the map, locating the small town northwest of Fort Worth. "That's some of the most expensive real estate around. What's the address?"

"It's 1555 Ottinger." Cassidy went to Google Maps, pulled up a satellite image of the house, and Beau whistled.

"Got to be twenty or thirty acres," he said. "Property's gated. House looks to be seven- or eight-thousand square feet. In today's market, place like that has to be eight or nine million."

"Hang on a minute, let me see who owns it."

Beau waited impatiently as Cassidy went into county records and cross-referenced the street address with the ownership parcels.

"The owner's name is Luca Aaron Reichlin. Sole and separate property. No other name on the tax rolls." She looked up. "Ever heard of him?"

Beau shook his head. "He's got to have some very big bucks to live out there, but no, I've never heard of him."

"We need to know who this guy is." Cassidy turned back to the computer and Googled his name. Nothing. No newspaper articles, nothing on PeopleFinder, nothing on Whitepages.com.

She kept looking, tapping away on the keyboard, finally glanced up at Beau. "No Facebook page, no Twitter account, no LinkedIn, no other social media."

She went to birth records for the state of Texas, found nothing. Went to a national birth record search that required payment, a site she had used before. Nothing.

She found him on a pay-for-use site that searched passport records. "Here he is. Luca Aaron Reichlin was born in Switzerland. Forty-five years old, American mother, German father, dual citizenship." She did a little more searching but nothing else popped up. All the while, the red dot in front of Reichlin's house didn't move.

"There's bound to be something more," Cassidy said. "But it's going to take me a while to find it." She looked up. "This guy keeps an unusually low profile. I wonder why?"

"I'd sure like to know what he and Vaughn are talking about."

"I know someone who might have info on him." Cassidy picked up her cell and punched a number in her contacts. "I'm calling Chase. Reichlin seems to move in the shadows, but he lives in Westlake, so clearly he travels in the higher echelons. Chase might know who he is."

"Maybe he's one of Vaughn's investors," Beau suggested.

"Could be." She put the phone on speaker and set it

down on the desk. "Chase, it's Cassidy. I'm with Beau. Sorry to bother you so late, but have you ever heard of a guy named Luca Reichlin, middle name Aaron?"

"Reichlin? Yeah, I know who he is. You think Reichlin's involved in this?"

"No idea. Vaughn just drove out to his house for a meeting. That's all we know."

"He's bad news, Cassidy." Worry roughened Chase's deep voice. "The guy is for sale to the highest bidder, completely conscienceless. Money is his god and nothing else matters. His name surfaces once in a while in some dark corner, but basically he keeps a very low profile. If I'm remembering right, for the past few years, he's been employed by some billionaire in Houston, but I don't know his name."

"You think there's a chance Reichlin could be connected to all of this?"

Chase fell silent. She could almost feel his mind spinning, going over the information they had, putting it all together.

"Reichlin's a facilitator but only at the highest levels. He deals with one client at a time. Whoever it is has to be mega-rich to afford him. Reichlin carries out orders, makes sure his client gets whatever he wants—legal or not. My guess, if all of this is connected, whatever's going down is big."

"Big enough for Reichlin to put a hit out on anyone who stands in the way of getting it done?" Beau asked.

"That big, yes. If he's protecting his client."

"How do we find out who Reichlin works for?"

"It won't be easy. If you're right and Mal Vaughn's involved, maybe he knows. More likely, Vaughn's only contact with the big-money man is through Reichlin. He may not even know the guy's name."

"We need to find out what these people are after," Cassidy said.

"Yes, you do. It's the only way you're going to end this."

"Thanks, Chase," Cassidy said. "At least we know more than we did."

"Keep me up-to-date and I'll do the same. You both be careful." Chase hung up the phone.

Beau looked down at the red dot pulsing on the computer screen. "We need to find out the name of Reichlin's client."

"I'll go to work on it right now," Cassidy said. "Maybe if I dig deep enough, I'll find something." She reached up and touched his cheek, ran her hand over the late-evening shadow along his jaw. "Why don't you get some sleep? No use both of us staying up half the night."

He should. He needed to be at the top of his game if they were going to figure all of this out. Unfortunately, he found himself reluctant to face his empty bed without her.

He faked a smile. "You aren't the only one who knows their way around a computer. I've got a few tricks of my own up my sleeve." Moving to his side of the desk, he sat down and went to work.

Chapter Thirty-One

Beau groaned at the sound determined to intrude on the slow, deep kiss he was enjoying. It was late, around midnight. Lying beneath him, Cassidy slid her arms around his neck and opened her warm body in invitation as he pressed her down in the mattress. His heavy erection nestled between her legs, the anticipation nearly as good as being inside her.

He was breathing raggedly and so was she, both of them fast-tracking toward the pleasure just out of reach and the sleep afterward they both so desperately needed.

She laced her fingers in the hair at the nape of his neck, and a fresh rush of heat slid through him. Her skin felt smooth and warm as his mouth traveled over her shoulder to feast on a delectable breast.

When the ringing intruded again, Beau swore and lifted himself away, sat up in bed and grabbed his cell phone off the nightstand. No way could he ignore it, not with the trouble swirling around them. Leaning down, he pressed a last kiss on Cassidy's warm lips.

"We aren't finished," he said softly, though for the moment, clearly they were. He looked down at the caller

ID, recognized the number, and every muscle in his body went tense. "Missy, what's going on? What's wrong?"

Missy started crying. "There's a man here, Beau. He's . . . he's got this ski mask over his head and he's got a gun. He says you . . . you owe him money."

Someone jerked the phone out of Missy's hand. "That's right, Reese. Your girlfriend was supposed to be dead in the middle of the street by now. She cost me fifteen thousand dollars and a world of trouble. I know who you are. I know you're filthy rich. Fifteen thousand's nothing to you, so now I want a million, and you're gonna bring it to me personally."

Anger and fear had him shaking. Beau's hand tightened around his cell. "You listen to me and you better listen good. Anything happens to Missy or the baby, you're a dead man. You hear me?"

"You're the one who should be listening. I need a ride out of the country. I'm on my way to ol' Mehico and you're gonna bring me the money to get there in that fancy helicopter of yours. If you don't, the girl and the kid are dead. Now keep your mouth shut and do what I say. And no police—you got that?"

Beau forced himself under control. "Yeah, I've got it." He needed to stay calm, think of Missy and Evie. He wondered where Josie was. It was just after midnight. He figured she could still be working, prayed she wouldn't go home and make things worse.

He pulled a deep breath into his lungs. "It'll take me a couple of hours to get the money together, get the chopper, and get there."

"You got ninety minutes." The phone went dead and Beau cursed.

He felt Cassidy's hand on his shoulder. "Beau, what is it? What's going on?"

The breath he'd been holding shuddered out. "The guy

who tried to kill you? He's got Missy and Evie. He wants a million bucks and a chopper."

"Oh, God."

"I've got to go." He rolled off the bed, strode over and grabbed his jeans, dragged them on and snagged a clean long-sleeved T-shirt. Behind him, he heard Cassidy run out the bedroom door and down the hall. By the time he'd finished dressing and started making calls, the first to his banker, Cassidy was rushing back into the room in jeans and a red plaid flannel shirt.

"I'm going with you."

"Not a good idea. You'll be safer here."

"I'm going. Missy and Evie might need me, Beau. Or Josie. Is Josie in the house, too?"

"I don't know. He didn't mention her." He started striding down the hall toward the garage and Cassidy fell in beside him.

"We need to call the café," she said, which he would have already done if he had been thinking more clearly. "We need to find out if Josie's still at work. If she is, we can't let her walk into the middle of this thing."

He glanced at Cassidy over his shoulder. "You're right. Can you call and find out?"

"Of course. You need me, Beau. Let me help you."

He swallowed. He always seemed to need her. He didn't like putting her in the middle of a bad situation, but at the moment, he had no choice. "All right, let's go."

Cassidy sat tensely in the Ferrari next to Beau. Tires squealing, he shot out of the garage, driving like a madman down the pavement toward the street, pausing only for a moment to speak to one of the guards, then taking Will Egan's frantic phone call when he learned Beau was leaving without Frank Marino.

"Don't worry, Marino's meeting us at the chopper," he informed Will over the speaker. They could make better time in the Ferrari and there wasn't room for Frank in the sports car. He explained the situation and ended with, "We'll figure things out as we go."

"You sure you won't need backup when you get there?"

"I don't want to set this guy off," Beau said. "As soon as he releases the hostages, I'll call the police."

"He could force them to go with him, Beau. He could shoot your helo pilot. Anything could happen."

Cassidy had run through the various scenarios with Beau as they had prepared to leave, including the ones Will mentioned.

"The guy isn't getting on the chopper," Beau said. "I won't let that happen. I just need to get him away from the girl and the baby."

Then they could deal with the hostage taker, the guy who had tried to kill Cassidy twice before.

"You realize this might just be a diversion to bring you out in the open," Will said. "Somewhere an assassin can get at you."

"We'll be ready if that's the case."

Cassidy's hand went to her waist. The little .380 in the holster clipped to her belt felt comforting. Cassidy was a good shot, and since Beau was good at just about everything, she figured he was more than competent with the Glock he was carrying.

She thought of what Will had said, that this could be a diversion to get them out in the open, but Cassidy had a feeling that wasn't what was going on. The guy who had tried to kill her wasn't a professional hit man. If he had been, she would be dead.

"Be careful," Will said.

"Count on it." Beau hung up the phone. They needed to get to the roof of the Tex/Am building, get on the chopper, and get to Pleasant Hill. But first they needed to pick up the money.

On the way, Cassidy phoned the café. It rang four times before the call was answered.

"Pleasant Hill Café," Josie's familiar voice said. "I'm sorry, we're closed."

Cassidy felt a wave of relief that the woman wasn't trapped in the house with a killer. "Josie, this is Cassidy Jones. Beau and I are on our way to Pleasant Hill. A problem's come up. We need you to wait for us in the café."

"What? We're closed. I'm just leaving for home."

"You can't leave, Josie. Beau will explain everything when we get there."

"Oh, God, something's wrong. What is it? What's going on?"

Cassidy glanced over at Beau, who was gripping the wheel as if he might tear it off the steering column, forcing himself to keep the Ferrari at a speed just above the limit. They couldn't afford to be stopped for a ticket.

"We need to talk in person," Cassidy said. "Promise me you won't leave the café until we get there."

"Oh, Lord Almighty—has something happened to my babies? What is it? Please, you have to tell me."

Cassidy's chest went tight. She didn't want to tell the woman the two people she loved most in the world were in danger, but whatever Josie was imagining might be worse than the truth.

"They're okay, Josie. There's a man in the house with them. He hasn't hurt them. He just wants money. Beau is bringing it. As soon as he gets it, the man will let Missy and Evie go."

Josie sobbed into the phone.

"We're coming, Josie. In the helicopter. It won't take us long to get there. Just stay calm and everything will be okay. You hear me?"

"My girls. My sweet babies."

"Josie, listen to me. Beau's going to take care of everything. He won't let anyone hurt them. You know that, right? He loves them. You just stay there. And whatever you do, don't call the police."

Josie whimpered.

"Promise me, Josie."

"I'll stay here. I won't call the cops or nobody else."

"Good, that's good. We'll see you soon." Cassidy ended the call, wiping her eyes with the tail of her flannel shirt. When she looked at Beau, his jaw was locked tight.

"She's okay for now," Cassidy said. "We just need to pick up the money and get there."

Beau sliced her a look. "There's a chance the money won't be enough. No way to know with a guy like that."

"Missy said he was wearing a ski mask. That means he doesn't want to be recognized. He wouldn't care about that if he was planning to kill them."

Beau's iron grip on his jaw eased a little. "You're right. We just need to get there." But he didn't sound completely convinced.

The money was waiting when he pulled the Ferrari up in front of the Dallas State Bank. The manager, sleepy-eyed and disconcerted, was there to personally hand over the heavy black canvas bag.

"This is highly unusual, Beau. Some of the bills are larger than you wanted. We didn't have much time. Is everything okay?" The bald, officious-looking manager shifted nervously from side to side.

"It will be. Thanks for handling this, Jim. I knew I could count on you. I'd appreciate your discretion."

"No problem. You know you can rely on Dallas State, Beau."

Beau grabbed the bag, popped the trunk, which was small but big enough to hold the bag of money, jumped back in the car, and they shot off down the street. The chopper was sitting on the roof when they reached the top floor of the Tex/Am building.

The elevator door slid open and Cassidy spotted Frank Marino, red hair glinting in the lights around the helipad. The rotors spun gently as Frank ran over to help her climb in. Beau tossed the bag of money into the chopper and followed. Frank climbed in behind them and slid closed the door.

"You sure you're ready for this?" Frank asked as they strapped themselves into their seats. "Like I said, might be smarter to bring in the police." Frank, a former police officer, had wanted to call in the authorities, but until they knew more, Beau refused to take the chance.

"No police," he said as he had before. "Not until we're sure they're safe." The roar of the engine and the whir of the rotors ended the conversation. They put on their headsets, but there wasn't much more to say.

Cassidy looked at Beau and her heart went out to him. Beau had adopted Missy and Evie as part of his family. Aside from Linc and Carly, they were all he had. Beau felt responsible for what was happening to them, though it wasn't really his fault. All he'd wanted was justice for his father. But Beau didn't see it that way.

The eighty-mile, twenty-five-minute flight was the longest of Cassidy's life, even with the chopper zooming at a hundred and seventy miles an hour over the darkened landscape. The blur of city lights faded to occasional pin-dots below as they traveled farther and farther into the rural countryside.

At Beau's instruction, the pilot headed straight for the park across the street from the house on Shady Lane. The bad news was, when they got there, the outside of the house was lit up like a giant summer carnival. Red and blue lights flashing, half a dozen patrol cars were parked at various angles in the street around the house, uniformed officers crouched next to their vehicles.

Beau swore softly. Marino made a hissing sound between his teeth. And Cassidy flat-out cursed.

Adrenaline pumped into Beau's veins, speeding up his heart rate. The last thing he wanted was for the guy in the house to panic. Crossing the grass toward the residence, he walked next to Cassidy while Frank covered from behind. He had just reached the opposite side of the road when a small group of uniformed officers stepped out of the shadows, blocking his way.

Beau recognized police chief Eric Warren, his solid jaw tight, clearly all business. Detective Tom Briscoe stood next to him, looking more worried than Beau had ever seen him.

"We've got a situation here, Beau," the chief said. "Which apparently you're aware of or you wouldn't be here."

"Are the girls all right? Missy and the baby?"

"Far as we know. The guy in there—he won't talk to anyone but you. Told us he was waiting for you. Said you'd be here any minute."

"How'd you know what was going on?"

"Neighbor saw a man wearing a ski mask through one of the windows and called 9-1-1. Neighbor said there was a woman and a baby in the house. We checked, found out Missy Kessler and her daughter had just moved in."

Beau looked over at the house. All the shades were drawn, and only a single lamp cast dim light into the living room.

"We're bringing in a hostage negotiator from Dallas," Chief Warren said. "Might be a while before he gets here."

"We don't need a hostage negotiator. I've got the money he wants. I'll talk to him, see if I can convince him to come out and get it."

"You're a civilian, Beau. You need to let us handle this."

Beau shook his head. "No way. I want those girls safe. I'll do whatever I have to in order to make that happen."

"Take it easy, okay? We all want the same thing here." The chief surveyed his men. "We're a little shorthanded.

We've got some kind of stomach bug going around. County sheriff handles SWAT. They're putting a team together now. Might take a while."

"*Jesus*. The sheriff handles SWAT? Howler's in charge?"

"Look, Beau, I know you and Sheriff Howler have some bad history, but SWAT falls under his jurisdiction. Like I said, we're all shorthanded, so I don't know how many men he can muster."

The last thing they needed were more men. Beau couldn't begin to imagine what was going on inside the house. And once Sheriff Howler arrived, he'd be in charge. Emmett Howler was the man who had arrested Beau the night he, Linc, and Kyle Howler, the sheriff's son, had tried to rob that convenience store. Even though it had been Kyle's idea, Howler still carried a grudge against Beau and Linc.

His stomach knotted. This was turning into a giant clusterfuck and Missy and Evie were going to be the ones to pay.

A feminine hand settled on his shoulder. He looked at Cassidy and the strength and resolve he saw in her pretty green eyes steadied him.

"They're going to be okay, Beau. We won't let anything happen to them."

He swallowed and nodded. He'd find a way to get them out of there. He had to.

"Is that bulge beneath your jacket what I think it is?" the chief asked.

"We're both armed, both permitted." In his case, carrying was probably not a good idea at the moment, seeing as he was currently under suspicion of murder. But the chief didn't press the issue.

Beau's phone rang. He dug it out of his jeans and looked at the screen. It was Missy's cell number. "It's him." Warren moved closer and Beau held the phone so the chief could listen.

"I'm here," Beau said. "Just landed in the park across the street."

"I thought I told you no cops."

"I didn't call them. One of the neighbors spotted you through the window and dialed 9-1-1."

"You got the money?"

"I've got it. Let Missy take the baby and leave, and you can have it."

A harsh laugh came over the line. "Yeah, like I'm gonna do that. What, you think I'm an idiot?"

Beau took a calming breath.

"Ask him his name," the chief quietly suggested.

"Who are you? What's your name?"

"None of your business. The money in the chopper?"

"Yes, it's waiting for you there. So what do you want me to call you?"

"I guess it don't matter. Since we're gonna be such good friends, you can call me Franco."

"All right, then, Franco."

"Leave the money where it is. We're getting ready to come out. I'm bringing the girl and the kid with me. Tell the pilot to get the chopper ready to go. Anybody tries to interfere, I shoot the girl."

The phone went dead and the knot in Beau's stomach tightened to the point of pain.

Chapter Thirty-Two

The baby was fussing, sensing her mother's fear. Missy held her gently, twirling from side to side, bouncing her a little, trying to comfort her. "It's all right, sweetheart. Mama's right here."

"Get the kid ready. We're leaving." After the police arrived, the man who had broken into their home had removed the ski mask he'd been wearing. He was average height, with olive skin, heavy eyebrows and a long, pointed nose. He'd told her to call him Franco.

"You're letting us go?" Hope rose inside her. She knew Beau had just arrived in his helicopter. Maybe everything was going to be okay.

"Not yet. Once we get to Mexico, I'll let you go."

A jolt of fear tore a strangled sound from her throat. "*Mexico!* You can't take us to Mexico! How will we get home?"

"Look. I wasn't gonna take you, okay? But now the cops are here, so I don't have any choice."

"Please. I'm begging you. Evie's too little for a trip like that. She might get sick. She might even die."

His black eyes swung to her face, taking in her long

blond hair and blue eyes, slid down over the curve of her breasts beneath the robe and nightgown she was wearing, took in her slender bare feet.

A shiver ran through her. She'd had a boyfriend in high school. She'd slept with Stewart. She knew when a man looked at a woman that way, he wanted to get between her legs.

"So . . . if you want," Franco said, "we could leave the baby in the house and you could come with me. Just you and me, you know? With all that money, we could have some real fun in Mexico."

Missy bit back a whimper. She couldn't imagine leaving her baby. She was too tiny, still breastfeeding. She needed her mama. But if Franco took them to Mexico, Evie could die. Missy's eyes filled. No matter what happened, her mom would take care of Evie. And Beau would make sure she had everything she needed. He was protective of Evie. Protective of both of them. She had to put her baby's safety first.

She pretended to smile but her lips trembled. "Okay, I'll go with you. I've got to get dressed. Then I'll just put Evie in her crib and get my things."

"Make it snappy. We don't have much time."

Missy started shaking. She fought not to cry as she left the room, but tears streamed down her cheeks. She swallowed against the thick lump clogging her throat and tried not to think she might never see her tiny baby daughter again.

"Try to stall him," Chief Warren said. "We aren't ready. We need to wait for SWAT, get men in position, be ready for this guy when he comes out."

"I don't think you're going to have time for that," Beau said. "I'm going in there and talk to him."

Warren clamped a hand on Beau's shoulder, stopping

him before he could move. "You're a civilian, Beau. I can't let you do that."

Beau shook off the chief's hand. "Let me help you, dammit. This is my fault. They wouldn't be in trouble if I hadn't been digging around, trying to find my father's killer."

"Sorry, that's not the way it works. We wait, hold our positions. We've already replaced your pilot with one of our men, in case gunfire breaks out. Once SWAT arrives, we can put a sniper in place, take him out if we have to."

At least his pilot was safe. One worry less. Beau's cell started ringing. He brought up his phone and held it so the chief could hear. "I'm listening."

"You've got five minutes to get the cops to back off. If I see even one of them when I open the door, I shoot the girl." The line went dead and Beau cursed. He thought of the young woman and her baby trapped in the house with a killer, and his mouth went dry.

He looked at Warren. "You heard what he said. You need to pull your men back. Get them far enough away that he can't see them." Movement off to the left caught his attention. A tall, broad-shouldered man materialized out of the darkness, moving toward him with long, confident strides. A rifle case hung from one of his big hands.

Joshua Cain. Linc's brother. Ex-military, former Marine special ops sniper. Beau had never been so glad to see anyone in his life.

"Linc thought you might need some backup," Josh said.

"How did he—"

"Guy named Marino called him, explained what was going on. Linc's in New Mexico or he'd be here with me."

Beau flicked a glance at Frank Marino, who shrugged but didn't apologize. At the moment it was impossible to be mad at the guy for overstepping his bounds.

"You're Cain," Chief Warren said to Josh. "Everybody in town knows what you did to protect our soldiers." Josh was a war hero. He was currently living at Blackland Ranch, trying to get his life back together after a brush with death that had ended his military career.

According to Linc, Josh wanted to leave his soldiering days behind and start over. Beau felt another stab of guilt for dragging Linc's brother into this.

"Your timing couldn't be better," Chief Warren said. "We've got a woman and baby held hostage in that house. The subject's just about to come out and head for the helo. SWAT isn't here yet and we're out of time. We could really use your help."

Something flickered in Josh's deep blue eyes. "That's why I'm here."

"Good. Joshua Cain, you're hereby deputized as an officer of the Pleasant Hill police force."

Josh just nodded. He turned to study the house, looked at the position of the helicopter sitting on the grass in the park, rotors spinning. He appeared to be drawing a mental line from the front door to the aircraft.

Without a word, he walked off toward the trees, moving as soundlessly as a ghost in the night. Beau blinked and Josh was gone.

"Where is he?" Warren asked.

"He's out there," Beau said. "Wherever he's supposed to be."

Chief Warren didn't argue. They had less than sixty seconds until the five-minute deadline was up. Warren checked to be sure his men, weapons drawn, were out of sight. The last police officer had just disappeared when Beau's phone rang.

"We're coming out," Franco said. "I better not see any police."

"No police," Beau said. "The chopper's ready to go just the way you wanted." He doubted the police officer at the

controls was actually going anywhere. This would be re-
solved one way or another before the helo left the ground.

"I need to see the money," Franco said. "The girl's with
me. I'm leaving the kid in the house."

Beau felt a trickle of relief. "That's good. Now you're
being smart." At least the baby would be safe. Unfortunately, the money was in the bag on the floor of the chopper.
The guy would have to board the aircraft to see it.

"Ready or not, here we come." Franco's voice held an
odd lightness, almost a note of excitement. Then the line
went dead.

The front door opened and a man with shaggy black hair
stepped out on the porch, Missy in front of him, his arm
clamped around her neck. A gun was pressed into the side
of her head. In the moonlight, her face was as white as the
sweater she was wearing. Her eyes were wild and tears
streamed down her cheeks.

Guilt swamped him. She was just a kid. The mother of a
newborn baby.

He felt Cassidy's presence beside him. She reached for
his hand, laced her fingers with his. The warmth of her touch
centered him, gave him a moment's peace. He squeezed her
fingers, then he let go and started walking.

Cassidy's heart nearly stopped beating when Beau
stepped out of the shadows, his hands in the air. Positioned
behind a tree, she drew her weapon and went into a shooting stance, her gun aimed at the hostage taker.

"I'm Reese," Beau said, walking into the moonlight
where Franco could see him as he approached the house. A
few feet away, Chief Warren quietly cursed. Cassidy's
palms went damp. She tightened her hold on the pistol.

"I'll get the money out of the chopper," Beau said,

"show you it's all there. But you can't leave till you let the girl go."

"Fuck you, Reese. I'm taking her with me. She's going of her own free will. Right, baby?"

Missy made a strangled sound in her throat, and Cassidy's chest clamped down. She kept her gun pointed at Franco, but she was too far away to risk any sort of shot.

Franco kept walking, forcing the girl in front of him as a shield, his arm still locked around her neck, gun pressed to her temple. "Stay back or I shoot her."

Hands held high, Beau froze where he stood. "The helicopter will have to land before you get to the border. It can only travel a little over four hundred miles without refueling. Piedras Negras and Nuevo Laredo are the closest Mexican towns. They're five hundred miles away."

Franco paused. "I don't believe you. You think I'm a fool? We're leaving and you better not try to stop us."

"Let the girl go and I'll arrange for you to refuel in San Antonio. No cops. The pilot will land and refuel and you'll be on your way."

"She's my insurance policy. She's going." Franco glanced around. He was still a good distance from the helicopter in the park across the street.

Franco started walking. As he stepped off the curb, a string of vehicle headlights appeared. Two sheriff's SUVs and a SWAT Bearcat careened around the corner, sirens blaring, roared down the road toward them, and slammed to a halt. Deputies in full tactical gear streamed out from the vehicles.

"I told you no police!" Franco screamed. Panic had him turning, swinging his big black semiautomatic pistol toward the deputies, firing off a string of bullets. Then the gun swung back toward Missy.

Cassidy watched in horror, too far away to make the

shot, and the deputies were not in position. Franco was going to kill Missy and there was nothing anyone could do.

A rifle shot sounded, the roar echoing into the darkness. Franco's head exploded in a rush of blood and bits of skull, and his lifeless body crumpled to the ground, the gun flying out of his hand as he hit the pavement. Missy started screaming, the sound a high, eerie wail of horror.

Beau raced toward her and the girl flew into his arms. She was covered with blood and hysterical. Cassidy ran toward the house.

"You're okay, Missy," Beau said, hugging her close, trying to calm her. "You're okay."

"My baby! I want my baby!"

"I'll get her!" Cassidy ran into the dwelling, but Evie wasn't in the living room. She ran for the bedroom, spotted the baby in her pink bassinet, waving her tiny arms and gurgling softly. Cassidy's heart clenched. She blinked back tears as she picked up the infant and cradled the baby in her arms.

"It's all right, sweetheart. You and your mama are safe." She loved babies, could imagine the beautiful babies she and Beau could make, felt a wave of sadness that it was never going to happen.

By the time she carried the infant outside, Josie was there, shouting for her daughter and crying. The café was close enough to hear the sirens. Apparently she figured she had waited long enough.

Beau handed the hysterical girl over to her mother and Missy began to sob in Josie's arms. Spotting Cassidy approaching with her infant daughter, Missy gave a soft cry and reached for her baby girl.

"Evie's fine," Cassidy said. "You're both okay."

"Evie . . ." Missy sobbed, carefully cuddling the infant in the crook of her arm. "My sweet little baby." Tears ran down her cheeks. She looked up at Beau. "I knew you'd come. You saved us. You've both been so good to us."

Beau just nodded, his features grim. Cassidy knew he blamed himself that Missy and Evie had ever been in danger. "They're okay," she said to him. "They're both okay."

Beau reached for her, pulled her into his arms. "It's over," he said, a shudder rippling through his tall, lean body. When he buried his face in her hair, Cassidy hung on hard.

"Missy and Evie are safe," she said. "Everybody's okay."

He swallowed. "If it hadn't been for Josh . . ." The words trailed off. *If it hadn't been for Josh, Missy would be dead.*

Chief Warren walked up and they broke apart. "Josh is giving a statement. You'll both need to do the same." He gave them a weary smile. "I'm glad the girl and her baby are okay."

It was over. Missy and Evie were safe and the hit-and-run driver who had tried to kill Cassidy was dead. The police knew his name now—Franco Giannetti. She breathed a sigh of relief.

"One down, one to go," Beau said, reminding her there was still a contract killer out there. Cassidy felt like collapsing on the ground, curling into a protective ball, and crying till she ran out of tears.

Instead, she walked next to Beau toward the waiting police.

Chapter Thirty-Three

They gave their statements at a picnic table in the park, trying to ignore the chaos around them, the flashing lights of the patrol cars, the ambulances, EMTs, sheriff's deputies, and SWAT.

After they'd finished, Beau went in search of Josh. Without him, Missy would be dead. He asked one of the policemen where to find him, but the officer said Josh had given his statement and left.

Beau didn't know Linc's brother well, but on the surface at least, Josh was the strong, silent type, a guy who probably didn't want any thanks. Or maybe he was still just trying to get his bearings in a world so different from the one he'd left behind.

Josh liked his privacy. Unfortunately, by tomorrow, his name would be all over the news.

Eventually, they were able to leave. By the time Beau, Cassidy, and Frank were aboard the chopper on their way back to Dallas, the sun was a big yellow ball rising over the flat Texas landscape, spilling faint gold light on the farms and towns below.

From the Tex/Am building, Beau drove the Ferrari back

to the house, with Marino following in the black SUV. Beau checked in with Will Egan while Marino took off for the studio apartment at the far end of the house.

Beau and Cassidy headed for the bedroom, desperate to get some sleep, both of them exhausted. Later, after they were rested, they would start over, try again to solve the mystery that was destroying their lives.

But only three short hours passed before their sleep was disturbed. Only three hours before Beau's cell rang with a call from Will Egan, warning him the FBI was about to show up at his door.

Beau cursed as he rolled out of bed. Eyes gritty from lack of sleep, he dressed in jeans, shrugged into a long-sleeved T-shirt, and headed down the hall, leaving Cassidy to dress and join him.

She walked into the kitchen a few minutes behind him in a pair of tailored slacks and a yellow turtleneck that outlined her pretty breasts. She looked feminine and professional. This was, after all, the FBI. Considering the situation, it should have been impossible to feel a jolt of sexual heat.

Beau ignored it, turned to the pot of coffee he had just finished brewing, poured three mugs full.

"Cassidy, this is Special Agent Quinn Taggart." He handed a mug to the agent, handed one to Cassidy. "Agent Taggart and I met a couple of years back when he worked a serial killer case involving one of our female employees. He also worked with Linc last year when he and Carly were having trouble."

Taggart took a drink of his coffee. "Looks like now you're the ones having trouble."

"Nice to meet you, Agent Taggart," Cassidy said.

"Pleasure's mine, Ms. Jones." Taggart was in his late thirties, thick-shouldered and barrel-chested, with short blond hair in a buzz cut. Dressed in a dark brown suit, yellow shirt, and a pair of polished wing tips, he pulled out a chair for Cassidy, one for himself, and they all sat down.

Cassidy took a drink of her coffee, apparently as desperate for a shot of caffeine as Beau was.

"Sorry I'm late," she said, "but would you mind repeating the reason you're here, Agent Taggart?"

"Actually, we were waiting for you to get here before we started." Taggart leaned across the table, his authority clear. "Let me begin by saying how glad I am last night's situation ended with everyone safe."

Beau grunted. "Everyone but Franco Giannetti."

One of the agent's blond eyebrows went up. "I stand corrected. Everyone except Giannetti. Actually, it would have been better for us if Franco had been arrested. As I understand it, that wasn't an option."

"No," Beau said flatly.

"We've been keeping an eye on Franco for a little over a week, hoping something would break. He only recently surfaced on our radar. No prior arrest record, nothing that alerted us to him right away. We didn't expect him to go rogue the way he did last night, which is why we weren't there to stop him."

"Why were you watching him?" Beau asked.

"One of our informants came forward with information that Franco was the man responsible for a string of hit-and-run murders, including the recent attempts on Ms. Jones's life. Unfortunately, we didn't have enough evidence to arrest him."

Beau flicked a glance at Cassidy, who seemed as intrigued by the FBI man's presence at the house as he was. Giannetti was dead. Why was Taggart there?

"Go on," Beau said.

"Aside from the man's hit-and-run, murder-for-hire scheme, we found out one of his paying customers was a man named Clifford Jennings. We were hoping, once we had Franco in custody, we could get him to roll on Jennings. Unfortunately, that isn't going to happen now."

Beau took a sip of his coffee, hoping the caffeine would kick his brain into gear. "So the man you're after is Clifford Jennings?"

"Yes and no. Jennings works for Malcolm Vaughn. I understand you've spoken to Vaughn, that you went to see him in regard to your father's murder."

"That's right," Beau said, keeping his answers simple till he knew what the hell was going on.

"The man we're interested in is one of Vaughn's largest investors," Taggart continued.

Cassidy caught Beau's eye, silently asking for his approval. Beau nodded. If they helped the feds, maybe the feds would help them.

"Vaughn's connected to a man named Luca Reichlin," she said. "He's not the guy you're looking for, but he might help you find him."

"We know about Reichlin. The man makes his money as a service provider, working at the highest levels. One client at a time, charges big bucks, and anything goes. Currently he's employed by a Texas billionaire named Jamal Nawabi."

Beau dredged up a memory from his sleep-deprived brain, something he had read or seen on TV. "I've heard of him. Lives in Houston."

"That's right. He lives there now, but Nawabi was born in Kabul, Afghanistan. Made his money in oil and gas and moved to Houston ten years ago. Net worth approximately thirteen billion."

Beau's eyebrows went up. "Definitely not chump change."

"No, it isn't."

"And the FBI is interested in Nawabi because . . . ?"

"Because lately his name has been surfacing in terrorist-related Internet chatter. We have no idea if it amounts to anything or not, but Nawabi lost his family during the war.

There's a chance he might want some kind of payback. We think it's possible he's involved with members of the same cell your friend Cain butted heads with last year. That's why I was assigned the case. We think someone from that cell may have been responsible for the terror attack last week in Houston."

Beau's head spun as he tried to put the pieces together. The Houston attack had been all over the news. And everyone in Texas knew about Cain's clash with the terrorists who had tried to smuggle stinger missiles into Dallas. But how were the attacks related to Franco Giannetti? It made no sense.

Maybe if he got a few more hours of sleep he'd be able to think more clearly.

Taggart turned to Beau. "We've asked the Howler County district attorney to hold off on any proceedings against you, Beau. We think your father's death may somehow be related to our investigation. The DA's agreed."

Relief eased some of the tension in his shoulders. "That's some good news at least."

"Unfortunately, Beau and I have an even bigger problem," Cassidy said. "Apparently there's a contract out on us. We think Mal Vaughn may be behind it."

Taggart frowned. "I thought Giannetti was the problem."

"Franco tried and failed," Beau said. "There's someone else out there now and it looks like the guy's a professional. Nearly took us out a few days ago."

"You report it?"

Beau nodded. "To Detective Briscoe in Pleasant Hill and also the Dallas PD."

"I met Will Egan, your head of security, when I arrived. I know Frank Marino. He's a good man."

"I've got round-the-clock protection," Beau said. "I'm doing everything I can to keep us safe."

Taggart glanced from one of them to the other. "Best thing you can do is hole up here until we figure this out."

"Give us a little time to digest all this," Beau said. "Maybe we can come up with something useful." *Maybe*. At the moment, none of the pieces seemed to fit together.

"That's the reason I'm here," Taggart said. "We're hoping, now that you understand the bigger picture, something will occur to you we might be able to use. You understand this is highly confidential. Our discussion doesn't go beyond this room?"

"Of course," he and Cassidy said in unison.

Taggart rose from his chair. "Call if you need me." He handed each of them a business card. Beau pulled out his cell and added the number to his contacts. Cassidy did the same.

"I'll be in touch," Taggart said. "In the meantime, you two be careful."

Beau walked Taggart to the door, then returned to the kitchen, where Cassidy sat sipping her coffee, looking almost as tired as he was.

"Let's go back to bed," he suggested, "get a couple more hours' sleep. Then we'll start over, take a look at everything we've got."

Cassidy managed a half-hearted smile. "That's an amazingly good idea."

Contract killers and terrorists, he thought. Could things get any worse?

Beau shuddered to think that, yeah, maybe they could.

Chapter Thirty-Four

After sleeping a few more hours, Cassidy felt a little better. It was midafternoon, the sun out but clouds beginning to build. Beau was already up, at work in his study.

She made a fresh pot of coffee, carried the thermal pot in with a couple of mugs, and poured them each a cup. She set Beau's down in front of him and turned to leave, but he caught her arm and tugged her down on his lap. A soft kiss turned slow and hot, and Cassidy's whole body lit up. The man really knew how to push her buttons.

"Thanks for the coffee," he said with another soft kiss. "Maybe it'll clear my head so we can figure this out."

Cassidy felt a little tug at her heart. She was in so deep with Beau. Way too deep. She wished there was something she could do.

Heading for her side of the desk, she opened her laptop and went to work. As soon as the screen lit up, she checked the GPS on Vaughn's car, then muffled a curse when she saw that the battery was dead. So was the battery-operated audio device that worked off her cell phone.

She'd been expecting it. Still, they were tools that could no longer be used.

"Anything?" Beau asked.

"Batteries are gone. We'll have to use the information we already have, go back over everything again."

His mouth flattened an instant before he went back to work. They started nosing around, going through files, hoping to spot something they had missed. After an hour of unsuccessful digging, Cassidy sat back in her chair.

"Let's take a break from the computer. What do you say we talk it out, run through our notes out loud, toss some ideas back and forth?"

Beau ran a hand over his face. "I don't know how much good it'll do, but maybe it'll help."

She picked up the yellow pad next to her laptop, and they headed for the table in the corner. She held up the notepad. "Old school," she said as she sat down across from him. "Let's start at the beginning."

Beau grumbled but nodded.

Determination and another cup of coffee fueled them as they delved through the information they had collected in the past few weeks. Cassidy printed the most recent information they had and they went over it verbally, sharing their thoughts aloud.

Beau got up to stretch, work the kinks out of his neck, then sat back down. Cassidy drummed her pencil on the table, drawing his attention.

"What is it?" he asked.

"We've gone over this again and again, but we always come to the same conclusion."

"Yeah," Beau said, frowning. "Zero, zip, nada."

"That's right. So let's try something new."

"Something new," Beau repeated. "I thought that's what we were doing. But all right, I'm game."

"Maybe the reason we keep coming up with zip is because

we've been looking at this the wrong way." Cassidy studied the notes she'd made on the pad, old ideas revived, new ones doodled on the thin blue lines, some scratched out, others rewritten.

"All this time we've been working the money angle," she said. "The loan your dad made with Vaughn, blackmailing George Larson into selling Green Gables, the building deal on the side, the arson fire for the insurance money, Jess Milford demanding money from Vaughn to keep quiet about what he knew."

"Money was what my father was all about."

"Right. Which is why we keep thinking the favor Vaughn's big client was after had to be something worth very large bucks. But what if money wasn't what the client wanted?"

Beau pondered the notion. "Taggart says Jamal Nawabi is Luca Reichlin's client. If Reichlin wanted a favor from Vaughn for his boss, it sure as hell wouldn't be money. He's already worth thirteen billion."

"Exactly. So let's make a leap and assume the Internet chatter is real. If Nawabi is part of a terrorist cell—"

"Terrorists don't need money, either. With all the oil they control, groups like Al-Qaeda and ISIS are swimming in dollars."

"So what do terrorists want?" Cassidy asked, working through the problem aloud.

"They want to destroy infidels. Anyone who doesn't believe the same way they do, Americans in particular."

Cassidy sat up straighter. "That's right, and to destroy infidels, they need access. *Access*, Beau. Access to planes to blow up the Twin Towers. Access to streets in the area where the Boston Marathon was being run."

"Nawabi would want access to . . . Jesus—what was the favor my father provided? Either knowingly or unknowingly, he gave Vaughn's client access to the capitol building!

What better terrorist target than blowing up the Texas State Capitol?"

Hurriedly digging through the printed material they had collected, he tugged out the sheet with the list of contractors hired to do deferred maintenance.

"What was the name of the company Scott Watson recommended?" He ran over the names on the list. "There it is— you circled it. Hardrock Trenching."

Her pulse started thrumming. "I remember it wasn't a very big company. It had to qualify under the Small Construction Participation Assistance Program."

"That's right." Beau shot up from his chair and pulled her to her feet. He tugged her over to her laptop. "Let's see if we can get the names of the people who own the company and a list of employees."

Excited now, thinking maybe they were finally on the right track, Cassidy sat down and started typing. "And we need to know exactly what job they are doing."

By a little after four P.M., they had the answers they had been looking for.

"Sonofabitch!" Beau studied the laptop screen over Cassidy's shoulder. "It's hard to wrap your head around, but there it is."

"We need to call Quinn Taggart," Cassidy said urgently.

"Better yet, let's pay him a visit. I don't think this is something we want to talk to him about on the phone."

Collecting their notes, making sure they had everything they needed, they set off in the Ferrari, Beau driving the car at breakneck speed toward FBI headquarters at One Justice Way, which on a Friday with heavy traffic took what seemed hours.

Cassidy refrained from mentioning that honking his horn and cutting in and out between cars wasn't going to get them there any faster. Beginning to know her, Beau flicked her a sideways glance and tapped the ~~breaks~~ brakes.

Cassidy flashed him a smile and for the first time in days, Beau smiled back.

"We're almost there," he said a few minutes later, turning off Storey Lane onto Justice Way.

Beau had called ahead, but Taggart wasn't there. He had an appointment somewhere else, but Beau had demanded a meeting, told the man's assistant it could be a matter of life or death. It was getting dark by the time the Ferrari parked in the lot of the federal complex and they walked through the main entrance into the big gray building.

"Agent Taggart's expecting you." An attractive middle-aged woman wearing tortoiseshell glasses sat behind a computer at the front desk. "Someone will be with you shortly."

So Taggart had returned, as Cassidy had figured he would.

A few minutes later a young woman with glossy black hair slicked into a knot at the back of her neck walked toward them. Dressed in a navy-blue skirt suit, white cotton blouse, and low-heeled shoes, typical FBI attire, she smiled as she approached.

"I'm Special Agent Margaret Dominguez. Agent Taggart is waiting for you upstairs. If you will please follow me." She was pretty, at least part Latina, with creamy skin and big brown eyes.

They rode in silence as the elevator swept them up to the fourth floor and the doors slid open. In a glass-fronted conference room, Quinn Taggart waited next to a long mahogany table.

"I didn't expect to hear from you so soon," he said, shaking hands with each of them.

"If things hadn't been happening so fast," Beau said, "we might have figured it out sooner."

Taggart indicated they should sit down, so they each took a seat in one of the rolling black vinyl chairs that lined the table. Beau set the manila folder they had compiled in front of him.

"Before we start," he said, "we'd like to know where you are with Malcolm Vaughn."

Taggart frowned. "Sorry, that's FBI business. I've given you more than I should have already."

Their lives were on the line. They needed to know what was going on with Vaughn, and as they had feared, the FBI wasn't going to tell them.

Beau rose from his chair and braced his hands on the table. "You don't have time to stonewall, Taggart. What's in this file is urgent. It could be a matter of life and death. Tell us what we need to know."

Cassidy noticed the faint tightening of Taggart's square jaw. He wasn't happy, but he was intrigued.

"We found a disposable phone in Franco Giannetti's car," the agent said. "There were calls between him and Clifford Jennings. We'll be able to get a warrant for Jennings, but we aren't quite ready to pick him up. If Jennings gives us what we need, we can bring Vaughn in. With luck, we can use him to go after Luca Reichlin. If Jamal Nawabi is connected to terrorism, our hope is Reichlin can help us prove it."

Beau sat back down in his chair and opened the file. "It might not matter. What we have in here will answer most of your questions." The information was also on the flash drive he handed to Taggart.

"This file contains a list of the companies currently working on deferred maintenance at the Texas State Capitol," Beau said. "I think you'll find one company of particular interest."

He pointed to the name circled on the list. "Hardrock Trenching. Senator Scott Watson—now deceased—recommended them at the request of my father—now also deceased. It was a favor done for Malcolm Vaughn as repayment for a portion of a loan."

"Go on," Taggart said, clearly interested now.

"Hardrock Trenching qualified through a special program for small contractors. We can't confirm since we don't have the same information you have, but we believe at least some of the employees' names will correspond with members of the terrorist cell you're investigating."

Taggart's gaze sharpened on Beau. A pulse beat excitedly at the side of his neck. "How do you know this?"

They knew because Cassidy had dug through Hardrock Trenching's bank accounts, employee tax withholdings, anything that would give them the names of the people working on the project, many of whom were Middle Eastern. She had also gone into the corporate records, which eventually led them to the name they were looking for—Jamal Nawabi.

Beau leaned back in his chair. "Let's just say we received the information through an anonymous source."

Taggart wasn't pleased. "That's your story?"

The glance Beau flicked Cassidy held a hint of amusement. "That's right, and we're sticking to it."

Taggart's mouth edged up, but only for a moment. "All right—for now. So you believe the men who work for this company are part of a terrorist cell."

"That's right. Turns out Hardrock Trenching is owned by a company named Mardax, which is owned by a corporation called Sandon. One of the owners of the Sandon Corporation is Jamal Nawabi."

"*What?*" Taggart's whole body went tense.

Cassidy spoke up. "If Nawabi is a terrorist, as you suspect, we think it's possible the men working for Hardrock Trenching are planning to destroy the Texas State Capitol."

Beau leaned toward Taggart. "For the most impact, it's likely to happen when the entire legislature is in session.

Which, though repairs are currently in progress—is going on now."

Taggart was out of his chair before Beau had finished his last sentence. "Stay right here." Striding through the door of the conference room, he disappeared outside.

Cassidy could hear him shouting orders as he headed down the hall. True, it sounded like something out of a TV movie, but the information they had compiled proved the threat was real.

"No matter what happens now," she said, "it's all out in the open. No point in Vaughn having us killed when the FBI knows everything we know."

Beau rose from his chair, pulled her up, and into his arms. "Once the FBI follows the chain of evidence that starts with my father's murder and ends with Jamal Nawabi, I should be completely in the clear and neither of us will be targets."

Beau bent his head and very gently kissed her. "It's almost over, baby, and I owe it all to you. If you hadn't shown up that day in my father's study, I'd probably be rotting in jail."

Cassidy rested her cheek against his shoulder. Just a few more days and Beau's name would be cleared. Her job would be finished. She could pack her bags and go home.

Her eyes stung. Even if Beau asked her to stay, she would refuse. She valued herself too highly to live in a dead woman's shadow.

She ignored the ache in her throat and the pain that settled deep inside her. She was in love with Beau, but she would have to give him up. There was nothing else she could do.

Chapter Thirty-Five

After they finished making love, Beau curled Cassidy against his side in bed. It had been a long, torturous day, but everything they had worked for was falling into place.

Cassidy had been quiet since they'd left the federal building. She was worried. So was he. Until Nawabi and the terrorists were stopped, anything could happen. Hundreds of lives could be lost.

He yawned, beginning to drift to sleep when his cell phone started ringing. He sighed at what was becoming an unwelcome habit. Beau snagged the phone.

"Turn on your TV," Agent Taggart said. "Bring up the news." Beau picked up the remote, clicked it on, and the screen lit up.

"What's going on?" Cassidy asked as Beau changed the channel.

"It's Taggart," he said. From then on there wasn't much need for explanation. Cameras rolled in Austin, showing teams of FBI agents swarming the Texas State Capitol. Bomb-sniffing dogs strained at their leashes. Lines of police vehicles and black FBI SUVs stretched as far as the camera lens could see.

Beau put the phone on speaker. "Fast work," he said.

"The session was over for the day, but construction work was continuing at night. Hardrock Trenching was doing maintenance under the capitol rotunda, digging trenches for a series of pipes for new underground plumbing. They were also planting bombs in the trenches—set to go off with manual detonators. Cell phones that could be exploded at any time."

"Jesus," Beau said.

"Bombs that could kill Lord knows how many people," Cassidy added.

"Hundreds, maybe more. Thanks to you and Cassidy, that isn't going to happen."

"What about Vaughn?" Cassidy asked.

"We're lining up evidence that connects Jennings, Vaughn, Luca Reichlin, and Jamal Nawabi. They'll all be facing charges very soon. Once things get underway, I'll speak to the DA in Howler County on your behalf, Beau. I don't think you'll have to worry about being charged in Senator Reese's murder."

Relief hit him hard, reminding him how worried he had been. "I appreciate that."

"You can watch some of what's happening on TV. As things progress, I'll keep you posted on the rest. Good night, both of you, and thanks again." The line went dead and for a while they watched events unfolding in Austin.

No mention was made of Jamal Nawabi; nor was there any reference to Luca Reichlin, Clifford Jennings, or Malcolm Vaughn.

Still, it was only a matter of time until all of it was over. "I feel like the weight of the world has been lifted off my shoulders," Beau said.

Pulling Cassidy down on the mattress, he kissed her. What started as a celebratory moment turned deeper, hotter. After everything that had happened, they seemed to need each other tonight. He didn't like how deeply involved he'd become, but he'd worry about that tomorrow.

Tomorrow, he told himself. It was still a day away.

It was late, almost two in the morning. Eliza Spears had been watching the sprawling contemporary home in the expensive Bluffview neighborhood from various locations, looking for exactly the right entry.

She had no idea why killing Beaumont Reese and his current bedmate, a private investigator named Cassidy Jones, was worth a quarter of a million bucks—the deal she had cut for her services—but she didn't care.

Ten days ago, she had received the call on a disposable phone, the usual procedure. Because the payoff that Jennings had agreed to was so big, she'd made an exception to some of her rules and taken the job; then she'd gone off the grid.

Three days ago, she'd spotted a house a few blocks away from the targets' location with a FOR RENT sign in front of a small, furnished apartment above a detached garage. The property was owned by an eighty-year-old widow who rarely ventured outdoors and was too rickety to climb the stairs.

"I don't really need the money," Mrs. Dabney had said. "I just hate seeing the apartment go to waste."

Eliza inwardly smiled. Being softhearted, the old woman hadn't been able to resist renting to Julie Simmons, a slender blond woman in her early thirties, a single woman who was supposedly four months pregnant and only needed to stay for a week or two before her place in Dallas was ready to move into.

The apartment provided the perfect base of operations, a spot to store her equipment, stake out Reese's house and both targets, and prepare. Now the time had come to utilize the information she had compiled.

Eliza moved silently through the darkness. A thick layer of clouds obscured a fingernail moon, giving her the cover she needed. Dressed completely in black, her blond wig gone, her short black hair stuffed under a black knit cap, face covered in greasepaint, she was tall enough to pass for the man her clients believed her to be.

Athletic and strong, her muscles honed from hours spent in the gym, she was former military, her army training invaluable for the far more lucrative career she had chosen. She figured in a year or two, she could live the life of luxury she had always wanted.

Eliza settled herself, focused on the task ahead. The money was better than good, the biggest job she'd ever undertaken. Her task was simply to eliminate Reese and Jones, exactly what Eliza planned to do.

She had waited long enough, prepared for every possibility. It wouldn't be easy, not with guards circling the property every fifteen minutes. Not with a bodyguard sleeping in the studio apartment at one end of the house while her targets slept in the other. But the way she had worked it out, it was doable.

Black canvas satchel in hand, she crossed a wide stretch of manicured lawn, careful to stay in the shadows of the trees scattered around the four-acre property, headed for the stream that meandered through it, and slipped down the bank.

Keeping low, each step placed soundlessly, she moved along the edge of the water with the stealth she'd been taught by the former special ops soldier she had trained with before she'd gone pro.

When the stream reached the point closest to the house, she checked her wristwatch and crouched below the bank, out of sight. A white circle of light appeared, approaching through the darkness, the guard right on time.

Eliza pressed against the bank, folding into herself, her

black clothes making her nearly invisible. The light swept closer, ran up and down both sides of the stream, then the guard moved on.

Eliza gave herself a couple of minutes to be sure the man was completely out of sight, then opened her satchel, pulled out her smartphone, and aimed it toward the house. The software she had downloaded disarmed the digital alarm system in less than three seconds, though red lights would continue to blink inside and out, giving the false impression the system was still armed.

The outside entrance to the studio at the far end of the house was her destination. She needed to dispose of the body-guard; then she could take care of Reese and the woman.

She smiled. She could almost smell the papery scent of money, touch the stacks of bills in her hand. She could almost feel the sun shining down as she lay on the beach in Cancún, sipping a salty margarita. It wouldn't be long now.

Eliza checked her weapon, a Walther PPQ, the silencer already in place. She smiled as she stuck it back in the bag and quietly moved forward.

Beau awoke slowly, his brain stirring to life in the darkened room lit only by the light of the moon outside. As he lay in his bedroom, next to Cassidy, he listened, straining to locate the sound that had roused him from a deep, dreamless sleep.

A soft click, a quiet glide of movement somewhere in the house had him rolling silently out of bed and dragging on his jeans. He opened the drawer in the nightstand beside the bed and lifted out his Glock. He didn't need to check to be sure it was loaded. Not since he'd found out someone was trying to kill them.

Beau started for the door, heard the mattress shift as Cassidy slid out of bed. He turned to see her slipping on her robe, knew the moment she saw the gun in his hand she would be arming herself.

It was probably nothing, just the house settling, or the wind blowing. Nothing to worry about. From the corner of his eye, he saw Cassidy come up behind him, her gun aimed at the ceiling, same as his. He pointed a finger at himself then down the hall toward the living room, pointed at her then down the hall in the opposite direction.

No way to know exactly where the sound had come from. No way to know if someone was actually inside the house. Or if there was more than one person.

They moved off in opposite directions. If it had been any other woman, he would have told her to stay in the bedroom, lock the door and keep safe, but this was Cassidy. He trusted her to know what she was doing. It occurred to him he trusted her as he hadn't trusted a woman in a very long time.

He paused at the end of the hall, listening for movement in the kitchen or living room. On the opposite side of the house, the studio apartment had its own kitchen and living area. No reason for Frank to come into the main part of the house at this hour of the night.

He heard the sound again, a kind of glide, almost indistinguishable and yet there was a rhythm to it, a progression that said the sound was moving forward, definitely heading for this end of the house.

The hairs on the back of his neck went up. Someone was inside and it wasn't Frank Marino. His gaze shot to the alarm on the wall next to the door leading out to the swimming pool. A tiny red light indicated the system was armed.

A soft glide, the faint shift of air. How had the intruder gotten inside the house undetected?

Beau flattened himself against the wall, his gun in a double-handed grip, legs braced slightly apart. He stood stock-still, letting the intruder get closer. Clearly the man was heading for the hallway leading to the bedrooms at the other end of the house.

Beau waited. Waited. If this was the assassin, he would be deadly. He sorted through his options, the most dangerous rising to the surface. He needed to take the man alive, needed to find out if it was Vaughn who was paying him, or if it was someone else. But if he made a mistake, it could get him killed, maybe get both of them killed.

His fingers tightened around the pistol grip. He was a good shot, better than good. He brought the gun up into position, aimed it toward the dark shape moving through the shadows. The pool lights lit the room with an eerie blue glow, but it wasn't enough to see. For an instant, the clouds parted, and a shaft of moonlight slid into the living room. A lean figure stepped into Beau's line of fire.

"Stop right where you are!"

The man darted and fired. At the same time Beau pulled off two quick rounds, ducking to the right, dodging the dull thump of the silenced bullets hitting the wall where he had just been standing. He heard the sound of running feet, heard the double tap of Cassidy's pistol, a shot striking the intruder in the knee and sending him crashing to the floor. The man's big black semiauto landed with a clatter and slid across the polished hardwood floor out of reach.

Beau and Cassidy both stepped out of the shadows, the barrels of their weapons aimed at the intruder, who lay on his back in a spreading pool of blood. Beau had aimed a little high, going for the man's shoulder and upper chest, determined to keep him alive. Cassidy's shots had both been aimed low.

Clutching his shoulder, the man groaned as Cassidy flipped a switch and the room lit up.

"Move an inch and I'll finish you," Beau warned.

The man didn't flinch, just lay there clutching his shoulder, his other hand reaching toward his bloody knee.

Cassidy hurried toward the phone in the kitchen. "I'll call security, have them call 9-1-1 while I check on Frank."

Beau fixed his attention on the assailant. "Did you kill Marino?" His gun remained steady as he studied the man's face, covered in black greasepaint beneath a black wool cap.

"I wasn't paid to . . . kill him." He took a ragged breath. "Since I don't work . . . for free, I loaded him up with . . . ketamine. The voice was high and soft, a female voice, Beau realized in shock. "He'll be out for a while but . . ." The woman sucked in a heavy breath of air. "He'll live."

"Who are you?"

Instead of answering, the woman hissed in pain and let her head fall back on the floor. "Look . . . it wasn't personal. A girl's got to . . . make a living, okay?"

"No, it isn't okay. Who do you work for?"

She took a ragged breath but didn't reply.

"We need an ambulance," Beau said. Whoever she was, they needed her alive; the FBI needed her alive.

"Ambulance is on its way," Cassidy said as she walked back into the living room.

Beau looked at her, thought how she could have been killed, and his chest clamped down. He forced himself to focus, push away thoughts of what might have happened.

Security arrived. Worried about the hit, Will Egan had been spending his nights on a cot out in the cabana. He strode in with a group of his men, silver hair sleep-rumpled, semiautomatic pistol pointed at the intruder.

"Frank's out cold," Cassidy said. "He's been drugged. I found a needle on the floor in his room. His breathing's even and his pulse is strong."

Beau felt a sweep of relief. He tipped his head toward the assailant. "Our hit man's a woman. According to her, Frank should be okay."

"I've got this," Egan said, gun held steady. Several other

security guards had their pistols aimed at the intruder, enough men that Beau finally felt comfortable lowering his weapon.

He turned to Cassidy. "We need to call Taggart," he said.

Cassidy nodded. "I was hoping with everything out in the open, we'd be safe. Apparently, the assassin didn't get the message."

"I guess not," Beau said. Arrests hadn't yet been made, though the case was rapidly progressing. He slid a glance toward the woman groaning in pain on the floor. "I think she got the message now."

Chapter Thirty-Six

Federal agents swarmed the house, along with EMTs and Dallas PD, but Agent Quinn Taggart went directly to the hospital where the female assassin was admitted to surgery for three bullet wounds: one to the upper chest, one to the shoulder, and one to the knee. A groggy, semiconscious Frank Marino was admitted for overnight observation.

Since the house was a crime scene, Beau and Cassidy packed overnight bags, grabbed their laptops, and Beau drove them to the nearby Highland Dallas hotel, taking a suite there instead of holing up in his private rooms at the Tex/Am office, where he would have to deal with employees in the morning.

The sun was coming up by the time they'd checked in at the front desk and taken the elevator up to the room. The suite was well furnished and spacious. Beau pulled the curtains in the bedroom, blocking out the early dawn sunlight, yawning as he stripped off his clothes and padded over to the bed.

"These all-nighters are getting to be a habit," Cassidy said, stripping off the T-shirt and jeans she had put on after the shooting.

Beau paused to watch her. Surely he was way too tired to be thinking of sex. Surely. But when Cassidy unhooked her bra, setting her pretty rose-tipped breasts free, when she shook her mane of dark curls back from her face, he felt a shot of lust that went straight to his groin.

No way, he told himself. Both of them needed rest even more than the hot wash of sexual release.

He glanced up to see her watching him the way he'd been watching her, her green eyes drifting over his chest, his abs, lower.

Beau bit back a groan as he started getting hard. "You're killing me here. You know that, right?"

Cassidy just smiled. "You're right. We need to get at least a few hours of sleep before we go home."

He loved that she enjoyed sex as much as he did, was smart and practical, yet in every way was a soft, sexy woman. He loved a lot of things about Cassidy Jones.

The thought made him frown. He slid into bed and pulled her close, but sex was off the table, at least for now.

Instead, as he stared up at the ceiling, he remembered the moment gunfire had erupted, the instant he had spotted Cassidy behind him in the hall and known she was putting her life on the line.

She was an investigator. Even if she weren't, Cassidy would never be willing to stay safely on the sidelines. She would live her life to the fullest, grab hold by the balls and hang on for the utter challenge of it.

He thought about Sarah, a homebody who had wanted nothing more than to have his babies, take care of him and the family they planned to raise together. Sarah shouldn't have died, but she had.

The odds were stacked even greater against a woman like Cassidy, a woman out in a tough world, not protected and sheltered at home. She could have been killed tonight, could have died so easily. Dread washed through him, terrible memories of death and loss.

Beau turned on his side, determined to block them, finally succeeded. Eventually exhaustion swept over him and he fell asleep. He didn't know how long he slept before he started to dream.

Footsteps echoed in the hall, a dark shape moved toward him. Someone was in the house! He turned, saw Cassidy in the passageway behind him, a pistol in her hand. Gunfire erupted. When Cassidy turned, he saw a neat black hole dead center in her forehead. A trickle of blood turned into a river of crimson, washing over her beautiful face.

A strangled cry locked in his throat and his chest clamped down. The image changed and the face no longer belonged to Cassidy. It was Sarah. His beloved Sarah, and she was dead. "Sarah!" he cried out. "Sarah!"

Then the woman was Cassidy again, and the agony of losing her was more painful than he ever could have imagined.

"Beau!" Someone shook his shoulder. "Wake up, Beau, you're dreaming!"

Jolted awake, he shot upright in bed.

"It's only a dream, Beau. Just a dream." Cassidy rested her palm against his cheek. "Everything's okay."

Perspiration covered his chest. He raked a hand through his sweat-damp black hair. "Sorry. I didn't mean to wake you."

"It's all right. Go back to sleep."

Beau nodded, still thinking of Cassidy and the dream. His breathing was still a little ragged. He wasn't sure he could fall asleep, but as soon as his head hit the pillow, his tired body had other ideas and he drifted back into slumber. This time he didn't dream.

* * *

Cassidy lay awake. Her eyes burned. Her throat felt tight. Her chest ached as if she had been running for miles. She fought not to cry, but tears leaked from beneath her lashes and slipped down her cheeks.

She had no one to blame but herself. She'd known the way Beau felt about Sarah, known he would always be in love with her. Known he had no room left in his heart for her. But hearing him call out Sarah's name in his sleep had brought it all home.

If she could, she would get dressed and leave the suite, get as far from Beau as she possibly could. She was in love with him. She had known it for some time. He was everything a woman could want in a man. Strong, brave, smart, capable, sexy as hell. He was everything Cassidy had ever wanted.

But he belonged to someone else, and that would never change. She closed her eyes and finally managed to block thoughts of him. She couldn't leave until this case was completely over and she knew for sure Beau was safe.

If you loved someone you didn't abandon them, no matter the reason. You stayed. You protected them. You put their life before your own.

Eventually, she fell asleep. But when Beau awoke and began to kiss the side of her neck, cup and caress her breasts, she pretended to be deeply asleep. Eventually, he gave up and padded in to the shower.

Cassidy started crying, turning into the pillow to muffle the sound of her tears. She couldn't have Beau. It didn't matter that her heart was broken. She had to accept things the way they were and move on.

When the shower went off, she took a shuddering breath and steeled herself. She thought of Beau, climbed out of bed, and silently began making plans to move back home.

* * *

Beau paced the floor of the living room in the suite, waiting for the call that would tell them the CSIs were done and they could go home. He glanced over at Cassidy, who sat at the walnut dining room table, sipping a cup of coffee, quiet, as she had been all morning.

Beau was worried about her. Clearly she was more upset about last night's shooting than she had first appeared. A tray loaded with pastries sat mostly untouched. Instead, the first stainless pot of coffee was empty and they were halfway through the second.

Beau poured more of the dark brew into his cup and sat down at the table just as his phone rang.

"Thought you'd appreciate an update." Quinn Taggart's deep voice rolled over the line.

"You bet. Let me put you on speaker." He set the phone on the table so both of them could hear.

"The shooter we arrested last night was a woman named Eliza Spears."

"A female assassin," Beau said with a shake of his head. "She confess to the murder attempt?"

"She confessed to a lot of things. The woman's a professional contract killer known as The Spear. Until last night, we thought The Spear was a man."

"Who's she work for?"

"Most of it's going to go public soon, so here's where we are. Clifford Jennings hired The Spear. We arrested him this morning. We're offering him a deal in return for testifying against Malcolm Vaughn. If he accepts, which we're fairly sure he will, we can arrest Vaughn for conspiracy to commit murder—among other charges."

Beau's pulse was thrumming. "You think Vaughn will give you something that will help you nail Jamal Nawabi?"

"Vaughn's a sleazeball. He looks out for himself—first, last, and always. He'll make whatever deal it takes to stay out of prison. I'm not sure he can help us with Nawabi, but it doesn't matter. We've got most of the members of the cell he was involved with in custody. Turns out they're not the loyal bunch you might imagine. A couple of them have already implicated Nawabi. This morning he was arrested for terrorism."

"That's good news," Cassidy said.

"Nawabi's lawyered up," Taggart continued. "But he's considered a flight risk, so he's cooling his heels in jail and he isn't going anywhere anytime soon."

Beau smiled.

"So far, the only one who's managed to escape the long arm of the law is Luca Reichlin. He's hightailed it out of the country to parts unknown."

"Always one snake able to slip off through the grass," Beau said.

"As far as the two of you are concerned, Reichlin's no longer a threat. Not with his boss in jail. The Spear is in custody and Vaughn likely will be by the end of the day. Aside from some additional questions that might come up, this is over for the two of you."

Beau sagged back in his chair. "Thank God."

"The CSIs have cleared the crime scene at your house. Your man Egan had a cleaning crew brought in this morning. You can go home anytime you want."

Beau glanced at Cassidy but couldn't read her face.

"We appreciate everything you've done," Taggart said. "If you ever need me, you know where to find me." The FBI man ended the call, and they both rose from their chairs.

Cassidy said nothing, just went in and started packing. Beau joined her a few minutes later. He tried to start a conversation in the car on their way back to the house, but Cassidy seemed distant, so he left her alone. He'd been worried about her all morning. He wasn't sure what was wrong, but something was on her mind.

"Hey," he said as he parked the Ferrari, got out, and walked into the kitchen. "You okay?"

She just nodded. "I'm fine, just tired."

"You sure?"

"It's been a long couple of days. I need a little time to work things out."

A long couple of days, to say the least. It was early afternoon. He had more than enough to do at the office. Maybe giving Cassidy a little time to herself wasn't a bad idea.

"Listen, if you're sure you're okay, I think I'll make a quick trip into the office. It's Saturday. Nobody'll be around. I can go in, get some stuff done, and come right back. What do you think?"

She smiled, but it didn't look quite real and she seemed strangely sad. "I think it's a good idea. I'm a big girl, remember?"

Fresh worry filtered through him. He bent his head and kissed her, wishing he knew what was wrong. "You're *my* girl. That's all that matters. That's something we need to talk about when I get back. Okay?"

He'd been thinking about it all morning, and one thing he knew, he wasn't ready to end things with Cassidy. There was no reason they couldn't continue to see each other. Maybe she'd even want to move in with him. It was a big step, but they could at least discuss it.

"I'll see you later." He gave her another soft kiss, but when the kiss ended, Cassidy pulled his head down and kissed him long and deep.

"Bye," she said softly. There was something in her voice . . . He couldn't put his finger on it, but he almost changed his mind and stayed. Would have if he didn't think a little time on her own might be exactly what she needed.

Plus, he hated to abandon Linc completely. A couple of hours of catching up and he could be back at the house. He'd stop and pick up Chinese takeout. They both liked

Chinese. Open a good bottle of wine and they'd make it a celebration. After everything they'd been through, they deserved a little fun.

He was smiling as he backed the Ferrari out of the garage and headed down the road. It was crazy, but he and Cassidy had spent so much time together, by the time he reached the office, he was already missing her.

There was a mountain of work on his desk when he arrived. The first thing he did was check his calendar. He sat back in surprise when he discovered it was Valentine's Day.

Perfect, he thought, smiling again. He'd like nothing better than to buy Cassidy a gift. Something pretty and feminine. A necklace, maybe, with a heart-shaped diamond pendant. No, she might take that the wrong way.

Maybe a bracelet. Something elegant. Emeralds would match her pretty green eyes. Didn't matter how much it cost. He called a jeweler friend, the owner of the Cartier store in the NorthPark Center, and told the man what he had in mind.

His friend said he had something he was sure Beau would like. It would be ready for him to pick up on his way home.

Beau returned to his schedule, made note of a couple of important client meetings, then planned some necessary staff updates. He managed to concentrate, but he was eager to give Cassidy her special Valentine's gift. She was special to him in every way, and he wanted her to know it.

Three hours after he'd arrived at the office, he left for home. Instead of Chinese, he'd ordered a gourmet dinner from Piero's, an Italian restaurant he and Linc favored, and had it delivered to the office.

He loaded the meal into the car, then stopped at the flower shop to pick up a bouquet of pink roses he had ordered and had waiting. Not red, that came too close to the L word, though he'd considered it for a while.

From the flower shop, he drove to Cartier to pick up his gift, a diamond and emerald tennis bracelet. He hoped she would like it.

He was smiling as he rolled up the driveway, clicked the opener, and drove into the garage. Unfortunately, Cassidy's little Honda wasn't parked in the Lamborghini's spot, where it had been moved. He wondered if maybe she'd had the same idea and gone after a gift for him. They thought so much alike it wouldn't surprise him.

Emptying the car, he carried everything into the house, which seemed strangely quiet without her there. The cleaning crew had moved a few things. He figured that was probably it.

He was heading for the wine cellar for a bottle of champagne to chill when he spotted the note on the kitchen table. It was from Cassidy, he saw, glancing at the signature at the bottom. He picked up the note and began to read.

My dearest Beau,

I know you're probably surprised to find me gone. But now that your name has been cleared and neither of us is in danger, it's time for me to move on. I want you to know that aside from some of the bad things that happened, I don't regret a single moment I spent with you.

That's the problem. I fell in love with you, Beau. I didn't plan it. It just happened. I know you can never love me back. I know you're still in love with Sarah and that isn't going to change. You were honest about that from the start.

I had to leave, Beau. I need a man who can love me with his whole heart, love me the way you love Sarah. I deserve that, and I won't settle for less.

Please don't call or try to get in touch in any way.

*I hope you remember me fondly as I will always
remember you. Have a good life, Beau.*
Your friend,
Cassidy

Beau sank down in one of the kitchen chairs. His stomach
felt hollow. A hard knot centered in his chest. He read the
note again. Cassidy loved him. And she was gone.

He knew without a shred of doubt she wouldn't be returning. She was right. She deserved a man who loved her
with all his heart. Cassidy was special. The most special
woman he had ever known.

Beau swallowed. His hand shook as he set the note back
down on the table. He rubbed his eyes, scrubbed a hand
over his face. He felt like he'd been hit with a brick.

He looked at the delicious meal he'd brought home, but
the smell of food made him nauseous. His mouth felt dry as
he reached into his jacket pocket, pulled out the blue velvet
box and flipped it open. Beautiful emeralds winked up at
him, reminding him of Cassidy's eyes. He wished he'd had
a chance to give it to her.

He wished for a lot of things, but none of them were
going to happen.

Leaving the food on the table next to the box, he walked
out of the house and climbed into the Ferrari. He needed to
clear his head, get some fresh air, put things back in per-
spective. What had happened was for the best. It would
have happened sooner or later.

He had known their relationship would eventually come
to an end. He just hadn't known it would hurt so badly.

Chapter Thirty-Seven

Three days after she moved out of Beau's house, Cassidy drove to Houston. She hadn't seen her dad in what felt like ages. Talking on the phone just wasn't the same.

She found him in his favorite brown recliner in front of the TV, watching an old John Wayne western. He was only average height, but he'd always been burly, with big arms and thick shoulders. Recently, he had grown one of those horseshoe mustaches the guys were all wearing. Even though there were gray stripes around his mouth, it looked good.

"Hey, honey, what are you doing here?" He came out of his chair and wrapped her in a big bear hug.

Cassidy managed to smile. "What, a girl can't just decide to come home and visit her old man?"

He snorted. "Old man, my ass."

She laughed. It felt good after all the useless tears. He took a step back to look at her and she wondered if he had heard something in her voice. He had always been amazingly perceptive.

"Something's happened. What is it?"

She should have known she couldn't fool him. She shrugged as if it were nothing, when it was everything. "I fell in love. It was stupid. It's over and eventually I'll be okay."

"Was it him? The race-car driver? The one your brothers and I used to watch?"

"It was him."

Her father's jaw tightened. "That rat bastard. I can tell he hurt you. I ought to kick his ass."

She actually felt a smile tugging at her lips. "It wasn't his fault. He's a great guy. He's just in love with someone else. Someone who died." She looked up at him, into his dark eyes. "You should know what that's like. You still love Mom."

He grunted. "I'll always love your mother, honey. So I guess I understand. I still don't like it, and I'd still like to kick his ass."

She brushed a kiss on his cheek. "You're the best dad ever."

He sighed. "I'm glad you think so, because there's something I need to tell you. I'm hoping it'll be okay with you."

Cassidy frowned, worry slipping through her. "What is it, Dad?"

"I met someone, honey. I really like her. I don't know how it'll all shake out, but I like being with her. She makes me smile and when she's around, I'm not lonely anymore."

Cassidy slid her arms around her father's neck and hugged him, managed to ignore the thick lump swelling in her throat. "I'm happy for you, Dad. Really happy." But somehow her dad's newfound happiness made her heartbreak even worse. She forced herself to smile. "So when do I get to meet her?"

"Soon, honey. I don't think Anna's quite ready for the whole family thing yet, but soon. I promise."

Cassidy nodded and turned away, hoping he wouldn't see the wetness in her eyes. Of course her father noticed.

"The man's a fool," he said gruffly. Cassidy made no

reply. Things were what they were, and nothing was going to change that.

She didn't stay the night. Her dad was having dinner with Anna, and Cassidy was ready to drive back to Dallas.

Eventually, she'd get past this. She'd get over Beau Reese and get on with her life. She just hoped it didn't take too many years.

Linc stormed into the office Wednesday morning. He'd been traveling all week. He strode up to Marty's desk, his jaw tight, one hand balled into a fist. "Where the hell is he?"

When the kid looked at him and kind of flinched, Linc took a deep breath and stepped away. "Sorry. I'm worried about him, is all."

"We're all a little worried," Marty said. "I think he's home. He's been coming in way early, working while it's still dark outside, then leaving before anyone gets here. It's not like him. Not at all."

"No, it isn't. Beau's more of a nighttime guy."

"You think maybe you could talk to him?" Marty asked, clearly hopeful.

"It's the girl, right? She ended things. He told me the day after it happened. Then he just disappeared."

"I really liked her," Marty said.

Linc grunted. "Apparently, so did Beau. I'll talk to him."

"Thanks, Mr. Cain."

He smiled faintly. "Don't you think it's time you started calling me Linc?"

Marty smiled, his black eyes tilting up at the corners. "Okay, Linc. Thanks." He was a good kid, a great employee, and he was completely loyal to Beau.

"Don't worry. Between us, we'll get him straightened

out." Linc turned and started walking, heading for his Mercedes in the underground garage.

It didn't take long to reach Beau's house. The guards were all gone, his friend's life no longer in danger. Things were back to normal. Except for Cassidy Jones.

As he reached the top of the drive, jammed the car into park and turned off the engine, the house looked empty. Linc had a feeling it wasn't. He walked to the door and knocked, but nobody answered. They had keys to each other's places. He used his and walked inside, calling out so he wouldn't be mistaken for another assassin and shot dead in the living room.

"Beau, I know you're in here. Where are you?"

Beau called back to him. "I'll come into the office tomorrow, okay? I'm not up to talking right now."

Linc ignored him, strode toward the sound of his voice and walked into the study. The curtains were closed, the room completely dark. Beau sprawled on the sofa in front of the fireplace, but no blaze burned in the hearth.

Linc walked over and opened the windows, letting in a shaft of bright light. Beau groaned as the sun hit him in the face, which was dark with beard stubble, his black hair greasy and uncombed.

"You look like hell," Linc said.

"Thanks."

"So I guess you and Cassidy split up."

Beau raked back his hair, which definitely needed a cut. "She ended things." He shrugged. "It would have happened sooner or later."

"Why is that?"

Beau sighed. "She said she deserved someone who wasn't in love with someone else."

Linc walked over to where Beau sat. "That someone else being a ghost, right?"

"I guess."

Linc sat down at the opposite end of the sofa. "You know what you're doing in this dark house?"

"Apparently you're going to tell me."

"You're right, I am. You're grieving, Beau. Only this time you aren't grieving for Sarah. You're grieving for Cassidy."

"Cassidy is nothing like Sarah."

"That's right. Sarah was just a kid. When you loved her, you were a kid, too, a boy in his twenties. Maybe if the two of you had married, you would have changed together over the years, but that didn't happen. You're a different man now. A strong man, Beau. It takes a strong woman to handle you, a woman like Cassidy Jones."

Beau sat up on the sofa. "What if she dies, just like Sarah? I couldn't go through that again, Linc."

"What if she doesn't die? What if the two of you have a great life together? That's the chance we all take, Beau."

For several seconds he said nothing. Then a breath whispered out. "Even if you're right, it's too late. Cassidy's gone and there's nothing I can do."

"That's not necessarily true. Listen to me, Beau. When Sarah died, it was out of your control. There was nothing you could do to change the outcome. This is different. If you love Cassidy, you can fix this. You can make it right."

Beau lifted his head but didn't say anything for the longest time. "How? How could I fix it?"

"Hell, I don't know. You're the salesman. If you want her, you figure out how to convince her. You can have Cassidy and the kind of life you once wanted—the life you deserve."

When Beau said nothing, Linc rose from the sofa. "Think about it. That's all I ask."

Beau remained silent, but Linc knew his friend. He would think things over, sort it all through in his head.

Eventually he'd figure things out, one way or another. Linc hoped he made the right decision.

Cassidy drove home after work. She'd been spending long hours at the office, anything to keep her mind off Beau. She tried not to wonder where he was or what he was doing, wonder if he ever thought of her. She tried not to wonder if he missed her.

She was tired as she rode the elevator up to her loft apartment. She hadn't been sleeping well and her appetite was gone. She used her key and opened the door, stepped inside and turned on the light. A gasp escaped as a familiar tall figure rose from the sofa.

Her heart jerked and started pounding. "Beau . . ."

"Hi," he said softly. He looked nervous, uneasy. She had never seen him quite that way. He tipped his head toward a huge bouquet of red roses. "They're for Valentine's Day. Better . . . ahh . . . late than never."

"How did you get in?"

"The building manager. Turns out he's a racing fan."

Under other circumstances, she might have smiled. Instead she steeled herself. She wanted to run to him, to feel those strong arms around her. She wanted to tell him how much she loved him.

She wouldn't. She couldn't stand the pain when he was gone. She had meant what she'd said in the note. She wouldn't settle for less than a man who loved her.

"I asked you not to call me, Beau. I need you to leave."

Beau ignored her, just stood there looking like her own secret fantasy, all lean muscle and gorgeous blue eyes. Those eyes swept over her now, as if they tried to absorb every detail.

"I really missed you," he said gruffly. "I missed you so damn much."

"Beau, please . . ."

"I went to the cemetery yesterday," he said. "I went to see Sarah."

A little sound escaped, a slice of agony she had hoped to hide.

Beau walked toward her. "I went to say good-bye, Cassidy. I wanted Sarah to know that after all these lonely years, I'd finally found someone I loved the way I loved her. Someone I loved totally and completely, with everything in my heart. I told Sarah about you, Cassidy. And I said good-bye."

She started to tremble as he reached her, drew her into his arms.

"I love you," he said. "I love you so much."

"Beau . . ." She started crying, slid her arms up around his neck and just hung on. "Oh, God, Beau." He kissed her. Kissed her until she couldn't breathe, until crying was impossible.

"I love you and I want you with me," he said. "Now and for always. When you're ready, I want us to get married."

She made a little sound, couldn't quite believe he was there. "Are . . . are you sure?"

"I've never been more sure of anything. Nothing feels right without you."

Cassidy wiped tears from her cheeks and looked up at him. "No, it doesn't."

"So that's a yes?"

She managed to nod.

The tension eased from Beau's shoulders. "I was afraid you'd say no. I thought I might say something wrong. Do something stupid and ruin any chance of getting you back."

Tears clogged her throat. "You could say just about anything as long as you said you loved me."

"I'm crazy in love with you. I need you, baby. Will you come home with me?"

She glanced around the loft. It wasn't her home anymore. Home was wherever Beau was. "Okay."

"We could have kids," he said. "I mean, if you want to."

She just nodded. "Kids. Yes, okay."

Beau kissed her, deeply then softly. "You must have missed me, too. You've never been quite this agreeable."

Cassidy laughed. She was going home with Beau. She might even marry him. "You better not get too used to it."

Beau laughed, soft, free and easy. She had never heard him laugh that way before. Cassidy went up on her toes and kissed him. She had never been so happy. It was amazing how much life could change between yesterday and tomorrow.

Epilogue

Beau sat behind the wheel of the brand-new Lamborghini Aventador he had just driven out of the showroom. It was exactly like the one he'd owned before, metallic slate gray with a burnt orange interior, V-12 engine, 740 horses, all the other specs the same. Cassidy wouldn't have it any other way.

"How's it drive?" she asked from the passenger seat, clearly eager to test the car herself.

"Like a screaming demon," he said, grinning as he drove the low-slung sports car out of the city. For the first few miles, he just enjoyed the feel of the wheel in his hands, the incredible power of the engine. A couple of times, when the road was clear, he let her run a little.

Forty miles from Pleasant Hill, he pulled the car over to the side of the road. "Why don't you give her a try, see what you think?"

She flashed him a grin, clearly excited. "You did make the insurance payment?"

Beau laughed. "Oh, yeah, baby. Since I knew you'd be driving her, I didn't want to take any chances."

She grinned as they climbed out and rounded the vehicle

to trade places. Beau caught the flash of diamonds and emeralds on her left hand. He'd traded the tennis bracelet for an engagement ring even before he'd gone to see her. He'd officially proposed during supper at Antoine's, which had turned into a spontaneous engagement party.

He didn't think he could fall more deeply in love, but once he'd let go of the past, he was completely toast. Maybe he'd suffered some form of survivor's guilt, regret that he had lived and Sarah had died. Whatever it was, Cassidy had shown him the way past it.

She slid into the driver's seat, put the Lambo in gear, and revved the engine. Laughing, she burned a little rubber as she pulled onto the road. They were on their way to Pleasant Hill, having lunch with Josie, Missy, and Evie.

He tried to get out for a visit at least every other week, loved watching the baby grow up. He couldn't wait till Cassidy got pregnant, though they had decided to put it off for a while, give themselves a little time together after the wedding.

Which was only two months away. He grinned to think of it.

Seemed like everything had settled into place the day Cassidy had come back to him. Quinn Taggart had called to tell him Malcolm Vaughn had been arrested. He was taking a plea deal that would land him in prison for at least twenty years. Jennings's sentence could go even longer.

Even with the most expensive attorneys money could buy, Jamal Nawabi wasn't getting out of prison. The only worry was that other members of the terrorist cell might still be out there, plotting and planning to do their worst.

Luca Reichlin was now in Interpol's sights. Taggart figured sooner or later he would make a mistake and they would arrest him.

Best of all, Malcolm Vaughn had inadvertently given Beau a parting gift. Mal had told Quinn Taggart he'd had no idea Jamal Nawabi was involved in terrorism, no idea why

Luca Reichlin wanted Hardrock Trenching to get the capitol maintenance contract. Even the murders were Reichlin's idea—eliminating any loose ends.

Vaughn was just trying to please his number-one client.

Taggart believed him.

Which meant former State Senator Stewart Reese had no idea terrorism was involved when he'd agreed to press Scott Watson for a favor.

Beau liked to think that no matter what his father had done in his life, there was a line he would never have crossed.

Beau hoped like hell it was the truth.

Don't miss the exciting conclusion of
Kat Martin's Texas Trilogy,

Beyond Control!

Iron River Ranch
Iron Springs, Texas

Victoria Bradford drove the old blue Chevy Malibu along the two-lane road. Up ahead, a sign hung above a narrow dirt track running off to the west, IRON RIVER RANCH.

"Are we there yet, Mama?" Ivy, her four-year-old daughter, had asked at least a dozen times since they'd left the Walmart parking lot in Iron Springs. The ten-mile drive didn't take long, but after being cooped up in the car for days, to Ivy, they couldn't reach their destination soon enough.

"We're very close, sweetheart. This is the turn, right here." Tory checked the gas gauge as the wheels left the pavement and started rumbling over the bumpy dirt road. Less than an eighth of a tank. She hoped the ranch wasn't much farther.

More than that, she prayed the job hadn't already been filled.

She sighed as the aging Malibu rolled along. She was basically in bumfrick Egypt, ten miles north of Nowhere

Springs, almost out of gas, with twenty-three dollars and thirty-three cents in her wallet.

Last night, without enough money for a motel room and afraid to use her credit cards for fear Damon would somehow track her, they'd slept in the car in the Walmart parking lot. As soon as the McDonald's opened, she had pulled into the drive-thru and bought Sausage McMuffins, then driven out to the ranch to somehow convince the owner to hire a woman with a four-year-old and no actual ranching experience.

She thought of the ad in the paper she had spotted last night on the counter in the Iron Springs Café. If she some-how managed to get the job, it would be perfect. Besides a steady paycheck and the ranch being way off the grid, the position included the use of a double-wide trailer.

After being on the road for the past three weeks, living out of motel rooms and suitcases, the trailer sounded like a palace.

"Look, Mama, there it is!" Ivy pointed toward the cluster of buildings up ahead, a couple of barns, several fenced training arenas, and a two-story home with dormer win-dows and a covered porch running the length of the front. A double-wide sat fifty yards away.

Surrounding the complex were vast stretches of open green pastureland where horses and cattle grazed, and there were ponds and woodlands in the distance, and dense clusters of trees.

The Chevy bumped over the last patch of road, pulled up in front of the house, and Tory quickly turned off the engine. No use wasting what little gas she had left.

"Mama, there's a man over there by the barn."

Her gaze swung in that direction. There was, indeed, a man. The noisy buzz of a saw covered the sounds of their arrival, giving her time to assess him.

Shirtless, he was working with his back to them, broad,

tanned, and muscled above a narrow waist that disappeared into a pair of faded jeans. The jeans hugged a round behind and long, powerful legs.

He was tall, she saw when he straightened away from his work and walked into the barn, with medium brown hair cut short. She got her first look at his face when he walked back out; he was handsome, with a solid jaw and masculine features, at least three days' growth of beard.

The front of him was just as impressive as the back, a broad chest with solid pecs, muscular biceps, and six-pack abs.

Unease filtered through her. This was a strong, powerful male. She knew firsthand what a man like that could do to a woman.

Tory forced down the notion. Not all men were like Damon. Before she'd met him, she had been married to a good and decent man, the father of her child. Jamie Bradford, her high school sweetheart, was one of the gentlest people she'd ever known. Her father, too, was a good man, before he'd fallen in love with his secretary and divorced her mother, leaving the two of them alone.

Tory took a courage-building breath. "Stay here, sweetheart." Cracking open the car door, she slid out from behind the wheel. "Don't worry, sweetheart. Everything's going to be okay."

She hoped.

Ivy sank down in her booster seat, trying to make herself invisible. Tory had survived the fights, arguments, and finally the brutal beating Damon had given her that had put her in the hospital. Though he had never hurt Ivy, the little girl had seen the results of his mistreatment, leaving her with an unnatural fear of men.

Tory glanced at the big, thick-chested male striding toward her, shrugging into a blue denim shirt. Ivy would be terrified of him. If there was any other way, she would climb back in the car and just drive away.

There wasn't. Tory started walking, meeting the man halfway. She glanced around but didn't see a soul besides the big man in front of her. Her uneasiness returned, but she forced it away.

"May I help you?" he asked, and she thought that at least he was polite.

"My name is Tory Ford. I'm looking for Joshua Cain. Is that you?" He had blue eyes and a cleft in his chin. From a purely physical standpoint, the man was flat-out hot.

"I'm Josh Cain. What can I do for you?"

"I saw your ad in the Iron Springs *Gazette*. You're looking for a stable hand. I'm here to apply for the job."

He just shook his head. "I'm afraid it's a man's job, Ms. Ford. Mucking out stalls and cleaning tack, feeding the livestock. It isn't something you'd want to do."

"Work isn't supposed to be fun, Mr. Cain. That's why they call it work. I can muck out stalls, clean tack, and feed stock as well as anyone else."

"Sorry. I'm looking for a man. I appreciate your coming out, but—"

"There are laws, Mr. Cain. Equal rights for women. Have you never heard of that? Lawsuits against discrimination?"

His jaw hardened. His eyebrows came down in a frown. "Are you kidding me? You're going to sue me because I won't hire you to shovel horseshit out of the barn?"

She could feel the heat creeping into her cheeks. With her fair skin and fiery red hair, there was no way to hide her embarrassment.

She looked him straight in the face. "I need this job, Mr. Cain. I need the house that comes with it." She forced herself to smile. "Why don't we compromise? You give me three days to prove I'm up to the job. If I'm not, I won't give you any more trouble. Three days. If you don't think I can handle the work, I'll leave. I won't argue, I'll just go."

A muscle jerked in his cheek. Obviously, he didn't like being pressured. He looked at her hard, then those condemning blue eyes traveled over her shoulder to something behind her.

"Who is *that*?"

She didn't have to turn to know Ivy had climbed out of the car. Like Tory, she was petite, but her hair was blond instead of red, and her eyes were blue instead of green.

"That's my daughter. She's only four." Desperate now, she could feel her heart throbbing softly inside her ribs. "We need a place, Mr. Cain. I'll work hard. I'll do whatever you need done. Just give me a chance."

He swore the F-word under his breath, not loud enough for Ivy to hear. Damon wouldn't have cared. She clung to the hope that represented.

"What do you plan to do with your daughter while you're working? You can't leave her in the house alone."

Tory glanced wildly around. She had known this would be a problem. Before, she'd had money enough to hire a sitter or there was day care for employees' kids.

She looked at the fenced yard off to the side in front of the trailer. The grass was sparse and in need of a trim. Maybe he'd had a dog or something, but it was clean and empty now. The weather was still good and there was a little gazebo with a table and benches in the middle. She'd be able to keep an eye on Ivy while she was working.

"She could play in the yard. She likes to color and she loves looking at kids' books. She wouldn't be any trouble. If this works out, I'll have money to pay for a sitter."

Cain looked at Ivy, paced away, then back. "Dammit."

"It's just three days. If I do a good job, you won't have to search for someone else."

He ran a hand over his short brown hair, paced away, then walked back. "Did you sleep in your car last night?"

She refused to answer. She didn't want charity from Cain or anyone else.

"Fine," he said. "You've got three days. But I'm not cutting you any slack. You do a man's job for a man's pay. If you can't hack it, you're out of here."

And from the look on his face, he was clearly hoping she would fail. Hell, maybe she would.

She managed to fake a smile. "Okay, it's a deal." She stuck out her hand to seal the bargain, for a moment didn't think he was going to shake. Then he sighed and took hold of her hand, not too hard, just firm enough to let her know he was in charge.

"You start tomorrow morning. Six A.M. sharp. There's enough food in the trailer to last a few days. I'll bring you a quart of milk. After that, board's on you. If you're still here, you'll need to make a trip into town for groceries."

Relief filtered through her, so strong it made her head swim. She had a place to stay where no one would look for her. She had a job, which meant food and money for necessities. If he kept her on, she'd find a sitter to watch Ivy. She'd have time to figure things out, make a new plan.

She took a step back, set an arm around her little girl's shoulders and drew her forward. "This is my daughter, Ivy. Ivy, this is Mr. Cain."

"Hello, Ivy," he said. He had an unusual voice, deep and resonant, but at the same time soft and oddly compelling.

Ivy shrank back.

"Say hello, honey," Tory said.

"I don't want to stay. I want to go." Clinging to Tory's waist, she burrowed into her.

"She's shy," Tory said.

"The trailer's unlocked," Cain said. "It's clean and ready to go."

"Thank you."

He turned and started striding back to the barn. She probably should be at least a little afraid of him. Oddly, she wasn't.

Then again, she hadn't been afraid of Damon, either.

Connect with Us

Visit us online at
KensingtonBooks.com
to read more from your favorite authors, see books
by series, view reading group guides, and more.

for sneak peeks, chances to win books and prize packs,
and to share your thoughts with other readers.

facebook.com/kensingtonpublishing
twitter.com/kensingtonbooks

Tell us what you think!

To share your thoughts, submit a review,
or sign up for our eNewsletters, please visit:
KensingtonBooks.com/TellUs.

More by Bestselling Author
Hannah Howell

Books by Bestselling Author
Fern Michaels

___**The Jury**	0-8217-7878-1	$6.99US/$9.99CAN
___**Sweet Revenge**	0-8217-7879-X	$6.99US/$9.99CAN
___**Lethal Justice**	0-8217-7880-3	$6.99US/$9.99CAN
___**Free Fall**	0-8217-7881-1	$6.99US/$9.99CAN
___**Fool Me Once**	0-8217-8071-9	$7.99US/$10.99CAN
___**Vegas Rich**	0-8217-8112-X	$7.99US/$10.99CAN
___**Hide and Seek**	1-4201-0184-6	$6.99US/$9.99CAN
___**Hokus Pokus**	1-4201-0185-4	$6.99US/$9.99CAN
___**Fast Track**	1-4201-0186-2	$6.99US/$9.99CAN
___**Collateral Damage**	1-4201-0187-0	$6.99US/$9.99CAN
___**Final Justice**	1-4201-0188-9	$6.99US/$9.99CAN
___**Up Close and Personal**	0-8217-7956-7	$7.99US/$9.99CAN
___**Under the Radar**	1-4201-0683-X	$6.99US/$9.99CAN
___**Razor Sharp**	1-4201-0684-8	$7.99US/$10.99CAN
___**Yesterday**	1-4201-1494-8	$5.99US/$6.99CAN
___**Vanishing Act**	1-4201-0685-6	$7.99US/$10.99CAN
___**Sara's Song**	1-4201-1493-X	$5.99US/$6.99CAN
___**Deadly Deals**	1-4201-0686-4	$7.99US/$10.99CAN
___**Game Over**	1-4201-0687-2	$7.99US/$10.99CAN
___**Sins of Omission**	1-4201-1153-1	$7.99US/$10.99CAN
___**Sins of the Flesh**	1-4201-1154-X	$7.99US/$10.99CAN
___**Cross Roads**	1-4201-1192-2	$7.99US/$10.99CAN

Available Wherever Books Are Sold!
Check out our website at **www.kensingtonbooks.com**